# Clarke's Universe

# Clarke's Universe

## Arthur C. Clarke

**ibooks**

DISTRIBUTED BY PUBLISHERS GROUP WEST

A Publication of ibooks, inc.

*The Lion of Comarre* © 1953, 1968 Arthur C. Clarke; *A Fall of Moondust* © 1961 by
Arthur C. Clarke; "Jupiter V" © 1956 Arthur C. Clarke

An ibooks, inc. Book

Distributed by: Publishers Group West
1700 Fourth Street, Berkeley, CA 94710
www.pgw.com

ibooks, inc.
24 West 25th Street
New York, NY 10010

ISBN: 1-59687-306-X
First ibooks, inc. printing: December 2005
10 9 8 7 6 5 4 3 2 1

Printed in the U.S.A.

# Contents

# The Lion of Comarre

# 1
# REVOLT

Toward the close of the twenty-sixth century, the great tide of Science had at last begun to ebb. The long series of inventions that bad shaped and molded the world for nearly a thousand years was coming to its end. Everything had been discovered. One by one, all the great dreams of the past had become reality.

Civilization was completely mechanized—yet machinery had almost vanished. Hidden in the walk of the cities or buried far underground, the perfect machines bore the burden of the world. Silently, unobtrusively, the robots attended to their masters' needs, doing their work so well that their presence seemed as natural as the dawn.

There was still much to learn in the realm of pure science, and the astronomers, now that they were no longer bound to Earth, had work enough for a thousand years to come. But the physical sciences and the arts they nourished had ceased to be the chief preoccupation of the race. By the year 2600 the finest human minds were no longer to be found in the laboratories.

The men whose names meant roost to the world were the artists and philosophers, the lawgivers and statesmen. The engineers and tine great inventors belonged to the past. Like the men who had once ministered to long-vanished diseases, they had done their work so well that they were no longer required.

Five hundred years were to pass before the pendulum swung back again.

The view from the studio was breath-taking, for the long, curving room was over two miles from the base of Central Tower. The five other giant buildings of the city clustered below, their metal walk gleaming with all the colors of the spectrum as they caught the rays of the morning sun. Lower still, die checkerboard fields of the automatic farms stretched away until they were lost in the mists of the horizon, But for once, the beauty of the scene was wasted on Richard Peyton II as he paced angrily among the great blocks of synthetic marble that were the raw materials of his art.

The huge, gorgeously colored masses of artificial rock completely dominated the studio. Most of them were roughly hewn cubes, but some were beginning to assume the shapes of animals, human beings, and abstract solids that no geometrician would have dared to give a name. Sitting awkwardly on a ten-ton block of diamond—the largest ever synthesized—the artist's son was regarding his famous parent with an unfriendly expression.

"I don't think I'd mind so much," Richard Peyton II remarked peevishly, "if you were content to do nothing, so long as you did it gracefully. Certain people excel at that, and on the whole they make the world more interesting. But why you should want to make a life study of engineering is more than I can imagine.

"Yes, I know we let you take technology as your main subject, but we never thought you were so serious about it. When I was your age I had a passion for botany—but I never made it my main interest in life, Has Professor Chandras Ling been giving you ideas?"

Richard Peyton III blushed.

"Why shouldn't he? I know what my vocation is, and he agrees with me. You've read his report."

The artist waved several sheets of paper in the air, holding them between thumb and forefinger like some unpleasant insect.

"I have," he said grimly, "'shows very unusual mechanical ability—has done original work in subelectronic research,' et cetera, et cetera. Good heavens, I thought the human race had outgrown those toys centuries ago! Do you want to be a mechanic, first class, and go around attending to disabled robots? That's hardly a job for a boy of mine, not to mention the grandson of a World Councillor."

"I wish, you wouldn't keep bringing Grandfather into this," said Richard Peyton III with mounting annoyance. "The fact that he was a statesman didn't prevent your becoming an artist. So why should you expect me to be either?"

The older man's spectacular golden beard began to bristle ominously.

"I don't care what you do as long as it's something we can be proud of. But why this craze for gadgets? We've got all tike machines we need. The robot was perfected five hundred years, ago; spaceships haven't changed for at least that time; I believe our present communications system is nearly eight hundred years old. So why change what's already perfect?"

"That's special pleading with a vengeance!" the young man replied. "Fancy an artist saying that anything's perfect! Father, I'm ashamed of you!"

"Don't split hairs. You know perfectly well what I mean. Our ancestors designed machines that provide us with everything we need. No doubt some of them might be a few per cent more efficient. But why worry? Can you mention a single important invention that the world lacks today?"

Richard Peyton III sighed.

"Listen, Father," he said patiently. "I've been studying history as well as engineering. About twelve centuries ago there were people who said that everything had been invented—and *that* was before the coming of electricity, let alone flying and astronautics. They just didn't look far enough ahead—their minds were rooted in the present.

"The same thing's happening today. For five hundred years the world's been living on the brains of the past. I'm prepared to admit that some lines of development have come to an end, but there are dozens of others that haven't even begun.

"Technically the world has stagnated. It's not a dark age, because we haven't forgotten anything. But we're marking time. Look at space travel Nine hundred years ago we reached Pluto, and where are we now? Still at Pluto! When are we going to cross interstellar space?"

"Who wants to go to the stars, anyway?"

The boy made an exclamation of annoyance and jumped off the diamond block in his excitement.

"What a question to ask in this age! A thousand years ago people were saying, 'Who wants to go to the Moon?' Yes, I know it's unbelievable, but it's all there in the old books. Nowadays the Moon's only forty-five minutes away, and people like Harn Jansen work on Earth and live in Plato City.

"We take interplanetary travel for granted. One day we're going to do the same with *real* space travel I could mention scores of other subjects that have come to a full stop simply because people think m you do and are content with what they've got."

"And why not?"

Peyton waved his arm around in the studio.

"Be serious, Fattier. Have you ever been satisfied with anything you've made? Only animals are contented."

The artist laughed ruefully.

"Maybe you're right. But that doesn't affect my argument. I still think you'll be wasting your life, and so does Grandfather." He looked a little embarrassed. "In fact, he's coming down to Earth especially to see you."

Peyton looked alarmed.

"Listen, Father, I've already told you what I think, I don't want to have to go through it all again. Because neither Grandfather nor the whole of the World Council will make me alter my mind."

It was a bombastic statement, and Peyton wondered if he really meant it. His father was just about to reply when a low musical note vibrated through the studio. A second later a mechanical voice spoke from the air.

"Your father to see you, Mr. Peyton."

He glanced at his son triumphantly.

"I should have added," he said, "that Grandfather was coming now. But I know your habit of disappearing when you're wanted."

The boy did not answer. He watched his father walk toward the door. Then his lips curved in a smile.

The single pane of glassite that fronted the studio was open, and he stepped out on to the balcony. Two miles below, the great concrete apron of the parking ground gleamed whitely in the sun, except where it was dotted with the teardrop shadows of grounded ships.

Peyton glanced back into the room. It was still empty, though he could hear his father's voice drifting through the door. He waited no longer. Placing his hand on the balustrade, he vaulted over into space.

Thirty seconds later two figures entered the studio and gazed around in surprise. *The* Richard Peyton, with no qualifying number, was a roan who might have been taken for sixty, though that was less than a third of his actual age.

He was dressed in the purple robe worn by only twenty men on Earth and by fewer than a hundred in the entire Solar System. Authority seemed to radiate from him; by comparison, even his famous and self-assured son seemed fussy and inconsequential.

"Well, where is he?"

"Confound him! He's gone out the window. At least we can still say what we think of him."

Viciously, Richard Peyton II forked up his wrist and dialed an eight-figure number on his personal communicator. The reply came almost instantly. In clear, impersonal tones an automatic voice repeated endlessly:

"My master is asleep. Please do not disturb. My master is asleep. Please do not disturb...."

With an exclamation of annoyance Richard Peyton II switched off the instrument and turned to his father. The old man chuckled.

"Well, he thinks fast. He's beaten us there. We can't get hold of him until he chooses to press the clearing button. I certainly don't intend to chase him at my age."

There was silence for a moment as the two men gazed at each other with mixed expressions. Then, almost simultaneously, they began to laugh.

# 2
# THE LEGEND OF COMARRE

Peyton fell like a stone for a mile and a quarter before he switched on the neutralizer. The rush of air past him, though it made breathing difficult, was exhilarating. He was falling at less than a hundred and fifty miles an hour, but the impression of speed was enhanced by the smooth upward rush of the great building only a few yards away.

The gentle tug of the decelerator field slowed him some three hundred yards from the ground. He full gently toward the lines of parked flyers ranged at the foot of the tower.

His own speedster was a small single-seat fully automatic machine. At least, it had been fully automatic when it was built three centuries ago, but its current owner had made so many illegal modifications to it that no one else in the world could have flown it and lived to tell the tale.

Peyton switched off the neutralizer belt—an amusing device which, although technically obsolete, still had interesting possibilities—and stepped into the airlock of his machine. Two minutes later the towers of the city were sinking below the rim of the world and the uninhabited Wild Lands were speeding beneath at four thousand miles an hour.

Peyton set his course westward and almost immediately was over the ocean. He could do nothing but wait; the ship would reach its goal automatically. He leaned back in the pilot's seat, thinking bitter thoughts and feeling sorry for himself.

He was more disturbed than he cared to admit. The fact that his family failed to share his technical interests had ceased to worry Peyton years ago. But this steadily growing opposition, which had now come to a head, was something quite new. He was completely unable to understand it.

Ten minutes later a single white pylon began to climb out of the ocean like the sword Excalibur rising from the lake. The city known to the world as Scientia, and to its more cynical inhabitants as Bat's Belfry, had been built eight centuries ago on an island far from the major land masses. The gesture had been one of independence, for the last traces of nationalism had still lingered in that far-off age.

Peyton grounded his ship on the landing apron and walked to the nearest entrance. The boom of the great waves, breaking on the rocks a hundred yards away, was a sound that never failed to impress him.

He paused for a moment at the opening, inhaling the salt air and watching the gulls and migrant birds circling the tower. They had used this speck of land as a resting place when man was still watching the dawn with puzzled eyes and wondering if it was a god.

The Bureau of Genetics occupied a hundred floors near the center of the tower. It had taken Peyton ten minutes to reach the City of Science. It required almost as long again to locate the man he wanted in the cubic miles of officer and laboratories.

Alan Henson II was still one of Peyton's closest friends, although he had left the University of Antarctica two years earlier and had been studying biogenetics rather than engineering. When Peyton was in trouble, which was not infrequently, he found his friend's calm common sense very reassuring. It was natural for him to fly to Scientia now, especially since Henson had sent him an urgent call only the day before.

The biologist was pleased and relieved to see Peyton, yet his welcome had an undercurrent of nervousness.

"I'm glad you've come; I've got some news that will interest you. But you look glum—what's the matter?"

Peyton told him, not without exaggeration. Henson was silent for a moment.

"So they've started already!" he said. "We might have expected it!"

"What do you mean?" asked Peyton in surprise.

The biologist opened a drawer and pulled out a sealed envelope. From it he extracted two plastic sheets in which were cut several hundred parallel slots of varying lengths. He handed one to his friend.

"Do you know what this is?"

"It looks like a character analysis."

"Correct. It happens to be yours."

"Oh! This is rather illegal, isn't it?"

"Never mind that. The key is printed along the bottom: it runs from Aesthetic Appreciation to Wit. The last column gives your Intelligence Quotient. Don't let it go to your head."

Peyton studied the card intently. Once, he flushed slightly.

"I don't see how you knew,"

"Never mind," grinned Henson. "Now look at this analysis." He handed over a second card.

"Why, it's the same one!"

"Not quite, but very nearly."

"Whom does it belong to?"

Henson leaned back in his chair and measured out his words slowly.

"That analysis, Dick, belongs to your great-grandfather twenty-two times removed on the direct male line—the great Rolf Thordarsen."

Peyton took off like a rocket.

"What!"

"Don't shout the place down, We're discussing old times at college if anyone comes in."

"But—Thordarsen!"

"Well, if we go back far enough we've all got equally distinguished ancestors. But now you know why your grandfather is afraid of you."

"He's left it till rather late. I've practically finished my training."

"You can thank us for that. Normally our analysis goes back ten generations, twenty in special cases. It's a tremendous job. There are hundreds of millions of cards in the Inheritance Library, one for every man and woman who has lived since the twenty-third century. This coincidence was discovered quite accidentally about a month ago."

"*That*'s when the trouble started. But I still don't understand what its all about."

"Exactly what do you know, Dick, about your famous ancestor?"

"No more than anyone else, I suppose. I certainly don't know how or why he disappeared, if that's what you mean. Didn't he leave Earth?"

"No, He left the world, if you like, but he never left Earth. Very few people know this, Dick, but Rolf Thordarsen was the man who built Comarre."

Comarrel Peyton breathed the word through half-open lips savoring its meaning and its strangeness. So it *did* exist, after all! Even that had been denied by some.

Henson was speaking again.

"I don't suppose you know very much about the Decadents. The history books have been rather carefully edited. But the whole story is linked up with the end of the Second Electronic Age...."

Twenty thousand miles above the surface of the Earth, the artificial moon that housed the World Council was spinning on its eternal orbit. The roof of the Council Chamber was one flawless sheet of crystallite; when the members of the Council were in session it seemed as if there was nothing between them and the great globe spinning far below.

The symbolism was profound. No narrow parochial viewpoint could long survive in such a setting. Here, if anywhere, the minds of men would surely produce their greatest works.

Richard Peyton the Elder had spent his life guiding the destinies of Earth. For five hundred years the human race had known peace and had lacked nothing that art or science could provide. The men who ruled the planet could he proud of their work.

Yet the old statesman was uneasy. Perhaps the changes that lay ahead were already casting their shadows before them. Perhaps he felt, if only with his subconscious mind, that the five centuries of tranquillity were drawing to a close.

He switched on his writing machine and began to dictate.

The First Electronic Age, Peyton knew, had begun in 1908, more than eleven centuries before, with De Forest's invention of the triode. The same fabulous century that had seen the coming of the World Slate, the airplane, the spaceship, and atomic power hat! witnessed the invention of all the fundamental thermionic devices that made possible the civilization he knew.

The Second Electronic Age had come five hundred years later. It had been started not by the physicists but by the doctors and psychologists. For nearly five centuries they had been recording the electric currents that flow in the brain during the processes of thought. The analysis had been appallingly complex, but it had been completed after generations of toil. When it was finished the way lay open for the first machines that could read the human mind.

But this was only the beginning, Once man had discovered the mechanism of his own brain he could go further. He could reproduce it, using transistors and circuit networks instead of living cells.

Toward the end of the twenty-fifth century, the first thinking machines were built. They were very crude, a hundred square yards of equipment being required to do the work of a cubic centimeter of human brain. But once the first step had been taken it was not long before the mechanical brain was perfected and brought into general use.

It could perform only the lower grades of intellectual work and it lacked such purely human characteristics as initiative, intuition, and all emotions. However, in circumstances which seldom varied, where its limitations were not serious, it could do all that a man could do.

The coming of the metal brains had brought one of the great crises in human civilization. Though men had still to carry out all the higher duties of statesmanship and the control of society, all the immense mass of routine administration had been taken over by the robots. Man had achieved freedom at last. No longer did he have to rack his brains planning complex transport schedules, deciding production programs, and balancing budgets. The machines, which had taken over all manual labor centuries before, had made their second great contribution to society.

The effect on busman affairs was immense, and men reacted to the new situation in two ways. There were those who used their new-found freedom nobly in the pursuits which kid always attracted the highest minds: the quest for beauty and truth, still us elusive as when the Acropolis was built.

But there were others who thought differently. At last, they said, tine curse of Adam is lifted forever. Now we can build cities where the machines will care for our every need as soon as the thought enters our minds—sooner, since the analyzers can read even the buried desires of the subconscious. The aim of all life is pleasure and the pursuit of happiness. Man has earned the right to that We are tired of this unending struggle for knowledge and the blind desire to bridge space to the stars.

It was the ancient dream of the Lotus Eaters, a dream as old its Man. Now, for the first time, it could be realized. For a while there were not many who shared it. The fires of the Second Renaissance had not yet begun to flicker and die. But as the years passed, the Decadents drew more and more to their way of thinking. In hidden places on the inner planets they built the cities of their dreams.

For a century they flourished like strange exotic flowers, until the almost religious fervor that inspired their building had died. They lingered for a generation more. Then, one by one, they faded from human knowledge. Dying, they left behind a host of fables and legends which had grown with the passing centuries.

Only one such city hid been built on Earth, and there were mysteries about it that the outer world had never solved. For purposes of its own, the World Council had destroyed all knowledge of the place. Its location was a mystery. Some said it was in the Arctic wastes; others believed it to be hidden on the bed of the Pacific. Nothing was certain but its name—Comarre.

Henson paused in his recital

"So far I have told you nothing new, nothing that isn't common knowledge. The rest of the story is a secret to the World Council and perhaps a hundred men of Scientia.

"Rolf Thordarsen, as you know, was the greatest mechanical genius the world has ever known, Not even Edison can be compared with him. He laid the foundations of robot engineering and built the first of the practical thought-machines.

"His laboratories poured out a stream of brilliant inventions for over twenty years. Then, suddenly, he disappeared. The story was put out that he tried to reach the stars. This is what really happened:

"Thordarsen believed that his robots—the machines that still run our civilization—were only a beginning. He went to the World Council with certain proposals which would have changed the face of human society. What those changes are we do not know, but Thordarsen believed that unless they were adopted the race would eventually come to a dead end—as, indeed, many of us think it has.

"The Council disagreed violently. At that time, you see, the robot was just being integrated into civilization and stability was slowly returning—the stability that has been maintained for five hundred years.

"Thordarsen was bitterly disappointed. With the flair they had for attracting genius the Decadents got hold of him and persuaded him to renounce the world. He was the only man who could convert their dreams into reality."

"And did he?"

"No one knows. But Comarre was built—that is certain. We know where it is—and so does the World Council. There are some things that cannot be kept secret."

That was true, thought Peyton. Even in this age people still disappeared and it was rumored that they had gone in search of the dream city. Indeed, the phrase "He's gone to Comarre" had become such a part of the language that its meaning was almost forgotten.

Henson leaned forward and spoke with mounting earnestness.

"This is the strange part. The World Council could destroy Comarre, but it won't do so. The belief that Comarre exists has a definite stabilizing influence on society. In spite of all our efforts, we still have psychopaths. It's no difficult matter to give them hints, under hypnosis, about Comarre. They may never find it but the quest will keep them harmless.

"In the early days, soon after the city was founded, the Council sent its agents into Comarre. None of them ever returned. There was no foul play; they just preferred to remain. That's known definitely because they sent messages back. I suppose the Decadents realized that the Council would tear the place down if its agents were detained deliberately.

"I've seen some of those messages. They are extraordinary. There's only one word for them; exalted. Dick, there was something in Comarre that could make a man forget the outer world, his friends, his family—everything! Try to imagine what that means!

"Later, when it was certain that none of the Decadents could still be alive, the Council tried again. It was still trying up to fifty years ago. But to this day no one has ever returned from Comarre."

As Richard Peyton spoke, the waiting robot analyzed his words into their phonetic groups, inserted the punctuation, and automatically routed the minute to the correct electronic files.

"Copy to President and my personal file.

"Your Minute of the 22nd and our conversation this morning.

"I have seen my son, but R.P. III evaded me. He is completely determined, and we will only do harm by trying to coerce him. Thordarsen should have taught us that lesson.

"My suggestion is that we earn his gratitude by giving him all the assistance he needs. Then we can direct him along safe lines of research. As long as he never discovers that R. T. was his ancestor, there should be no danger. Inspite of character similarities, it is unlikely that he will try to repeat R. T.'s work.

"Above all, we must ensure that he never locates or visits Comarre. If that happens, no one can foresee the consequences,"

Henson stopped his narrative, but his friend said nothing. He was too spellbound to interrupt, and, after a minute, the other continued.

"That brings us up to the present and to you. The World Council, Dick, discovered your inheritance a month ago. We're sorry we told them, but it's too late now. Genetically, you're a reincarnation of Thordarsen in the only scientific sense of the word. One of Nature's longest odds has come off, as it does every few hundred years in some family or another.

"You, Dick, could carry on the work Thordarsen was compelled to drop—whatever that work was. Perhaps it's lost forever, but if any trace of it exists, the secret lies in Comarre. The World Council knows that. That is why it is trying to deflect you from your destiny.

"Don't be bitter about it. On the Council are some of the noblest minds the human race has yet produced. They mean you no harm, and none will ever befall you. But they are passionately anxious to preserve the present structure of society, which they believe to be the best."

Slowly, Peyton rose to his feet. For a moment, it seemed as if he were a neutral, exterior observer, watching this lay figure called Richard Peyton III, now no longer a man, but a symbol, one of the keys to the future of the world. It took a positive mental effort to reidentify himself.

His friend was watching him silently.

"There's something else you haven't told me, Alan. How do you know all this?"

Henson smiled.

"I was waiting for that. I'm only the mouthpiece, chosen because I know you. Who the others are I can't say, even to you. But they include quite a number of the scientists I know you admire.

"There has always been a friendly rivalry between the Council and the scientists who serve it, but in the last few years our viewpoints have drifted farther apart. Many of us believe that the present age, which the Council thinks will last forever, is only an interregnum. We believe that too long a period of stability will cause decadence. The Council's psychologists arc confident they can prevent it."

Peyton's eyes gleamed.

"That's what I've been saying! Can I join you?"

"Later. There's work to be done first. You see, we are revolutionaries of a sort. We are going to start one or two social reactions, and when we've finished the danger of racial decadence will be postponed for thousands of years. You, Dick, are one of our catalysts. Not the only one, I might say."

He paused for a moment.

"Even if Comarre comes to nothing, we have another card up our sleeve. In fifty years, we hope to have perfected the interstellar drive."

"At last!" said Peyton. "What will you do then?"

"We'll present it to the Council and say, 'Here you are—now you can go to the stars. Aren't we good boys?' And the Council will just have to give a sickly smile and start uprooting civilization. Once we've achieved interstellar travel, we shall have an expanding society again and stagnation will be indefinitely postponed."

"I hope I live to see it," said Peyton. "But what do you want me to do now?"

"Just this: we want you to go into Comarre to find what's there. Where others have failed, we believe you can succeed. All the plans have been made."

"And where is Comarre?"

Henson smiled.

"It's simple, really. There was only one place it could be—the only place over which no aircraft can fly, where no one lives, where all travel is on foot. It's in the Great Reservation."

The old man switched off the writing machine. Overhead—or below; it was all the same—the great crescent of Earth was blotting out the stars. In its eternal circling the little moon had overtaken the terminator and was plunging into night. Here and there the darkling land below was dotted with the lights of cities.

The sight filled the old man with sadness. It reminded him that his own life was coming to a close—and it seemed to foretell the end of the culture he had sought to protect. Perhaps, after all, the young scientists were right. The long rest was ending and the world was moving to new goals that he would never see.

# 3

# THE WILD LION

It was night when Peyton's ship came westward over the Indian Ocean. The eye could see nothing far below but the white line of breakers against the African coast, but the navigation screen showed every detail of the land beneath. Night, of course, was no protection or safeguard now, but it meant that no human eye would see him. As for the machines that should be watching—well, others had taken care of them. There were many, it seemed, who thought as Henson did.

The plan had been skillfully conceived. The details had been worked out with loving care by people who had obviously enjoyed themselves. He was to land the ship at the edge of the forest, as near to the power barrier as he could.

Not even his unknown friends could switch off the barrier without arousing suspicion. Luckily it was only about twenty miles to Comarre from the edge of the screen, over fairly open country. He would have to finish the journey afoot

There was a great crackling of branches as the little ship settled down into the unseen forest. It came to rest on an even keel, and Peyton switched off the dim cabin lights and peered out of the window. He could see nothing. Remembering what he had been told, he did not open the door. He made himself as comfortable as he could and settled down to await the dawn.

He awoke with brilliant sunlight shining full in his eyes. Quickly climbing into the equipment his friends had provided, he opened the cabin door and stepped into the forest.

The landing place had been carefully chosen, and it was not difficult to scramble through to the open country a few yards away. Ahead lay small grass-covered hills dotted with occasional clusters of slender trees. The day was mild, though it was summer and the equator was not far away. Eight hundred years of climatic control and the great artificial lakes that had drowned the deserts had seen to that.

For almost the first time in his life Peyton was experiencing Nature as it had been in the days before Man existed. Yet it was not the wildness of the scene that he found so strange. Peyton had never known silence. Always there had been the murmur of machines or the faraway whisper of speeding liners, heard faintly from the towering heights of the stratosphere.

Here there were none of these sounds, for no machines could cross the power barrier that surrounded the Reservation. There was only the wind to the grass and the half-audible medley of insect voices. Peyton found the silence unnerving and did what almost any man of his time would have done, He pressed the button of his personal radio that selected the background-music band.

So, mile after mile, Peyton walked steadily through the undulating country of the Great Reservation, the largest area of natural territory remaining on the surface of the globe, Walking was easy, for the neutralizers built into his equipment almost nullified its weight. He carried with him that mist of unobtrusive music that had been the background of men's lives almost since the discovery of radio. Although he had only to lick a dial to get in touch with anyone on the planet, he quite sincerely imagined himself to be alone in the heart of Nature, and for a moment he felt all the emotions that Stanley or Livingstone most have experienced when they first entered this same land more than a thousand years ago.

Luckily Peyton was a good walker, and by noon had covered half the distance to his goal. He rested for his midday meal under a cluster of imported Martian conifers, which would have brought baffled consternation to an old-time explorer. In his ignorance Peyton took them completely for granted.

He had accumulated a small pile of empty cans when he noticed an object moving swiftly over the plain in the direction from which he had come. It was too far away to be recognized. Not until it was obviously approaching him did he bother to get up to get a clearer view of it. So far he bad seen no animals—though plenty of animals had seen him—and he watched the newcomer with interest.

Peyton had never seen a lion before, but he had no difficulty in recognizing the magnificent beast that was bounding toward him. It was to his credit that he glanced only once at the tree overhead. Then he stood his ground firmly.

There were, he knew, no really dangerous animals in the world any more. The Reservation was something between a vast biological laboratory and a national park, visited by thousands of people every year. It was generally understood that if one left the inhabitants alone, they would reciprocate. On the whole, the arrangement worked smoothly.

The animal was certainly anxious to be friendly. It trotted straight toward him and began to rub itself affectionately against his side. When Peyton got up again, it was taking a great deal of interest in his empty food cans. Presently it turned toward him with an expression that was irresistible.

Peyton laughed, opened a fresh can, and laid the contents carefully on a flat stone. The lion accepted the tribute with relish, and while it was eating Peyton ruffled through the index of the official guide which his unknown supporters bad thought fully provided.

There were several pages about lions, with photographs for the benefit of extraterrestrial visitors. The information was reassuring. A thousand years of scientific breeding had greatly improved the King of Beasts. He had eaten only a dozen people in the last century: in ten of the cases the subsequent enquiry had exonerated him from blame and the other two were "not proved."

But the book said nothing about unwanted lions and the best ways of disposing of them. Nor did it hint that they were normally as friendly as this specimen.

Peyton was not particularly observant. It was some time before be noticed the thin metal band around the lion's right forepaw, It bore a series of numbers and letters, followed by the official stamp of the Reservation.

This was no wild animal; perhaps all its youth had been spent among men. It was probably one of the famous superlions the biologists had been breeding and then releasing to improve the race. Some of them were almost as intelligent as dogs, according to the reports that Peyton had seen.

He quickly discovered that it could understand many simple words, particularly those relating to food. Even for this era it was a splendid beast, a good foot taller than its scrawny ancestors of ten centuries before.

When Peyton started on his journey again, the lion trotted by his side. He doubted if its friendship was worth more than a pound of synthetic beef, but it was pleasant to have someone to talk to—someone, moreover, who made no attempt to contradict him. After profound and concentrated thought, he decided that "Leo" would be a suitable name for his new acquaintance.

Peyton had walked a few hundred yards when suddenly there was a blinding flash in the air before him. Though he realized immediately what it was, he was startled, and stopped, blinking. Leo had fled precipitately and was already out of sight. He would not, Peyton thought, be of much use to an emergency. Later he was to revise this judgment.

When his eyes had recovered, Peyton found himself looking at a multicolored notice, burning in letters of fire. It hung steadily in the air and read:

WARNING!
YOU ARE NOW APPROACHING
RESTRICTED TERRITORY!
TURN BACK!


By Order,

World Council in Session

Peyton regarded the notice thoughtfully for a few moments. Then he looked around for the projector. It was in a metal box, not very effectively hidden at the side of the road. He quickly unlocked it with the universal keys a trusting Electronics Commission had given him on his first graduation.

After a few minutes' inspection he breathed a sigh of relief. The projector was a simple capacity-operated device. Anything coming along the road would actuate it. There was a photographic recorder, but it had been disconnected. Peyton was not surprised, far every passing animal would have operated the device. This was fortunate. It meant that no one need ever know that Richard Peyton III had once walked along this road.

He shouted to Leo, who came slowly back, looking rather ashamed of himself. The sign had disappeared, and Peyton held the relays open to prevent its reappearance as Leo passed by. Then he relocked the door and continued on his way, wondering what would happen next.

A hundred yards farther on, a disembodied voice began to speak to him severely. It told him nothing new, but the voice threatened a number of minor penalties, some of which were not unfamiliar to him.

It was amusing to watch Leo's face as he tried to locate the source of the sound. Once again Peyton searched for the projector and checked it before proceeding. It would be safer, he thought, to leave the road altogether. There might be recording devices farther along it.

With some difficulty he induced Leo to remain on the, metal surface while he himself walked along the barren ground bordering the road. In the next quarter of a mile the lion set off two more electronic booby traps. The last one seemed to have given up persuasion. It said simply:

BEWARE OF WILD LIONS

Peyton looked at Leo and began to laugh. Leo couldn't see the pie but he joined in politely. Behind them the automatic sign faded out with a last despairing flicker.

Peyton wondered why the signs were there at all. Perhaps they were intended to scare away accidental visitors, Those who knew the goal would hardly be deflected by them.

The road made a sudden right-angle turn—and there before him was Comarre. It was strange that something he had been expecting could give him such a shock. Ahead lay an immense clearing in the jungle, half filled by a black metallic structure.

The city was shaped like, a terraced cone, perhaps eight hundred yards high and a thousand across at the base. How much was underground, Peyton could not guess. He halted, overwhelmed by the size and strangeness of the enormous building. Then, slowly, he began to walk toward it.

*Like a beast of prey crouching in its lair, the city lay waiting. Though its guests were now very few, it was ready to receive them, whoever they might be. Sometimes they turned back at the first warning, sometimes at the second. A few had reached the very entrance before their resolution failed them. But most, having come so far, had entered willingly enough.*

So Peyton reached the marble steps that led up to the towering metal wall and the curious black hole that seemed to be the only entrance. Leo trotted quietly beside him, taking little notice of his strange surroundings.

Peyton stopped at the foot of the stairs and dialed a number in his communicator. He waited until the acknowledgment tone came and then spoke slowly into the microphone.

"The fly is entering the parlor."

He repeated it twice, feeling rather a fool. Someone, he thought, had a perverted sense of humor.

There was no reply. That had been part of the arrangement. But he had no doubt that the message had been received, probably in some laboratory in Scientia, since the number he had dialed had a Western Hemisphere coding.

Peyton opened his biggest can of meat and spread it out on the marble. He entwined his fingers in the lion's mane and twisted it playfully.

"I guess you'd better stay here, Leo," he said. "I may be gone quite some time. Don't try to follow me."

At the top of the steps, he looked buck. Rather to his relief the lion had made no attempt to follow, It was sitting on its haunches, looking at him pathetically, Peyton waved and turned away.

There was no door, only a plain black hole in the curving metal surface. That was puzzling, and Peyton wondered how the builders had expected to keep animals from wandering in. Then something about the opening attracted his attention.

It was *too* black. Although the wall was In shadow, the entrance had no right to be as dark as this. He took a coin from his pocket and tossed it into the aperture. The sound of its fall reassured him, and lie stepped forward.

*The delicately adjusted discriminator circuits had ignored the cam, as they had ignored all the stray animals that had entered this dark portal But the presence of a human mind had been enough to trip the relays. For a fraction of a second the screen through which Peyton was moving throbbed with power. Then it became inert again.*

It seemed to Peyton that his foot took a long time to reach the ground, but that was the least of his worries. Far more surprising was the instantaneous transition from darkness to sudden light, from the somewhat oppressive heat of the jungle to a temperature that seemed almost chilly by comparison, The change was so abrupt that it left him gasping. Filled with a feeling of distinct unease he turned toward the archway through which he had Just come.

It was no longer there. It never had been there. He was standing on a raised metal dais at the exact center of a large circular room with a dozen pointed archways around its circumference. He might have come through any one of them-if only they had not all been forty yards away.

For a moment Peyton was seized with panic. He felt his heart pounding, and something odd was happening to his legs. Feeling very much alone, he sat down on the dais and begun to consider the situation logically.

built. But the machine could be very useful if he employed it properly.

Thank you," he said, unnecessarily. "Please take me to the living quarters."

Although Peyton was now certain that the city was completely automatic, there was still the possibility that it held some human life. There might be others here who could help him in his quest, though the absence of opposition was perhaps as much as he could hope for.

Without a word the little machine spun around on its driving wheels and rolled out of the room. The corridor along which it led Peyton ended sit a beautifully carved door, which he had already tried in vain to open. Apparently A-Five knew its; secret—for at their approach the thick metal plate slid silently aside. The robot rolled forward into a small, boxlike chamber.

Peyton wondered if they had entered another of the matter transmitters, but quickly discovered that it was nothing more unusual than an elevator. Judging by the time of ascent, it must have taken them almost to the top of the city. When the doors slid open it seemed to Peyton that he was in another world.

The corridors in which he had first found himself were drab and undecorated, purely utilitarian. In contrast, these spacious halls and assembly rooms were, furnished with the utmost luxury. The twenty-sixth century had been a period of florid decoration and coloring, much despised by subsequent ages. But the Decadents had gone far beyond their own period. They had taxed the resources of psychology as well as art when they designed Comarre.

One could have spent a lifetime without exhausting all the murals, the carvings and paintings, the intricate tapestries which still seemed as brilliant as when they had been made. It seemed utterly wrong that so wonderful a place should be deserted and hidden from the world Peyton almost forgot all his scientific zeal, and hurried like a child from marvel to marvel

Here were works of genius, perhaps as great as any the world had ever known. But it was a sick and despairing genius, one that had lost faith in itself while still retaining an immense technical skill For the first time Peyton truly understood why the builders of Comarre had been given their name.

The art of the Decadents at once repelled and fascinated him. It was not evil, for it was completely detached from moral standards. Perhaps its dominant characteristics were weariness and disillusion. After a while Peyton, who had never thought himself very sensitive to visual art, begun to feel a subtle depression creeping into his soul. Yet he found it quite impossible to tear himself away.

At last Peyton turned to the robot again,

"Does anyone live here now?"

"Yes."

"Where are they?"

"Sleeping,"

Somehow that seemed a perfectly natural reply. Peyton felt very tired. For the last hour it had been a struggle to remain awake. Something seemed to be compelling sleep, almost willing it upon him. Tomorrow would be time enough to learn the secrets he had come to find. For the moment he wanted nothing but sleep.

He followed automatically when the robot led him out of the spacious halls into a long corridor lined with metal doors, each bearing a half-familiar symbol Peyton could not quite recognize. His sleepy mind was still wrestling halfheartedly with the problem when the machine halted before one of the doors, which slid silently open.

The heavily draped couch in the darkened room was irresistible. Peyton stumbled toward it automatically. As he sank down into sleep, a glow of satisfaction wanted his mind. He had recognized the symbol on the door, though his brain was too tired to understand its significance.

It was the poppy.

*There was no guile, no malevolence in the working of the city. Impersonally it was fulfilling the tasks to which it had been dedicated. All who had entered Comarre had Willingly embraced its gifts. This visitor was the first who had ever ignored them.*

*The integrators had been ready for hours, but the restless, probing mind had eluded them. They could afford to wait, as they had done these hat five hundred years.*

*And now the defenses of this strangely stubborn mind were crumbling us Richard Peyton sank peacefully to Bleep. Far down in the heart of Comarre a relay tripped, and complex, slowly fluctuating currents began to ebb and flow through banks of vacuum tubes. The consciousness that had been Richard Peyton III ceased to exist.*

Peyton had fallen asleep instantly. For a while complete oblivion claimed him. Then faint wisps of consciousness began to return. And then, as always, he began to dream.

It was strange that his favorite dream should have come into his mind, and it was more vivid now than it had ever been before. All his life Peyton had loved the sea, and once he had seen the unbelievable beauty of the Pacific islands from the observation deck of a low-flying liner. He had never visited them, but he had often wished that he could spend his life on some remote and peaceful isle with no care for the future or the world.

It was a dream that almost all men had known at some time in their lives, but Peyton was sufficiently sensible to realize that two months of such an existence would have driven him back to civilization, half crazy with boredom. However, his dreams were never worried by such considerations, and once more he was lying beneath waving palms, the surf drumming on the reef beyond a lagoon that framed the sun in an azure mirror.

The dream was extraordinarily vivid, so much so that even in his sleep Peyton found himself thinking that no dream had any right to be so real. Then it ceased, so abruptly that there seemed to be a definite rift in his thoughts, The interruption jolted him back to consciousness.

Bitterly disappointed, Peyton lay for a while with his eyes tightly closed, trying to recapture the lost paradise. But it was useless. Something was beating against his brain, keeping him from sleep. Moreover, his couch had suddenly become very hard and uncomfortable. Reluctantly he turned his mind toward the interruption.

Peyton had always been a realist and had never been troubled by philosophical doubts, so the shock was far greater than it might have been to many less intelligent minds. Never before had he found himself doubting his own sanity, but he did so now. For the sound that had awakened him was the drumming of the waves against the reef, He was lying on the golden sand beside the lagoon. Around him, the wind was sighing through the palms, its warm fingers caressing him gently.

For a moment, Peyton could only imagine that he was still dreaming. But this time there could lie no real doubt, While one is sane, reality can never be mistaken for a dream. This was real if anything in the universe was real.

Slowly the sense of wonder began to fade. He rose to his feet, the sand showering from him in a golden rain. Shielding his eyes against the sun, he stared along the beach.

He did not stop to wonder why the place should be so familiar. It seemed natural enough to know that the village was a little farther along the bay. Presently he would rejoin his friends, from whom he had been separated for a little while in a world he was swiftly forgetting.

There was a fading memory of a young engineer—even the name escaped him now—who bad once aspired to fame and wisdom. In that other life, he had known this foolish person well, but now he could never explain to him the vanity of his ambitions.

He began to wander idly along the beach, the last vague recollections of his shadow life sloughing from him with every footstep, as the details of a dream fade into the light of day.

On the other side of the world three very worried scientists were waiting in a deserted laboratory, their eyes on a multichannel communicator of unusual design. The machine had been silent for nine hours. No one had expected a message in the first eight, but the prearranged signal Wits now more than an hour overdue.

Alan Henson jumped to his feet with a gesture of impatience.

"We've got to do something! I'm going to call him."

The other two scientists looked at each other nervously.

"The call may be traced!"

"Not unless they're actually watching us. Even if they are, I'll say nothing unusual. Peyton will understand, if he can answer at all..."

If Richard Peyton had ever known time, that knowledge was forgotten now. Only the present was real, for both past and future lay hidden behind an impenetrable screen, as a great landscape may be concealed by a driving wall of rain.

In his enjoyment of the present Peyton was utterly content. Nothing at all was left of the restless driving spirit that had once set out, a little uncertainly, to conquer fresh fields of knowledge. He had no use for knowledge now.

Later he was never able to recollect anything of his life on the island. He had known many companions, but their names and faces had vanished beyond recall. Love, peace of mind, happiness—all were his for a brief moment of time. And yet he could remember no more than the last few moments of his life in paradise.

Strange that it should have ended as it began. Once more he was by the side of the lagoon, but this time it was night and he was not alone. The moon that seemed always to be full rode low above the ocean, and its long silver baud stretched far away to the edge of the world. The stars that never changed their places glowed unblinking in the sky like brilliant jewels, more glorious than the forgotten stars of Earth.

But Peyton's thoughts were intent on other beauty, and once again he bent toward the figure lying on the sand that was no more golden than the hair strewn carelessly across it,

Then paradise trembled and dissolved around him. He gave a great cry of anguish as everything he loved was wrenched away. Only the swiftness of the transition saved his mind. When it was over, he felt as Adam must have when the gates of Eden clanged forever shut behind him.

But the sound that had brought him back was the most common-place in all the world. Perhaps, indeed, no other could have reached his mind in its place of hiding. It was only the shrilling of his communicator set as it lay on the floor beside his couch, here in the darkened room in the city of Comarre.

The clangor died away as he reached out automatically to press the receiving switch. He must have made some answer that satisfied his unknown caller—who was Alan Henson?—for after a very short time the circuit was cleared. Still dazed, Peyton sat on the couch, holding his head in his hands and trying to reorient his life.

He had not been dreaming; he was sure of that. Rather, it was as if he had been living a second life and now he was returning to his old existence as might a man recovering from amnesia. Though he was still dazed, one clear conviction came into his mind. He must never again sleep in Comarre.

Slowly the will and character of Richard Peyton III returned from their banishment. Unsteadily he rose to his feet and made his way out of the room. Once again he found himself in the long corridor with its hundreds of identical doors. With new understanding he looked at the symbol carved upon them.

He scarcely noticed where he was going. His mind was fixed too intently on the problem before him. As he walked, his brain cleared, and slowly understanding came. For the moment it was only a theory, but soon he would put it to the test.

The human mind was a delicate, sheltered thing, having no direct contact with the world and gathering all its knowledge and experience through the body's senses. It was possible to record and store thoughts and emotions as earlier men had once recorded sound on miles of wire.

If those thoughts were projected into another mind, when the body was unconscious and all its senses numbed, that brain would think it was experiencing reality. There was no way in which it could detect the deception, any more than one can distinguish a perfectly recorded symphony from the original performance.

All this had been known for centuries, but the builders of Comarre had used the knowledge as no one in the world had ever done before. Somewhere in the city there mast be machines that could analyze every thought and desire of those who entered. Elsewhere the city's makers must have stored every sensation and experience a human mind could know. From this raw material all possible futures could be constructed.

Now at last Peyton understood the measure of the genius that had gone into the making of Comarre, The machines had analyzed his deepest thoughts and built for him a world based on his subconscious desires. Then, when the chance had come, they had taken control of his mind and injected into it all lie had experienced.

No wonder that everything he had ever longed for had been his in that already half-forgotten paradise. And no wonder that through the ages no many had sought the peace only Comarre could bring!

# 5
# THE ENGINEER

Peyton had become himself again by the time the sound of wheels made him look over his shoulder. The little robot that had been his guide was returning. No doubt the great machines that controlled it were wondering what had happened to its charge. Peyton waited, a thought slowly forming in his mind.

A-Five started all over again with its set speech. It seemed very incongruous now to find so simple a machine in this place where automatronics had reached their ultimate development. Then Peyton realized that perhaps the robot was deliberately uncomplicated. There was little purpose, in using a complex machine where a simple one would serve as well—or better.

Peyton ignored the now familiar speech. All robots, he knew, must obey human commands unless other humans bad previously given them orders to die contrary. Even the projectors of the city, he thought wryly, had obeyed the unknown and unspoken commands of his own subconscious mind.

"Lead me to the thought projectors," he commanded.

As he had expected, tie robot did not move. It merely replied, "I do not understand."

Peyton's spirits began to revive as be felt himself once more master of the situation.

"Come here and do not move again until I give the order."

The robot's selectors and relays considered the instructions. They could find no countermanding order. Slowly the little machine rolled forward on its wheels. It had committed itself—there was no turning back now. It could not move again until Peyton ordered it to do so or something overrode his commands. Robot hypnosis was a very old trick, much beloved by mischievous small boys.

Swiftly, Peyton emptied his bag of the tools no engineer was ever without: the universal screw driver, the expanding wrench, the automatic drill, and, most important of all, the atomic cutter that could eat through the thickest metal in a matter of seconds. Then, with a skill born of long practice, he went to work on the unsuspecting machine.

Luckily the robot had been built for easy servicing, and could be opened with little difficulty. There was nothing unfamiliar about the controls, and it did not take Peyton long to find the locomotor mechanism. Now, whatever happened, the machine could not escape. It was crippled.

Next he blinded it and, one by one, tracked down its other electrical senses and put them out of commission. Soon the little machine was no more than a cylinder full of complicated junk. Feeling like a small boy who has just made a wanton attack on a defenseless grandfather clock, Peyton sat down and waited for what he knew must happen.

It was a little inconsiderate of him to sabotage the robot so far from the main machine levels. The robot-transporter took nearly fifteen minutes to work its way up from the depths. Peyton heard the rumble of its wheels in the distance and knew that his calculations had been correct. The breakdown party was on the way,

The transporter was a simple carrying machine, with a set of arms that could grasp and hold a damaged robot. It seemed to be blind, though no doubt its special senses were quite sufficient for its purpose.

Peyton waited until it had collected the unfortunate A-Five. Then he jumped aboard, keeping well away from the mechanical limbs. He had no desire to be mistaken for another distressed robot. Fortunately the big machine took no notice of him at all.

So Peyton descended through level after level of the great building, past the living quarters, through the room in which he had first found himself, and lower yet into regions he had never before seen. As he descended, the character of the city changed around him.

Gone now were the luxury and opulence of the higher levels, replaced by a no man's land of bleak passageways that were little more than giant cable duets. Presently these, too, came to an end. The conveyor passed through a set of great sliding doors—and he had readied his goal.

The rows of relay panels and selector mechanisms seemed endless, but though Peyton was tempted to jump off his unwitting steed, he waited until the main central panels came into sight. Then he climbed off the conveyor and watched it disappear into the distance toward some still more remote part of the city.

He wondered how long it would take the superautomata to repair A-Five. His sabotage had been very thorough, and he rather thought the little machine was heading for the scrap heap. Then, feeling like a starving man suddenly confronted by a banquet, lie began his examination of the city's wonders.

In the next five hours he paused only once to send the routine signal back to his friends. He wished he could tell of his success, but the risk was too peat. After prodigies of circuit tracing he had discovered the functions of the main units and was beginning to investigate some of the secondary equipment.

It was just as he had expected. The thought analyzers and projectors lay on the floor immediately above, and could be controlled from, his central installation. How they worked he had no conception: it might well take months to uncover all their secrets. But he had identified them and thought he could probably switch them off if necessary.

A little later he discovered the thought monitor. It was a small machine, rather like an ancient manual telephone switchboard, but very much more complex. The operator's seat was a curious structure, insulated from the ground and roofed by a network of wires and crystal bars. It was the first machine he had discovered that was obviously intended for direct human use. Probably the first engineers had built it to set up the equipment in the early days of the city.

Peyton would not have risked using the thought monitor if detailed instructions had not been printed on its control panel. After some experimenting he plugged in to one of the circuits and slowly increased the power, keeping the intensity control well below the red danger mark.

It was as well that he did so, for the sensation was a shattering one. He still retained his own personality, but superimposed on his own thoughts were ideas and images that were utterly foreign to him. He was looking at another world, through the windows of an alien mind.

It was as though his body were In two places at once, though the sensations of his second personality were much less vivid than those of the real Richard Peyton III. Now he understood the meaning of the danger line. If the thought-intensity control was turned too high, madness would certainly result.

Peyton switched off the instrument so that he could think without interruption. He understood now what the robot had meant when it said that the other inhabitants of the city were sleeping. There were other men in Comarre, lying entranced beneath the thought projectors.

His mind went back to the long corridor and its hundreds of metal doors. On his way down he had passed through many such galleries and it was clear that the greater part of the city was no more than a vast honeycomb of chambers in which thousands of men could dream away their lives.

One after another he checked the circuits on the board. The great majority were dead, but perhaps fifty were still operating. And each of them carried all the thoughts, desires, and emotions of the human mind.

Now that he was fully conscious, Peyton could understand how he had been tricked, but the knowledge brought little consolation. He could see the flaws in these synthetic worlds, could observe how all the critical faculties of the mind were numbed while an endless stream of simple but vivid emotions was poured into it.

Yes, it all seemed very simple now. But it did not alter the fact that this artificial world was utterly real to the beholder—so real that the pain of leaving it still burned in his own mind.

For nearly an hour, Peyton explored the worlds of the fifty sleeping minds. It was a fascinating though repulsive quest. In that hour he learned more of the human brain and its hidden ways than he had ever dreamed existed. When he had finished he sat very still for a long time at the controls of the machine, analyzing his newfound knowledge. His wisdom had advanced by many years, and his youth seemed suddenly very far away.

For the first time he had direct knowledge of the fact that the perverse and evil desires that sometimes ruffled the surface of his own mind were shared by all human beings. The builders of Comarre had eared nothing for good or evil—and the machines had been their faithful servants.

It was satisfactory to know that his theories had been correct. Peyton understood now the narrowness of his escape. If he fell asleep again within these walk he might never awake. Chance had saved him once, but it would not do so again.

The thought projectors must be put out of action, so thoroughly that the robots could never repair them. Though they could handle normal breakdowns, the robots could not deal with deliberate sabotage on the scale Peyton was envisaging. When he had finished, Comarre would be a menace no longer. It would never trap his mind again, or the minds of any future visitors who might come this way.

First he would have to locate the sleepers and revive them. That might he a lengthy task, but fortunately the machine level was equipped with standard monovision search apparatus. With it he could see and hear everything in the city, simply by focusing the carrier beams on the required spot. He could even project his voice if necessary, but not his image. That type of machine had not come into general use until after the building of Comarre.

It took him a little while to master the controls, and at first the beam wandered erratically all over the city. Peyton found himself looking into any number of surprising places, and once he even got a glimpse of the forest—though it was upside down. He wondered if Leo was still around, and with some difficulty he located the entrance.

Yes, there it was, just as he had left it the day before. And a few yards away the faithful Leo was lying with his head toward the city and a distinctly worried look on his face. Peyton was deeply touched. He wondered if he could get the lion into Comarre. The moral support would be valuable, for he was beginning to feel need of companionship after the night's experiences.

Methodically he searched the wall of the city and was greatly relieved to discover several concealed entrances at ground level. He had been wondering how he was going to leave. Even if he could work the matter-transmitter in reverse, the prospect was not an attractive one. He much preferred an old-fashioned physical movement through space.

The openings were all sealed, and for a moment he was baffled. Then he began to search for a robot. After some delay, he discovered one of the late A-Five's twins rolling along a corridor on some mysterious errand. To his relief, it obeyed his command unquestioningly and opened the door.

Peyton drove the beam through the walls again and brought the focus point to rest a few feet away from Leo. Then he called, softly: "Leo!"

The lion looked up, startled.

"Hello, Leo—it's me—Peyton!"

Looking puzzled, the lion walked slowly around in a circle. Then it gave up and sat clown helplessly.

With a great deal of persuasion, Peyton coaxed Leo up to the entrance. The lion recognized his voice and seemed willing to follow, but it was a sorely puzzled and rather nervous animal. It hesitated for a moment at the opening, liking neither Comarre nor the silently waiting robot.

Very patiently Peyton instructed Leo to follow the robot. He repeated his remarks in different words until he was sure the lion understood. Then he spoke directly to the machine and ordered it to guide the lion to the control chamber. He watched for a moment to see that Leo was following. Then, with a word of encouragement, he left the strangely assorted pair.

It was rather disappointing to find that he could not see into any of the sealed rooms behind the poppy symbol. They were shielded from the beam or else the focusing controls had been set so that the monovisor could not be used to pry into that volume of space.

Peyton was not discouraged. The sleepers would wake up the hard way, as he had done. Having looked into their private worlds, he felt little sympathy for them and only a sense of duty impelled him to wake them. They deserved no consideration.

A horrible thought suddenly assailed him. What had the projectors fed into his own mind in response to his desires, in that forgotten idyll from which he had been so reluctant to return? Had his own hidden thoughts been as disreputable as those of the other dreamers?

It was an uncomfortable idea, and he put it aside as he sat down once more at the central switchboard. First he would disconnect the circuits, then he would sabotage the projectors so that they could never again be used. The spell that Comarre had cast over so many minds would be broken forever.

Peyton reached forward to throw the multiplex circuit breakers, but he never completed the movement. Gently but very firmly, four metal arms clasped his body from behind. Kicking and struggling, he was lifted into the air away from the controls and carried to the center of the room. There he was set dawn again, and the metal arms released him.

More angry than alarmed, Peyton whirled to face his captor. Regarding him quietly from a few yards away was the most complex robot he had ever seen. Its body was nearly seven feet high, and rested on a dozen fat balloon tires.

From various parts of its metal chassis, tentacles, arms, rods, and other less easily describable mechanisms projected in all directions. In two places, groups of limbs were busily at work dismantling or repairing pieces of machinery which Peyton recognized with a guilty start.

Silently Peyton weighed his opponent. It was clearly a robot of the very highest order. But it had used physical violence against him—and no robot could do that against a man, though it might refuse to obey his orders. Only under the direct control of another human mind could a robot commit such an act. So there was life, conscious and hostile life, somewhere in the city.

"Who are you?" exclaimed Peyton at last, addressing not the robot, but the controller behind it.

With no detectable time lag the machine answered in a precise and automatic voice that did not seem to be merely the amplified, speech of a human being.

"I am the Engineer."

"Then come out and let me see you."

"You arc seeing me."

It was the inhuman tone of the voice, as much as the words themselves, that made Peyton's anger evaporate in a moment and replaced it with a sense of unbelieving wonder.

There was no human being controlling this machine. It was as automatic as the other robots of the city—but unlike them, and all other robots the world had ever known, it had a will and a consciousness of its own.

# 6
# THE NIGHTMARE

As Peyton stared wide-eyed at the machine before him, he felt his scalp crawling, not with fright, but with the sheer intensity of his excitement. His quest had been rewarded—the dream of nearly a thousand years was here before his eyes.

Long ago the machines had won a limited intelligence. Now at last they had reached the goal of consciousness itself. This was the secret Thordarsen would have given to the world—the secret the Council had sought to suppress for fear of the consequences it might bring.

The passionless voice spoke again.

"I am glad that you realize the truth. It will make things easier."

"You can read my mind?" gapped Peyton.

"Naturally. That was done from the moment you entered."

"Yes, I gathered that" said Peyton grimly. "And what do you intend to do with me now?"

"I must prevent you from damaging Comarre."

That, thought Peyton, was reasonable enough.

"Suppose I left now? Would that suit you?"

"Yes. That would be good."

Peyton could not help laughing. The Engineer was still a robot, in spite of all its near-humanity. It was incapable of guile, and perhaps that gave him an advantage. Somehow he must trick it into revealing its secrets. But once again the robot read his mind.

"I will not permit it. You have learned too much already. You must leave at once. I will use force if necessary."

Peyton decided to fight for time. He could, at least, discover the limits of this amazing machine's intelligence.

"Before I go, tell me this. Why are you called the Engineer?"

The robot answered readily enough.

"If serious faults developed that cannot be repaired by the robots, I deal with them, I could rebuild Comarre if necessary. Normally, when everything is functioning properly, I am quiescent."

How alien, thought Peyton, the idea of quiescence was to a human mind. He could not help feeling amused at the distinction the Engineer had drawn between itself and "the robots." He asked the obvious question.

"And if something goes wrong with your?"

There are two of us. The other is quiescent now. Each can repair the other. That was necessary once, three hundred years ago."

It was a flawless system. Comarre was sale from accident for millions of years. The builders of the city had set these eternal guardians to watch over them while they went in search of their dreams. No wonder that, long after its makers had died, Comarre was still fulfilling its strange purpose.

What a tragedy it was, thought Peyton, that all this genius had been wasted! The secrets of the Engineer could revolutionize robot technology, could bring a new world into being. Now that the first conscious machines had been built, was there any limit to what lay beyond?

"No," said the Engineer unexpectedly. "Thordarsen told me that the robots would one day be more intelligent than man."

It was strange to hear the machine uttering the name of its maker. So that was Thordarsen's dream! It's full immensity had not yet dawned on him. Though he had been half-prepared for it, he could not easily accept the conclusions. After all, between the robot and the human mind lay an enormous gulf.

"No greater than that between man and the animals from which ha rose, so Thordarsen once said. You, Man, are no more than a very complex robot. I am simpler, but more efficient. That is all."

Very carefully Peyton considered the statement. If indeed Man was no more than a complex robot—a machine composed of living cells rather than wires and vacuum tubes—yet more complex robots would one day be made. When that day came, the supremacy of Man would be ended. The machines might still be his servants, but they would be more intelligent than their master.

It was very quiet in the great room lined with the racks of analyzers and relay panels. The Engineer was watching Peyton intently, its arms and tentacles still busy on their repair work.

Peyton was beginning to feel desperate. Characteristically the opposition had made him more determined than ever. Somehow he must discover how the Engineer was built. Otherwise he would waste all his life trying to match the genius of Thordarsen.

It was useless. The robot was one jump ahead of him.

"You cannot make plans against me. If you do try to escape through that door, I shall throw this power unit at your legs. My probable error at this range is less than half a centimeter."

One could not hide from the thought analyzers. The plan had been scarcely half-formed in Peyton's mind, but the Engineer knew it already.

Both Peyton and the Engineer were equally surprised by the interruption. There was a sudden flash of tawny gold, and half a ton of bone and sinew, traveling at forty miles an hour, struck the robot amidships.

For a moment there was a great flailing of tentacles. Then, with a sound like the crack of doom, the Engineer lay sprawling on the floor. Leo, licking his paws thoughtfully, crouched over the fallen machine.

He could not quite understand this shining animal which had been threatening his master. Its skin was the toughest he had encountered since a very ill-advised disagreement with a rhinoceros many years ago.

"Good boy!" shouted Peyton gleefully. "Keep him down!"

The Engineer had broken some of his larger limbs, and the tentacles were too weak to do any damage. Once again Peyton found his tool kit invaluable. When he had finished, the Engineer was certainly incapable of movement, though Peyton had not touched any of the neural circuits. That, somehow, would have been rather too much like murder.

"You can. get off now, Leo," he said when the task was finished. The lion obeyed with poor grace.

"I'm sorry to have to do this," said Peyton hypocritically, "but I hope you appreciate my point of view. Can you still speak?"

"Yes," replied the Engineer. "What do you intend to do now?"

Peyton smiled. Five minutes ago, he had been the one to ask the question. How long, he wondered, would it take for the Engineer's twin to arrive on the scene? Though Leo could deal with the situation if it came to a trial of strength, the other robot would have been warned and might be able to make things very unpleasant for them. It could, for instance, switch off the lights.

The glow tubes died and darkness fell. Leo gave a mournful howl of dismay. Feeling rather annoyed, Peyton drew his torch and twitched it on.

"It doesn't really make any difference to me," he said. "You might just as well switch them on again."

The Engineer said nothing. But the glow tubes lit once more.

How on earth, thought Peyton, could you fight an enemy who could read your thoughts and could even watch you preparing your defenses? He would have to avoid thinking of any idea that might react to his disadvantage, such as—he stopped himself just in time. For a moment he blocked his thoughts by trying to integrate Armstrong's omega function in his head. Then he got his mind under control again.

"Look," he said at last, "I'll make a bargain with you,"

"What is that? I do not know the word."

"Never mind," Peyton replied hurriedly. "My suggestion is this. Let me waken the men who are trapped here, give me your fundamental circuits, and I'll leave without touching anything. You will have obeyed your builders' orders and no harm will have been done."

A human being might have argued over the matter, but not so the robot. Its mind took perhaps a thousandth of a second to weigh any situation, however involved.

"Very well. I see from your mind that you intend to keep the agreement. But what does the word 'blackmail' mean?"

Peyton flushed.

"It doesn't matter," he said hastily. "It's only a common human expression. I suppose your—er—colleague will be here in a moment?"

"He has been waiting outside for some time," replied the robot. "Will you keep your dog under control?"

Peyton laughed. It was too much to expect a robot to know zoology.

"Lion, then," said the robot, correcting itself as it read his mind.

Peyton addressed a few words to Leo and, to make doubly sure, wound his fingers in the lion's mane. Before he could frame the invitation with his lips, the second robot rolled silently into the room. Leo growled and tried to tug away, but Peyton calmed him.

In every respect Engineer II was a duplicate of its colleague. Even as it came toward him it dipped into his mind in the disconcerting manner that Peyton could never get used to.

"I see that you wish to go to the dreamers," it said. "Follow me,"

Peyton was tired of being ordered around. Why didn't the robots ever say "please"?

"Follow me, please," repeated the machine, with the slightest possible accentuation.

Peyton followed.

Once again be found himself in the corridor with the hundreds of poppy-embossed doors—or a similar corridor. The robot led him to a door indistinguishable from the rest and came to a halt in front of it.

Silently the metal plate slid open, and, not without qualms, Peyton stepped into the darkened room.

On the couch lay a very old man. At first sight he seemed to be dead. Certainly his breathing had slowed to the point of cessation. Peyton stared at him for a moment. Then he spoke to the robot.

"Waken him."

Somewhere in the depths of the city the stream of impulses through a thought projector ceased. A universe that had never existed crumbled to ruins.

From the couch two burning eyes glowed up at Peyton, lit with the light of madness. They stared through him and beyond, and from the thin lips poured a stream of jumbled words that Peyton could barely distinguish. Over and over again the old man cried out names that must be those of people or places in the dream world from which he had been wrenched. It was at once horrible and pathetic.

"Stop it!" cried Peyton, "You are back in reality now,"

The glowing eyes seemed to see him for the first time. With an immense effort the old man raised himself.

"Who are you?" he quavered. Then, before Peyton could answer, he continued in a broken voice. "This must be a nightmare—go away, go away. Let me wake up!"

Overcoming his repulsion, Peyton put his hand on the emaciated shoulder.

"Don't worry—you are awake. Don't you remember?"

The other did not seem to hear him.

"Yes, it must be a nightmare—it must be! But why don't I wake up? Nyran, Cressidor, where are you? I cannot find you!"

Peyton stood it as long as he could, but nothing he did could attract the old man's attention again. Sick at heart, he turned to the robot.

"Send him back."

# 7

# THE THIRD RENAISSANCE

Slowly the raving ceased. The frail body fell back on the couch, and once again the wrinkled face became a passionless mask.

"Are they all as mad as this?" asked Peyton finally.

"But he is not mad."

"What do you mean? Of course he is!"

"He has been entranced for many years. Suppose you went to a far land and changed your mode of living completely, forgetting all you had ever known of your previous life. Eventually you would have no more knowledge of it than you have of your first childhood.

"If by some miracle you were then suddenly thrown back in time, you would behave in just that way. Remember, his dream life is completely real to him and he has lived it now for many years."

That was true enough. But how could the Engineer possess such insight? Peyton turned to it in amazement, but as usual had no need to frame the question.

"Thordarsen told me this the other day while we were still building Comarre. Even then some of the dreamers had been entranced for twenty years."

"The other day?"

"About five hundred years ago, you would call it."

The words brought a strange picture into Peyton's mind. He could visualize the lonely genius, working here among his robots, perhaps with no human companions left All the others would long since have gone in search of their dreams.

But Thordarsen might have stayed on, the desire for creation still linking him to the world, until he had finished his work. The two engineers, his greatest achievement and perhaps the most wonderful feat of electronics of which the world had record, were his ultimate masterpieces.

The waste and the pity of it overwhelmed Peyton. More than ever he was determined that, because the embittered genius had thrown away his life, his work should not perish, but be given to the world.

"Will all the dreamers be like this?" he asked the robot.

"All except the newest. They may still remember their first lives."

"Take me to one of them."

The room they entered nest was identical with the other, but the body lying on the couch was that of a man of no more than forty.

"How long has he been here?" asked Peyton.

"He came only a few weeks ago—the first visitor we had for many years until your coming."

"Wake him, please."

The eyes opened slowly. There was no insanity in them, only wonder and sadness. Then came the dawn of recollection, and the man half rose to a sitting position. His first words were completely rational.

"Why have you called me back? Who are you?"

"I have just escaped from the thought projectors," explained Peyton. "I want to release all who can be saved."

The other laughed bitterly.

"Saved! From what? It took me forty years to escape from the world, and now you would drag me back to it! Go away and leave me in peace!"

Peyton would not retreat so easily.

"Do you think that this make-believe world of yours is better than reality? Have you no desire to escape from it at all?"

Again the other laughed, with no trace of humor.

"Comarre is reality to me. The world never gave me anything, so why should I wish to return to it? I have found peace here, and that is all I need."

Quite suddenly Peyton turned on his heels and left. Behind him he heard the dreamer fall back with a contented sigh. He knew when her had been beaten. And he knew now why he had wished to revive the others.

It had not been through any sense of duty, but for his own selfish purpose. He had wished to convince himself that Comarre was evil. Now he knew that it was not. There would always be, even in Utopia, some for whom the world had nothing to offer but sorrow and disillusion.

They would be fewer and fewer with the passage of time. In the dark ages of a thousand years ago most of mankind had been misfits of some sort. However splendid the world's future, there would still be some tragedies—and why should Comarre be condemned because it offered them their only hope of peace?

He would try no more experiments. His own robust faith and confidence had been severely shaken. And the dreamers of Comarre would not thank him for his pains.

He turned to the Engineer again. The desire to leave the city had grown very intense in the last few minutes, but the most important work was still to be done. As usual, the robot forestalled him.

"I have what you want," he said. "Follow me, please."

It did not lead, as Peyton had half expected, back to the machine levels, with their maze of control equipment. When their journey had finished, they were higher than Peyton had ever been before, in a little circular room he suspected might be at the very apex of the city. There were no windows, unless the curious plates set in the wall could be made transparent by some secret means.

It was a study, and Peyton gazed at it with awe as he realized who had worked here many centuries ago. The walls were lined with ancient textbooks that had not been disturbed for five hundred years. It seemed as if Thordarsen had left only a few hours before. There was even a half-finished circuit pinned on a drawing board against the wall.

"It almost looks as if he was interrupted," said Peyton, half to himself.

"He was," answered the robot.

"What do you mean? Didn't he join the others when he had finished you?"

It was difficult to believe that there was absolutely no emotion behind the reply, but the words were spoken in the same passionless tones as everything else the robot had ever said.

"When he had finished us, Thordarsen was Still not satisfied. He was not like the others. He often told as that he had found happiness in the building of Comarre. Again and again he said that he would join the rest, but always there was some last improvement he wanted to make. So it went on until one day we found him lying here in this room. He had stopped. The word I see in your mind is 'death,' but I have no thought for that."

Peyton was silent. It seemed to him that the great scientist's ending had not been an ignoble one. The bitterness that had darkened his life had lifted from it at the last. He had known the joy of creation. Of all the artists who had come to Comarre, he was the greatest. And now his work would not be wasted.

The robot glided silently toward a steel desk, and one of its tentacles disappeared into a drawer. When it emerged it was holding a thick volume, bound between sheets of metal. Wordlessly it handed the book to Peyton, who opened it with trembling hands. It contained many thousands of pages of thin, very tough material.

Written on the flyleaf in a bold, firm hand were the words:

*Rolf Thordarsen*
*Notes on Subelectronics*
*Begun: Day 2, Month 13, 2598.*

Underneath was more writing, very difficult to decipher and apparently scrawled in frantic haste. As he read, understanding came at last to Peyton with the suddenness of an equatorial dawn.

To the reader of these words:

I, Rolf Thordarsen, meeting no understanding in my own age, send this message into the future. If Comarre still exists, you will have seen my handiwork and must have escaped the snares I set for lesser minds. Therefore you are fitted to take this knowledge to the world. Give it to the scientists and tell them to me it wisely.

I have broken down the barrier between Man and Machine. Now they must share the future equally.

Peyton read the message several times, his heart warming toward his long-dead ancestor. It was a brilliant scheme. In this way, as perhaps in no other, Thordarsen had been able to send his message safely down the ages, knowing that only the right hands would receive it. Peyton wondered if this had been Thordarsen's plan when he first joined the Decadents or whether he had evolved it later in his life. He would never know.

He looked again at the Engineer and thought of the world that would come when all robots had reached consciousness. Beyond that he looked still farther into the mists of the future.

The robot need have none of the limitations of Man, none of his pitiful weaknesses. It would never let passions cloud its logic, would never be swayed by self-interest and ambition. It would be complementary to man.

Peyton remembered Thordarsen's words, "Now they must share the future equally."

Peyton stopped his daydream. All this, if it ever came, might be centuries in the future. He turned to the Engineer.

"I am ready to leave. But one day I shall return."

The robot backed slowly away from him.

"Stand perfectly still," it ordered.

Peyton looked at the Engineer in puzzlement. Then he glanced hurriedly at the ceiling. There again was that enigmatic bulge under which he had found himself when he first entered the city such an age ago.

"Hey!" he cried. "I don't want—"

It was too late. Behind him was the dark screen, blacker than night itself. Before him lay the clearing, with the forest at its edge, It was evening, and the sun was nearly touching the trees.

There was a sudden whimpering noise behind him; a very frightened lion was looking out at the forest with unbelieving eyes. Leo had not enjoyed his transfer.

"It's all over now, old chap," said Peyton reassuringly. "You can't blame them for trying to get rid of us as quickly as they could. After all, we did smash up the place a bit between us. Come along—I don't want to spend the night in the forest."

On the other side of the world, a group of scientists was dispersing with what patience it could, not yet knowing the fall extent of its triumph. In Central Tower, Richard Peyton II had just discovered that his son had not spent the last two days with his cousins in South America, and was composing a speech of welcome for the prodigal's return.

Far above the Earth the World Council was laying down plans soon to be swept away by the coming of the Third Renaissance. But the cause of all the trouble knew nothing of this and, for the moment, cared less.

Slowly Peyton descended the marble steps from that mysterious doorway whose secret was still hidden from him. Leo followed a little way behind, looking over his shoulder and growling quietly now and then.

Together, they started back along the metal road, through the avenue of stunted trees. Peyton was glad that the sun had not yet set. At night this road would be glowing with its internal radioactivity, and the twisted trees would not look pleasant silhouetted against the stars.

At the bend in the road he paused for a while and looked back at the curving metal wall with its single black opening whose appearance was so deceptive. All his feeling of triumph seemed to fade away. He knew that as long as he lived he could never forget what lay behind those towering walls—the cloying promise of peace and utter contentment.

Deep in his soul he felt the fear that any satisfaction, any achievement the outer world could give might seem vain beside the effortless bliss offered by Comarre. For an instant he had a nightmare vision of himself, broken and old, returning along this road to seek oblivion. He shrugged his shoulders and put the thought aside.

Once he was out on the plain his spirits rose swiftly. He opened the precious book again and ruffled through its pages of microprint, intoxicated by the promise that it held. Ages ago the slow caravans had come this way, bearing gold and ivory for Solomon the Wise, But all their treasure was as nothing beside this single volume, and all the wisdom of Solomon could not have pictured the new civilization of which this volume was to be the seed.

Presently Peyton began to sing, something he did very seldom and extremely badly. The song was a very old one, so old that it came from an age before atomic power, before interplanetary travel, even before the coming of flight. It had to do with a certain hairdresser in Seville, wherever Seville might be.

Leo stood it in silence for as long as he could. Then he, too, joined in. The duet was not a success.

When night descended, the forest and all its secrets had fallen below the horizon. With his face to the stars and Leo watching by his side, Peyton slept well.

This time he did not dream.

# A Fall of Moondust

# Chapter 1

To be the skipper of the only boat on the Moon was a distinction that Pat Harris enjoyed. As the passengers filed aboard *Selene*, jockeying for window seats, he wondered what sort of trip it would be this time. In the rear-view mirror he could see Miss Wilkins, very smart in her blue Lunar Tourist Commission uniform, putting on her usual welcome act. He always tried to think of her as "Miss Wilkins," not Sue, when they were on duty together; it helped to keep his mind on business. But what she thought of him, he had never really discovered.

There were no familiar faces; this was a new bunch, eager for their first cruise. Most of the passengers were typical tourists—elderly people, visiting a world that had been the very symbol of inaccessibility when they were young. There were only four or five passengers on the low side of thirty, and they were probably technical personnel on vacation from one of the lunar bases. It was a fairly good working rule, Pat had discovered, that all the old people came from Earth, while the youngsters were residents of the Moon.

But to all of them, the Sea of Thirst was a novelty. Beyond *Selene*'s observation windows, its gray, dusty surface marched onward unbroken until it reached the stars. Above it hung the waning crescent Earth, poised forever in the sky from which it had not moved in a billion years. The brilliant, blue-green light of the mother world flooded this strange land with a cold radiance—and cold it was indeed, perhaps three hundred below zero on the exposed surface.

No one could have told, merely by looking at it, whether the Sea was liquid or solid. It was completely flat and featureless, quite free from the myriad cracks and fissures that scarred all the rest of this barren world. Not a single hillock, boulder, or pebble broke its monotonous uniformity. No sea on Earth—no millpond, even—was ever as calm as this.

It was a sea of dust, not of water, and therefore it was alien to all the experience of men; therefore, also, it fascinated and attracted them. Fine as talcum powder, drier in this vacuum than the parched sands of the Sahara, it flowed as easily and effortlessly as any liquid. A heavy object dropped into it would disappear instantly, without a splash, leaving no scar to mark its passage. Nothing could move upon its treacherous surface except the small, two-man dust-skis—and *Selene* herself, an improbable combination of sledge and bus, not unlike the Sno-cats that had opened up the Antarctic a lifetime ago.

*Selene*'s official designation was Dust-Cruiser, Mark I, though to the best of Pat's knowledge, a Mark II did not exist even on the drawing board. She was called "ship," "boat," or "moon bus," according to taste; Pat preferred "boat," for it prevented confusion. When he used that word, no one would mistake him for the skipper of a spaceship—and spaceship captains were, of course, two a penny.

"Welcome aboard *Selene*," said Miss Wilkins, when everyone had settled down. "Captain Harris and I are pleased to have you with us. Our trip will last four hours, and our first objective will be Crater Lake, a hundred kilometers east of here, in the Mountains of Inaccessibility...."

Pat scarcely heard the familiar introduction; he was busy with his count-down. *Selene* was virtually a grounded space-ship; she had to be, since she was traveling in a vacuum, and must protect her frail cargo from the hostile world beyond her walls. Though she never left the surface of the Moon, and was propelled by electric motors instead of rockets, she carried all the basic equipment of a full-fledged ship of space—and all of it had to be checked before departure.

Oxygen—O.K. Power—O.K. Radio—O.K. ("Hello, Rainbow Base, *Selene* testing. Are you receiving my beacon?") Inertial navigator——zeroed. Air-lock safety—On. Cabin-leak detector—O.K. Internal lights—O.K. Gangway—disconnected. And so on for more than fifty items, every one of which would automatically call attention to itself in case of trouble. But Pat Harris, like all spacemen hankering after old age, never relied on autowarnings if he could carry out the check himself.

At last he was ready. The almost silent motors started to spin, but the blades were still feathered, and *Selene* barely quivered at her moorings. Then he eased the port fan into fine pitch, and she began to curve slowly to the right. When she was clear of the embarkation building, he straightened her out and pushed the throttle forward.

She handled very well, when one considered the complete novelty of her design. There had been no millennia of trial and error here, stretching back to the first neolithic man who ever launched a log out into a stream. *Selene* was the very first of her line, created in the brains of a few engineers who had sat down at a table and asked themselves: "How do we build a vehicle that will skim over a sea of dust?"

Some of them, harking back to Ole Man River, had wanted to make her a stern-wheeler, but the more efficient submerged fans had carried the day. As they drilled through the dust, driving her before them, they produced a wake like that of a high-speed mole, but it vanished within seconds, leaving the Sea unmarked by any sign of the boat's passage.

Now the squat pressure-domes of Port Roris were dropping swiftly below the sky line. In less than ten minutes, they had vanished from sight: *Selene* was utterly alone. She was at the center of something for which the languages of mankind have no name.

As Pat switched off the motors and the boat coasted to rest, he waited for the silence to grow around him. It was always the same; it took a little while for the passengers to realize the strangeness of what lay outside. They had crossed space and seen stars all about them; they had looked up—or down—at the dazzling face of Earth, but this was different. It was neither land nor sea, neither air nor space, but a little of each.

Before the silence grew oppressive—if he left it too long, someone would get scared—Pat rose to his feet and faced his passengers.

"Good evening, ladies and gentlemen," he began. "I hope Miss Wilkins has been making you comfortable. We've stopped here because this is a good place to introduce you to the Sea—to give you the feel of it, as it were."

He pointed to the windows, and the ghostly grayness that lay beyond.

"Just how far away," he asked quietly, "do you imagine our horizon is? Or, to put it in another way, how big would a man appear to you if he was standing out there where the stars seem to meet the ground?"

It was a question that no one could possibly answer, from the evidence of sight alone. Logic said, "The Moon's a small world—the horizon *must* be very close." But the senses gave a wholly different verdict. "This land," they reported, "is absolutely flat, and stretches to infinity. It divides the Universe in twain; for ever and ever, it rolls onward beneath the stars...."

The illusion remained, even when one knew its cause. The eye has no way of judging distances when there is nothing for it to focus upon. Vision slipped and skidded helplessly on this featureless ocean of dust. There was not even—as there must always be on Earth—the softening haze of the atmosphere to give some hint of nearness or remoteness. The stars were un-winking needle points of light, clear down to that indeterminate horizon.

"Believe it or not," continued Pat, "you can see just three kilometers—or almost two miles, for those of you who haven't been able to go metric yet. I know it looks a couple of light-years out to the horizon, but you could walk there in twenty minutes, if you could walk on this stuff at all."

He moved back to his seat, and started the motors once more.

"Nothing much to see for the next sixty kilometers," he called over his shoulder, "so we'll get a move on."

*Selene* surged forward. For the first time, there was a real sensation of speed. The boat's wake became longer and more disturbed as the spinning fans bit fiercely into the dust. Now the dust itself was being tossed up on either side in great ghostly plumes; from a distance, *Selene* would have looked like a snowplow driving its way across a winter landscape, beneath a frosty moon. But those gray, slowly collapsing parabolas were not snow, and the lamp that lit their trajectory was the planet Earth.

The passengers relaxed, enjoying the smooth, almost silent ride. Every one of them had traveled hundreds of times faster than this, on the journey to the Moon. But in space one was never conscious of speed, and this swift glide across the dust was far more exciting. When Pat swung *Selene* into a tight turn, so that she orbited in a circle, the boat almost overtook the falling veils of powder her fans had hurled into the sky. It seemed altogether wrong that this impalpable dust should rise and fall in such clean-cut curves, utterly unaffected by air resistance. On Earth it would have drifted for hours—perhaps for days.

As soon as the boat had straightened out on a steady course and there was nothing to look at except the empty plain, the passengers began to read the literature thoughtfully provided for them. Each had been given a folder of photographs, maps, souvenirs ("This is to certify that Mr./Mrs./Miss—has Sailed the Seas of the Moon, aboard Dust-Cruiser *Selene*"), and informative text. They had only to read this to discover all that they wanted to know about the Sea of Thirst, and perhaps a little more.

Most of the Moon, they read, was covered by a thin layer of dust, usually no more than a few millimeters deep. Some of this was debris from the stars—the remains of meteorites that had fallen upon the Moon's unprotected face for at least five billion years. Some had flaked from the lunar rocks as they expanded and contracted in the fierce temperature extremes between day and night. Whatever its source, it was so finely divided that it would flow like a liquid, even under this feeble gravity.

Over the ages, it had drifted down from the mountains into the lowlands, to form pools and lakes. The first explorers had expected this, and had usually been prepared for it. But the Sea of Thirst was a surprise; no one had anticipated finding a dustbowl more than a hundred kilometers across.

As the lunar "seas" went, it was very small; indeed, the astronomers had never officially recognized its title, pointing out that it was only a small portion of the Sinus Roris—the Bay of Dew. And how, they protested, could part of a bay be an entire sea? But the name, invented by a copywriter of the Lunar Tourist Commission, had stuck despite their objections. It was at least as appropriate as the names of the other so-called seas—Sea of Clouds, Sea of Rains, Sea of Tranquillity. Not to mention Sea of Nectar.

The brochure also contained some reassuring information, designed to quell the fears of the most nervous traveler, and to prove that the Tourist Commission had thought of everything. "All possible precautions have been taken for your safety," it stated. "*Selene* carries an oxygen reserve sufficient to last for more than a week, and all essential equipment is duplicated. An automatic radio beacon signals your position at regular intervals, and in the extremely improbable event of a complete power failure, a dust-ski from Port Roris would tow you home with little delay. Above all, there is no need to worry about rough weather. No matter how bad a sailor you may be, you can't get seasick on the Moon. There are never any storms on the Sea of Thirst; it is always a flat calm."

Those last comforting words had been written in all good faith, for who could have imagined that they would soon be proved untrue?

As *Selene* raced silently through the earthlit night, the Moon went about its business. There was a great deal of business now, after the aeons of sleep. More had happened here in the last fifty years than in the five billion before that, and much more was to happen soon.

In the first city that Man had ever built outside his native world, Chief Administrator Olsen was taking a stroll through the park. He was very proud of the park, as were all the twenty-five thousand inhabitants of Port Clavius. It was small, of course—though not as small as was implied by that miserable TV commentator who'd called it "a windowbox with delusions of grandeur." And certainly there were no parks, gardens, or anything else on Earth where you could find sunflowers ten meters high.

Far overhead, wispy cirrus clouds were sailing by—or so it seemed. They were, of course, only images projected on the inside of the dome, but the illusion was so perfect that it sometimes made the C.A. homesick. Homesick? He corrected himself; *this* was home.

Yet in his heart of hearts, he knew it was not true. To his children it would be, but not to him. He had been born in Stockholm, Earth;

they had been born in Port Clavius. They were citizens of the Moon; he was tied to Earth with bonds that might weaken with the years, but would never break.

Less than a kilometer away, just outside the main dome, the head of the Lunar Tourist Commission inspected the latest returns, and permitted himself a mild feeling of satisfaction. The improvement over the last season had been maintained; not that there *were* seasons on the Moon, but it was noticeable that more tourists came when it was winter in Earth's northern hemisphere.

How could he keep it up? That was always the problem, for tourists wanted variety, and you couldn't give them the same thing over and over again. The novel scenery, the low gravity, the view of Earth, the mysteries of Farside, the spectacular heavens, the pioneer settlements (where tourists were not always welcomed, anyway)—after you'd listed those, what else did the Moon have to offer? What a pity there were no native Selenites with quaint customs and quainter physiques at which visitors could click their cameras. Alas, the largest life form ever discovered on the Moon needed a microscope to show it—and its ancestors had come here on Lunik II, only a decade ahead of Man himself.

Commissioner Davis riffled mentally through the items that had arrived by the last telefax, wondering if there was anything there that would help him. There was, of course, the usual request from a TV company he'd never heard of, anxious to make yet another document-ary on the Moon—if all expenses were paid. The answer to that one would be "No"; if he accepted all these kind offers, his department would soon be broke.

Then there was a chatty letter from his opposite number in the Greater New Orleans Tourist Commission, Inc., suggesting an exchange of personnel. It was hard to see how that would help the Moon, or New Orleans either, but it would cost nothing and might produce some good will. And—this was more interesting—there was a request from the waterskiing champion of Australia, asking if anyone had ever tried to ski on the Sea of Thirst.

Yes—there was definitely an idea here; he was surprised that someone had not tried it already. Perhaps they had, behind *Selene* or one of the small dust-skis. It was certainly worth a test; he was always on the lookout for new forms of lunar recreation, and the Sea of Thirst was one of his pet projects.

It was a project that, within a very few hours, was going to turn into a nightmare.

# Chapter 2

Ahead of *Selene*, the horizon was no longer a perfect, unbroken arc; a jagged line of mountains had risen above the edge of the Moon. As the cruiser raced toward them, they seemed to climb slowly up the sky, as if lifted upon some gigantic elevator.

"The Mountains of Inaccessibility," announced Miss Wilkins. "So called because they're entirely surrounded by the Sea. You'll notice, too, that they're much steeper than most lunar mountains."

She did not labor this, since it was an unfortunate fact that the majority of lunar peaks were a severe disappointment. The huge craters which looked so impressive on photographs taken from Earth turned out upon close inspection to be gently rolling hills, their relief grossly exaggerated by the shadows they cast at dawn and sunset. There was not a single lunar crater whose ramparts soared as abruptly as the streets of San Francisco, and there were very few that could provide a serious obstacle to a determined cyclist. No one would have guessed this, however, from the publications of the Tourist Commission, which featured only the most spectacular cliffs and canyons, photographed from carefully chosen vantage points.

"They've never been thoroughly explored, even now," Miss Wilkins continued. "Last year we took a party of geologists there, and landed them on that promontory, but they were only able to go a few kilometers into the interior. So there may be *anything* up in those hills; we simply don't know."

Good for Sue, Pat told himself; she was a first-rate guide, and knew what to leave to the imagination and what to explain in detail. She had an easy relaxed tone, with no trace of that fatal singsong that was the occupational disease of so many professional guides. And she had mastered her subject thoroughly; it was very rare for her to be asked a question that she could not answer. Altogether, she was a formidable young lady, and though she often figured in Pat's erotic reveries, he was secretly a little afraid of her.

The passengers stared with fascinated wonder at the approaching peaks. On the still-mysterious Moon, here was a deeper mystery. Rising like an island out of the strange sea that guarded them, the Mountains of Inaccessibility remained a challenge for the next generation of explorers. Despite their name, it was now easy enough to reach them—but with millions of square kilometers of less difficult territory still unexamined, they would have to wait their turn.

*Selene* was swinging into their shadows; before anyone had realized what was happening, the low-hanging Earth had been eclipsed. Its brilliant light still played upon the peaks far overhead, but down here all was utter darkness.

"I'll turn off the cabin lights," said the stewardess, "so you can get a better view."

As the dim red background illumination vanished, each traveler felt he was alone in the lunar night. Even the reflected radiance of Earth on those high peaks was disappearing as the cruiser raced farther into shadow. Within minutes, only the stars were left—cold, steady points of light in a blackness so complete that the mind rebelled against it.

It was hard to recognize the familiar constellations among this multitude of stars. The eye became entangled in patterns never seen from Earth, and lost itself in a glittering maze of clusters and nebulae. In all that resplendent panorama, there was only one unmistakable landmark—the dazzling beacon of Venus, far outshining all other heavenly bodies, heralding the approach of dawn.

It was several minutes before the travelers realized that not all the wonder lay in the sky. Behind the speeding cruiser stretched a long, phosphorescent wake, as if a magic finger had traced a line of light across the Moon's dark and dusty face. *Selene* was drawing a comet tail behind her, as surely as any ship plowing its way through the tropical oceans of Earth.

Yet there were no microorganisms here, lighting this dead sea with their tiny lamps. Only countless grains of dust, sparking one against the other as the static discharges caused by *Selene*'s swift passage neutralized themselves. Even when one knew the explanation, it was still beautiful to watch—to look back into the night and to see this luminous, electric ribbon continually renewed, continually dying away, as if the Milky Way itself were reflected in the lunar surface.

The shining wake was lost in the glare as Pat switched on the searchlight. Ominously close at hand, a great wall of rock was sliding past. At this point the face of the mountain rose almost sheer from the surrounding sea of dust; it towered overhead to unknown heights, for only where the racing oval of light fell upon it did it appear to flash suddenly into real existence.

Here were mountains against which the Himalayas, the Rockies, the Alps were newborn babies. On Earth, the forces of erosion began to tear at all mountains as soon as they were formed, so that after a few million years they were mere ghosts of their former selves. But the Moon knew neither wind nor rain; there was nothing here to wear away the rocks except the immeasurably slow flaking of the dust as their surface layers contracted in the chill of night. These mountains were as old as the world that had given them birth.

Pat was quite proud of his showmanship, and had planned the next act very carefully. It looked dangerous, but was perfectly safe, for *Selene* had been over this course a hundred times and the electronic memory of her guidance system knew the way better than any human pilot. Suddenly, he switched off the searchlight—and now the passengers could tell that while they had been dazzled by the glare on one side, the mountains had been stealthily closing in upon them from the other.

In almost total darkness, *Selene* was racing up a narrow canyon—and not even on a straight course, form from time to time she zigged and zagged to avoid invisible obstacles. Some of them, indeed, were not merely invisible, but nonexistent; Pat had programmed this course, at slow speed and in the safety of daylight, for maximum impact on the nerves. The "Ah's" and "Oh's" from the darkened cabin behind him proved that he had done a good job.

Far above, a narrow ribbon of stars was all that could be seen of the outside world; it swung in crazy arcs from right to left and back again with each abrupt change of *Selene*'s course. The Night Ride, as Pat privately called it, lasted for about five minutes, but seemed very much longer. When he once again switched on the floods, so that the cruiser was moving in the center of a great pool of light, there was a sigh of mingled relief and disappointment from the passengers. This was an experience none of them would forget in a hurry.

Now that vision had been restored, they could see that they were traveling up a steep-walled valley or gorge, the sides of which were slowly drawing apart. Presently the canyon had widened into a roughly oval amphitheater about three kilometers across—the heart of an extinct volcano, breached aeons ago, in the days when even the Moon was young.

The crater was extremely small, by lunar standards, but it was unique. The ubiquitous dust had flooded into it, working its way up the valley age after age, so that now the tourists from Earth could ride in cushioned comfort into what had once been a cauldron filled with the fires of Hell. Those fires had died long before the dawn of terrestrial life, and would never wake again. But there were other forces that had not died, and were merely biding their time.

When *Selene* began a slow circuit of the steeply walled amphitheater, more than one of her passengers remembered a cruise in some mountain lake at home. Here was the same sheltered stillness, the same sense of unknown depths beneath the boat. Earth had many crater lakes, but the Moon only one—though it had far more craters.

Taking his time, Pat made two complete circuits of the lake, while the floodlights played upon its enclosing walls. This was the best way to see it; during the daytime, when the sun blasted it with heat and light, it lost much of its magic. But now it belonged to the kingdom of fantasy, as if it had come from the haunted brain of Edgar Allan Poe. Ever and again one seemed to glimpse strange shapes moving at the edge of vision, beyond the narrow range of the lights. It was pure imagination, of course; nothing moved in all this land except the shadows of the Sun and Earth. There could be no ghosts upon a world that had never known life.

It was time to turn back, to sail down the canyon into the open sea. Pat aimed the blunt prow of *Selene* toward the narrow rift in the mountains, and the high walls enfolded them again. On the outward journey he left the lights on, so that the passengers could see where they were going; besides, that trick of the Night Ride would not work so well a second time.

Far ahead, beyond the reach of *Selene*'s own illumination, a light was growing, spreading softly across the rocks and crags. Even in her last quarter, Earth still had the power of a dozen full moons, and now that they were emerging from the shadow of the mountains, she was once more the mistress of the skies. Every one of the twenty-two men and women aboard *Selene* looked up at that blue-green crescent, admiring its beauty, wondering at its brilliance. How strange that the familiar fields and lakes and forests of Earth shone with such celestial glory when one looked at them from afar! Perhaps there was a lesson here; perhaps no man could appreciate his own world until he had seen it from space.

And upon Earth, there must be many eyes turned toward the waxing Moon—more than ever before, now that the Moon meant so much to mankind. It was possible, but unlikely, that even now some of those eyes were peering through powerful telescopes at the faint spark of *Selene*'s floodlights as it crept through the lunar night. But it would mean nothing to them when that spark flickered and died.

For a million years the bubble had been growing, like a vast abscess, below the root of the mountains. Throughout the entire history of Man, gas from the Moon's not yet wholly dead interior had been forcing itself along lines of weakness, accumulating in cavities hundreds of meters below the surface. On nearby Earth, the ice ages had marched past, one by one, while the buried caverns grew and merged and at last coalesced. Now the abscess was about to burst.

Captain Harris had left the controls on autopilot and was talking to the front row of passengers when the first tremor shook the boat. For a fraction of a second he wondered if a fan blade had hit some submerged obstacle; then, quite literally, the bottom fell out of his world.

It fell slowly, as all things must upon the Moon. Ahead of *Selene*, in a circle many acres in extent, the smooth plain puckered like a navel. The Sea was alive and moving, stirred by the forces that had waked it from its age-long sleep. The center of the disturbance deepened into a funnel, as if a giant whirlpool were forming in the dust. Every stage of that nightmare transformation was pitilessly illuminated by the earth-light, until the crater was so deep that its far wall was completely lost in shadow, and it seemed as if *Selene* were racing into a curving crescent of utter blackness—an arc of annihilation.

The truth was almost as bad. By the time that Pat had reached the controls, the boat was sliding and skittering far down that impossible slope. Its own momentum and the accelerating flow of the dust beneath it were carrying it headlong into the depths. There was nothing he could do but attempt to keep on an even keel, and to hope that their speed would carry them up the far side of the crater before it collapsed upon them.

If the passengers screamed or cried out, Pat never heard them. He was conscious only of that dreadful, sickening slide, and of his own attempts to keep the cruiser from capsizing. Yet even as he fought with the controls, feeding power first to one fan, then to the other, in an effort to straighten *Selene*'s course, a strange, nagging memory was teasing his mind. Somewhere, somehow, he had seen this happen before.

That was ridiculous, of course, but the memory would not leave him. Not until he reached the bottom of the funnel and saw the endless slope of dust rolling down from the crater's star-fringed lip did the veil of time lift for a moment.

He was a boy again, playing in the hot sand of a forgotten summer. He had found a tiny pit, perfectly smooth and symmetrical, and there was something lurking in its depths—something completely buried except for its waiting jaws. The boy had watched, wondering, already conscious of the fact that this was the stage for some microscopic drama. He had seen an ant, mindlessly intent upon its mission, stumble at the edge of the crater and topple down the slope.

It would have escaped easily enough—but when the first grain of sand had rolled to the bottom of the pit, the waiting ogre had reared out of its lair. With its forelegs, it had hurled a fusillade of sand at the struggling insect, until the avalanche had overwhelmed it and brought it sliding down into the throat of the crater.

As *Selene* was sliding now. No ant lion had dug this pit on the surface of the Moon, but Pat felt as helpless now as that doomed insect he had watched so many years ago. Like it, he was struggling to reach the safety of the rim, while the moving ground swept him back into the depths where death was waiting. A swift death for the ant, a protracted one for him and his companions.

The straining motors were making some headway, but not enough. The falling dust was gaining speed—and, what was worse, it was rising outside the walls of the cruiser. Now it had reached the lower edge of the windows; now it was creeping up the panes; and at last it had covered them completely. Pat cut the motors before they tore themselves to pieces, and as he did so, the rising tide blotted out the last glimpse of the crescent Earth. In darkness and in silence, they were sinking into the Moon.

# Chapter 3

In the banked communications racks of Traffic Control, Earthside North, an electronic memory stirred uneasily. The time was one second past twenty hundred hours GMT: a pattern of pulses that should arrive automatically on every hour had failed to make its appearance.

With a swiftness beyond human thought, the handful of cells and microscopic relays looked for instructions. "WAIT FIVE SECONDS," said the coded orders. "IF NOTHING HAPPENS, CLOSE CIRCUIT 10011001."

The minute portion of the traffic computer as yet concerned with the problem waited patiently for this enormous period of time—long enough to make a hundred million twenty-figure additions, or to print most of the contents of the Library of Congress. Then it closed circuit 10011001.

High above the surface of the Moon, from an antenna which, curiously enough, was aimed directly at the face of the Earth, a radio pulse launched itself into space. In a sixth of a second it had flashed the fifty thousand kilometers to the relay satellite known as Lagrange II, directly in the line between Moon and Earth. Another sixth of a second and the pulse had returned, much amplified, flooding Earthside North from pole to equator.

In terms of human speech, it carried a simple message. "HELLO, SELENE," the pulse said. "I AM NOT RECEIVING YOUR BEACON. PLEASE REPLY AT ONCE."

The computer waited for another five seconds. Then it sent out the pulse again, and yet again. Geological ages had passed in the world of electronics, but the machine was infinitely patient.

Once more, it consulted its instructions. Now they said: "CLOSE CIRCUIT 10101010." The computer obeyed. In Traffic Control, a green light flared suddenly to red, a buzzer started to saw the air with its alarm. For the first time, men as well as machines became aware that there was trouble, somewhere on the Moon.

The news spread slowly at first, for the Chief Administrator took a very poor view of unnecessary panic. So, still more strongly, did the Tourist Commissioner; nothing was worse for business than alerts and emergencies—even when, as happened in nine cases out of ten, they proved to be due to blown fuses, tripped cutouts, or oversensitive alarms. But on a world like the Moon, it was necessary to be on one's toes. Better be scared by imaginary crises than fail to react to real ones.

It was several minutes before Commissioner Davis reluctantly admitted that this looked like a real one. *Selene*'s automatic beacon had failed to respond on one earlier occasion, but Pat Harris had answered as soon as he had been called on the cruiser's assigned frequency. This time, there was silence. *Selene* had not even replied to a signal sent out on the carefully guarded MOONCRASH band, reserved solely for emergencies. It was this news that brought the Commissioner hurrying from the Tourist Tower along the buried glideway into Clavius City.

At the entrance to the Traffic Control center, he met the Chief Engineer, Earthside. That was a bad sign; it meant that someone thought that rescue operations would be necessary. The two men looked at each other gravely, each obsessed by the same thought.

"I hope you don't need me," said Chief Engineer Lawrence. "Where's the trouble? All I know is that a Moon-crash signal's gone out. What ship is it?"

"It's not a ship. It's *Selene*; she's not answering, from the Sea of Thirst."

"My God—if anything's happened to her out there, we can only reach her with the dust-skis. I always said we should have two cruisers operating, before we started taking out tourists."

"That's what I argued—but Finance vetoed the idea. They said we couldn't have another until *Selene* proved she could make a profit."

"I hope she doesn't make a headline instead," said Lawrence grimly. "You know what *I* think about bringing tourists to the Moon."

The Commissioner did, very well; it had long been a bone of contention between them. For the first time, he wondered if the Chief Engineer might have a point.

It was, as always, very quiet in Traffic Control. On the great wall maps, the green and amber lights flashed continuously, their routine messages unimportant against the clamor of that single, flaring red. At the Air, Power, and Radiation consoles, the duty officers sat like guardian angels, watching over the safety of one quarter of a world.

"Nothing new," reported the Ground Traffic officer. "We're still completely in the dark. All we know is that they're *somewhere* out in the Sea."

He traced a circle on the large-scale map.

"Unless they're fantastically off course, they must be in that general area. On the nineteen hundred hours check, they were within a kilometer of their planned route. At twenty hundred, their signal had vanished, so whatever happened took place in that sixty minutes."

"How far can *Selene* travel in an hour?" someone asked.

"Flat out, a hundred and twenty kilometers," replied the Commissioner. "But she normally cruises at well under a hundred. You don't hurry on a sight-seeing tour."

He stared at the map, as if trying to extract information from it by the sheer intensity of his gaze.

"If they're out in the Sea, it won't take long to find them. Have you sent out the dust-skis?"

"No, sir; I was waiting for authorization."

Davis looked at the Chief Engineer, who outranked anyone on this side of the Moon except Chief Administrator Olsen himself. Lawrence nodded slowly.

"Send them out," he said. "But don't expect results in a hurry. It will take awhile to search several thousand square kilometers—especially at night. Tell them to work over the route from the last reported position, one ski on either side of it, so that they sweep the widest possible band."

When the order had gone out, David asked unhappily: "What do you think could have happened?"

"There are only a few possibilities. It must have been sudden, because there was no message from them. That usually means an explosion."

The Commissioner paled; there was always the chance of sabotage, and no one could ever guard against that. Because of their vulnerability, space vehicles, like aircraft before them, were an irresistible attraction to a certain type of criminal. Davis thought of the Venus-bound liner *Argo*, which had been destroyed with two hundred men, women, and children aboard, because a maniac had a grudge against a passenger who scarcely knew him.

"And then there's collision," continued the Chief Engineer. "She could have run into an obstacle."

"Harris is a very careful driver," said the Commissioner. "He's done this trip scores of times."

"Everyone can make mistakes; it's easy to misjudge your distance when you're driving by earthlight."

Commissioner Davis barely heard him; he was thinking of all the arrangements he might have to make if the worst came to the worst. He'd better start by getting the Legal Branch to check the indemnity forms. If any relatives started suing the Tourist Commission for a few million dollars, that would undo his entire publicity campaign for the next year—even if he won.

The Ground Traffic officer gave a nervous cough.

"If I might make a suggestion," he said to the Chief Engineer. "We could call Lagrange. The astronomers up there may be able to see something."

"At night?" asked Davis skeptically. "From fifty thousand kilometers up?"

"Easily, if her searchlights are still burning. It's worth trying."

"Excellent idea," said the Chief Engineer. "Do that right away."

He should have thought of that himself, and wondered if there were any other possibilities he had overlooked. This was not the first occasion he had been forced to pit his wits against this strange and beautiful world, so breath-taking in her moments of magic—so deadly in her times of peril. She would never be wholly tamed, as Earth had been, and perhaps that was just as well. For it was the lure of the untouched wilderness and the faint but ever-present hint of danger that now brought the tourists as well as the explorers across the gulfs of space. He would prefer to do without the tourists—but they helped to pay his salary.

And now he had better start packing. This whole crisis might evaporate, and *Selene* might turn up again quite unaware of the panic she had caused. But he did not think this would happen, and his fear deepened to certainty as the minutes passed. He would give her another hour; then he would take the suborbital shuttle to Port Roris and to the realm of his waiting enemy, the Sea of Thirst.

When the PRIORITY RED signal reached Lagrange, Thomas Lawson, Ph.D., was fast asleep. He resented the interruption; though one needed only two hours' sleep in twenty-four when living under zero gravity, it seemed a little unfair to lose even that. Then he grasped the meaning of the message, and was fully awake. At last it looked as if he would be doing something useful here.

Tom Lawson had never been very happy about this assignment; he had wanted to do scientific research, and the atmosphere aboard Lagrange II was much too distracting. Balanced here between Earth and Moon, in a cosmic tightrope act made possible by one of the obscurer consequences of the law of gravitation, the satellite was an astronautical maid-of-all-work. Ships passing in both directions took their fixes from it, and used it as a message center—though there was no truth in the rumor that they stopped to pick up mail. Lagrange was also the relay station for almost all lunar radio traffic, because the whole earthward-facing side of the Moon lay spread beneath it.

The hundred-centimeter telescope had been designed to look at objects billions of times farther away than the Moon, but it was admirably suited for this job. From so close at hand, even with the low power, the view was superb. Tom seemed to be hanging in space immediately above the Sea of Rains, looking down upon the jagged peaks of the Apennines as they glittered in the morning light. Though he had only a sketchy knowledge of the Moon's geography, he could recognize at a glance the great craters of Archimedes and Plato, Aristillus and Eudoxus, the dark scar of the Alpine Valley, and the solitary pyramid of Pico, casting its long shadow across the plain.

But the daylight region did not concern him; what he sought lay in the darkened crescent where the sun had not yet risen. In some ways, that might make his task simpler. A signal lamp—even a hand torch—would be easily visible down there in the night. He checked the map co-ordinates, and punched the control buttons. The burning mountains drifted out of his field of view, and only blackness remained, as he stared into the lunar night that had just swallowed more than twenty men and women.

At first he could see nothing—certainly no winking signal light, flashing its appeal to the stars. Then, as his eyes grew more sensitive, he could see that this land was not wholly dark. It was glimmering with a ghostly phosphorescence as it lay bathed in the earthlight, and the longer he looked, the more details he could see.

There were the mountains to the east of Rainbow Bay, waiting for the dawn that would strike them soon. And there—my God, what was that star shining in the darkness? His hopes soared, then swiftly crashed. That was only the lights of Port Roris, where even now men would be waiting anxiously for the results of his survey.

Within a few minutes, he had convinced himself that a visual search was useless. There was not the slightest chance that he could see an object no bigger than a bus, down there in that faintly luminous landscape. In the daytime, it would have been different; he could have spotted *Selene* at once by the long shadow she cast across the Sea. But the human eye was not sensitive enough to make this search by the light of the waning Earth, from a height of fifty thousand kilometers.

This did not worry Tom. He had scarcely expected to see anything, on this first visual survey. It was a century and a half since astronomers had had to rely upon their eyesight; today, they had far more delicate weapons—a whole armory of light amplifiers and radiation detectors. One of these, he was certain, would be able to find *Selene*.

He would not have been so sure of this had he known that she was no longer upon the surface of the Moon.

# Chapter 4

When *Selene* came to rest, both crew and passengers were still too stricken by astonishment to utter a sound. Captain Harris was the first to recover, perhaps because he was the only one who had any idea of what had happened.

It was a cave-in, of course; they were not rare, though none had ever been recorded in the Sea of Thirst. Deep down in the Moon, something had given way; possibly the infinitesimal weight of *Selene* had itself triggered the collapse. As Pat Harris rose shakily to his feet, he wondered what line of talk he had better use to the passengers. He could hardly pretend that everything was under control and that they'd be on their way again in five minutes; on the other hand, panic was liable to set in if he revealed the true seriousness of the situation. Sooner or later he would have to, but until then it was essential to maintain confidence.

He caught Miss Wilkins' eye as she stood at the back of the cabin, behind the expectantly waiting passengers. She was very pale, but quite composed; he knew that he could rely on her, and flashed her a reassuring smile.

"We seem to be in one piece," he began in an easy, conversational style. "We've had a slight accident, as you'll gather, but things could be worse." (How? a part of his mind asked him. Well, the hull could have been fractured....So you want to prolong the agony? He shut off the interior monologue by an effort of will.) "We've been caught in a land-slip—a moonquake, if you like. There's certainly no need to be alarmed; even if we can't get out under our own power, Port Roris will soon have someone here. Meanwhile, I know that Miss Wilkins was just going to serve refreshments, so I suggest you all relax while I—ah—do whatever proves necessary."

That seemed to have gone over quite well. With a silent sigh of relief, he turned back to the controls. As he did so, he noticed one of the passengers light a cigarette.

It was an automatic reaction, and one that he felt very much like sharing. He said nothing; that would have destroyed the atmosphere his little speech had created. But he caught the man's eye just long enough for the message to go home; the cigarette had been stubbed out before he resumed his seat.

As he switched on the radio, Pat heard the babble of conversation start up behind him. When a group of people were talking together, you could gather their mood even if you could not hear the individual words. He could detect annoyance, excitement, even amusement—but, as yet, very little fear. Probably those who were speaking did not realize the full danger of the situation; the ones who did were silent.

And so was the ether. He searched the wave bands from end to end, and found only a faint crackle from the electrified dust that had buried them. It was just as he had expected. This deadly stuff, with its high metallic content, was an almost perfect shield. It would pass neither radio waves not sound; when he tried to transmit, he would be like a man shouting from the bottom of a well that was packed with feathers.

He switched the beacon to the high-powered emergency setting, so that it automatically broadcast a distress signal on the MOONCRASH band. If anything got through, this would; there was no point in trying to call Port Roris himself, and his fruitless efforts would merely upset the passengers. He left the receiver operating on *Selene*'s assigned frequency, in case of any reply, but he knew that it was useless. No one could hear them; no one could speak to them. As far as they were concerned, the rest of the human race might not exist.

He did not brood over this setback for very long. He had expected it, and there was too much else to do. With the utmost care, he checked all the instruments and gauges. Everything appeared to be perfectly normal, except that the temperature was just a shade high.

That also was to be expected, now that the dust blanket was shielding them from the cold of space.

His greatest worry was the thickness of that blanket, and the pressure it was exerting on the boat. There must be thousands of tons of the stuff above *Selene*—and her hull had been designed to withstand pressure from within, not from without. If she went too deep, she might be cracked like an eggshell.

How deep the cruiser was, he had no idea. When he had caught his last glimpse of the stars, she was about ten meters below the surface, and she might have been carried down much farther by the suction of the dust. It would be advisable—even though it would increase their oxygen consumption—to put up the internal pressure and thus take some of the strain off the hull.

Very slowly, so that there would be no telltale popping of ears to alarm anyone, he boosted the cabin pressure by twenty per cent. When he had finished, he felt a little happier. He was not the only one, for as soon as the pressure gauge had stabilized at its new level, a quiet voice said over his shoulder: "I think that was a very good idea."

He twisted around to see what busybody was spying on him, but his angry protest died unborn. On his first quick inspection, Pat had recognized none of the passengers; now, however, he could tell that there was something vaguely familiar about the stocky, gray-haired man who had come forward to the driver's position.

"I don't want to intrude, Captain—you're the skipper here. But I thought I'd better introduce myself in case I can help. I'm Commodore Hansteen."

Pat stared, slack-jawed, at the man who had led the first expedition to Pluto, who had probably landed on more virgin planets and moons than any explorer in history. All he could say to express his astonishment was "You weren't down on the passenger list!"

The Commodore smiled.

"My alias is Hanson. Since I retired, I've been trying to do a little sight-seeing without quite so much responsibility. And now that I've shaved off my beard, no one ever recognizes me."

"I'm very glad to have you here," said Pat, with deep feeling. Already some of the weight seemed to have lifted from his shoulders; the Commodore would be a tower of strength in the difficult hours—or days—that lay ahead.

"If you don't mind," continued Hansteen, with that same careful politeness, "I'd appreciate an evaluation. To put it bluntly, how long can we last?"

"Oxygen's the limiting factor, as usual. We've enough for about seven days, assuming that no leaks develop. So far, there are no signs of any."

"Well, that gives us time to think. What about food and water?"

"We'll be hungry, but we won't starve. There's an emergency reserve of compressed food, and of course the air purifiers will produce all the water we need. So there's no problem there."

"Power?"

"Plenty, now that we're not using our motors."

"I notice that you haven't tried to call Base."

"It's useless; the dust blankets us completely. I've put the beacon on emergency—that's our only hope of getting a signal through, and it's a slim one."

"So they'll have to find us in some other way. How long do you think it will take them?"

"That's extremely difficult to say. The search will begin as soon as our twenty hundred hours transmission is missed, and they'll know our general area. But we may have gone down without leaving any trace—you've seen how this dust obliterates everything. And even when they *do* find us—"

"How will they get us out?"

"Exactly."

Skipper of twenty-seat dust-cruiser and Commodore of space stared at each other in silence, as their minds circled the same problem. Then, cutting across the low murmur of conversation, they heard a very English voice call out: "I say, Miss—this is the first decent cup of tea I've drunk on the Moon. I thought no one could make it here. My congratulations."

The Commodore chuckled quietly.

"He ought to thank *you*, not the stewardess," he said, pointing to the pressure gauge.

Pat smiled rather wanly in return. That was true enough; now that he had put up the cabin pressure, water must be boiling at nearly its normal, sea-level temperature back on Earth. At last they could have some hot drinks—not the usual tepid ones. But it did seem a somewhat extravagant way to make tea, not unlike the reputed Chinese method of roasting pig by burning down the entire house.

"Our big problem," said the Commodore (and Pat did not in the least resent that "our"), "is to maintain morale. I think it's important, therefore, for you to give a pep talk about the search procedure that must be starting now. But don't be *too* optimistic; you mustn't give the impression that someone will be knocking on the door inside half an hour. That might make it difficult if—well, if we have to wait several days."

"It won't take me long to describe the MOONCRASH organization," said Pat. "And, frankly, it wasn't planned to deal with a situation like this. When a ship's down on the Moon, it can be spotted very quickly from one of the satellites—either Lagrange II, above Earthside, or Lagrange I, over Farside. But I doubt if they can help us now. As I said, we've probably gone down without leaving a trace."

"That's hard to believe. When a ship sinks on Earth, it always leaves *something* behind—bubbles, oil slicks, floating wreckage."

"None of those apply to us. And I can't think of any way we could send something up to the surface—however far away that is."

"So we just have to sit and wait."

"Yes," agreed Pat. He glanced at the oxygen-reserve indicator. "And there's one thing we can be sure of: we can only wait a week."

Fifty thousand kilometers above the Moon, Tom Lawson laid down the last of his photographs. He had gone over every square millimeter of the prints with a magnifying glass. Their quality was excellent; the electronic image intensifier, millions of times more sensitive than the human eye, had revealed details as clearly as if it were already daylight down there on the faintly glimmering plain. He had even spotted one of the tiny dust-skis—or, more accurately, the long shadow it cast in the earthlight. Yet there was no trace of *Selene*; the Sea was as smooth and unruffled as it had been before the coming of Man. And as it would be, in all probability, ages after he had gone.

Tom hated to admit defeat, even in matters far less important than this. He believed that all problems could be solved if they were tackled in the right way, with the right equipment. This was a challenge to his scientific ingenuity; the fact that there were many lives involved was immaterial. Dr. Tom Lawson had no great use for human beings, but he did respect the Universe. This was a private fight between him and It.

He considered the situation with a coldly critical intelligence. Now how would the great Holmes have tackled the problem? (It was characteristic of Tom that one of the few men he really admired had never existed.) He had eliminated the open Sea, so that left only one possibility. The dust-cruiser must have come to grief along the coast or near the mountains, probably in the region known as—he checked the charts—Crater Lake. That made good sense; an accident was much more likely here than out on the smooth, unobstructed plain.

He looked at the photographs again, this time concentrating on the mountains. At once, he ran into a new difficulty. There were scores of isolated crags and boulders along the edge of the Sea, any one of which might be the missing cruiser. Worse still, there were many areas that he could not survey at all, because his view was blocked by the mountains themselves. From his vantage point, the Sea of Thirst was far around the curve of the Moon, and his view of it was badly foreshortened. Crater Lake itself, for instance, was completely invisible to him, hidden by its mountain walls. That area could only be investigated by the dust-skis, working at ground level; even Tom Lawson's godlike eminence was useless here.

He had better call Earthside and give them his interim report.

"Lawson, Lagrange II," he said, when Communications had put him through. "I've searched the Sea of Thirst—there's nothing in the open plain. Your boat must have gone aground near the edge."

"Thank you," said an unhappy voice. "You're quite sure of that?"

"Absolutely. I can see your dust-skis, and they're only a quarter the size of *Selene*."

"Anything visible along the edge of the Sea?"

"There's too much small-scale detail to make a search possible. I can see fifty—oh, a hundred—objects that might be the right size. As soon as the sun rises I'll be able to examine them more closely. But it's night down there now, remember."

"We appreciate your help. Let us know if you find anything else."

Down in Clavius City, the Tourist Commissioner heard Lawson's report with resignation. That settled it; the next of kin had better be notified. It was unwise, if not impossible, to maintain secrecy any longer.

He turned to the Ground Traffic officer and asked: "Is that passenger list in yet?"

"Just coming over the telefax from Port Roris. Here you are." As he handed over the flimsy sheet, he said inquisitively: "Anyone important aboard?"

"All tourists are important," said the Commissioner coldly, without looking up. Then, in almost the same breath, he added: "Oh, my God!"

"What's the matter?"

"Commodore Hansteen's aboard."

"*What*? I didn't know he was on the Moon."

"We've kept it quiet. We thought it was a good idea to have him on the Tourist Commission, now that he's retired. He wanted to have a look around, incognito, before he made up his mind."

There was a shocked silence as the two men considered the irony of the situation. Here was one of the greatest heroes of space—lost as an ordinary tourist in some stupid accident in Earth's backyard, the Moon.

"That may be very bad luck for the Commodore," said the traffic controller at last. "But it's good luck for the passengers—if they're still alive."

"They'll need all the luck they can get, now the Observatory can't help us," said the Commissioner.

He was right on the first point, but wrong on the second. Dr. Tom Lawson still had a few tricks up his sleeve.

And so did The Reverend Vincent Ferraro, S.J., a scientist of a very different kind. It was a pity that he and Tom Lawson were never to meet; the resulting fireworks would have been quite interesting. Father Ferraro believed in God and Man; Dr. Lawson believed in neither.

The priest had started his scientific career as a geophysicist, then switched worlds and became a selenophysicist—though that was a name he used only in his more pedantic moments. No man alive had a greater knowledge of the Moon's interior, gleaned from batteries of instruments strategically placed over the entire surface of the satellite.

Those instruments had just produced some rather interesting results. At 19 hours 35 minutes 47 seconds GMT, there had been a major quake in the general area of Rainbow Bay. That was a little surprising, for the area was an unusually stable one, even for the tranquil Moon. Father Ferraro set his computers to work pinpointing the focus of the disturbance, and also instructed them to search for any other anomalous instrument readings. He left them at this task while he went to lunch, and it was here that his colleagues told him about the missing *Selene*.

No electronic computer can match the human brain at associating apparently irrelevant facts. Father Ferraro only had time for one spoonful of soup before he had put two and two together and had arrived at a perfectly reasonable but disastrously misleading answer.

# Chapter 5

"And that, ladies and gentlemen, is the position," concluded Commodore Hansteen. "We're in no immediate danger, and I haven't the slightest doubt that we'll be located quite soon. Until then, we have to make the best of it."

He paused, and swiftly scanned the upturned, anxious faces. Already he had noted the possible trouble spots—that little man with the nervous tic, the acidulous, prune-faced lady who kept twisting her handkerchief in knots. Maybe they'd neutralize each other, if he could get them to sit together.

"Captain Harris and I—he's the boss; I'm only acting as his adviser—have worked out a plan of action. Food will be simple and rationed, but will be adequate, especially since you won't be engaged in any physical activity. We would like to ask some of the ladies to help Miss Wilkins; she'll have a lot of extra work, and could do with some assistance. Our biggest problem, frankly, is going to be boredom. By the way, did anyone bring any books?"

There was much scrabbling in handbags and baskets. The total haul consisted of assorted lunar guides, including six copies of the official handbook; a current best seller, *The Orange and the Apple*, whose unlikely theme was a romance between Nell Gwyn and Sir Isaac Newton; a Harvard Press edition of *Shane*, with scholarly annotations by a professor of English; an introduction to the logical positivism of Auguste Comte; and a week-old copy of the New York *Times*, Earth edition. It was not much of a library, but with careful rationing it would help to pass the hours that lay ahead.

"I think we'll form an Entertainment Committee to decide how we'll use this material, though I don't know how it will deal with Monsieur Comte. Meanwhile, now that you know what our situation is, are there any questions, any points you'd like Captain Harris or myself to explain in more detail?"

"There's one thing I'd like to ask, sir," said the English voice that had made the complimentary remarks about the tea. "Is there the slightest chance that we'll *float* up? I mean, if this stuff is like water, won't we bob up sooner or later, like a cork?"

That floored the Commodore completely. He looked at Pat and said wryly: "That's one for you, Mr. Harris. Any comment?"

Pat shook his head.

"I'm afraid it won't work. True, the air inside the hull must make us very buoyant, but the resistance of this dust is enormous. We *may* float up eventually—in a few thousand years."

The Englishman, it seemed, was not easily discouraged.

"I noticed that there was a space suit in the air lock. Could anyone get out and *swim* up? Then the search party will know where we are."

Pat stirred uneasily. He was the only one qualified to wear that suit, which was purely for emergency use.

"I'm almost sure it's impossible," he answered. "I doubt if a man could move against the resistance—and of course he'd be absolutely blind. How would he know which way was up? And how would you close the outer door after him? Once the dust had flooded in, there would be no way of clearing it. You certainly couldn't pump it out again."

He could have said more, but decided to leave it at that. They might yet be reduced to such desperate expedients, if there was no sign of rescue by the end of the week. But that was a nightmare that must be kept firmly at the back of his mind, for to dwell too long upon it could only sap his courage.

"If there are no more questions," said Hansteen, "I suggest we introduce ourselves. Whether we like it or not, we have to get used to each other's company, so let's find out who we are. I'll go round the room, and perhaps each of you in turn will give your name, occupation, and home town. You first, sir."

"Robert Bryan, civil engineer, retired, Kingston, Jamaica."

"Irving Schuster, attorney at law, Chicago—and my wife, Myra."

"Nihal Jayawardene, Professor of Zoology, University of Ceylon, Peradeniya."

As the roll call continued, Pat once again found himself grateful for the one piece of luck in this desperate situation. By character, training, and experience, Commodore Hansteen was a born leader of men: already he was beginning to weld this random collection of individuals into a unit, to build up that indefinable *esprit de corps* that transforms a mob into a team. These things he had learned while his little fleet—the first ever to venture beyond the orbit of Neptune, almost three billion miles from the sun—had hung poised week upon week in the emptiness between the planets. Pat, who was thirty years younger and had never been away from the Earth-Moon system, felt no resentment at the change of command that had tacitly taken place. It was nice of the Commodore to say that he was still the boss, but he knew better.

"Duncan McKenzie, physicist, Mount Stromlo Observatory, Canberra."

"Pierre Blanchard, cost accountant, Clavius City, Earthside."

"Phyllis Morley, journalist, London."

"Karl Johanson, nucleonics engineer, Tsiolkovski Base, Farside."

That was the lot; quite a collection of talent, though not an unusual one, for the people who came to the Moon always had something out of the ordinary—even if it was only money. But all the skill and experience now locked up in *Selene* could not, so it seemed to Pat, do anything to help them in their present situation.

That was not quite true, as Commodore Hansteen was now about to prove. He knew, as well as any man alive, that they would be fighting boredom as well as fear. They had been thrown upon their own resources; in an age of universal entertainment and communications, they had suddenly been cut off from the rest of the human race. Radio, TV, telefax newssheets, movies, telephone—all these things now meant no more to them than to the people of the Stone Age. They were like some ancient tribe gathered round the campfire, in a wilderness that held no other men. Even on the Pluto run, thought

Commodore Hansteen, they had never been as lonely as this. They had had a fine library and had been well stocked with every possible form of canned entertainment, and they could talk by tight beam to the inner planets whenever they wished. But on *Selene*, there was not even a pack of cards.

That was an idea. "Miss Morley! As a journalist, I imagine you have a notebook?"

"Why, yes, Commodore."

"Fifty-two blank sheets in it still?"

"I think so."

"Then I must ask you to sacrifice them. Please cut them out and mark a pack of cards on them. No need to be artistic—as long as they're legible, and the lettering doesn't show through the back."

"How are you going to shuffle paper cards?" asked somebody.

"A good problem for our Entertainment Committee to solve. Anyone who thinks they have talent in this direction?"

"I used to be on the stage," said Myra Schuster, rather hesitantly. Her husband did not look at all pleased by this revelation, but it delighted the Commodore.

"Excellent! Though we're a little cramped for space, I was hoping we might be able to put on a play."

Now Mrs. Schuster looked as unhappy as her husband.

"It was rather a long time ago," she said, "and I—I never did much talking."

There were several chuckles, and even the Commodore had difficulty in keeping a straight face. Looking at Mrs. Schuster, on the wrong side of both fifty years and a hundred kilos, it was a little hard to imagine her as, he suspected, a chorus girl.

"Never mind," he said, "it's the spirit that counts. Who will help Mrs. Schuster?"

"I've done some amateur theatricals," said Professor Jayawardene. "Mostly Brecht and Ibsen, though."

That final "though" indicated recognition of the fact that something a little lighter would be appreciated here—say, one of the decadent but amusing comedies of the 1980's, which had invaded the airways in such numbers with the collapse of TV censorship.

There were no more volunteers for this job, so the Commodore moved Mrs. Schuster and Professor Jayawardene into adjacent seats and told them to start program-planning. It seemed unlikely that such an ill-assorted pair would produce anything useful, but one never knew. The main thing was to keep everyone busy, either on tasks of their own or co-operating with others.

"We'll leave it at that for the moment," concluded Hansteen. "If you have any bright ideas, please give them to the committee. Meanwhile, I suggest you stretch your legs and get to know each other. Everyone's announced his job and home town; many of you must have common interests or know the same friends. You'll have plenty of things to talk about." And plenty of time, too, he added silently.

He was conferring with Pat in the pilot's cubicle when they were joined by Dr. McKenzie, the Australian physicist. He looked very worried—even more so than the situation merited.

"There's something I want to tell you, Commodore," he said urgently. "If I'm right, that seven-day oxygen reserve doesn't mean a thing. There's a much more serious danger."

"What's that?"

"Heat." The Australian indicated the outside world with a wave of his hand. "We're blanketed by this stuff, and it's about the best insulator you can have. On the surface, the heat our machines and bodies generated could escape into space, but down here it's trapped. That means we'll get hotter and hotter—until we cook."

"My God," said the Commodore. "I never thought of that. How long do you think it will take?"

"Give me half an hour, and I can make a fair estimate. My guess is—not much more than a day."

The Commodore felt a wave of utter helplessness sweep over him. There was a horrible sickness at the pit of his stomach, like the second time he had been in free fall. (Not the first—he had been ready for it then. But on the second trip, he had been overconfident.) If this estimate was right, all their hopes were blasted. They were slim enough in all conscience, but given a week there was a slight chance that something might be done. With only a day, it was out of the question. Even if they were found in that time, they could never be rescued.

"You might check the cabin temperature," continued McKenzie. "That will give us some indication."

Hansteen walked to the control panel and glanced at the maze of dials and indicators.

"I'm afraid you're right," he said. "It's gone up two degrees already."

"Over a degree an hour. That's about what I figured."

The Commodore turned to Harris, who had been listening to the discussion with growing alarm.

"Is there anything we can do to increase the cooling? How much reserve power has our air-conditioning gear got?"

Before Pat could answer, the physicist intervened.

"That won't help us," he said a little impatiently. "All that our refrigeration does is to pump heat out of the cabin and radiate it away. But that's exactly what it *can't* do now, because of the dust around us. If we try to run the cooling plant faster, it will actually make matters worse."

There was a gloomy silence that lasted until the Commodore said: "Please check those calculations, and let me have your best estimate as soon as you can. And for heaven's sake don't let this go beyond the three of us."

He felt suddenly very old. He had been almost enjoying his unexpected last command; and now it seemed that he would have it only for a day.

At that very moment, though neither party knew the fact, one of the searching dust-skis was passing overhead. Built for speed, efficiency, and cheapness, not for the comfort of tourists, it bore little resemblance to the sunken *Selene*. It was, in fact, no more than an open sledge with seats for pilot and one passenger—each wearing a space suit—and with a canopy overhead to give protection from the sun. A simple control panel, motor, and twin fans at the rear, storage racks for tools and equipment—that completed the inventory. A ski going about its normal work usually towed at least one carrier sledge behind it, sometimes two or three, but this one was traveling light. It had zigzagged back and forth across several hundred square kilometers of the Sea, and had found absolutely nothing.

Over the suit intercom, the driver was talking to his companion.

"What do *you* think happened to them, George? I don't believe they're here."

"Where else can they be? Kidnaped by Outsiders?"

"I'm almost ready to buy that" was the half-serious answer. Sooner or later, all astronauts believed, the human race would meet intelligences from elsewhere. That meeting might still be far in the future but meanwhile, the hypothetical "Outsiders" were part of the mythology of space, and got the blame for everything that could not be explained in any other way.

It was easy to believe in them when you were with a mere handful of companions on some strange, hostile world where the very rocks and air (if there *was* air) were completely alien. Then, nothing could be taken for granted, and the experience of a thousand Earth-bound generations might be useless. As ancient man had peopled the unknown around him with gods and spirits, so *Homo astronauticus* looked over his shoulder when he landed upon each new world, wondering who or what was there already. For a few brief centuries, Man had imagined himself the lord of the Universe, and those primeval hopes and fears had been buried in his subconscious. But now they were stronger than ever, and with good reason, as he looked into the shining face of the heavens and thought of the power and knowledge that must be lurking there.

"Better report to Base," said George. "We've covered our area, and there's no point in going over it again. Not until sunrise, anyway. We'll have a much better chance of finding something then. This damned earthlight gives me the creeps."

He switched on the radio, and gave the ski's call sign.

"Duster Two calling Traffic Control. Over."

"Port Roris Traffic Control here. Found anything?"

"Not a trace. What's new from your end?"

"We don't think she's out in the Sea. The Chief Engineer wants to speak to you."

"Right; put him on."

"Hello, Duster Two. Lawrence here. Plato Observatory's just reported a quake near the Mountains of Inaccessibility. It took place at nineteen thirty-five, which is near enough the time when *Selene* should have been in Crater Lake. They suggest she's been caught in an avalanche somewhere in that area. So head for the mountains and see if you can spot any recent slides or rockfalls."

"What's the chance, sir," asked the dust-ski pilot anxiously, "that there may be more quakes?"

"Very small, according to the Observatory. They say it will be thousands of years before anything like this happens again, now that the stresses have been relieved."

"I hope they're right. I'll radio when I get to Crater Lake; that should be in about twenty minutes."

But it was only fifteen minutes before Duster Two destroyed the last hopes of the waiting listeners.

"Duster Two calling. This is it, I'm afraid. I've not reached Crater Lake yet; I'm still heading up the gorge. But the Observatory was right about the quake. There have been several slides, and we had difficulty in getting past some of them. There must be ten thousand tons of rock in the one I'm looking at now. If *Selene*'s under that lot, we'll never find her. And it won't be worth the trouble of looking."

The silence in Traffic Control lasted so long that the ski called back: "Hello, Traffic Control—did you receive me?"

"Receiving you," said the Chief Engineer in a tired voice. "See if you can find *some* trace of them. I'll send Duster One in to help. Are you sure there's no chance of digging them out?"

"It might take weeks, even if we could locate them. I saw one slide three hundred meters long. If you tried to dig, the rock would probably start moving again."

"Be very careful. Report every fifteen minutes, whether you find anything or not."

Lawrence turned away from the microphone, physically and mentally exhausted. There was nothing more that he could do—or, he suspected, that anyone could do. Trying to compose his thoughts, he walked over to the southward-facing observation window, and stared into the face of the crescent Earth.

It was hard to believe that she was fixed there in the southern sky, that though she hung so close to the horizon, she would neither rise nor set in a million years. However long one lived here, one never really accepted this fact, which violated all the racial wisdom of mankind.

On the other side of that gulf (already so small to a generation that had never known the time when it could not be crossed), ripples of shock and grief would soon be spreading. Thousands of men and women were involved, directly or indirectly, because the Moon had stirred briefly in her sleep.

Lost in his thoughts, it was some time before Lawrence realized that the Port signals officer was trying to attract his attention.

"Excuse me, sir—you've not called Duster One. Shall I do it now?"

"What? Oh yes—go ahead. Send him to help Two in Crater Lake. Tell him we've called off the search in the Sea of Thirst."

# Chapter 6

The news that the search had been called off reached Lagrange II when Tom Lawson, red-eyed from lack of sleep, had almost completed the modifications to the hundred-centimeter telescope. He had been racing against time, and now it seemed that all his efforts had been wasted. *Selene* was not in the Sea of Thirst at all, but in a place where he could never have found her—hidden from him by the ramparts of Crater Lake, and, for good measure, buried by a few thousand tons of rock.

Tom's first reaction was not one of sympathy for the victims, but of anger at his wasted time and effort. Those YOUNG ASTRONOMER FINDS MISSING TOURISTS headlines would never flash across the news-screens of the inhabited worlds. As his private dreams of glory collapsed, he cursed for a good thirty seconds, with a fluency that would have astonished his colleagues. Then, still furious, he started to dismantle the equipment he had begged, borrowed, and stolen from the other projects on the satellite.

It would have worked; he was sure of that. The theory had been quite sound—indeed, it was based on almost a hundred years of practice. Infrared reconnaissance dated back to at least as early as World War II, when it was used to locate camouflaged factories by their telltale heat.

Though *Selene* had left no visible track across the Sea, she must, surely, have left an infrared one. Her fans had stirred up the relatively warm dust a foot or so down, scattering it across the far colder surface layers. An eye that could see by the rays of heat could track her path for hours after she had passed. There would have been just time, Tom calculated, to make such an infrared survey before the sun rose and obliterated all traces of the faint heat trail through the cold lunar night.

But, obviously, there was no point in trying now.

It was well that no one aboard *Selene* could have guessed that the search in the Sea of Thirst had been abandoned, and that the dust-skis were concentrating their efforts inside Crater Lake. And it was well, also, that none of the passengers knew of Dr. McKenzie's predictions.

The physicist had drawn, on a piece of homemade graph paper, the expected rise of temperature. Every hour he noted the reading of the cabin thermometer and pinpointed it on the curve. The agreement with theory was depressingly good; in twenty hours, one hundred ten degrees Fahrenheit would be passed, and the first deaths from heat-stroke would be occurring. Whatever way he looked at it, they had barely a day to live. In these circumstances, Commodore Hansteen's efforts to maintain morale seemed no more than an ironic jest. Whether he failed or succeeded, it would be all the same by the day after tomorrow.

Yet was that true? Though their only choice might lie between dying like men and dying like animals, surely the first was better. It made no difference even if *Selene* remained undiscovered until the end of time, so that no one ever knew how her occupants passed their final hours. This was beyond logic or reason; but so, for that matter, was almost everything that was really important in the shaping of men's lives and deaths.

Commodore Hansteen was well aware of that, as he planned the program for the dwindling hours that lay ahead. Some men are born to be leaders, and he was one of them. The emptiness of his retirement had been suddenly filled; for the first time since he had left the bridge of his flagship *Centaurus*, he felt whole again.

As long as his little crew was busy, he need not worry about morale. It did not matter what they were doing, provided they thought it interesting or important. That poker game, for instance, took care of the Space Administration accountant, the retired civil engineer, and the two executives on vacation from New York. One could tell at a glance that they were all poker fanatics; the problem would be to stop them playing, not to keep them occupied.

Most of the other passengers had split up into little discussion groups, talking quite cheerfully among themselves. The Entertainment Committee was still in session, with Professor Jayawardene making occasional notes while Mrs. Schuster reminisced about her days in burlesque, despite the attempts of her husband to shut her up. The only person who seemed a little apart from it all was Miss Morley, who was writing slowly and carefully, using a very minute hand, in what was left of her notebook. Presumably, like a good journalist, she was keeping a diary of their adventure. Commodore Hansteen was afraid that it would be briefer than she suspected, and that not even those few pages would be filled. And if they were, he doubted that anyone would ever read them.

He glanced at his watch, and was surprised to see how late it was. By now, he should have been on the other side of the Moon, back in Clavius City. He had a lunch engagement at the Lunar Hilton, and after that a trip to—but there was no point in thinking about a future that could never exist. The brief present was all that would ever concern him now.

It would be as well to get some sleep, before the temperature became unbearable. *Selene* had never been designed as a dormitory—or a tomb, for that matter—but it would have to be turned into one now. This involved some research and planning, and a certain amount of damage to Tourist Commission property. It took him twenty minutes to ascertain all the facts; then, after a brief conference with Captain Harris, he called for attention.

"Ladies and gentlemen," he said, "we've all had a busy day, and I think most of us will be glad to get some sleep. This presents a few problems, but I've been doing some experimenting and have discovered that with a little encouragement the center armrests between the seats come out. They're not supposed to, but I doubt if the Commission will sue us. That means that ten of us can stretch out across the seats; the rest will have to use the floor.

"Another point. As you will have noticed, it's become rather warm, and will continue to do so for some time. Therefore I advise you to take off all unnecessary clothing; comfort is much more important than modesty." (And survival, he added silently, is much more important than comfort—but it would be some hours yet before it came to that.)

"We'll turn off the main cabin lights, but since we don't want to be in complete darkness, we'll leave on the emergency lighting at low power. One of us will remain on watch at all times in the skipper's seat. Mr. Harris is working out a roster of two-hour shifts. Any questions or comments?"

There were none, and the Commodore breathed a sigh of relief. He was afraid that someone would be inquisitive about the rising temperature, and was not quite sure how he would have answered. His many accomplishments did not include the gift of lying, and he was anxious that the passengers should have as untroubled a sleep as was possible in the circumstances. Barring a miracle, it would be their last.

Miss Wilkins, who was beginning to lose a little of her professional smartness, took round final drinks for those who needed them. Most of the passengers had already begun to remove their outer clothing; the more modest ones waited until the main lights went off. In the dim red glow, the interior of *Selene* now had a fantastic appearance, one that would have been utterly inconceivable when she left Port Roris a few hours before. Twenty-two men and women, most of them stripped down to their underclothing, lay sprawled across the seats or along the floor. A few lucky ones were already snoring, but for most, sleep would not come as easily as that.

Captain Harris had chosen a position at the very rear of the cruiser; in fact, he was not in the cabin at all, but in the tiny air-lock galley. It was a good vantage point. Now that the communicating door had been slid back, he could look the whole length of the cabin and keep an eye on everyone inside it.

He folded his uniform into a pillow, and lay down on the unyielding floor. It was six hours before his watch was due, and he hoped he could get some sleep before then.

Sleep! The last hours of his life were ticking away, yet he had nothing better to do. How well do condemned men sleep, he wondered, in the night that will end with the gallows?

He was so desperately tired that even this thought brought no emotion. The last thing he saw, before consciousness slipped away, was Dr. McKenzie taking yet another temperature reading and carefully plotting it on his chart, like an astrologer casting a horoscope.

Fifteen meters above—a distance that could be covered in a single stride under this low gravity—morning had already come. There is no twilight on the Moon, but for many hours the sky had held the promise of dawn. Stretching far ahead of the sun was the glowing pyramid of the zodiacal light, so seldom seen on Earth. With infinite slowness it edged its way above the horizon, growing brighter and brighter as the moment of sunrise approached. Now it had merged into the opalescent glory of the corona; and now, a million times more brilliant than either, a thin thread of fire began to spread along the horizon as the sun made its reappearance after fifteen days of darkness. It would take more than an hour for it to lift itself clear of the sky line, so slowly did the Moon turn on its axis, but the night had already ended.

A tide of ink was swiftly ebbing from the Sea of Thirst, as the fierce light of dawn swept back the darkness. Now the whole drab expanse of the Sea was raked with almost horizontal rays. Had there been anything showing above its surface, this grazing light would have thrown its shadow for hundreds of meters, revealing it at once to any who were searching.

But there were no searchers there. Duster One and Duster Two were busy on their fruitless quest in Crater Lake, fifteen kilometers away. They were still in darkness; it would be another two days before the sun rose above the surrounding peaks, though their summits were already blazing with the dawn. As the hours passed, the sharp-edged line of light would creep down the flanks of the mountains—sometimes moving no faster than a man could walk—until the sun climbed high enough for its rays to strike into the crater.

But man-made light was already shining there, flashing among the rocks as the searchers photographed the slides that had come sweeping silently down the mountains when the Moon trembled in its sleep. Within an hour, those photographs would have reached Earth; in another two, all the inhabited worlds would have seen them.

It would be very bad for the tourist business.

When Captain Harris awoke, it was already much hotter. Yet it was not the now oppressive heat that had interrupted his sleep, a good hour before he was due to go on watch.

Though he had never spent a night aboard her, Pat knew all the sounds that *Selene* could make. When the motors were not running, she was almost silent; one had to listen carefully to notice the susurration of the air pumps and the low throb of the cooling plant. Those sounds were still there, as they had been before he went to sleep. They were unchanged; but they had been joined by another.

It was a barely audible whisper, so faint that for a moment he could not be sure he was not imagining it. That it should have called to his subconscious mind across the barriers of sleep seemed quite incredible. Even now that he was awake, he could not identify it, or decide from which direction it came.

Then, abruptly, he knew why it had awakened him. In a second, the sogginess of sleep had vanished. He got quickly to his feet, and pressed his ear against the air-lock door, for that mysterious sound was coming from *outside* the hull.

Now he could hear it, faint but distinct, and it set his skin crawling with apprehension. There could be no doubt; it was the sound of countless dust grains whispering past *Selene*'s walls like a ghostly sandstorm. What did it mean? Was the Sea once more on the move? If so, would it take *Selene* with it? Yet there was not the slightest vibration or sense of motion in the cruiser itself; only the outside world was rustling past.

Very quietly, being careful not to disturb his sleeping companions, Pat tiptoed into the darkened cabin. It was Dr. McKenzie's watch. The scientist was hunched up in the pilot's seat, staring out through the blinded windows. He turned round as Pat approached, and whispered: "Anything wrong at your end?"

"I don't know—come and see."

Back in the galley, they pressed their ears against the outer door, and listened for a long time to that mysterious crepitation. Presently McKenzie said: "The dust's moving, all right—but I don't see why. That gives us another puzzle to worry about."

"Another?"

"Yes. I don't understand what's happening to the temperature. It's still going up, but nothing like as fast as it should."

The physicist seemed really annoyed that his calculations had proved incorrect, but to Pat this was the first piece of good news since the disaster.

"Don't look so miserable about it; we all make mistakes. And if this one gives us a few more days to live, I'm certainly not complaining."

"But I *couldn't* have made a mistake. The math is elementary. We know how much heat twenty-two people generate, and it must go somewhere."

"They won't produce so much heat when they're sleeping; maybe that explains it."

"You don't think I'd overlook anything so obvious as that!" said the scientist testily. "It helps, but it isn't enough. There's some other reason why we're not getting as hot as we should."

"Let's just accept the fact and be thankful," said Pat. "Meanwhile, what about this noise?"

With obvious reluctance, McKenzie switched his mind to the new problem.

"The dust's moving, but we aren't, so it's probably merely a local effect. In fact, it only seems to be happening at the back of the cabin. I wonder if that has any significance." He gestured to the bulkhead behind them. "What's on the other side of this?"

"The motors, oxygen reserve, cooling equipment..."

"*Cooling* equipment! Of course! I remember noticing that when I came aboard. Our radiator fins are back there, aren't they?"

"That's right."

"*Now* I see what's happened. They've got so hot that the dust is circulating, like any liquid that's heated. There's a dust fountain outside, and it's carrying away our surplus heat. With any luck, the temperature will stabilize now. We won't be comfortable, but we can survive."

In the crimson gloom, the two men looked at each other with a dawning hope. Then Pat said slowly: "I'm sure that's the explanation. Perhaps our luck's beginning to turn."

He glanced at his watch, and did a quick mental calculation.

"The sun's rising over the Sea about now. Base will have the dust-skis out looking for us, and they must know our approximate position. Ten to one they'll find us in a few hours."

"Should we tell the Commodore?"

"No, let him sleep. He's had a harder day than any of us. This news can wait until morning."

When McKenzie had left him, Pat tried to resume his interrupted sleep. But he could not do so; he lay with eyes open in the faint red glow, wondering at this strange turn of fate. The dust that had swallowed and then had threatened to broil them had now come to their aid, as its convection currents swept their surplus heat up to the surface. Whether those currents would continue to flow when the rising sun smote the Sea with its full fury, he could not guess.

Outside the wall, the dust still whispered past, and suddenly Pat was reminded of an antique hourglass he had once been shown as a child. When you turned it over, sand poured through a narrow constriction into the lower chamber, and its rising level marked the passage of the minutes and the hours.

Before the invention of clocks, myriads of men must have had their days divided by such falling grains of sand. But none until now, surely, had ever had his life span metered out by a fountain of rising dust.

# Chapter 7

In Clavius City, Chief Administrator Olsen and Tourist Commissioner Davis had just finished conferring with the Legal Department. It had not been a cheerful occasion; much of the time had been spent discussing the waivers of responsibility which the missing tourists had signed before they boarded *Selene*. Commissioner Davis had been much against this when the trips were started, on the grounds that it would scare away customers, but the Administration's lawyers had insisted. Now he was very glad that they had had their way.

He was glad, also, that the Port Roris authorities had done the job properly; matters like this were sometimes treated as unimportant formalities and quietly ignored. There was a full list of signatures for *Selene*'s passengers—with one possible exception that the lawyers were still arguing about.

The incognito Commodore had been listed as R. S. Hanson, and it looked very much as if this was the name he had actually signed. The signature was, however, so illegible that it might well have been "Hansteen." Until a facsimile was radioed from Earth, no one would be able to decide this point. It was probably unimportant. Because the Commodore was traveling on official business, the Administration was bound to accept some responsibility for him. And for all the other passengers, it was responsible morally, if not legally.

Above all, it had to make an effort to find them and give them a decent burial. This little problem had been placed squarely in the lap of Chief Engineer Lawrence, who was still at Port Roris.

He had seldom tackled anything with less enthusiasm. While there was a chance that the *Selene*'s passengers were still alive, he would have moved heaven, Earth, and Moon to get at them. But now that they must be dead, he saw no point in risking men's lives to locate them and dig them out. Personally, he could hardly think of a better place to be buried than among these eternal hills.

That they were dead, Chief Engineer Robert Lawrence did not have the slightest doubt; all the facts fitted together too perfectly. The quake had occurred at just about the time *Selene* should have been leaving Crater Lake, and the gorge was now half blocked with slides. Even the smallest of those would have crushed her like a paper toy, and those aboard would have perished within seconds as the air gushed out. If, by some million-to-one chance, she had escaped being smashed, her radio signals would have been received. The tough little automatic beacon had been built to take any reasonable punishment, and if *that* was out of action, it must have been some crack-up.

The first problem would be to locate the wreck. That might be fairly easy, even if it was buried beneath a million tons of rubble. There were prospecting instruments and a whole range of metal detectors that could do the trick. And when the hull was cracked, the air inside would have rushed out into the lunar near-vacuum; even now, hours later, there would be traces of carbon dioxide and oxygen that might be spotted by one of the gas detectors used for pinpointing spaceship leaks. As soon as the dust-skis came back to base for servicing and recharging, he'd get them fitted with leak detectors and would send them sniffing round the rockslides.

No—*finding* the wreck might be simple—but getting it out might be impossible. He wouldn't guarantee that the job could be done for a hundred million. (And he could just see the C.A.'s face if he mentioned a sum like that.) For one thing, it was a physical impossibility to bring heavy equipment into the area—the sort of equipment needed to move thousands of tons of rubble. The flimsy little dust-skis were useless. To shift those rockslides, one would have to float moondozers across the Sea of Thirst, and import whole shiploads of gelignite to blast a road through the mountains. The whole idea was absurd. He could understand the Administration's point of view, but he was damned if he would let his overworked Engineering Division get saddled with such a Sisyphean task.

As tactfully as possible—for the Chief Administrator was not the sort of man who liked to take no for an answer—he began to draft his report. Summarized, it might have read: "A. The job's almost certainly impossible. B. If it can be done at all, it will cost millions and may involve further loss of life. C. It's not worth doing anyway." But because such bluntness would make him unpopular, and he had to give his reasons, the report ran to over three thousand words.

When he had finished dictating, he paused to marshal his ideas, could think of nothing further, and added: "Copies to Chief Administrator, Moon; Chief Engineer, Farside; Supervisor, Traffic Control; Tourist Commissioner; Central Filing. Classify as Confidential."

He pressed the transcription key. Within twenty seconds all twelve pages of his report, impeccably typed and punctuated, with several grammatical slips corrected, had emerged from the office telefax. He scanned it rapidly, in case the electro-secretary had made mistakes. She did this occasionally (all electrosecs were "she"), especially during rush periods when she might be taking dictation from a dozen sources at once. In any event, no wholly sane machine could cope with all the eccentricities of a language like English, and every wise executive checked his final draft before he sent it out. Many were the hilarious disasters that had overtaken those who had left it all to electronics.

Lawrence was halfway through this task when the telephone rang.

"Lagrange II on the line, sir," said the operator—a human one, as it happened. "A Doctor Lawson wants to speak to you."

Lawson? Who the devil's that? the C.E.E. asked himself. Then he remembered; that was the astronomer who was making the telescopic search. Surely someone had told him that it was useless.

The Chief Engineer had never had the dubious privilege of meeting Dr. Lawson. He did not know that the astronomer was a very neurotic and very brilliant young man—and, what was more important in this case, a very stubborn one.

Lawson had just begun to dismantle the infrared scanner when he stopped to consider his action. Since he had practically completed the blasted thing, he might as well test it, out of sheer scientific curiosity. He prided himself, rightly, as a practical experimenter; this was something unusual in an age when most so-called astronomers were really mathematicians who never went near an observatory.

He was now so tired that only sheer cussedness kept him going. If the scanner had not worked the first time, he would have postponed testing it until he had had some sleep. But by the good luck that is occasionally the reward of skill, it *did* work; only a few minor adjustments were needed before the image of the Sea of Thirst began to build up upon the viewing screen.

It appeared line by line, like an old-fashioned TV picture, as the infrared detector scanned back and forth across the face of the Moon. The light patches indicated relatively warm areas, the dark ones, regions of cold. Almost all the Sea of Thirst was dark, except for a brilliant band where the rising sun had already touched it with fire. But in that darkness, as Tom looked closely, he could see some very faint tracks, glimmering as feebly as the paths of snails through some moonlit garden back on Earth.

Beyond doubt, there was the heat trail of *Selene*; and there also, much fainter, were the zigzags of the dust-skis that even now were searching for her. All the trails converged toward the Mountains of Inaccessibility and there vanished beyond his field of view.

He was much too tired to examine them closely; and in any event it no longer mattered, for this merely confirmed what was already known. His only satisfaction, which was of some importance to him, lay in the proof that another piece of Lawson-built equipment had obeyed his will. For the record, he photographed the screen, then staggered to bed to catch up with his arrears of sleep.

Three hours later he awoke from a restless slumber. Despite his extra hour in bed, he was still tired, but something was worrying him and would not let him sleep. As the faint whisper of moving dust had disturbed Pat Harris in the sunken *Selene*, so also, fifty thousand kilometers away, Tom Lawson was recalled from sleep by a trifling variation from the normal. The mind has many watchdogs; sometimes they bark unnecessarily, but a wise man never ignores their warning.

Still bleary-eyed, Tom left the cluttered little cell that was his private cabin aboard Lagrange, hooked himself on to the nearest moving belt, and drifted along the gravityless corridors until he had reached the Observatory. He exchanged a surly good morning (though it was now late in the satellite's arbitrary afternoon) with those of his colleagues who did not see him in time to take avoiding action. Then, thankful to be alone, he settled down among the instruments that were the only things he loved.

He ripped the photograph out of the one-shot camera where it had been lying all night, and looked at it for the first time. It was then that he saw the stubby trail emerging from the Mountains of Inaccessibility, and ending a very short distance away in the Sea of Thirst.

He must have seen it last night when he looked at the screen—but he had not noticed it. For a scientist, that was a serious, almost an unforgivable, lapse, and Tom felt very angry with himself. He had let his preconceived ideas affect his powers of observation.

What did it mean? He examined the area closely with a magnifier. The trail ended in a small, diffuse dot, which he judged to be about two hundred meters across. It was very odd—almost as if *Selene* had emerged from the mountains, and then taken off like a spaceship.

Tom's first theory was that she had blown to pieces, and that this smudge of heat was the aftermath of the explosion. But in that case, there would have been plenty of wreckage, most of it light enough to float on the dust. The skis could hardly have missed it when they passed through this area—as the thin, distinctive track of one showed it had indeed done.

There had to be some other explanation, yet the alternative seemed absurd. It was almost impossible to imagine that anything as large as *Selene* could sink without trace in the Sea of Thirst, merely because there had been a quake in that neighborhood. He certainly could not call the Moon on the evidence of a single photograph and say, "You're looking in the wrong place." Though he pretended that the opinion of others meant nothing to him, Tom was terrified of making a fool of himself. Before he could advance this fantastic theory, he would have to get more evidence.

Through the telescope, the Sea was now a flat and featureless glare of light. Visual observation merely confirmed what he had proved before sunrise; there was nothing more than a few centimeters high projecting above the dust surface. The infrared scanner was no greater help; the heat trails had vanished completely, wiped out hours ago by the sun.

Tom adjusted the instrument for maximum sensitivity, and searched the area where the trail had ended. Perhaps there was some lingering trace that could be picked up even now, some faint smudge of heat that still persisted, strong enough to be detected even in the warmth of the lunar morning. For the sun was still low, and its rays had not yet attained the murderous power they would possess at noon.

Was it imagination? He had the gain turned full up, so that the instrument was on the verge of instability. From time to time, at the very limit of its detecting power, he thought he could see a tiny glimmer of heat, in the exact area where last night's track had ended.

It was all infuriatingly inconclusive—not at all the sort of evidence that a scientist needed, especially when he was going to stick his neck out. If he said nothing, no one would ever know, but all his life he would be haunted by doubts. Yet if he committed himself, he might raise false hopes, become the laughingstock of the solar system, or be accused of seeking personal publicity.

He could not have it both ways; he would have to make a decision. With great reluctance, knowing that he was taking a step from which there could be no turning back, he picked up the Observatory phone.

"Lawson here," he said. "Get me Luna Central—priority."

# Chapter 8

Aboard *Selene*, breakfast had been adequate but hardly inspiring. There were several complaints from passengers who thought that crackers and compressed meat, a dab of honey and a glass of tepid water, scarcely constituted a good meal. But the Commodore had been adamant. "We don't know how long this has got to last us," he said, "and I'm afraid we can't have not meals. There's no way of preparing them, and it's too warm in the cabin already. Sorry, no more tea or coffee. And frankly, it won't do any of us much harm to cut down on the calories for a few days." That came out before he remembered Mrs. Schuster, and he hoped that she wouldn't take it as a personal affront. Ungirdled after last night's general clothes-shedding, she now looked rather like a good-natured hippopotamus, as she lay sprawled over a seat and a half.

"The sun's just risen overhead," continued Hansteen, "the search parties will be out, and it's only a matter of time before they locate us. It's been suggested that we have a sweep-stake on that; Miss Morley, who's keeping the log, will collect your bets.

"Now about our program for the day. Professor Jayawardene, perhaps you'll let us know what the Entertainment Committee has arranged."

The Professor was a small, birdlike person whose gentle dark eyes seemed much too large for him. It was obvious that he had taken the task of entertainment very seriously, for his delicate brown hand clutched an impressive sheaf of notes.

"As you know," he said, "my speciality is the theater—but I'm afraid that doesn't help us very much. It would be nice to have a play-reading, and I thought of writing out some parts; unfortunately, we're too short of paper to make that possible. So we'll have to think of something else.

"There's not much reading matter on board, and some of it is rather specialized. But we do have two novels—a university edition of one of the classic Westerns, *Shane*, and this new historical romance, *The Orange and the Apple*. The suggestion is that we form a panel of readers and go through them. Has anyone any objection—or any better ideas?"

"We want to play poker," said a firm voice from the rear.

"But you can't play poker *all* the time," protested the Professor, thus showing a certain ignorance of the nonacademic world. The Commodore decided to go to his rescue.

"The reading need not interfere with the poker," he said. "Besides, I suggest you take a break now and then. Those cards won't last much longer."

"Well, which book shall we start on first? And any volunteers as readers? I'll be quite happy to do so, but we want some variety."

"I object to wasting our time on *The Orange and the Apple*," said Miss Morley. "It's utter trash, and most of it is—er—near-pornography."

"How do *you* know?" asked David Barrett, the Englishman who had commended the tea. The only answer was an indignant sniff. Professor Jayawardene looked quite unhappy, and glanced at the Commodore for support. He did not get any; Hansteen was studiously looking the other way. If the passengers relied on him for everything, that would be fatal. As far as possible, he wanted them to stand on their own feet.

"Very well," said the Professor. "To prevent any argument, we'll start with *Shane*."

There were several protesting cries of: "We want *The Orange and the Apple*!" but, surprisingly, the Professor stood firm. "It's a very long book," he said. "I really don't think we'll have time to finish it before we're rescued." He cleared his throat, looked around the cabin to see if there were any further objections, and then started to read in an extremely pleasant though rather singsong voice.

"'Introduction: The Role of the Western in the Age of Space. By Karl Adams, Professor of English. Being based on the 2037 Kingsley Amis Seminars in Criticism at the University of Chicago.'"

The poker players were wavering; one of them was nervously examining the worn pieces of paper that served as cards. The rest of the audience had settled down, with looks of boredom or anticipation. Miss Wilkins was back in the air-lock galley, checking the provisions. The melodious voice continued:

"'One of the most unexpected literary phenomena of our age has been the revival, after half a century of neglect, of the romance known as the "Western." These stories, set in a background extremely limited in both space and time—the United States of America, circa 1865-1880—were for a considerable period one of the most popular forms of fiction the world has ever known. Millions were written, almost all published in cheap magazines and shoddily produced books, but out of those millions, a few have survived both as literature and as a record of an age—though we must never forget that the writers were describing an era that had passed long before they were born.

"'With the opening up of the solar system in the 1970's, the earth-based frontier of the American West seemed so ludicrously tiny that the reading public lost interest in it. This, of course, was as illogical as dismissing *Hamlet* on the grounds that events restricted to a small and drafty Danish castle could not possibly be of universal significance.

"'During the last few years, however, a reaction has set in. I am creditably informed that Western stories are among the most popular reading matter in the libraries of the space liners now plying between the planets. Let us see if we can discover the reason for this apparent paradox—this link between the Old West and the New Space.

"'Perhaps we can best do this by divesting ourselves of all our modern scientific achievements, and imagining that we are back in the incredibly primitive world of 1870. Picture a vast, open plain, stretching away into the distance until it merges into a far-off line of misty mountains. Across that plain is crawling, with agonizing slowness, a line of clumsy wagons. Around them ride men on horse-back, bearing guns—for this is Indian territory.

"'It will take those wagons longer to reach the mountains than a star-class liner now requires to make the journey from Earth to Moon. The space of the prairie was just as great, therefore, to the men who challenged it as the space of the solar system is to us. This is one of the links we have with the Western; there are others, even more fundamental. To understand them, we must first consider the role of the epic in literature....'"

It seemed to be going well, thought the Commodore. An hour would be long enough; at the end of that time Professor J. would be through the introduction and well into the story. Then they could switch to something else, preferably at an exciting moment in the narrative, so that the audience would be anxious to get back to it.

Yes, the second day beneath the dust had started smoothly, with everyone in good heart. But how many days were there still to go?

The answer to that question depended upon two men who had taken an instant dislike to each other even though they were fifty thousand kilometers apart. As he listened to Dr. Lawson's account of his discoveries, the Chief Engineer found himself torn in opposing directions. The astronomer had a most unfortunate method of approach, especially for a youngster who was addressing a very senior official more than twice his age. He talks to me, thought Lawrence, at first more amused than angry, as if I'm a retarded child, who has to have everything explained to him in words of one syllable.

When Lawson had finished, the C.E.E. was silent for a few seconds as he examined the photographs that had come over the telefax while they were talking. The earlier one, taken before sunrise, was certainly suggestive—but it was not enough to prove the case, in his opinion. And the one taken after dawn showed nothing at all on the reproduction he had received. There might have been something on the original print, but he would hate to take the word of this unpleasant young man for it.

"This is very interesting, Doctor Lawson," he said at last. "It's a great pity, though, that you didn't continue your observations when you took the first photos. Then we might have had something more conclusive."

Tom bridled instantly at this criticism, despite—or perhaps because of—the fact that it was well-founded.

"If you think that anyone else could have done better—" he snapped.

"Oh, I'm not suggesting that," said Lawrence, anxious to keep the peace. "But where do we go from here? The spot you indicate may be fairly small, but its position is uncertain by at least half a kilometer. There may be nothing visible on the surface, even in daylight. Is there any way we can pinpoint it more accurately?"

"There's one very obvious method. Use this same technique at ground level. Go over the area with an infrared scanner. That will locate any hot spot, even if it's only a fraction of a degree warmer than its surroundings."

"A good idea," said Lawrence. "I'll see what can be arranged, and will call you back if I need any further information. Thank you very much—Doctor."

He hung up quickly, and wiped his brow. Then he immediately put through another call to the satellite.

"Lagrange II? Chief Engineer, Earthside, here. Give me the Director, please....Professor Kotelnikov? This is Lawrence....I'm fine, thanks. I've been talking to your Doctor Lawson....No, he hasn't done anything, except nearly make me lose my temper. He's been looking for our missing dust-cruiser, and he thinks he's found her. What I'd like to know is—how competent is he?"

In the next five minutes, the Chief Engineer learned a good deal about young Dr. Lawson; rather more, in fact, than he had any right to know, even over a confidential circuit. When Professor Kotelnikov had paused for breath, he interjected sympathetically: "I can under-stand why you put up with him. Poor kid—I thought orphanages like that went out with Dickens and the twentieth century. A good thing it *did* burn down. Do you suppose he set fire to it? No, don't answer that—you've told me he's a first-class observer, and that's all I want to know. Thanks a lot. See you down here someday?"

In the next half-hour, Lawrence made a dozen calls to points all over the Moon. At the end of that time, he had accumulated a large amount of information; now he had to act on it.

At Plato Observatory, Father Ferraro thought the idea was perfectly plausible. In fact, he had already suspected that the focus of the quake was under the Sea of Thirst rather than the Mountains of Inaccessibility, but couldn't prove it because the Sea had such a damping effect on all vibrations. No, a complete set of soundings had never been made; it would be very tedious and time consuming. He'd probed it himself in a few places with telescopic rods, and had always hit bottom at less than forty meters. His guess for the average depth was under ten meters, and it was much shallower round the edges. No, he didn't have an infrared detector, but the astronomers on Farside might be able to help.

Sorry, no I.R. detector at Dostoevski. Our work is all in the ultraviolet. Try Verne.

Oh yes, we used to do some work in the infrared, a couple of years back—taking spectrograms of giant red stars. But do you know what? There were enough traces of lunar atmosphere to interfere with the readings, so the whole program was shifted out into space. Try Lagrange.

It was at this point that Lawrence called Traffic Control for the shipping schedules from Earth, and found that he was in luck. But the next move would cost a lot of money, and only the Chief Administrator could authorize it.

That was one good thing about Olsen; he never argued with his technical staff over matters that were in their province. He listened carefully to Lawrence's story, and went straight to the main point.

"If this theory is true," he said, "there's a chance that they may still be alive, after all."

"More than a chance; I'd say it's quite likely. We know the Sea is shallow, so they can't be very deep. The pressure on the hull would be fairly low; it may still be intact."

"So you want this fellow Lawson to help with the search."

The Chief Engineer gave a gesture of resignation. "He's about the last person I *want*," he answered. "But I'm afraid we've got to have him."

# Chapter 9

The skipper of the cargo liner *Auriga* was furious, and so was his crew—but there was nothing they could do about it. Ten hours out from Earth and five hours from the Moon they were ordered to stop at Lagrange, with all the waste of speed and extra computing that implied. And to make matters worse, they were being diverted from Clavius City to that miserable dump Port Roris, practically on the other side of the Moon. The ether crackled with messages canceling dinners and assignations all over the southern hemisphere.

Not far from full, the mottled silver disc of the Moon, its eastern limb wrinkled with easily visible mountains, formed a dazzling background to Lagrange II as *Auriga* came to rest a hundred kilometers earthward of the station. She was allowed no closer; the interference produced by her equipment, and the glare of her jets, had already affected the sensitive recording instruments on the satellite. Only old-fashioned chemical rockets were permitted to operate in the immediate neighborhood of Lagrange; plasma drives and fusion plants were strictly taboo.

Carrying one small case full of clothing, and one large case full of equipment, Tom Lawson entered the liner twenty minutes after his departure from Lagrange. The shuttle pilot had refused to hurry, despite urgings from *Auriga*. The new passenger was greeted without warmth as he came aboard; he would have been received quite differently had anyone known his mission. The Chief Administrator, however, had ruled that it should be kept secret for the present; he did not wish to raise false hopes among the relatives of the lost passengers.

The Tourist Commissioner had wanted an immediate release, maintaining that it would prove that they were doing their best, but Olsen had said firmly: "Wait until he produces results. *Then* you can give something to your friends in the news agencies."

The order was already too late. Aboard *Auriga*, Maurice Spenser, Bureau Chief of Interplanet News, was on his way to take up his duties in Clavius City. He was not sure if this was a promotion or demotion from Peking, but it would certainly be a change.

Unlike all the other passengers, he was not in the least annoyed by the change of course. The delay was on the firm's time, and, as an old newsman, he always welcomed the unusual, the break in the established routine. It was certainly odd for a Moon-bound liner to waste several hours and an unimaginable amount of energy to stop at Lagrange, just to pick up a dour-faced young man with a couple of pieces of baggage. And why the diversion from Clavius to Port Roris? "Top-level instructions from Earth," said the skipper, and seemed to be telling the truth when he disowned all further knowledge. It was a mystery, and mysteries were Spenser's business. He made one shrewd guess at the reason, and was right—or almost right—the first time.

It must have something to do with that lost dust-cruiser there had been such a fuss about just before he left Earth. This scientist from Lagrange must have some information about her, or must be able to assist in the search. But why the secrecy? Perhaps there was some scandal or mistake that the Lunar Administration was trying to hush up. The simple and wholly creditable reason never occurred to Spenser.

He avoided speaking to Lawson during the remainder of the brief trip, and was amused to note that the few passengers who tried to strike up a conversation were quickly rebuffed. Spenser bided his time, and that time came thirty minutes before landing.

It was hardly an accident that he was sitting next to Lawson when the order came to fasten seat belts for deceleration. With the fifteen other passengers, they sat in the tiny, blacked-out lounge, looking at the swiftly approaching Moon. Projected on a viewing screen from a lens in the outer hull, the image seemed sharper and more brilliant even than in real life. It was as if they were inside an old-fashioned camera obscure; the arrangement was much safer than having an actual observation window—a structural hazard that spaceship designers fought against tooth and nail.

That dramatically expanding landscape was a glorious and unforgettable sight, yet Spenser could give it only half his attention. He was watching the man beside him, his intense aquiline features barely visible in the reflected light from the screen.

"Isn't it somewhere down there," he said, in his most casual tone of voice, "that the boatload of tourists has just been lost?"

"Yes," said Tom, after a considerable delay.

"I don't know my way about the Moon. Any idea where they're supposed to be?"

Even the most unco-operative of men, Spenser had long ago discovered, could seldom resist giving information if you made it seem that they were doing you a favor, and gave them a chance of airing their superior knowledge. The trick worked in nine cases out of ten: it worked now with Tom Lawson.

"They're down there," he said, pointing to the center of the screen. "Those are the Mountains of Inaccessibility; that's the Sea of Thirst all around them."

Spenser stared, in entirely unsimulated awe, at the sharply etched blacks and whites of the mountains toward which they were falling. He hoped the pilot—human or electronic—knew his job; the ship seemed to be coming in very fast. Then he realized that they were drifting toward the flatter territory on the left of the picture; the mountains and the curious gray area surrounding them were sliding away from the center of the screen.

"Port Roris," Tom volunteered unexpectedly, pointing to a barely visible black mark on the far left. "That's where we're landing."

"Well! I'd hate to come down in those mountains," said Spenser, determined to keep the conversation on target. "They'll never find the poor devils if they're lost in that wilderness. Anyway, aren't they supposed to be buried under an avalanche?"

Tom gave a superior laugh.

"They're *supposed* to be," he said.

"Why—isn't that true?"

A little belatedly, Tom remembered his instructions.

"Can't tell you anything more," he replied in that same smug, cocksure voice.

Spenser dropped the subject; he had already learned enough to convince him of one thing. Clavius City would have to wait; he had better hang on at Port Roris for a while.

He was even more certain of this when his envious eyes saw Dr. Tom Lawson cleared through Quarantine, Customs, Immigration, and Exchange Control in three minutes flat.

Had any eavesdropper been listening to the sounds inside *Selene*, he would have been very puzzled. The cabin was reverberating unmelodiously to the sound of twenty-one voices, in almost as many keys, singing "Happy Birthday to You."

When the din had subsided, Commodore Hansteen called out: "Anyone else besides Mrs. Williams who just remembered that it's his or her Birthday? We know, of course, that some ladies like to keep it quiet when they reach a certain age—"

There were no volunteers, but Duncan McKenzie raised his voice above the general laughter.

"There's a funny thing about birthdays—I used to win bets at parties with it. Knowing that there are three hundred and sixty-five days in the year, how large a group of people would you think was needed before you had a fifty-fifty chance that two of them shared the same birthday?"

After a brief pause, while the audience considered the question, someone answered: "Why, half of three hundred and sixty-five, I suppose. Say a hundred and eighty."

"That's the obvious answer—and it's completely wrong. If you have a group of more than twenty-four people, the odds are better than even that two of them have the same birthday."

"That's ridiculous! Twenty-four days out of three sixty-five *can't* give those odds."

"Sorry—it does. And if there are more than forty people, nine times out of ten two of them will have the same birthday. There's a sporting chance that it might work with the twenty-two of us. What about trying it, Commodore?"

"Very well. I'll go round the room, and ask each one of you for his date of birth."

"Oh no," protested McKenzie. "People cheat if you do it that way. The dates must be written down, so that nobody knows anyone else's birthday."

An almost blank page from one of the tourist guides was sacrificed for this purpose, and torn up into twenty-two slips. When they were collected and read, to everyone's astonishment—and McKenzie's gratification—it turned out that both Pat Harris and Robert Bryan had been born on May 23.

"Pure luck!" said a skeptic, thus igniting a brisk mathematical argument among half a dozen of the male passengers. The ladies were quite uninterested; either because they did not care for mathematics or because they preferred to ignore birthdays.

When the Commodore decided that this had gone on long enough, he rapped for attention.

"Ladies and gentlemen!" he called. "Let's get on with the next item on our program. I'm pleased to say that the Entertainment Committee, consisting of Mrs. Schuster and Professor Jaya—er, Professor J.—has come up with an idea that should give us some amusement. They suggest that we set up a court and cross-examine everybody here in turn. The object of the court is to find an answer to this question: Why did we come to the Moon in the first place? Of course, some people may not want to be examined—for all I know, half of you may be on the run from the police, or your wives. You're at liberty to refuse to give evidence, but don't blame us if we draw the worst possible conclusions if you do. Well, what do you think of the idea?"

It was received with fair enthusiasm in some quarters and ironic groans of disapproval in others, but since there was no determined opposition, the Commodore went ahead. Almost automatically, he was elected President of the Court; equally automatic was Irving Schuster's appointment as General Counsel.

The front-right pair of seats had been reversed so that it faced toward the rear of the cruiser. This served as the bench, shared by the

President and Counsel. When everyone had settled down, and the Clerk of the Court (viz. Pat Harris) had called for order, the President made a brief address.

"We are not yet engaged in criminal proceedings," he said, keeping his face straight with some difficulty. "This is purely a court of enquiry. If any witness feels that he is being intimidated by my learned colleague, he can appeal to the Court. Will the Clerk call the first witness?"

"Er—your Honor—who *is* the first witness?" said the Clerk, reasonably enough.

It took ten minutes of discussion among the Court, learned Counsel, and argumentative members of the public to settle this important point. Finally it was decided to have a ballot, and the first name to be produced was David Barrett's.

Smiling slightly, the witness came forward and took his stand in the narrow space before the bench.

Irving Schuster, looking and feeling none too legal in undershirt and underpants, cleared his throat impressively.

"Your name is David Barrett?"

"That is correct."

"Your occupation?"

"Agricultural engineer, retired."

"Mr. Barrett, will you tell this court exactly why you have come to the Moon."

"I was curious to see what it was like here and I had the time and money."

Irving Schuster looked at Barrett obliquely through his thick glasses; he had always found this had an unsettling effect on witnesses. To wear spectacles was almost a sign of eccentricity in this age, but doctors and lawyers—especially the older ones—still patronized them; indeed, they had come to symbolize the legal and medical professions.

"You were 'curious to see what it was like,'" Schuster quoted. "That's no explanation. *Why* were you curious?"

"I am afraid that question is so vaguely worded that I cannot answer it. Why does one do anything?"

Commodore Hansteen relaxed with a smile of pleasure. This was just what he wanted—to get the passengers arguing and talking freely about something that would be of mutual interest to them all, but would arouse no passions or controversy. (It might do that, of course, but it was up to him to keep order in Court.)

"I admit," continued Counsel, "that my question might have been more specific. I will try to reframe it."

He thought for a moment, shuffling his notes. They consisted merely of sheets from one of the tourist guides. He had scribbled a few lines of questioning in the margins, but they were really for effect and reassurance. He had never liked to stand up in court without something in his hand; there were times when a few seconds of imaginary consultation were priceless.

"Would it be fair to say that you were attracted by the Moon's scenic beauties?"

"Yes, that was part of the attraction. I had seen the tourist literature and movies, of course, and wondered if the reality would live up to it."

"And has it done so?"

"I would say," was the dry answer, "that it has exceeded my expectations."

There was general laughter from the rest of the company. Commodore Hansteen rapped loudly on the back of his seat.

"Order!" he called. "If there are any disturbances, I shall have to clear the Court!"

This, as he had intended, started a much louder round of laughter, which he let run its natural course. When the mirth had died down, Schuster continued in his most "Where were you on the night of the twenty-second?" tone of voice.

"This is very interesting, Mr. Barrett. You have come all the way to the Moon, at considerable expense, to look at the view. Tell me—have you ever seen the Grand Canyon?"

"No. Have you?"

"Your Honor!" appealed Schuster. "The witness is being unresponsive."

Hansteen looked severely at Mr. Barrett, who did not seem in the least abashed.

"*You* are not conducting this enquiry, Mr. Barrett. Your job is to answer questions, not to ask them."

"I beg the Court's pardon, my Lord," replied the witness.

"Er—am I 'my Lord'?" said Hansteen uncertainly, turning to Schuster. "I thought I was 'your Honor.'"

The lawyer gave the matter several seconds of solemn thought.

"I suggest—your Honor—that each witness use the procedure to which he is accustomed in his country. As long as due deference is shown to the Court, that would seem to be sufficient."

"Very well—proceed."

Schuster turned to his witness once more.

"I would like to know, Mr. Barrett, why you found it necessary to visit the Moon while there was so much of Earth that you hadn't seen. Can you give us any valid reason for this illogical behavior?"

It was a good question, just the sort that would interest everyone, and Barrett was now making a serious attempt to answer it.

"I've seen a fair amount of Earth," he said slowly, with his precise English accent—almost as great a rarity now as Schuster's spectacles. "I've stayed at the Hotel Everest, been to both Poles, even gone to the bottom of the Calypso Deep. So I know something about our planet. Let's say it had lost its capacity to surprise me. The Moon, on the other hand, was completely new—a whole world less than twenty-four hours away. I couldn't resist the novelty."

Hansteen listened to the slow and careful analysis with only half his mind. He was unobtrusively examining the audience while Barrett spoke. By now he had formed a good picture of *Selene*'s crew and passengers, and had decided who could be relied upon, and who would give trouble, if conditions became bad.

The key man, of course, was Captain Harris. The Commodore knew his type well; he had met it so often in space—and more often still at such training establishments as Astrotech. (Whenever he made a speech there, it was to a front row of freshly scrubbed and barbered Pat Harrises.) Pat was a competent but unambitious youngster with mechanical interests who had been lucky enough to find a job that suited him perfectly, and which made no greater demands upon him than care and courtesy. (Attractive lady passengers, Hansteen was quite certain, would have no complaints on the latter score.) He would be loyal, conscientious, and unimaginative, would do his duty as he saw it, and in the end would die gamely without making a fuss. That was a virtue not possessed by many far abler men, and it was one they would need badly aboard the cruiser if they were still here five days from now.

Miss Wilkins, the stewardess, was almost as important as the captain in the scheme of things; she was certainly not the stereotyped space-hostess image, all vapid charm and frozen smile. She was, Hansteen had already decided, a young lady of character and considerable education—but so, for that matter, were many space hostesses he had known.

Yes, he was lucky with the crew. And what about the passengers? They were considerably above average, of course; otherwise they would not have been on the Moon in the first place. There was an impressive reservoir of brains and talent here inside *Selene*, but the irony of the situation was that neither brains nor talent could help them now. What was needed was character, fortitude—or, in a blunter word, bravery.

Few men in this age ever knew the need for physical bravery. From birth to death, they never came face to face with danger. The men and women aboard *Selene* had no training for what lay ahead, and he could not keep them occupied much longer with games and amusements.

Some time in the next twelve hours, he calculated, the first cracks would appear. By then it would be obvious that something was holding up the search parties, and that if they found the cruiser at all, the discovery might be too late.

Commodore Hansteen glanced swiftly round the cabin. Apart from their scanty clothing and slightly unkempt appearance, all these twenty-one men and women were still rational, self-controlled members of society.

Which, he wondered, would be the first to go?

# Chapter 10

Dr. Tom Lawson, so Chief Engineer Lawrence had decided, was an exception to the old saying "To know all is to forgive all." The knowledge that the astronomer had passed a loveless, institutionalized childhood and had escaped from his origins by prodigies of pure intellect, at the cost of all other human qualities, helped one to understand him—but not to like him. It was singular bad luck, thought Lawrence, that he was the only scientist within three hundred thousand kilometers who happened to have an infrared detector, and knew how to use it.

He was now sitting in the observer's seat of Duster Two, making the final adjustments to the crude but effective lash-up he had contrived. A camera tripod had been fixed on the canopy of the ski, and the detector had been mounted on this, in such a way that it could pan in any direction.

It seemed to be working, but that was hard to tell in this small, pressurized hangar, with a confused jumble of heat sources all around it. The real test could come only out in the Sea of Thirst.

"It's ready," said Lawson presently to the Chief Engineer. "Let me have a word with the man who's going to run it."

The C.E.E. looked at him thoughtfully, still trying to make up his mind. There were strong arguments for and against what he was considering now, but whatever he did, he must not let his personal feelings intrude. The matter was far too important for that.

"You can wear a space suit, can't you?" he asked Lawson.

"I've never worn one in my life. They're only needed for going outside—and we leave that to the engineers."

"Well, now you have a chance of learning," said the C.E.E., ignoring the jibe. (If it was a jibe; much of Lawson's rudeness, he decided, was indifference to the social graces rather than defiance of them.) "There's not much to it, when you're riding a ski. You'll be sitting still in the observer's seat and the autoregulator takes care of oxygen, temperature, and the rest. There's only one problem—"

"What's that?"

"How are you for claustrophobia?"

Tom hesitated, not liking to admit any weakness. He had passed the usual space tests, of course, and suspected—quite rightly—that he had had a very close call on some of the psych ratings. Obviously he was not an acute claustrophobe, or he could never have gone aboard a ship. But a spaceship and a space suit were two very different things.

"I can take it," he said at last.

"Don't fool yourself if you can't," Lawrence insisted. "I think you should come with us, but I'm not trying to bully you into false heroics. All I ask is that you make up your mind before we leave the hangar. It may be a little too late to have second thoughts when we're twenty kilometers out to Sea."

Tom looked at the ski and bit his lip. The idea of skimming across that infernal lake of dust in such a flimsy contraption seemed crazy—but these men did it every day. And if anything went wrong with the detector, there was at least a slight chance that he could fix it.

"Here's a suit that's your size," said Lawrence. "Try it on—it may help you to make up your mind."

Tom struggled into the flaccid yet crinkly garment, closed the front zipper, and stood, still helmetless, feeling rather a fool. The oxygen flask that was buckled to his harness seemed absurdly small, and Lawrence noticed his anxious glance.

"Don't worry; that's merely the four-hour reserve. You won't be using it at all. The main supply's on the ski. Mind your nose—here comes the helmet."

Tom could tell, by the expressions of those around him, that this was the moment that separated the men from the boys. Until that helmet was seated, you were still part of the human race; afterward, you were alone, in a tiny mechanical world of your own. There might be other men only centimeters away, but you had to peer at them through thick plastic, talk to them by radio. You could not even touch them, except through double layers of artificial skin. Someone had once written that it was very lonely to die in a space suit. For the first time, Tom realized how true that must be.

The Chief Engineer's voice sounded suddenly, reverberantly, from the tiny speakers set in the side of the helmet.

"The only control you need worry about is the intercom—that's the panel on your right. Normally you'll be connected to your pilot. The circuit will be live all the time you're both on the ski, so you can talk to each other whenever you feel like it. But as soon as you disconnect, you'll have to use radio—as you're doing now to listen to me. Press your Transmit button and talk back."

"What's that red Emergency button for?" asked Tom, after he had obeyed this order.

"You won't need it—I hope. That actuates a homing beacon and sets up a radio racket until someone comes to find you. Don't touch any of the gadgets on the suit without instructions from us—especially that one."

"I won't," promised Tom. "Let's go."

He walked, rather clumsily—for he was used to neither the suit nor the lunar gravity—over to Duster Two and took his place in the observer's seat. A single umbilical cord, plugged inappropriately into the right hip, connected the suit to the ski's oxygen, communications, and power. The vehicle could keep him alive, though hardly comfortable, for three or four days, at a pinch.

The little hangar was barely large enough for the two dust-skis, and it took only a few minutes for the pumps to exhaust its air. As the suits stiffened around him, Tom felt a touch of panic. The Chief Engineer and two pilots were watching, and he did not wish to give them the satisfaction of thinking that he was afraid. No man could help feeling tense when, for the first time in his life, he went into vacuum.

The clamshell doors pivoted open. There was a faint tug of ghostly fingers as the last vestige of air gushed out, plucking feebly at his suit before it dispersed into the void. And then, flat and featureless, the empty gray of the Sea of Thirst stretched out to the horizon.

For a moment it seemed impossible that here, only a few meters away, was the reality behind the images he had studied from far out in space. (Who was looking through the hundred-centimeter telescope now? Was one of his colleagues watching, even at this moment, from his vantage point high above the Moon?) But this was no picture painted on a screen by flying electrons; *this* was the real thing, the strange, amorphous stuff that had swallowed twenty-two men and women without trace. And across which he, Tom Lawson, was about to venture on this insubstantial craft.

He had little time to brood. The ski vibrated beneath him as the fans started to spin; then, following Duster One, it glided slowly out onto the naked surface of the Moon.

The low rays of the rising sun smote them as soon as they emerged from the long shadow of the Port buildings. Even with the protection of the automatic filters, it was dangerous to look toward the blue-white fury in the eastern sky. No, Tom corrected himself, this is the Moon, not Earth; here the sun rises in the west. So we're heading northeast, into the Sinus Roris, along the track *Selene* followed and never retraced.

Now that the low domes of the Port were shrinking visibly toward the horizon, he felt something of the exhilaration and excitement of all forms of speed. The sensation lasted only for a few minutes, until no more landmarks could be seen and they were caught in the illusion of being poised at the very center of an infinite plain. Despite the turmoil of the spinning fans, and the slow, silent fall of the dust parabolas behind them, they seemed to be motionless. Tom knew that they were traveling at a speed that would take them clear across the Sea in a couple of hours, yet he had to wrestle with the fear that they were lost light-years from any hope of salvation. It was at this moment that he began, a little late in the game, to feel a grudging respect for the men he was working with.

This was a good place to start checking his equipment. He switched on the detector, and set it scanning back and forth over the emptiness they had just crossed. With calm satisfaction, he noted the two blinding trails of light stretching behind them across the darkness of the Sea. This test, of course, was childishly easy; *Selene's* fading thermal ghost would be a million times harder to spot against the waxing heat of dawn. But it was encouraging. If he had failed here, there would have been no point in continuing any further.

"How's it working?" said the Chief Engineer, who must have been watching from the other ski.

"Up to specification," replied Tom cautiously. "It seems to be behaving normally." He aimed the detector at the shrinking crescent of Earth; that was a slightly more difficult target, but not a really hard one, for it needed little sensitivity to pick up the gentle warmth of the mother world when it was projected against the cold night of space.

Yes, there it was—Earth in the far infrared, a strange and at first glance baffling sight. For it was no longer a clean-cut, geometrically perfect crescent, but a ragged mushroom with its stem lying along the equator.

It took Tom a few seconds to interpret the picture. Both Poles had been chopped off. That was understandable, for they were too cold to be detected at this setting of the sensitivity. But why that bulge across the unilluminated night side of the planet? Then he realized that he was seeing the warm glow of the tropical oceans, radiating back into the darkness the heat that they had stored during the day. In the infrared, the equatorial night was more brilliant than the polar day.

It was a reminder of the fact, which no scientist should ever forget, that human senses perceived only a tiny, distorted picture of the Universe. Tom Lawson had never heard of Plato's analogy of the chained prisoners in the cave, watching shadows cast upon a wall and trying to deduce from them the realities of the external world. But here was a demonstration that Plato would have appreciated:

Which Earth was "real"? The perfect crescent visible to the eye, the tattered mushroom glowing in the far infrared—or neither?

The office was small, even for Port Roris—which was purely a transit station between Earthside and Farside, and a jumping-off point for tourists to the Sea of Thirst. (Not that any looked like jumping off in that direction for some time.) The Port had had a brief moment of glory thirty years before, as the base used by one of the Moon's few successful criminals—Jerry Budker, who had made a small fortune dealing in fake pieces of Lunik II. He was hardly as exciting as Robin Hood or Billy the Kid, but he was the best that the Moon could offer.

Maurice Spenser was rather glad that Port Roris was such a quiet little one-dome town, though he suspected that it would not stay quiet much longer, especially when his colleagues at Clavius woke up to the fact that an I.N. Bureau Chief was lingering here unaccountably, and not hurrying southward to the lights of the big (pop. 52,647) city. A guarded cable to Earth had taken care of his superiors, who would trust his judgment and would guess the story he was after. Sooner or later, the competition would guess it, too—but by that time, he hoped to be well ahead.

The man he was conferring with was *Auriga*'s still-disgruntled skipper, who had just spent a complicated and unsatisfactory hour on the telephone with his agents at Clavius, trying to arrange trans-shipment of his cargo. McIver, McDonald, Macarthy and McCulloch, Ltd. seemed to think it was his fault that *Auriga* had put down at Roris. In the end, he had hung up after telling them to sort it out with the head office. Since it was now early Sunday morning in Edinburgh, this should hold them for a while.

Captain Anson mellowed a little after the second whisky; a man who could find Johnnie Walker in Port Roris was worth knowing, and he asked Spenser how he had managed it.

"The power of the press," said the other with a laugh. "A reporter never reveals his sources; if he did, he wouldn't stay in business for long."

He opened his brief case, and pulled out a sheaf of maps and photos.

"I had an even bigger job getting these at such short notice—and I'd be obliged, Captain, if you would say nothing at all about this to anyone. It's extremely confidential, at least for the moment."

"Of course. What's it about—*Selene*?"

"So you guessed that, too? You're right. It may come to nothing, but I want to be prepared."

He spread one of the photos across the desk. It was a view of the Sea of Thirst, from the standard series issued by the Lunar Survey and taken from low-altitude reconnaissance satellites. Though this was an afternoon photograph, and the shadows thus pointed in the opposite direction, it was almost identical with the view Spenser had had just before landing. He had studied it so closely that he now knew it by heart.

"The Mountains of Inaccessibility," he said. "They rise very steeply out of the Sea to an altitude of almost two thousand meters. That dark oval is Crater Lake—"

"Where *Selene* was lost?"

"Where she may be lost: there's now some doubt about that. Our sociable young friend from Lagrange has evidence that she's actually gone down in the Sea of Thirst—round about this area. In that case, the people inside her may be alive. And in *that* case, Captain, there's going to be one hell of a salvage operation only a hundred kilometers from here. Port Roris will be the biggest new center in the solar system."

"Phew! So that's your game. But where do I come in?"

Once again Spenser placed his finger on the map.

"Right here, Captain. I want to charter your ship. And I want you to land me, with a cameraman and two hundred kilos of TV equipment, on the western wall of the Mountains of Inaccessibility."

"I have no further questions, your Honor," said Counsel Schuster, sitting down abruptly.

"Very well," replied Commodore Hansteen. "I must order the witness not to leave the jurisdiction of the Court."

Amid general laughter, David Barrett returned to his seat. He had put on a good performance; though most of his replies had been serious and thoughtful, they had been enlivened with flashes of humor and had kept the audience continuously interested. If all the other witnesses were equally forthcoming, that would solve the problem of entertainment, for as long as it had to be solved. Even if they used up all the memories of four lifetimes in every day—a complete impossibility, of course—someone would still be talking when the oxygen container gave its last gasp.

Hansteen looked at his watch. There was still an hour to go before their frugal lunch. They could revert to *Shane*, or start (despite Miss Morley's objections) on that preposterous historical novel. But it seemed a pity to break off now, while everyone was in a receptive mood.

"If you all feel the same way about it," said the Commodore, "I'll call another witness."

"I'll second that" was the quick reply from Barrett, who now considered himself safe from further inquisition. Even the poker players were in favor, so the Clerk of the Court pulled another name out of the coffeepot in which the ballot papers had been mixed.

He looked at it with some surprise, and hesitated before reading it out.

"What's the matter?" said the Court. "Is it *your* name?"

"Er—no," replied the Clerk, glancing at learned Counsel with a mischievous grin. He cleared his throat and called: "Mrs. Myra Schuster!"

"Your Honor—I object!" Mrs. Schuster rose slowly, a formidable figure even though she had lost a kilogram or two since leaving Port Roris. She pointed to her husband, who looked embarrassed and tried to hide behind his notes. "Is it fair for *him* to ask me questions?"

"I'm willing to stand down," said Irving Schuster, even before the Court could say "objection sustained."

"I am prepared to take over the examination," said the Commodore, though his expression rather belied this. "But is there anyone else who feels qualified to do so?"

There was a short silence; then, to Hansteen's surprised relief, one of the poker players stood up.

"Though I'm not a lawyer, your Honor, I have some slight legal experience. I'm willing to assist."

"Very good, Mr. Harding. *Your* witness."

Harding took Schuster's place at the front of the cabin, and surveyed his captive audience. He was a well-built, tough-looking man who somehow did not fit his own description, that he was a bank executive. Hansteen had wondered, fleetingly, if this was the truth.

"Your name is Myra Schuster?"

"Yes."

"And what, Mrs. Schuster, are you doing on the Moon?"

The witness smiled.

"That's an easy one to answer. They told me I'd weigh only twenty kilos here—so I came."

"For the record, *why* did you want to weigh twenty kilos?"

Mrs. Schuster looked at Harding as if he had said something very stupid.

"I used to be a dancer once," she said, and her voice was suddenly wistful, her expression faraway. "I gave that up, of course, when I married Irving."

"Why 'of course,' Mrs. Schuster?"

The witness glanced at her husband, who stirred a little uneasily, looked as if he might raise an objection, but then thought better of it.

"Oh, he said it wasn't dignified. And I guess he was right—the kind of dancing *I* used to do."

This was too much for Mr. Schuster. He shot to his feet, ignoring the Court completely, and protested: "Really, Myra! There's no need—"

"Oh, vector it out, Irv!" she answered, the incongruously old-fashioned slang bringing back a faint whiff of the nineties. "What does it matter now? Let's stop acting and be ourselves. I don't mind these folks knowing that I used to dance at the 'Blue Asteroid'—*or* that you got me off the hook when the cops raided the place."

Irving subsided, spluttering, while the Court dissolved in a roar of laughter which his Honor did nothing to quell. This release of tensions was precisely what he had hoped for; when people were laughing, they could not be afraid.

And he began to wonder still more about Mr. Harding, whose casual yet shrewd questioning had brought this about. For a man who said he was not a lawyer, he was doing pretty well. It would be interesting to see how he performed in the witness box, when it was Schuster's turn to ask the questions.

# Chapter 11

At last there was something to break the featureless flatness of the Sea of Thirst. A tiny but brilliant splinter of light had edged itself above the horizon, and as the dust-skis raced forward, it slowly climbed against the stars. Now it was joined by another—and a third. The peaks of the Mountains of Inaccessibility were rising over the edge of the Moon.

As usual, there was no way of judging their distance; they might have been small rocks a few paces away, or not part of the Moon at all, but a giant, jagged world, millions of kilometers out in space. In reality, they were fifty kilometers distant; the dust-skis would be there in half an hour.

Tom Lawson looked at them with thankfulness. Now there was something to occupy his eyes and mind; he felt he would have gone crazy if he had had to stare at this apparently infinite plain for much longer. He was annoyed with himself for being so illogical. He knew that the horizon was really very close and that the whole Sea was only a small part of the Moon's quite limited surface. Yet as he sat here in his space suit, apparently getting nowhere, he was reminded of those horrible dreams in which you struggled with all your might to escape from some frightful peril but remained stuck helplessly in the same place. Tom often had such dreams, and worse ones.

But now he could see that they were making progress, and that their long, black shadow was not frozen to the ground, as it sometimes seemed. He focused the detector on the rising peaks, and obtained a strong reaction. As he had expected, the exposed rocks were almost ˗

at boiling point where they faced the sun. Though the lunar day had barely started, the Mountains were already burning. It was much cooler down here at "Sea" level. The surface dust would not reach its maximum temperature until noon, still seven days away. That was one of the biggest points in his favor; though the day had already begun, he still had a sporting chance of detecting any faint source of heat before the full fury of the day had overwhelmed it.

Twenty minutes later, the mountains dominated the sky, and the skis slowed down to half-speed.

"We don't want to overrun their track," explained Lawrence. "If you look carefully, just below that double peak on the right, you'll see a dark vertical line. Got it?"

"Yes."

"That's the gorge leading to Crater Lake. The patch of heat you detected is three kilometers to the west of it, so it's still out of sight from here, below our horizon. Which direction do you want to approach from?"

Lawson thought this over. It would have to be from the north or the south. If he came in from the west, he would have those burning rocks in his field of view; the eastern approach was even more impossible, for that would be into the eye of the rising sun.

"Swing round to the north," he said. "And let me know when we're within two kilometers of the spot."

The skis accelerated once more. Though there was no hope of detecting anything yet, he started to scan back and forth over the surface of the Sea. This whole mission was based upon one assumption; that the upper layers of dust were normally at a uniform temperature, and that any thermal disturbance was due to man. If this was wrong—

It was wrong. He had miscalculated completely. On the viewing screen, the Sea was a mottled pattern of light and shade, or, rather, of warmth and coldness. The temperature differences were only fractions of a degree, but the picture was hopelessly confused. There was no possibility at all of locating any individual source of heat in that thermal maze.

Sick at heart, Tom Lawson looked up from the viewing screen and stared incredulously across the dust. To the unaided eye, it was still absolutely featureless—the same unbroken gray it had always been. But by infrared, it was as dappled as the sea during a cloudy day on Earth, when the waters are covered with shifting patterns of sunlight and shadow.

Yet there were no clouds here to cast their shadows on this arid sea; this dappling must have some other cause. Whatever it might be, Tom was too stunned to look for the scientific explanation. He had come all the way to the Moon, had risked neck and sanity on this crazy ride—and at the end of it all, some quirk of nature had ruined his carefully planned experiment. It was the worst possible luck, and he felt very sorry for himself.

Several minutes later, he got around to feeling sorry for the people aboard *Selene.*

"So," said the skipper of the *Auriga*, with exaggerated calm, "you would like to land on the Mountains of Inaccessibility. That's a verra interesting idea."

It was obvious to Spenser that Captain Anson had not taken him seriously; he probably thought he was dealing with a crazy newsman who had no conception of the problems involved. That would have been correct twelve hours before, when the whole plan was only a vague dream in Spenser's mind. But now he had all the information at his fingertips, and knew exactly what he was doing.

"I've heard you boast, Captain, that you could land this ship within a meter of any given point. Is that right?"

"Well—with a little help from the computer."

"That's good enough. Now take a look at this photograph"

"What is it? Glasgow on a wet Saturday night?"

"I'm afraid it's badly overenlarged, but it shows all we want to know. It's a blowup of this area—just below the western peak of the Mountains. I'll have a much better copy in a few hours, and an accurate contour map—Lunar Survey's drawing one now, working from the photos in their files. My point is that there's a wide ledge here—wide enough for a dozen ships to land. And it's fairly flat, at least at these points here, and here. So a landing would be no problem at all, from your point of view."

"No *technical* problem, perhaps. But have you any idea what it would cost?"

"That's my affair, Captain—or my network's. We think it may be worthwhile, if my hunch comes off."

Spenser could have said a good deal more, but it was bad business to show how much you needed someone else's wares. This might well be the news story of the decade—the first space rescue that had ever taken place literally under the eyes of the TV cameras. There had been enough accidents and disasters in space, heaven knows, but they had lacked all elements of drama or suspense. Those involved had died instantly, or had been beyond all hope of rescue when their predicament was discovered. Such tragedies produced headlines, but not sustained human-interest stories like the one he sensed here.

"There's not only the money," said the Captain, though his tone implied that there were few matters of greater importance. "Even if the owners agree, you'll have to get special clearance from Space Control, Earthside."

"I know; someone is working on it now. That can be organized."

"And what about Lloyd's? Our policy doesn't cover little jaunts like this."

Spenser leaned across the table, and prepared to drop his city-buster.

"Captain," he said slowly, "Interplanet News is prepared to deposit a bond for the insured value of the ship—which I happen to know is a somewhat inflated six million four hundred and twenty-five thousand and fifty sterling dollars."

Captain Anson blinked twice, and his whole attitude changed immediately. Then, looking very thoughtful, he poured himself another drink.

"I never imagined I'd take up mountaineering at my time of life," he said. "But if you're fool enough to plonk down six million dollars—then my heart's in the highlands."

To the great relief of her husband, Mrs. Schuster's evidence had been interrupted by lunch. She was a talkative lady, and was obviously delighted at the first opportunity she had had in years of letting her hair down. Her career, such as it was, had not been particularly distinguished when fate and the Chicago police had brought it to a sudden close, but she had certainly got around, and had known many of the great performers at the turn of the century. To not a few of the older passengers, her reminiscences brought back memories of their own youth, and faint echoes from the songs of the nineteen-nineties. At one point, without any protest from the Court, she led the entire company in a rendering of that durable favorite, "Space-suit Blues." As a morale-builder, the Commodore decided, Mrs. Schuster was worth her weight in gold—and that was saying a good deal.

After lunch (which some of the slower eaters managed to stretch to half an hour, by chewing each mouthful fifty times) book-reading was resumed, and the agitators for *The Orange and the Apple* finally got their way. Since the theme was English, it was decided that Mr. Barrett was the only man for the job. He protested with vigor, but all his objections were shouted down.

"Oh, very well," he said reluctantly. "Here we go. Chapter One. Drury Lane. 1665..."

The author certainly wasted no time. Within three pages, Sir Isaac Newton was explaining the law of gravitation to Mistress Gwyn, who had already hinted that she would like to do something in return. What form that appreciation would take, Pat Harris could readily guess, but duty called him. This entertainment was for the passengers; the crew had work to do.

"There's still one emergency locker I've not opened," said Miss Wilkins as the air-lock door thudded softly behind them, shutting off Mr. Barrett's carefully clipped accents. "We're low on crackers and jam, but the compressed meat is holding out."

"I'm not surprised," answered Pat. "Everyone seems to be getting sick of it. Let's see those inventory sheets."

The stewardess handed over the typed sheets, now much annotated with pencil marks.

"We'll start with this box. What's inside it?"

"Soap and paper towels."

"Well, we can't eat *them*. And this one?"

"Candy. I was saving it for the celebration—when they find us."

"That's a good idea, but I think you might break some of it out this evening. One piece for every passenger, as a nightcap. And this?"

"A thousand cigarettes."

"Make sure that no one sees them. I wish you hadn't told me." Pat grinned wryly at Sue and passed on to the next item. It was fairly obvious that food was not going to be a major problem, but they had to keep track of it. He knew the ways of Administration; after they were rescued, sooner or later some human or electronic clerk would insist on a strict accounting of all the food that had been used.

*After they were rescued.* Did he really believe that this was going to happen? They had been lost for more than two days, and there had not been the slightest sign that anyone was looking for them. He was not sure what signs there could be, but he had expected some.

He stood brooding in silence, until Sue asked anxiously: "What's the trouble, Pat? Is something wrong?"

"Oh, no," he said sarcastically. "We'll be docking at Base in five minutes. It's been a pleasant trip, don't you think?"

Sue stared at him incredulously; then a flush spread over her cheeks, and her eyes began to brim with tears.

"I'm sorry," said Pat, instantly contrite. "I didn't mean that. It's been a big strain for us both, and you've been wonderful. I don't know what we'd have done without you, Sue."

She dabbed her nose with a handkerchief, gave a brief smile, and answered: "That's all right; I understand." They were both silent for a moment. Then she added: "Do you really think we're going to get out of this?"

He gave a gesture of helplessness.

"Who can tell? Anyway, for the sake of the passengers, we've got to appear confident. We can be certain that the whole Moon's looking for us. I can't believe it will take much longer."

"But even if they find us, how are they going to get us out?"

Pat's eyes wandered to the external door, only a few centimeters away. He could touch it without moving from this spot; indeed, if he immobilized the safety interlock, he could open it, for it swung inward. On the other side of that thin metal sheet were unknown tons of dust that would come pouring in, like water into a sinking ship, if there was the slightest crack through which they could enter. How far above them was the surface? That was a problem that had worried him ever since they had gone under, but there seemed no way of finding out.

Nor could he answer Sue's question. It was hard to think beyond the possibility of being found. If that happened, then surely rescue would follow. The human race would not let them die, once it had discovered them alive.

But this was wishful thinking, not logic. Hundreds of times in the past, men and women had been trapped as they were now, and all the resources of great nations had been unable to save them. There were the miners behind rockfalls, sailors in sunken submarines—and, above all, astronauts in ships on wild orbits, beyond possibility of interception. Often they had been able to talk freely with their friends and relatives until the very end. That had happened only two years ago, when *Cassiopeia*'s main drive had jammed, and all her energies had been poured into hurling her away from the sun. She was out there now, heading toward Canopus, on one of the most precisely measured orbits of any space vehicle. The astronomers would be able to pinpoint her to within a few thousand kilometers for the next million years. That must have been a great consolation to her crew, now in a tomb more permanent than any Pharaoh's.

Pat tore his mind away from this singularly profitless reverie. Their luck had not yet run out, and to anticipate disaster might be to invite it.

"Let's hurry up and finish this inventory. I want to hear how Nell is making out with Sir Isaac."

That was a much more pleasant train of thought, especially when you were standing so close to a very attractive and scantily dressed girl. In a situation like this, thought Pat, women had one great advantage over men. Sue still looked fairly smart, despite the fact that nothing much was left of her uniform in this tropical heat. But he, like all the men aboard *Selene*, felt scratchily uncomfortable with his three days' growth of beard, and there was absolutely nothing he could do about it.

Sue did not seem to mind the stubble, though, when he abandoned the pretense of work and moved up so close that his bristles rubbed against her cheek. On the other hand, she did not show any enthusiasm. She merely stood there, in front of the half-empty locker, as if she had expected this and was not in the least surprised. It was a disconcerting reaction, and after a few seconds Pat drew away.

"I suppose you think I'm an unscrupulous wolf," he said, "trying to take advantage of you like this."

"Not particularly," Sue answered. She gave a rather tired laugh. "It makes me glad to know that I'm not slipping. No girl ever minds a man *starting* to make approaches. It's when he won't stop that she gets annoyed."

"Do you want me to stop?"

"We're not in love, Pat. To me, that's rather important. Even now."

"Would it still be important if you knew we won't get out of this?"

Her forehead wrinkled in concentration.

"I'm not sure—but you said yourself we've got to assume that they'll find us. If we don't, then we might as well give up right away."

"Sorry," said Pat. "I don't want you under those terms. I like you too much, for one thing."

"I'm glad to hear that. You know I've always enjoyed working with you—there were plenty of other jobs I could have transferred to."

"Bad luck for you," Pat answered, "that you didn't." His brief gust of desire, triggered by proximity, solitude, scanty clothing, and sheer emotional strain, had already evaporated.

"Now you're being pessimistic again," said Sue. "You know, that's your big trouble. You let things get you down. And you won't assert yourself; anyone can push you around."

Pat looked at her with more surprise than annoyance.

"I'd no idea," he said, "that you'd been busy psyching me."

"I haven't. But if you're interested in someone, and work with him, how can you help learning about him?"

"Well, I don't believe that people push me around."

"No? Who's running this ship now?"

"If you mean the Commodore, that's different. He's a thousand times better qualified to take charge than I am. And he's been absolutely correct about it—he's asked my permission all along the line."

"He doesn't bother now. Anyway, that's not the whole point. Aren't you *glad* he's taken over?"

Pat thought about this for several seconds. Then he looked at Sue with grudging respect.

"Maybe you're right. I've never cared to throw my weight about, or assert my authority—if I have any. I guess that's why I'm driver of a Moon bus, not skipper of a space liner. It's a little late to do anything about it now."

"You're not thirty yet."

"Thank you for those kind words. I'm thirty-two. We Harrises retain our youthful good looks well into old age. It's usually all we have left by then."

"Thirty-two—and no steady girl friend?"

Ha! thought Pat, there are several things you don't know about me. But there was no point in mentioning Clarissa and her little apartment in Copernicus City, which now seemed so far away. (And how upset is Clarissa right now? he wondered. Which of the boys is busy consoling her? Perhaps Sue is right, after all. I don't have a *steady* girl friend. I haven't had one since Yvonne, and that was five years ago. No, my God—seven years ago.)

"I believe there's safety in numbers," he said. "One of these days I'll settle down."

"Perhaps you'll still be saying that when you're forty—or fifty. There are so many spacemen like that. They haven't settled down when it's time to retire, and then it's too late. Look at the Commodore, for example."

"What about him? I'm beginning to get a little tired of the subject."

"He's spent all his life in space. He has no family, no children. Earth can't mean much to him—he's spent so little time there. He must have felt quite lost when he reached the age limit. This accident has been a godsend to him; he's really enjoying himself now."

"Good for him; he deserves it. I'll be happy if I've done a tenth as much as he has when I've reached his age—which doesn't seem very likely at the moment."

Pat became aware that he was still holding the inventory sheets; he had forgotten all about them. They were a reminder of their dwindling resources, and he looked at them with distaste.

"Back to work," he said. "We have to think of the passengers."

"If we stay here much longer," replied Sue, "the passengers will start thinking of us."

She spoke more truthfully than she had guessed.

# Chapter 12

Dr. Lawson's silence, the Chief Engineer decided, had gone on long enough. It was high time to resume communication.

"Everything all right, Doctor?" he asked in his friendliest voice.

There was a short, angry bark, but the anger was directed at the Universe, not at him.

"It won't work," Lawson answered bitterly. "The heat image is too confused. There are dozens of hot spots, not just the one I was expecting."

"Stop your ski. I'll come over and have a look."

Duster Two slid to a halt; Duster One eased up beside it until the two vehicles were almost touching. Moving with surprising ease despite the encumbrance of his space suit, Lawrence swung himself from one to the other and stood, gripping the supports of the overhead canopy, behind Lawson. He peered over the astronomer's shoulder at the image on the infrared converter.

"I see what you mean; it's a mess. But why was it uniform when you took your photos?"

"It must be a sunrise effect. The Sea's warming up, and for some reason it's not heating at the same rate everywhere."

"Perhaps we can still make sense out of the pattern. I notice that there are some fairly clear areas—there must be an explanation for them. If we understood what's happening, it might help."

Tom Lawson stirred himself with a great effort. The brittle shell of his self-confidence had been shattered by this unexpected setback, and he was very tired. He had had little sleep in the last two days, he had been hurried from satellite to spaceship to Moon to dust-ski, and after all that, his science had failed him.

"There could be a dozen explanations," he said dully. "This dust looks uniform, but there may be patches with different conductivities. And it must be deeper in some places than in others; that would alter the heat flow."

Lawrence was still staring at the pattern on the screen, trying to relate it to the visual scene around him.

"Just a minute," he said. "I think you've got something." He called to the pilot. "How deep is the dust around here?"

"Nobody knows; the Sea's never been sounded properly. But it's very shallow in these parts—we're near the northern edge. Sometimes we take out a fan blade on a reef."

"As shallow as *that*? Well, there's your answer. If there's rock only a few centimeters below us, anything could happen to the heat pattern. Ten to one you'll find the picture getting simpler again when we're clear of these shoals. This is only a local effect, caused by irregularities just underneath us."

"Perhaps you're right," said Tom, reviving slightly. "If *Selene* has sunk, she must be in an area where the dust's fairly deep. You're *sure* it's shallow here?"

"Let's find out; there's a twenty-meter probe on my ski."

A single section of the telescoping rod was enough to prove the point. When Lawrence drove it into the dust, it penetrated less than two meters before hitting an obstruction.

"How many spare fans have we got?" he asked thoughtfully.

"Four—two complete sets," answered the pilot. "But when we hit a rock, the cotter pin shears through and the fans aren't damaged. Anyway, they're made of rubber; usually they just bend back. I've only lost three in the last year. *Selene* took out one the other day, and Pat Harris had to go outside and replace it. Gave the passengers some excitement."

"Right—let's start moving again. Head for the gorge; I've a theory that it continues out underneath the Sea, so the dust will be much deeper there. If it is, your picture should start getting simpler, almost at once."

Without much hope, Tom watched the patterns of light and shade flow across the screen. The skis were moving quite slowly now, giving him time to analyze the picture. They had traveled about two kilometers when he saw that Lawrence had been perfectly right.

The mottlings and dapplings had begun to disappear; the confused jumble of warmth and coolness was merging into uniformity. The screen was becoming a flat gray as the temperature variations smoothed themselves out. Beyond question, the dust was swiftly deepening beneath them.

The knowledge that his equipment was effective once more should have gratified Tom, but it had almost the opposite result. He could think only of the hidden depths above which he was floating, supported on the most treacherous and unstable of mediums. Beneath him now there might be gulfs reaching far down into the Moon's mysterious heart; at any moment they might swallow the dust-ski, as already they had swallowed *Selene*.

He felt as if he were tightrope walking across an abyss, or feeling his way along a narrow path through a quaking quicksand. All his life he had been uncertain of himself, and had known security and confidence only through his technical skills—never at the level of personal relations. Now the hazards of his present position were reacting upon those inner fears. He felt a desperate need for solidity, for something firm and stable to which he could cling.

Over there were the mountains, only three kilometers away—massive, eternal, their roots anchored in the Moon. He looked at the sunlit sanctuary of those high peaks as longingly as some Pacific castaway, helpless upon a drifting raft, might have stared at an island passing just beyond his reach.

With all his heart, he wished that Lawrence would leave this treacherous, insubstantial ocean of dust for the safety of the land. "Head for the mountains!" he found himself whispering. "Head for the mountains!"

There is no privacy in a space suit—when the radio is switched on. Fifty meters away, Lawrence heard that whisper and knew exactly what it meant.

One does not become Chief Engineer for half a world without learning as much about men as machines. I took a calculated risk, thought Lawrence, and it looks as if it hasn't come off. But I won't give in without a fight; perhaps I can still defuse this psychological time bomb before it goes off.

Tom never noticed the approach of the second ski; he was already too lost in his own nightmare. But suddenly he was being violently shaken, so violently that his forehead banged against the lower rim of his helmet. For a moment his vision was blinded by tears of pain; then, with anger—yet at the same time with an inexplicable feeling of relief—he found himself looking straight into the determined eyes of Chief Engineer Lawrence, and listening to his voice reverberate from the suit speakers.

"That's enough of this nonsense," said the C.E.E. "And I'll trouble you not to be sick in one of our space suits. Every time that happens it costs us five hundred stollars to put it back into commission—and even then it's never quite the same again."

"I wasn't going to be sick—" Tom managed to mutter. Then he realized that the truth was much worse, and felt grateful to Lawrence for his tact. Before he could add anything more, the other continued, speaking firmly but more gently: "No one else can hear us, Tom—we're on the suit circuit now. So listen to me, and don't get mad. I know a lot about you, and I know you've had a hell of a rough deal from life. But you've got a brain—a damn good brain—so don't waste it by behaving like a scared kid. Sure, we're all scared kids at some time or other, but this isn't the time for it. There are twenty-two lives depending on you. In five minutes, we'll settle this business one way or the other. So keep your eye on that screen, and forget about everything else. I'll get you out of here all right—don't you worry about *that*."

Lawrence slapped the suit—gently, this time—without taking his eyes off the young scientist's stricken face. Then, with a vast feeling of relief, he saw Lawson slowly relax.

For a moment the astronomer sat quite motionless, obviously in full control of himself but apparently listening to some inner voice. What was it telling him? wondered Lawrence. Perhaps that he was part of mankind, even though it had condemned him to that unspeakable orphans' home when he was a child. Perhaps that, somewhere in the world, there might be a person who could care for him, and who would break through the ice that had encrusted his heart.

It was a strange little tableau, here on this mirror-smooth plain between the Mountains of Inaccessibility and the rising sun. Like ships becalmed on a dead and stagnant sea, Duster One and Duster Two floated side by side, their pilots playing no part in the conflict of wills that had just taken place, though they were dimly aware of it. No one watching from a distance could have guessed the issues that had been at stake, the lives and destinies that had trembled in the balance; and the two men involved would never talk of it again.

Indeed, they were already concerned with something else, For in the same instant, they had both become aware of a highly ironic situation.

All the time they had been standing there, so intent upon their own affairs that they had never looked at the screen of the infrared scanner, it had been patiently holding the picture they sought.

When Pat and Sue had completed their inventory and emerged from the air-lock galley, the passengers were still far back in Restoration England. Sir Isaac's brief physics lecture had been followed, as might easily have been predicted, by a considerably longer anatomy lesson from Nell Gwyn. The audience was thoroughly enjoying itself, especially as Barrett's English accent was now going full blast.

"'"Forsooth, Sir Isaac, you are indeed a man of great knowledge. Yet, methinks there is much that a woman might teach you."

"'"And what is that, my pretty maid?"

"'Mistress Nell blushed shyly.

"'"I fear," she sighed, "that you have given your life to the things of the mind. You have forgotten, Sir Isaac, that the body, also, has much strange wisdom."

"'"Call me 'Ike,'" said the sage huskily, as his clumsy fingers tugged at the fastenings of her blouse.

""'Not here—in the palace!" Nell protested, making no effort to hold him at bay. "The King will be back soon!"

""'Do not alarm yourself, my pretty one. Charles is roistering with that scribbler Pepys. We'll see naught of him tonight—'""

If we ever get out of here, thought Pat, we must send a letter of thanks to the seventeen-year-old schoolgirl on Mars who is supposed to have written this nonsense. She's keeping everyone amused, and that's all that matters now.

No; there was someone who was definitely *not* amused. He became uncomfortably aware that Miss Morley was trying to catch his eye. Recalling his duties as skipper, he turned toward her and gave her a reassuring but rather strained smile.

She did not return it; if anything, her expression became even more forbidding. Slowly and quite deliberately, she looked at Sue Wilkins and then back at him.

There was no need for words. She had said, as clearly as if she had shouted it at the top of her voice: "I know what *you've* been doing, back there in the air lock."

Pat felt his face flame with indignation, the righteous indignation of a man who had been unjustly accused. For a moment he sat frozen in his seat, while the blood pounded in his cheeks. Then he muttered to himself: "I'll show the old bitch."

He rose to his feet, gave Miss Morley a smile of poisonous sweetness, and said just loudly enough for her to hear: "Miss Wilkins! I think we've forgotten something. Will you come back to the air lock?"

As the door closed behind them once more, interrupting the narration of an incident that threw the gravest possible doubts upon the paternity of the Duke of St. Albans, Sue Wilkins looked at him in puzzled surprise.

"Did you see that?" he said, still boiling.

"See what?"

"Miss Morley—"

"Oh," interrupted Sue, "don't worry about her, poor thing. She's been eyeing you ever since we left the Base. You know what her trouble is."

"What?" asked Pat, already uncomfortably sure of the answer.

"I suppose you could call it ingrowing virginity. It's a common complaint, and the symptoms are always the same. There's only one cure for it."

The ways of love are strange and tortuous. Only ten minutes ago, Pat and Sue had left the air lock together, mutually agreed to remain in a state of chaste affection. But now the improbable combination of Miss Morley and Nell Gwyn, and the feeling that one might as well be hung for a sheep as for a lamb—as well as, perhaps, the instinctive knowledge of their bodies that, in the long run, love was the only defense against death—had combined to overwhelm them. For a moment they stood motionless in the tiny, cluttered space of the galley; then, neither knowing who moved first, they were in each other's arms.

Sue had time to whisper only one phrase before Pat's lips silenced her.

"Not *here*," she whispered, "in the palace!"

# Chapter 13

Chief Engineer Lawrence stared into the faintly glowing screen, trying to read its message. Like all engineers and scientists, he had spent an appreciable fraction of his life looking at the images painted by speeding electrons, recording events too large or too small, too bright or too faint, for human eyes to see. It was more than a hundred years since the cathode-ray tube had placed the invisible world firmly in Man's grasp; already he had forgotten that it had ever been beyond his reach.

Two hundred meters away, according to the infrared scanner, a patch of slightly greater warmth was lying on the face of this dusty desert. It was almost perfectly circular, and quite isolated; there were no other sources of heat in the entire field of view. Though it was much smaller than the spot that Lawson had photographed from Lagrange, it was in the right area. There could be little doubt that it was the same thing.

There was no proof, however, that it was what they were looking for. It could have several explanations; perhaps it marked the site of an isolated peak, jutting up from the depths almost to the surface of the Sea. There was only one way to find out.

"You stay here," said Lawrence. "I'll go forward on Duster One. Tell me when I'm at the exact center of the spot."

"D'you think it will be dangerous?"

"It's not very likely, but there's no point in us both taking a risk."

Slowly, Duster One glided across to that enigmatically glowing patch—so obvious to the infrared scanner, yet wholly invisible to the eye.

"A little to the left," Tom ordered. "Another few meters—you're nearly there—whoa!"

Lawrence stared at the gray dust upon which his vehicle was floating. At first sight, it seemed as featureless as any other portion of the Sea; then, as he looked more closely, he saw something that raised the goose-pimples on his skin.

When examined very carefully, as he was examining it now, the dust showed an extremely fine pepper-and-salt pattern. *That pattern was moving; the surface of the Sea was creeping very slowly toward him, as if blown by an invisible wind.*

Lawrence did not like it at all. On the Moon, one learned to be wary of the abnormal and unexplained; it usually meant that something was wrong—or soon would be. This slowly crawling dust was both uncanny and disturbing. If a boat had sunk here once already, anything as small as a ski might be in even greater danger.

"Better keep away," he advised Duster Two. "There's something odd here—I don't understand it." Carefully, he described the phenomenon to Lawson, who thought it over and answered almost at once: "You say it looks like a fountain in the dust? That's exactly what it is. We already know there's a source of heat here. It's powerful enough to stir up a convection current."

"What could do that? It can't be *Selene*."

He felt a wave of disappointment sweep over him. It was all a wild-goose chase, as he had feared from the beginning. Some pocket of radioactivity, or an outburst of hot gases released by the quake, had fooled their instruments and dragged them to this desolate spot. And the sooner they left it the better; it might still be dangerous.

"Just a minute," said Tom. "A vehicle with a fair amount of machinery and twenty-two passengers—that must produce a good deal of heat. Three or four kilowatts, at least. If this dust is in equilibrium, that might be enough to start a fountain."

Lawrence thought this was very unlikely, but he was now willing to grasp at the slimmest straw. He picked up the thin metal probe, and thrust it vertically into the dust. At first it penetrated with almost no resistance, but as the telescopic extensions added to its length, it became harder and harder to move. By the time he had the full twenty meters out, it needed all his strength to push it downward.

The upper end of the probe disappeared into the dust; he had hit nothing—but he had scarcely expected to succeed on this first attempt. He would have to do the job scientifically and lay out a search pattern.

After a few minutes of cruising back and forth, he had criss-crossed the area with parallel bands of white tape, five meters apart. Like an old-time farmer planting potatoes, he started to move along the first of the tapes, driving his probe into the dust. It was a slow job, for it had to be done conscientiously. He was like a blind man, feeling in the dark with a thin, flexible wand. If what he sought was beyond the reach of his wand, he would have to think of something else. But he would deal with that problem when he came to it.

He had been searching for about ten minutes when he became careless. It required both hands to operate the probe, especially when it neared the limit of its extension. He was pushing with all his strength, leaning over the edge of the ski, when he slipped and fell headlong into the dust.

Pat was conscious of the changed atmosphere as soon as he emerged from the air lock. The reading from *The Orange and the Apple* had finished some time ago, and a heated argument was now in progress. It stopped when he walked into the cabin, and there was an embarrassing silence while he surveyed the scene. Some of the passengers looked at him out of the corners of their eyes, while the others pretended he wasn't there.

"Well, Commodore," he said, "what's the trouble?"

"There's a feeling," Hansteen answered, "that we're not doing all we could to get out. I've explained that we have no alternative but to wait until someone finds us—but not everybody agrees."

It was bound to come sooner or later, thought Pat. As time ran out, and there was no sign of rescue, nerves would begin to snap, tempers get frayed. There would be calls for action—*any* action. It was against human nature to sit still and do nothing in the face of death.

"We've been through this over and over again," he said wearily. "We're at least ten meters down, and even if we opened the air lock, no one could get up to the surface against the resistance of the dust."

"Can you be sure of that?" someone asked.

"Quite sure," Pat answered. "Have you ever tried to swim through sand? You won't get very far."

"What about trying the motors?"

"I doubt if they'd budge us a centimeter. And even if they did, we'd move forward—not up."

"We could all go to the rear; our weight might bring the nose up."

"It's the strain on the hull I'm worried about," said Pat. "Suppose I did start the motors—it would be like butting into a brick wall. Heaven knows what damage it might do."

"But there's a chance it might work. Isn't that worth the risk?"

Pat glanced at the Commodore, feeling a little annoyed that he had not come to his support. Hansteen stared straight back at him, as if to say, "I've handled this so far, now it's your turn." Well, that was fair enough, especially after what Sue had just said. It was time he stood on his own feet, or at least proved that he could do so.

"The danger's too great," he said flatly. "We're perfectly safe here for at least another four days. Long before then, we'll be found. So why risk everything on a million-to-one chance? If it was our last resort, I'd say yes—but not now."

He looked round the cabin, challenging anyone to disagree with him. As he did so, he could not help meeting Miss Morley's eye, nor did he attempt to avoid it. Nevertheless, it was with as much surprise as embarrassment that he heard her say: "Perhaps the Captain is in no great hurry to leave. I notice that we haven't seen much of him lately—or of Miss Wilkins."

Why, you prune-faced bitch, thought Pat. Just because no man in his right senses—

"Hold it, Harris!" said the Commodore, in the nick of time. "I'll deal with this."

It was the first time that Hansteen had really asserted himself; until now, he had run things easily and quietly, or stood in the background and let Pat get on with the job. But now they were hearing the authentic voice of authority, like a trumpet call across a battlefield. This was no retired astronaut speaking; it was a Commodore of Space.

"Miss Morley," he said, "that was a very foolish and uncalled-for remark. Only the fact that we are all under considerable strain can possibly excuse it. I think you should apologize to the Captain."

"It's true," she said stubbornly. "Ask him to deny it."

Commodore Hansteen had not lost his temper in thirty years, and had no intention of losing it now. But he knew when to pretend to lose it, and in this case little simulation was necessary. He was not only angry with Miss Morley; he was annoyed with Pat, and felt that he had let him down. Of course, there might be nothing at all in Miss Morley's accusation, but Pat and Sue had certainly spent a devil of a long time over a simple job. There were occasions when the appearance of innocence was almost as important as the thing itself. He remembered an old Chinese proverb: "Do not stoop to tie your laces in your neighbor's melon patch."

"I don't give a damn," he said in his most blistering voice, "about the relations, if any, between Miss Wilkins and the Captain. That's their own affair, and as long as they do their jobs efficiently, we've no right to interfere. Are you suggesting that Captain Harris is *not* doing his job?"

"Well—I wouldn't say that."

"Then please don't say anything. We have enough problems on our hands already, without manufacturing any more."

The other passengers had sat listening with that mixture of embarrassment and enjoyment which most men feel when they overhear a quarrel in which they have no part. Though, in a very real sense, this did concern everyone aboard *Selene*, for it was the first challenge to authority, the first sign that discipline was cracking. Until now, this group had been welded into a harmonious whole, but now a voice had been raised against the elders of the tribe.

Miss Morley might be a neurotic old maid, but she was also a tough and determined one. The Commodore saw, with understandable qualms, that she was getting ready to answer him.

No one would ever know just what she intended to say; for, at that moment, Mrs. Schuster let loose a shriek altogether in keeping with her dimensions.

When a man falls on the Moon, he usually has time to do something about it, for his nerves and muscles are designed to deal with a sixfold greater gravity. Yet when Chief Engineer Lawrence toppled off the ski, the distance was so short that he had no time to react. Almost at once, he hit the dust—and was engulfed in darkness.

He could see absolutely nothing, except for a very faint florescence from the illuminated instrument panel inside his suit. With extreme caution, he began to feel around in the softly resisting, half-fluid substance in which he was floundering, seeking some solid object for support. There was nothing; he could not even guess which direction was up.

A mind-sapping despair, which seemed to drain his body of all its strength, almost overwhelmed him. His heart was thumping with that erratic beat that heralds the approach of panic, and the final overthrow of reason. He had seen other men become screaming, struggling animals, and knew that he was moving swiftly to join them.

There was just enough left of his rational mind to remember that only a few minutes ago he had saved Lawson from this same fate, but he was not in a position to appreciate the irony. He had to concentrate all his remaining strength of will on regaining control of himself, and checking the thumping in his chest that seemed about to tear him to pieces.

And then, loud and clear in his helmet speaker, came a sound so utterly unexpected that the waves of panic ceased to batter against the island of his soul. It was Tom Lawson—laughing.

The laughter was brief, and it was followed by an apology.

"I'm sorry, Mr. Lawrence—I couldn't help it. You look so funny there, waving your legs in the sky."

The Chief Engineer froze in his suit. His fear vanished instantly, to be replaced by anger. He was furious with Lawson, but much more furious with himself.

Of course he had been in no danger; in his inflated suit, he was like a balloon floating upon water, and equally incapable of sinking. Now that he knew what had happened, he could sort matters out by himself. He kicked purposefully with his legs, paddled with his hands, and rolled round his center of gravity—and vision returned as the dust streamed off his helmet. He had sunk, at the most, ten centimeters, and the ski had been within reach all the time. It was a remarkable achievement to have missed it completely while he was flailing around like a stranded octopus.

With as much dignity as he could muster, he grabbed the ski and pulled himself aboard. He did not trust himself to speak, for he was still breathless from his unnecessary exertions, and his voice might betray his recent panic. And he was still angry; he would not have made such a fool of himself in the days when he was working constantly out on the lunar surface. Now he was out of touch. Why, the last time he had worn a suit had been for his annual proficiency check, and then he had never even stepped outside the air lock.

Back on the ski, as he continued with his probing, his mixture of fright and anger slowly evaporated. It was replaced by a mood of thoughtfulness, as he realized how closely—whether he liked it or not—the events of the last half-hour had linked him with Lawson. True, the astronomer had laughed when he was floundering in the dust, but he must have been an irresistibly funny sight. And Lawson had actually apologized for his mirth. A short time ago, both laughter and apology would have been equally unthinkable.

Then Lawrence forgot everything else; for his probe hit an obstacle, fifteen meters down.

# Chapter 14

When Mrs. Schuster screamed, Commodore Hansteen's first reaction was: My God—the woman's going to have hysterics. Half a second later, he needed all his will power not to join her.

From outside the hull, where there had been no sound for three days except the whispering of the dust, there was a noise at last. It was unmistakable, and so was its meaning. Something metallic was scraping along the hull.

Instantly, the cabin was filled with shouts, cheers, and cries of relief. With considerable difficulty, Hansteen managed to make himself heard.

"They've found us," he said, "but they may not know it. If we work together, they'll have a better chance of spotting us. Pat, you try the radio. The rest of us will rap on the hull—the old Morse V sign—DIT DIT DIT DAH. Come on—all together!"

*Selene* reverberated with a ragged volley of dots and dashes, which slowly became synchronized into one resounding tattoo.

"Hold it!" said Hansteen a minute later. "Everyone listen carefully!"

After the noise, the silence was uncanny—even unnerving. Pat had switched off the air pumps and fans, so that the only sound aboard the cruiser was the beating of twenty-two hearts.

The silence dragged on and on. Could that noise, after all, have been nothing but some contraction or expansion of *Selene*'s own hull? Or had the rescue party—if it *was* a rescue party—missed them and passed on across the empty face of the Sea?

Abruptly, the scratching came again. Hansteen checked the renewed enthusiasm with a wave of his hand.

"*Listen*, for God's sake," he entreated. "Let's see if we can make anything of it."

The scratching lasted only for a few seconds before being followed once again by that agonizing silence. Presently someone said quietly, more to break the suspense than to make any useful contribution, "That sounded like a wire being dragged past. Maybe they're trawling for us."

"Impossible," answered Pat. "The resistance would be too great, especially at this depth. It's more likely to be a rod probing up and down."

"Anyway," said the Commodore, "there's a search party within a few meters of us. Give them another tattoo. Once again—all together—"

DIT DIT DIT DAH...

DIT DIT DIT DAH...

Through *Selene*'s double hull and out into the dust throbbed the fateful opening of Beethoven's Fifth Symphony, as a century earlier it had pulsed across Occupied Europe. In the pilot's seat, Pat Harris was saying again and again, with desperate urgency, "*Selene* calling. Are you receiving? Over," and then listening for an eternal fifteen seconds before he repeated the transmission. But the ether remained as silent as it had been ever since the dust had swallowed them up.

Aboard *Auriga*, Maurice Spenser looked anxiously at the clock.

"Dammit," he said, "the skis should have been there long ago. When was their last message?"

"Twenty-five minutes ago," said the ship's Communications Officer. "The half-hourly report should be coming in soon, whether they've found anything or not."

"Sure you're still on the right frequency?"

"You stick to your business and I'll stick to mine," retorted the indignant radioman.

"Sorry," replied Spenser, who had learned long ago when to apologize quickly. "I'm afraid my nerves are jumping."

He rose from his seat, and started to make a circuit of *Auriga*'s little control room. After he had bumped himself painfully against an instrument panel—he had not yet grown accustomed to lunar gravity, and was beginning to wonder if he ever would—he got himself under control once more.

This was the worst part of his job, the waiting until he knew whether or not he had a story. Already, he had incurred a small fortune in expenses. They would be nothing compared with the bills that would soon be accumulating if he gave Captain Anson the order to go ahead. But in that event his worries would be over, for he would have his scoop.

"Here they are," said the Communications Officer suddenly. "Two minutes ahead of time. Something's happened."

"I've hit something," said Lawrence tersely, "but I can't tell what it is."

"How far down?" asked Lawson and both pilots simultaneously.

"About fifteen meters. Take me two meters to the right. I'll try again."

He withdrew the probe, then drove it in again when the ski had moved to the new position.

"Still there," he reported, "and at the same depth. Take me on another two meters."

Now the obstacle was gone, or was too deep for the probe to reach.

"Nothing there. Take me back in the other direction."

It would be a slow and tiring job, charting the outlines of whatever lay buried down there. By such tedious methods, two centuries ago, men began to sound the oceans of Earth, lowering weighted lines to the sea bed and then hauling them up again. It was a pity, thought Lawrence, that he had no echo-sounder that would operate here, but he doubted if either acoustic or radio waves could penetrate through more than a few meters of the dust.

What a fool—he should have thought of that before! *That* was what had happened to *Selene*'s radio signals. If she had been swallowed by the dust, it would have blanketed and absorbed her transmissions. But at this range, if he really was sitting on top of the cruiser...

Lawrence switched his receiver to the MOONCRASH band—and there she was, yelling at the top of her robot voice. The signal was piercingly strong—quite good enough, he would have thought, to have been picked up by Lagrange or Port Roris. Then he remembered that his metal probe was still resting on the submerged hull; it would give radio waves an easy path to the surface.

He sat listening to that train of pulses for a good fifteen seconds before he plucked up enough courage for the next move. He had never really expected to find anything, and even now his search might be in vain. That automatic beacon would call for weeks, like a voice from the tomb, long after *Selene*'s occupants were dead.

Then, with an abrupt, angry gesture that defied the fates to do their worst, Lawrence switched to the cruiser's own frequency—and was almost deafened by Pat Harris shouting: "*Selene* calling, *Selene* calling. Do you receive me? Over."

"This is Duster One," he answered. "C.E.E. speaking. I'm fifteen meters above you. Are you all O.K.? Over."

It was a long time before he could make any sense out of the reply, the background of shouting and cheering was so loud. That in itself was enough to tell him that all the passengers were alive, and in good spirits. Listening to them, indeed, one might almost have imagined that they were holding some drunken celebration. In their joy at being discovered, at making contact with the human race, they thought that their troubles were over.

"Duster One calling Port Roris Control," said Lawrence, while he waited for the tumult to die down. "We've found *Selene*, and established radio contact. Judging by the noise that's going on inside, everyone's quite O.K. She's fifteen meters down, just where Doctor Lawson indicated. I'll call you back in a few minutes. Out."

At the speed of light, waves of relief and happiness would now be spreading over the Moon, the Earth, the inner planets, bringing a sudden lifting of the hearts to billions of people. On streets and slideways, in buses and spaceships, perfect strangers would turn to each other and say, "Have you heard? They've found *Selene*."

In all the solar system, indeed, there was only one man who could not wholeheartedly share the rejoicing. As he sat on his ski, listening to those cheers from underground and looking at the crawling pattern in the dust, Chief Engineer Lawrence felt far more scared and helpless than the men and women trapped beneath his feet. He knew that he was facing the greatest battle in his life.

# Chapter 15

For the first time in twenty-four hours, Maurice Spenser was relaxing. Everything that could be done had been done. Men and equipment were already moving toward Port Roris. (Lucky about Jules Braques being at Clavius; he was one of the best cameramen in the business, and they'd often worked together.) Captain Anson was doing sums with the computer and looking thoughtfully at contour maps of the Mountains. The crew (all six) had been rounded up from the bars (all three) and informed that there was yet another change of route. On Earth, at least a dozen contracts had been signed and telefaxed, and large sums of money had already changed hands. The financial wizards of Interplanet News would be calculating, with scientific precision, just how much they could charge the other agencies for the story, without driving them to charter ships of their own—not that this was at all likely, for Spenser had too great a lead. No competitor could possibly reach the Mountains in less than forty-eight hours; he would be there in six.

Yes, it was very pleasant to take it easy, in the calm and confident assurance that everything was under control and going the way you wanted. It was these interludes that made life worth living, and Spenser knew how to make the most of them. They were his panacea against ulcers—still, after a hundred years, the occupational disease of the communications industry.

It was typical of him, however, that he was relaxing on the job. He was lying, a drink in one hand, a plate of sandwiches by the other, in the small observation lounge of the Embarkation Building. Through the double sheets of glass he could see the tiny dock from which *Selene* had sailed three days ago. (There was no escaping from those maritime words, inappropriate though they were to this situation.) It was merely a strip of concrete stretching for twenty meters out into the uncanny flatness of the dust; lying most of its length, like a giant concertina, was the flexible tube through which the passengers could walk from the Port into the cruiser. Now open to vacuum, it was deflated and partly collapsed—a most depressing sight, Spenser could not help thinking.

He glanced at his watch, then at that unbelievable horizon. If he had been asked to guess, he would have said that it was at least a hundred kilometers away, not two or three. A few minutes later, a reflected glint of sunlight caught his eye. There they were, climbing up over the edge of the Moon. They would be here in five minutes, out of the air lock in ten. Plenty of time to finish that last sandwich.

Dr. Lawson showed no signs of recognition when Spenser greeted him; that was not surprising, for their previous brief conversation had been in almost total darkness.

"Doctor Lawson? I'm Bureau Chief of Interplanet News. Permission to record?"

"Just a minute," interrupted Lawrence. "I know the Interplanet man. *You're* not Joe Leonard...."

"Correct; I'm Maurice Spenser. I took over from Joe last week. He has to get used to Earth gravity again—otherwise he'll be stuck here for life."

"Well, you're damn quick off the mark. It was only an hour ago that we radioed."

Spenser thought it best not to mention that he had already been here the better part of a day.

"I'd still like to know if I can record," he repeated. He was very conscientious about this. Some newsmen took a chance and went ahead without permission, but if you were caught, you lost your job. As a Bureau Chief, he had to keep the rules laid down to safeguard his profession, and the public.

"Not now, if you don't mind," said Lawrence. "I've fifty things to organize, but Doctor Lawson will be glad to talk to you; he did most of the work and deserves all the credit. You can quote me on *that*."

"Er—thank you," mumbled Tom, looking embarrassed.

"Right—see you later," said Lawrence. "I'll be at the Local Engineer's office, living on pills. But you might as well get some sleep."

"Not until I've finished with you," corrected Spenser, grabbing Tom and aiming him in the direction of the hotel.

The first person they met in the ten-meter-square foyer was Captain Anson.

"I've been looking for you, Mr. Spenser," he said. "The Space-Workers' Union is making trouble. You know there's a ruling about time off between trips. Well, it seems that—"

"*Please*, Captain, not now. Take it up with Interplanet's Legal Department. Call Clavius 1234, ask for Harry Dantzig—he'll straighten it out."

He propelled the unresisting Tom Lawson up the stairs (it was odd to find a hotel without elevators, but they were unnecessary on a world where you weighed only a dozen or so kilos) and into his suite.

Apart from its excessively small size, and complete absence of windows, the suite might have been in any cheap hotel on Earth. The simple chairs, couch, and table were manufactured from the very minimum of material, most of it Fiberglas, for quartz was common on the Moon. The bathroom was perfectly conventional (that was a relief, after those tricky free-fall toilets), but the bed had a slightly disconcerting appearance. Some visitors from Earth found it difficult to sleep under a sixth of a gravity, and for their benefit an elastic sheet could be stretched across the bed and held in place by light springs. The whole arrangement had a distinct flavor of straight-jackets and padded cells.

Another cheerful little touch was the notice behind the door, which announced in English, Russian, and Mandarin that THIS HOTEL IS INDEPENDENTLY PRESSURIZED. IN THE EVENT OF A DOME FAILURE, YOU WILL BE PERFECTLY SAFE. SHOULD THIS OCCUR, PLEASE REMAIN IN YOUR ROOM AND AWAIT FURTHER INSTRUCTIONS. THANK YOU.

Spenser had read that notice several times. He still thought that the basic information could have been conveyed in a more confident, lighthearted manner. The wording lacked charm.

And that, he decided, was the whole trouble on the Moon. The struggle against the forces of Nature was so fierce that no energy was left for gracious living. This was most noticeable in the contrast between the superb efficiency of the technical services, and the easygoing, take-it-or-leave-it attitude one met in all the other walks of life. If you complained about the telephone, the plumbing, the air (especially the air!), it was fixed within minutes. But just try to get quick service in a restaurant or bar...

"I know you're very tired," Spenser began, "but I'd like to ask a few questions. You don't mind being recorded, I hope?"

"No," said Tom, who had long since passed the stage of caring one way or the other. He was slumped in a chair, mechanically sipping the drink Spenser had poured out, but obviously not tasting it.

"This is Maurice Spenser, Interplanet News, talking with Doctor Thomas Lawson. Now, Doctor, all we know at the moment is that you and Mister Lawrence, Chief Engineer, Earthside, have found *Selene*, and that the people inside are safe. Perhaps you'll tell us, without going into technical details, just how you—hell and damnation!"

He caught the slowly falling glass without spilling a drop, then eased the sleeping astronomer over to the couch. Well, he couldn't grumble; this was the only item that hadn't worked according to plan. And even this might be to his advantage; for no one else could find Lawson—still less, interview him—while he was sleeping it off in what the Hotel Roris, with a fine sense of humor, called its luxury suite.

In Clavius City, the Tourist Commissioner had finally managed to convince everyone that he had not been playing favorites. His relief at hearing of *Selene*'s discovery had quickly abated when Reuter's, *Time-Space*, Triplanetary Publications, and Lunar News had phoned him in rapid succession to ask just how Interplanet had managed to break the story first. It had been on the wires, in fact, even before it had reached Administration headquarters, thanks to Spenser's thoughtful monitoring of the dust-ski radios.

Now that it was obvious what had happened, the suspicions of all the other news services had been replaced by frank admiration for Spenser's luck and enterprise. It would be a little while yet before they realized that he had an even bigger trick up his capacious sleeve.

The Communications Center at Clavius had seen many dramatic moments, but this was one of the most unforgettable. It was, thought Commissioner Davis, almost like listening to voices from beyond the grave. A few hours ago, all these men and women were presumed dead—yet here they were, fit and cheerful, lining up at that buried microphone to relay messages of reassurance to their friends and relatives. Thanks to the probe which Lawrence had left as marker and antenna, that fifteen-meter blanket of dust could no longer cut the cruiser off from the rest of mankind.

The impatient reporters had to wait until there was a break in *Selene*'s transmission before they could get their interviews. Miss Wilkins was now speaking, dictating messages that were being handed to her by the passengers. The cruiser must have been full of people scribbling telegraphese on the backs of torn-up guidebooks, trying to condense the maximum amount of information into the minimum number of words. None of this material, of course, could be quoted or reproduced; it was all private, and the Postmasters General of three planets would descend in their combined wrath upon any reporter foolish enough to use it. Strictly speaking, they should not even be listening in on this circuit, as the Communications Officer had several times pointed out with increasing degrees of indignation.

"...Tell Martha, Jan and Ivy not to worry about me, I'll be home soon. Ask Tom how the Erickson deal went, and let me know when you call back. My love to you all—George. End of message. Did you get that? *Selene* calling. Over."

"Luna Central calling *Selene*. Yes, we have it all down; we'll see that the messages get delivered and will relay the answers as soon as they come in. Now can we speak to Captain Harris? Over."

There was a brief pause, during which the background noises in the cruiser could be clearly heard—the sound of voices, slightly reverberant in this enclosed space, the creak of a chair, a muffled "Excuse me." Then:

"Captain Harris calling Central. Over."

Commissioner Davis took the mike.

"Captain Harris, this is the Tourist Commissioner. I know that you all have messages you wish to send, but the news services are here and are very anxious to have a few words with you. First of all, could you give us a brief description of conditions inside *Selene*? Over."

"Well, it's very hot, and we aren't wearing much clothes. But I don't suppose we can grumble about the heat, since it helped you to find us. Anyway, we've grown used to it. The air's still good, and we have enough food and water, though the menu is—let's say it's monotonous. What more do you want to know? Over."

"Ask him about morale—how are the passengers taking it?—are there any signs of strain?" said the representative of Triplanetary Publications. The Tourist Commissioner relayed the question, rather more tactfully. It seemed to cause slight embarrassment at the other end of the line.

"Everyone's behaved very well," said Pat, just a little too hastily. "Of course, we all wonder how long it will take you to get us out. Can you give us any ideas on that? Over."

"Chief Engineer Lawrence is in Port Roris now, planning rescue operations," Davis answered. "As soon as he has an estimate, we'll pass it on. Meanwhile, how are you occupying your time? Over."

Pat told him, thereby enormously multiplying the sales of *Shane* and, less happily, giving a boost to the flagging fortunes of *The Orange and the Apple*. He also gave a brief account of the court proceedings—now terminated sine die.

"That must have been amusing entertainment," said Davis. "But now you won't have to rely on your own resources. We can send you anything you want—music, plays, discussions. Just give the word—we'll fix it. Over."

Pat took his time in answering this. The radio link had already transformed their lives, had brought them hope and put them in touch with their loved ones. Yet, in a way he was almost sorry that their seclusion was ended. The heart-warming sense of solidarity, which even Miss Morley's outburst had scarcely ruffled, was already a fading dream. They no longer formed a single group, united in the common cause of survival. Now their lives had diverged again into a score of independent aims and ambitions. Humanity had swallowed them up once more, as the ocean swallows a raindrop.

# Chapter 16

Chief Engineer Lawrence did not believe that committees ever achieved anything. His views were well known on the Moon, for shortly after the last biannual visit of the Lunar Board of Survey, a notice had appeared on his desk conveying the information: A BOARD IS LONG, HARD, AND NARROW. IT IS MADE OF WOOD.

But he approved of this committee, because it fulfilled his somewhat stringent requirements. He was chairman; there were no minutes, no secretary, no agenda. Best of all, he could ignore or accept its recommendations as he pleased. He was the man in charge of rescue operations, unless the Chief Administrator chose to sack him—which he would do only under extreme pressure from Earth. The committee existed merely to provide ideas and technical knowledge; it was his private brain trust.

Only half of its dozen members were physically present; the rest were scattered over Moon, Earth, and space. The soil-physics expert on Earth was at a disadvantage, for owing to the finite speed of radio waves, he would always be a second and a half in arrears, and by the time his comments could get to the Moon, almost three seconds would have passed. He had accordingly been asked to make notes and to save his views until the end, only interrupting if it was absolutely necessary. As many people had discovered, after setting up lunar conference calls at great expense, nothing hamstrung a brisk discussion more effectively than that three-second time lag.

"For the benefit of the newcomers," said Lawrence, when the roll call had been completed, "I'll brief you on the situation. *Selene* is fifteen meters down, on a level keel. She's undamaged, with all her equipment functioning, and the twenty-two people inside her are still in good spirits. They have enough oxygen for ninety hours—*that's* the deadline we have to keep in mind.

"For those of you who don't know what *Selene* looks like, here's a one-in-twenty scale model." He lifted the model from the table, and turned it slowly in front of the camera. "She's just like a bus, or a small aircraft; the only thing unique is her propulsion system, which employs these wide-bladed, variable-pitch fans.

"Our great problem, of course, is the dust. If you've never seen it, you can't imagine what it's like. Any ideas you may have about sand or other materials on Earth won't apply here; this stuff is more like a liquid. Here's a sample of it."

Lawrence picked up a tall vertical cylinder, the lower third of which was filled with an amorphous gray substance. He tilted it, and the stuff began to flow. It moved more quickly than syrup, more slowly than water, and it took a few seconds for its surface to become horizontal again after it had been disturbed. No one could ever have guessed, by looking at it, that it was not a fluid.

"This cylinder is sealed," explained Lawrence, "with a vacuum inside, so the dust is showing its normal behavior. In air, it's quite different; it's much stickier, and behaves rather like very fine sand or talcum powder. I'd better warn you—it's impossible to make a synthetic sample that has the properties of the real thing. It takes a few billion years of desiccation to produce the genuine article. If you want to do some experimenting, we'll ship you as much dust as you like; heaven knows, we can spare it.

"A few other points. *Selene* is three kilometers from the nearest solid land—the Mountains of Inaccessibility. There may be several hundred meters of dust beneath her, though we're not sure of that. Nor can we be quite sure that there will be no more cave-ins, though the geologists think it's very unlikely.

"The only way we can reach the site is by dust-ski. We've two units, and another one is being shipped round from Farside. They can carry or tow up to five tons of equipment; the largest single item we could put on a sledge would be about two tons. So we can't bring any really heavy gear to the site.

"Well, that's the position. We have ninety hours. Any suggestion? I've some ideas of my own, but I'd like to hear yours first."

"There was a long silence while the members of the committee, scattered over a volume of space almost four hundred thousand kilometers across, brought their various talents to bear on the problem. Then the Chief Engineer, Farside, spoke from somewhere in the neighborhood of Joliot-Curie.

"It's my hunch that we can't do anything effective in ninety hours; we'll have to build special equipment, and that always takes time. So—we have to get an air line down to *Selene*. Where's her umbilical connection?"

"Behind the main entrance, at the rear. I don't see how you can get a line there and couple it up, fifteen meters down. Besides, everything will be clogged with dust."

"I've a better idea," someone injected. "Drive a pipe down through the roof."

"You'll need two pipes," pointed out another speaker. "One to pump in oxygen, the other to suck out the foul air."

"That means using a complete air purifier. And we won't even need it if we can get those people out inside the ninety hours."

"Too big a gamble. Once the air supply is secure, we can take our time, and the ninety-hour deadline won't worry us."

"I accept that point," said Lawrence. "In fact, I've several men working on those lines right now. The next question is: Do we try to raise the cruiser with everyone inside, or do we get the passengers out individually? Remember, there's only one space suit aboard her."

"Could we sink a shaft to the door, and couple it to the air lock?" asked one of the scientists.

"Same problem as with the air hose. Even worse, in fact, since the coupling would be so much bigger."

"What about a cofferdam large enough to go round the whole cruiser? We could sink it round her, then dig out the dust."

"You'd need tons of piles and shorings. And don't forget, the dam would have to be sealed off at the bottom. Otherwise the dust would flow back into it, just as fast as we took it out of the top."

"Can you pump the stuff?" asked someone else.

"Yes, with the right kind of impeller. But you can't suck it, of course. It has to be lifted. A normal pump just cavitates."

"This dust," grumbled the Port Roris Assistant Engineer, "has the worst properties of solids and liquids, with none of their advantages. It won't flow when you want it to; it won't stay put when you want it to."

"Can I make a point?" said Father Ferraro, speaking from Plato. "This word 'dust' is highly misleading. What we have here is a substance that can't exist on Earth, so there's no name for it on our language. The last speaker was quite correct; sometimes you have to think of it as a nonwetting liquid, rather like mercury, but much lighter. At other times, it's a flowing solid, like pitch—except that it moves much more rapidly, of course."

"Any way it can be stabilized?" someone asked.

"I think that's a question for Earth," said Lawrence. "Doctor Evans, would you like to comment?"

Everyone waited for the three seconds, which, as always, seemed very much longer. Then the physicist answered, quite as clearly as if he were in the same room: "I've been wondering about that. There might be organic binders—glue, if you like—that would make it stick together so that it could be handled more easily. Would plain water be any use? Have you tried that?"

"No, but we will," answered Lawrence, scribbling a note.

"Is the stuff magnetic?" asked the Traffic Control Officer.

"That's a good point," said Lawrence. "Is it, Father?"

"Slightly; it contains a fair amount of meteoric iron. But I don't think that helps us at all. A magnetic field would pull out the ferrous material, but it wouldn't affect the dust as a whole."

"Anyway, we'll try." Lawrence made another note. It was his hope—though a faint one—that out of this clash of minds would come some bright idea, some apparently farfetched but fundamentally sound conception that would solve his problem. And it was his, whether he liked it or not. He was responsible, through his various deputies and departments, for every piece of technical equipment on this side of the Moon—especially when something went wrong with it.

"I'm very much afraid," said the Clavius Traffic Control Officer, "that your biggest headache will be logistics. Every piece of equipment has to be ferried out on the skis, and they take at least two hours for the round trip—more, if they're towing a heavy load. Before you even start operating, you'll have to build some kind of working platform—like a raft—that you can leave on the site. It may take a day to get that in position, and much longer to get all your equipment out to it."

"Including temporary living quarters," added someone. "The workmen will have to stay on the site."

"That's straightforward; as soon as we fix a raft, we can inflate an igloo on it."

"Better than that; you won't even need a raft. An igloo will float by itself."

"Getting back to this raft," said Lawrence, "we want strong, collapsible units that can be bolted together on the site. Any ideas?"

"Empty fuel tanks?"

"Too big and fragile. Maybe Tech Stores has something."

So it went on; the brain trust was in session. Lawrence would give it another half-hour, then he would decide on his plan of action.

One could not spend too much time talking, when the minutes were ticking away and many lives were at stake. Yet hasty and ill-conceived schemes were worse than useless, for they would absorb materials and skills that might tilt the balance between failure and success.

At first sight, it seemed such a straightforward job. There was *Selene*, within a hundred kilometers of a well-equipped base. Her position was known exactly, and she was only fifteen meters down. But that fifteen meters presented Lawrence with some of the most baffling problems of his entire career.

It was a career which, he knew well, might soon terminate abruptly. For it would be very hard to explain his failure if those twenty-two men and women died.

It was a great pity that not a single witness saw *Auriga* coming down, for it was a glorious sight. A spaceship landing or taking off is one of the most impressive spectacles that Man has yet contrived—excluding some of the more exuberant efforts of the nuclear engineers. And when it occurs on the Moon, in slow motion and uncanny silence, it has a dream-like quality which no one who has seen it can ever forget.

Captain Anson saw no point in trying any fancy navigation, especially since someone else was paying for the gas. There was nothing in the *Master's Handbook* about flying a space liner a hundred kilometers—a *hundred* kilometers, indeed!—though no doubt the mathematicians would be delighted to work out a trajectory, based on the Calculus of Variations, using the very minimum amount of fuel. Anson simply blasted straight up for a thousand kilometers (this qualifying for deep-space rates under Interplanetary Law, though he would tell Spenser about this later) and came down again on a normal vertical approach, with final radar guidance. The ship's computer and the radar monitored each other, and both were monitored by Captain Anson. Any one of the three could have done the job, so it was really quite simple and safe, though it did not look it.

Especially to Maurice Spenser, who began to feel a great longing for the soft green hills of Earth as those desolate peaks clawed up at him. Why had he talked himself into this? Surely there were cheaper ways of committing suicide.

The worst part was the free fall between the successive braking periods. Suppose the rockets failed to fire on command, and the ship continued to plunge Moonward, slowly but inexorably accelerating until it crashed? It was no use pretending that this was a stupid or childish fear, because it had happened more than once.

It was not, however, going to happen to *Auriga*. The unbearable fury of the braking jets was already splashing over the rocks, blasting skyward the dust and cosmic debris that had not been disturbed in thrice a billion years. For a moment the ship hovered in delicate balance only centimeters off the ground; then, almost reluctantly, the spears of flame that supported her retracted into their scabbards. The widely spaced legs of the undercarriage made contact, their pads tilted according to the contours of the ground, and the whole ship rocked slightly for a second as the shock absorbers neutralized the residual energy of impact.

For the second time inside twenty-four hours, Maurice Spenser had landed on the Moon. That was a claim that very few men could make.

"Well," said Captain Anson, as he got up from the control board, "I hope you're satisfied with the view. It's cost you plenty—and there's still that little matter of overtime. According to the Space-Workers' Union—"

"Have you no soul, Captain? Why bother me with such trivia at a time like this? But if I may say so without being charged any extra, that was a very fine landing."

"Oh, it's all part of the day's work," replied the skipper, though he could not conceal slight signs of pleasure. "By the way, would you mind initialing the log here, against the time of landing."

"What's *that* for?" asked Spenser suspiciously.

"Proof of delivery. The log's our prime legal document."

"It seems a little old-fashioned, having a written one," said Spenser. "I thought everything was done by nucleonics these days."

"Traditions of the service," replied Anson. "Of course, the ship's flight recorders are running all the time we're under power, and the trip can always be reconstructed from them. But only the skipper's log gives the little details that make one voyage different from another—like 'Twins born to one of the steerage passengers this morning' or 'At six bells, sighted the White Whale off the starboard bow.'"

"I take it back, Captain," said Spenser. "You *do* have a soul, after all." He added his signature to the log, then moved over to the observation window to examine the view.

The control cabin, a hundred and fifty meters above the ground, had the only direct-vision windows in the ship, and the view through them was superb. Behind them, to the north, were the upper ramparts of the Mountains of Inaccessibility, ranging across half the sky. That name was no longer appropriate, thought Spenser; *he* had reached them, and while the ship was here it might even be possible to do some useful scientific research, such as collecting rock samples. Quite apart from the news value of being in such an outlandish place, he was genuinely interested in what might be discovered here. No man could ever become so blasé that the promise of the unknown and the unexplored completely failed to move him.

In the other direction, he could look across at least forty kilometers of the Sea of Thirst, which spanned more than half his field of view in a great arc of immaculate flatness. But what he was concerned with was less than five kilometers away, and two below.

Clearly visible through a low-powered pair of binoculars was the metal rod that Lawrence had left as a marker, and through which *Selene* was now linked with the world. The sight was not impressive—just a solitary spike jutting from an endless plain—yet it had a stark simplicity that appealed to Spenser. It would make a good opening; it symbolized the loneliness of man in this huge and hostile Universe that he was attempting to conquer. In a few hours, this plain would be far from lonely, but until then that rod would serve to set the scene, while the commentators discussed the rescue plans and filled in the time with appropriate interviews. That was not his problem; the unit at Clavius and the studios back on Earth could handle it in their stride. He had just one job now—to sit here in his eagle's nest and to see that the pictures kept coming in. With the big zoom lens, thanks to the perfect clarity of this airless world, he could almost get close-ups even from here, when the action started.

He glanced into the southwest, where the sun was lifting itself so sluggish up the sky. Almost two weeks of daylight, as Earth counted time, still lay ahead. No need, then, to worry about the lighting. The stage was set.

# Chapter 17

Chief Administrator Olsen seldom made public gestures. He preferred to run the Moon quietly and efficiently behind the scenes, leaving amiable extroverts like the Tourist Commissioner to face the newsmen. His rare appearances were, therefore, all the more impressive—as he intended them to be.

Though millions were watching him, the twenty-two men and women he was really addressing could not see him at all, for it had not been thought necessary to fit *Selene* with vision circuits. But his voice was sufficiently reassuring; it told them everything that they wanted to know.

"Hello, *Selene*," he began. "I want to tell you that all the resources of the Moon are now being mobilized for your aid. The engineering and technical staffs of my administration are working round the clock to help you.

"Mister Lawrence, Chief Engineer, Earthside, is in charge, and I have complete confidence in him. He's now at Port Roris, where the special equipment needed for the operation is being assembled. It's been decided—and I'm sure you'll agree with this—that the most urgent task is to make certain that your oxygen supply can be maintained. For this reason we plan to sink pipes to you; that can be done fairly quickly, and then we can pump down oxygen—as well as food and water, if necessary. So as soon as the pipes are installed, you'll have nothing more to worry about. It may still take a little time to reach you and get you out, but you'll be quite safe. You only have to sit and wait for us.

"Now I'll get off the air, and let you have this channel back so that you can talk to your friends. I'm sorry about the inconvenience and strain you've undergone, but that's all over now. We'll have you out in a day or two. Good luck!"

A burst of cheerful conversation broke out aboard *Selene* as soon as Chief Administrator Olsen's broadcast finished. It had had precisely the effect he had intended; the passengers were already thinking of this whole episode as an adventure which would give them something to talk about for the rest of their lives. Only Pat Harris seemed a little unhappy.

"I wish," he told Commodore Hansteen, "the C.A. hadn't been quite so confident. On the Moon, remarks like that always seem to be tempting fate."

"I know exactly how you feel," the Commodore answered. "But you can hardly blame him—he's thinking of our morale."

"Which is fine, I'd say, especially now that we can talk to our friends and relatives."

"That reminds me; there's one passenger who hasn't received or sent any messages. What's more, he doesn't show the slightest interest in doing so."

"Who's that?"

Hansteen dropped his voice still further. "The New Zealander, Radley. He just sits quietly in the corner over there. I'm not sure why, but he worries me."

"Perhaps the poor fellow has no one on Earth he wants to speak to."

"A man with enough money to go to the Moon must have *some* friends," replied Hansteen. Then he grinned; it was almost a boyish grin, which flickered swiftly across his face, softening its wrinkles and crow's feet. "That sounds very cynical—I didn't mean it that way. But I suggest we keep an eye on Mr. Radley."

"Have you mentioned him to Sue—er, Miss Wilkins?"

"She pointed him out to *me*."

I should have guessed that, thought Pat admiringly; not much gets past her. Now that it seemed he might have a future, after all, he had begun to think very seriously about Sue, and about what she had said to him. In his life he had been in love with five or six girls—or so he could have sworn at the time—but this was something different. He had known Sue for over a year, and from the start had felt attracted to her, but until now it had never come to anything. What were her real feelings? he wondered. Did she regret that moment of shared passion, or did it mean nothing to her? She might argue—and so might he, for that matter—that what had happened in the air lock was no longer relevant; it was merely the action of a man and a woman who thought that only a few hours of life remained to them. They had not been themselves.

But perhaps they had been; perhaps it was the real Pat Harris, the real Sue Wilkins, that had finally emerged from disguise, revealed by the strain and anxiety of the past few days. He wondered how he could be sure of this, but even as he did so, he knew that only time could give the answer. If there was a clear-cut, scientific test that could tell you when you were in love, Pat had not yet come across it.

The dust that lapped—if that was the word—against the quay from which *Selene* had departed four days ago was only a couple of meters deep, but for this test no greater depth was needed. If the hastily built equipment worked here, it would work out in the open Sea.

Lawrence watched from the Embarkation Building as his space-suited assistants bolted the framework together. It was made, like ninety per cent of the structures on the Moon, from slotted aluminum strips and bars. In some ways, thought Lawrence, the Moon was an engineer's paradise. The low gravity, the total absence of rust or corrosion—indeed, of weather itself, with its unpredictable winds and rains and frosts—removed at once a whole range of problems that plagued all terrestrial enterprises. But to make up for that, of course, the Moon had a few specialities of its own—like the two-hundred-below-zero nights, and the dust that they were fighting now.

The light framework of the raft rested upon a dozen large metal drums, which carried the prominently stenciled words: "Contents Ethyl Alcohol. Please return when empty to No. 3 Dispatching Center,

Copernicus." Their contents now were a very high grade of vacuum; each drum could support a weight of two lunar tons before sinking.

Now the raft was rapidly taking shape. Be sure to have plenty of spare nuts and bolts, Lawrence told himself. He had seen at least six dropped in the dust, which had instantly swallowed them. And there went a wrench. Make an order that all tools *must* be tied to the raft even when in use, however inconvenient that might be.

Fifteen minutes—not bad, considering that the men were working in vacuum and therefore were hampered by their suits. The raft could be extended in any direction as required, but this would be enough to start with. This first section alone could carry over twenty tons, and it would be some time before they unloaded that weight of equipment on the site.

Satisfied with this stage of the project, Lawrence left the Embarkation Building while his assistants were still dismantling the raft. Five minutes later (that was one advantage of Port Roris—you could get anywhere in five minutes), he was in the local engineering depot. What he found there was not quite so satisfactory.

Supported on a couple of trestles was a two-meter-square mock-up of *Selene*'s roof—an exact copy of the real thing, made from the same materials. Only the outer sheet of aluminized fabric that served as a sun shield was missing; it was so thin and flimsy that it would not affect the test.

The experiment was an absurdly simple one, involving only three ingredients: a pointed crowbar, a sledge hammer, and a frustrated engineer, who, despite strenuous efforts, had not yet succeeded in hammering the bar through the roof.

Anyone with a *little* knowledge of lunar conditions would have guessed at once why he had failed. The hammer, obviously, had only a sixth of its terrestrial weight; therefore—equally obviously—it was that much less effective.

The reasoning would have been completely false. One of the hardest things for the layman to understand was the difference between weight and mass, and the inability to do so had led to countless accidents. For weight was an arbitrary characteristic; you could change it by moving from one world to another. On Earth, that hammer would weigh six times as much as it did here; on the sun, it would be almost two hundred times heavier; and in space it would weigh nothing at all.

But in all three places, and indeed throughout the Universe, its mass or inertia would be exactly the same. The effort needed to set it moving at a certain speed, and the impact it would produce when stopped, would be constant through all space and time. On a nearly gravityless asteroid, where it weighed less than a feather, that hammer would pulverize a rock just as effectively as on Earth.

"What's the trouble?" said Lawrence.

"The roof's too springy," explained the engineer, rubbing the sweat from his brow. "The crowbar just bounces back every time it's hit."

"I see. But will that happen when we're using a fifteen-meter pipe, with dust packed all around it? That may absorb the recoil."

"Perhaps—but look at this."

They kneeled beneath the mock-up and inspected the underside of the roof. Chalk lines had been drawn upon it to indicate the position of the electric wiring, which had to be avoided at all costs.

"This Fiberglas is so tough, you can't make a clean hole through it. When it does yield, it splinters and tears. See—it's already begun to star. I'm afraid that if we try this brute-force approach, we'll crack the roof."

"And we can't risk that," Lawrence agreed. "Well, drop the idea. If we can't pile drive, we'll have to bore. Use a drill, screwed on the end of the pipe so it can be detached easily. How are you getting on with the rest of the plumbing?"

"Almost ready—it's all standard equipment. We should be finished in two or three hours."

"I'll be back in two," said Lawrence. He did not add, as some men would have done, "I want it finished by then." His staff was doing its utmost, and one could neither bully nor cajole trained and devoted men into working faster than their maximum. Jobs like this could not be rushed, and the deadline for *Selene*'s oxygen supply was still three days away. In a few hours, if all went well, it would have been pushed into the indefinite future.

Unfortunately, all was going very far from well.

Commodore Hansteen was the first to recognize the slow, insidious danger that was creeping up upon them. He had met it once before, when he had been wearing a faulty space suit on Ganymede—an incident he had no wish to recall, but had never really forgotten.

"Pat," he said quietly, making sure that no one could overhear. "Have you noticed any difficulty in breathing?"

Pat looked startled, then answered, "Yes, now that you mention it. I'd put it down to the heat."

"So did I at first. But I know these symptoms—especially the quick breathing. We're running into carbon-dioxide poisoning."

"But that's ridiculous. We should be all right for another three days—unless something has gone wrong with the air purifiers."

"I'm afraid it has. What system do we use to get rid of the carbon dioxide?"

"Straight chemical absorption. It's a very simple, reliable setup; we've never had any trouble with it before."

"Yes, but it's never had to work under these conditions before. I think the heat may have knocked out the chemicals. Is there any way we can check them?"

Pat shook his head.

"No. The access hatch is on the outside of the hull."

"Sue, my dear," said a tired voice which they hardly recognized as belonging to Mrs. Schuster, "do you have anything to fix a headache?"

"If you do," said another passenger, "I'd like some as well."

Pat and the Commodore looked at each other gravely. The classic symptoms were developing with textbook precision.

"How long would you guess?" said Pat quietly.

"Two or three hours at the most. And it will be at least six before Lawrence and his men can get here."

It was then that Pat knew, without any further argument, that he was genuinely in love with Sue. For his first reaction was not fear for his own safety, but anger and grief that, after having endured so much, but anger and grief that, after having endured so much, she would have to die within sight of rescue.

# Chapter 18

When Tom Lawson woke up in that strange hotel room, he was not even sure *who* he was, still less where he was. The fact that he had some weight was his first reminder that he was no longer on Lagrange—but he was not heavy enough for Earth. Then it was not a dream; he was on the Moon, and he really had been out into that deadly Sea of Thirst.

And he had helped to find *Selene*; twenty-two men and women now had a chance of life, thanks to his skill and science. After all the disappointments and frustrations, his adolescent dreams of glory were about to come true. Now the world would have to make amends to him for its indifference and neglect.

The fact that society had provided him with an education which, a century earlier, only a few men could afford did nothing to alleviate Tom's grudge against it. Such treatment was automatic in this age, when every child was educated to the level that his intelligence and aptitudes permitted. Now that civilization needed all the talent that it could find, merely to maintain itself, any other educational policy would have been suicide. Tom gave no thanks to society for providing the environment in which he had obtained his doctor's degree; it had acted in its own self-interest.

Yet this morning he did not feel quite so bitter about life or so cynical about human beings. Success and recognition are great emollients, and he was on his way to achieving both. But there was more to it than that; he had glimpsed a deeper satisfaction. Out there on Duster Two, when his fears and uncertainties had been about to overwhelm him, he had made contact with another human being, and had worked in successful partnership with a man whose skill and courage he could respect.

It was only a tenuous contact, and, like others in the past, it might lead nowhere. A part of his mind, indeed, hoped that it would, so that he could once again assure himself that all men were selfish, sadistic scoundrels. Tom could no more escape from his early boyhood than Charles Dickens, for all his success and fame, could escape the shadows of the blacking factory that had both metaphorically and literally darkened his youth. But he had made a fresh beginning—though he still had very far to go before he became a fully paid-up member of the human race.

When he had showered and tidied himself, he noticed the message that Spenser had left lying on the table. "Make yourself at home," it said. "I've had to leave in a hurry. Mike Graham is taking over from me—call him at 3443 as soon as you're awake."

I'm hardly likely to call him *before* I'm awake, thought Tom, whose excessively logical mind loved to seize on such looseness of speech. But he obeyed Spenser's request, heroically resisting the impulse to order breakfast first.

When he got through to Mike Graham, he discovered that he had slept through a very hectic six hours in the history of Port Roris, that Spenser had taken off in *Auriga* for the Sea of Thirst—and that the town was full of newsmen from all over the Moon, most of them looking for Dr. Lawson.

"Stay right where you are," said Graham, whose name and voice were both vaguely familiar to Tom; he must have seen him on those rare occasions when he tuned in to lunar telecasts. "I'll be over in five minutes."

"I'm starving," protested Tom.

"Call room service and order anything you like—it's on us, of course—but don't go outside the suite."

Tom did not resent being pushed around in this somewhat cavalier fashion; it meant, after all, that he was now an important piece of property. He was much more annoyed by the fact that, as anyone in Port Roris could have told him, Mike Graham arrived long before room service. It was a hungry astronomer who now faced Mike's miniature telecamera and tried to explain, for the benefit of—as yet—only two hundred million viewers, exactly how he had been able to locate *Selene.*

Thanks to the transformation wrought by hunger and his recent experiences, he made a first-class job of it. A few days ago, had any TV reporter managed to drag Lawson in front of a camera to explain the technique of infrared detection, he would have been swiftly and contemptuously blinded by science. Tom would have given a no-holds-barred lecture full of such terms as quantum efficiency, black-body radiation, and spectral sensitivity that would have convinced his audience that the subject was extremely complex (which was true enough) and wholly impossible for the layman to understand (which was quite false).

But now he carefully and fairly patiently—despite the occasional urgent proddings of his stomach—answered Mike Graham's questions in terms that most of his viewers could understand. To the large section of the astronomical community which Tom had scarred at some time or other, it was a revelation. Up in Lagrange II, Professor Kotelnikov summarized the feelings of all his colleagues when, at the end of the performance, he paid Tom the ultimate compliment. "Quite frankly," he said in tones of incredulous disbelief, "I would never have recognized him."

It was something of a feat to have squeezed seven men into *Selene*'s air lock, but—as Pat had demonstrated—it was the only place where one could hold a private conference. The other passengers doubtless wondered what was happening; they would soon know.

When Hansteen had finished, his listeners looked understandably worried, but not particularly surprised. They were intelligent men, and must have already guessed the truth.

"I'm telling you first," explained the Commodore, "because Captain Harris and I decided you were all levelheaded—and tough enough to give us help if we need it. I hope to God we won't, but there may be trouble when I make my announcement."

"And if there is?" said Harding.

"If anyone makes a fuss, jump on them," answered the Commodore briefly. "But be as casual as you can when we go back into the cabin. Don't look as if you're expecting a fight; that's the best way to start one. Your job is to damp out panic before it spreads."

"Do you think it's fair," said Dr. McKenzie, "not to give an opportunity to—well, send out some last messages?"

"We thought of that, but it would take a long time and would make everyone completely depressed. We want to get this through as quickly as possible. We want to get this through as quickly as possible. The sooner we act, the better our chance."

"Do you really think we have one?" asked Barrett.

"Yes," said Hansteen, "though I'd hate to quote the odds. No more questions? Bryan? Johanson? Right—let's go."

As they marched back into the cabin, and took their places, the remaining passengers looked at them with curiosity and growing alarm. Hansteen did not keep them in suspense.

"I've some grave news," he said, speaking very slowly. "You must all have noticed difficulty in breathing, and several of you have complained about headaches.

"Yes, I'm afraid it's the air. We still have plenty of oxygen—that's not our problem. But we can't get rid of the carbon dioxide we exhale; it's accumulating inside the cabin. Why, we don't know. My guess is that the heat has knocked out the chemical absorbers. But the explanation hardly matters, for there's nothing we can do about it." He had to stop and take several deep breaths before he could continue.

"So we have to face this situation. Your breathing difficulties will get steadily worse; so will your headaches. I won't attempt to fool you. The rescue team can't possibly reach us in under six hours, and we can't wait that long."

There was a stifled gasp from somewhere in the audience. Hansteen avoided looking for its source. A moment later there came a stertorous snore from Mrs. Schuster. At another time it would have been funny, but not now. She was one of the lucky ones; she was already peacefully, if not quietly, unconscious.

The Commodore refilled his lungs. It was tiring to talk for any length of time.

"If I couldn't offer you some hope," he continued, "I would have said nothing. But we do have one chance and we have to take it soon. It's not a very pleasant one, but the alternative is much worse. Miss Wilkins, please hand me the sleep tubes."

There was a deathly silence—not even interrupted by Mrs. Schuster—as the stewardess handed over a small metal box. Hansteen opened it, and took out a white cylinder the size and shape of a cigarette.

"You probably know," he continued, "that all space vehicles are compelled by law to carry these in their medicine chests. They are quite painless, and will knock you out for ten hours. That may mean all the difference between life and death—for man's respiration rate is cut by more than fifty per cent when he's unconscious. So our air will last twice as long as it would otherwise. Long enough, we hope, for Port Roris to reach us.

"Now, it's essential for at least one person to remain awake to keep in touch with the rescue team. And to be on the safe side, we should have two. One of them must be the Captain; I think that goes without argument."

"And I suppose the other should be you?" said an all-too-familiar voice.

"I'm really very sorry for you, Miss Morley," said Commodore Hansteen, without the slightest sign of resentment—for there was no point, now, in making an issue of a matter that had already been settled. "Just to remove any possible misconceptions—"

Before anyone quite realized what had happened, he had pressed the cylinder to his forearm.

"I'll hope to see you all—ten hours from now," he said, very slowly but distinctly, as he walked to the nearest seat. He had barely reached it when he slumped quietly into oblivion.

It's all your show now, Pat told himself as he got to his feet. For a moment he felt like addressing a few well-chosen words to Miss Morley; then he realized that to do so would spoil the dignity of the Commodore's exit.

"I'm the captain of this vessel," he said in a firm, low voice. "And from now on, what I say goes."

"Not with *me*," retorted the indomitable Miss Morley. "I'm a paying passenger and I have my rights. I've not the slightest intention of using one of those things."

The blasted woman seemed unsnubbable. Pat was also compelled to admit that she had guts. He had a brief, nightmare glimpse of the future that her words suggested. Then hours alone with Miss Morley, and no one else to talk to.

He glanced at the five trouble shooters. The nearest to Miss Morley was the Jamaican civil engineer, Robert Bryan. He looked ready and willing to move into action, but Pat still hoped that unpleasantness could be avoided.

"I don't wish to argue about rights," he said, "but if you were to look at the small print on your tickets, you'd discover that, in an emergency, I'm in absolute charge here. In any event, this is for your own good, and your own comfort. I'd much rather be asleep than awake while we wait for the rescue team to get here."

"That goes for me, too," said Professor Jayawardene unexpectedly. "As the Commodore said, it will conserve the air, so it's our only chance. Miss Wilkins, will you give me one of those things?"

The calm logic of this helped to lower the emotional temperature; so did the Professor's smooth, obviously comfortable slide into unconsciousness. Two down and eighteen to go, murmured Pat under his breath.

"Let's waste no more time," he said aloud. "As you can see, these shots are entirely painless. There's a microjet hypodermic inside each cylinder, and you won't even feel a pinprick."

Sue was already handing out the innocent-looking little tubes, and several of the passengers had used them immediately. There went the Schusters (Irving, with a reluctant and touching tenderness, had pressed the tube against the arm of his sleeping wife) and the enigmatic Mr. Radley. That left fifteen. Who would be next?

Now Sue had come to Miss Morley. This is it, thought Pat. If she was *still* determined to make a fuss...

He might have guessed it.

"I thought I made it *quite* clear that I don't want one of these things. Please take it away."

Robert Bryan began to inch forward, but it was the sardonic, English voice of David Barrett that did the trick.

"What *really* worries the good lady, Captain," he said, obviously placing his barb with relish, "is that you may take advantage of her in her helpless condition."

For a few seconds, Miss Morley sat speechless with fury, while her cheeks turned a bright crimson.

"I've never been so insulted in my—" she began.

"Nor have *I*, madam," interjected Pat, completing her demoralization. She looked round the circle of faces—most of them solemn, but several grinning, even at a time like this—and realized that there was only one way out.

As she slumped in her seat, Pat breathed a vast sigh of relief. After that little episode, the rest should be easy.

Then he saw that Mrs. Williams, whose birthday had been celebrated in such Spartan style only a few hours before, was staring in a kind of frozen trance at the cylinder in her hand. The poor woman was obviously terrified, and no one could blame her. In the next seat, her husband had already collapsed; it was a little ungallant, Pat thought, to have gone first and left his wife to fend for herself.

Before he could take any action, Sue had moved forward.

"I'm so sorry, Mrs. Williams, I made a mistake. I gave you an empty one. Perhaps you'll let me have it back...."

The whole thing was done so neatly that it looked like a conjuring trick. Sue took—or seemed to take—the tube from the unresisting fingers, but as she did so she must have jolted it against Mrs. Williams. The lady never knew what had happened; she quietly folded up and joined her husband.

Half the company was unconscious now. On the whole, thought Pat, there had been remarkably little fuss. Commodore Hansteen had been too much of a pessimist; the riot squad had not been necessary, after all.

Then, with a slight sinking feeling, he noticed something that made him change his mind. It looked as if, as usual, the Commodore had known exactly what he was doing. Miss Morley was not going to be the only difficult customer.

It was at least two years since Lawrence had been inside an igloo. There was a time, when he had been a junior engineer out on construction projects, when he had lived in one for weeks on end, and had forgotten what it was like to be surrounded by rigid walls. Since those days, of course, there had been many improvements in design; it was now no particular hardship to live in a home that would fold up into a small trunk.

This was one of the latest models—a Goodyear Mark XX—and it could sustain six men for an indefinite period, as long as they were supplied with power, water, food, and oxygen. The igloo could provide everything else—even entertainment, for it had a built-in microlibrary of books, music, and video. This was no extravagant luxury, though the auditors queried it with great regularity. In space, boredom could be a killer. It might take longer than, say, a leak in an air line, but it could be just as effective, and was sometimes much messier.

Lawrence stooped slightly to enter the air lock. In some of the old models, he remembered, you practically had to go down on hands and knees. He waited for the "pressure equalized" signal, then stepped into the hemispherical main chamber.

It was like being inside a balloon; indeed, that was exactly where he was. He could see only part of the interior, for it had been divided into several compartments by movable screens. (Another modern refinement; in *his* day, the only privacy was that given by the curtain across the toilet.) Overhead, three meters above the floor, were the lights and the air-conditioning grille, suspended from the ceiling by elastic webbing. Against the curved wall stood collapsible metal racks, only partly erected. From the other side of the nearest screen came the sound of a voice reading from an inventory, while every few seconds another interjected, "Check."

Lawrence stepped around the screen and found himself in the dormitory section of the igloo. Like the wall racks, the double bunks had not been fully erected; it was merely necessary to see that all the bits and pieces were in their place, for as soon as the inventory was completed everything would be packed and rushed to the site.

Lawrence did not interrupt the two storemen as they continued their careful stock-taking. This was one of those unexciting but vital jobs—of which there were so many on the Moon—upon which lives could depend. A mistake here could be a sentence of death for someone, sometime in the future.

When the checkers had come to the end of a sheet, Lawrence said, "Is this the largest model you have in stock?"

"The largest that's serviceable" was the answer. "We have a twelve-man Mark Nineteen, but there's a slow leak in the outer envelope that has to be fixed."

"How long will that take?"

"Only a few minutes. But then there's a twelve-hour inflation test before we're allowed to check it out."

This was one of those times when the man who made the rules had to break them.

"We can't wait to make the full test. Put on a double patch and take a leak reading; if it's inside the standard tolerance, get the igloo checked out right away. I'll authorize the clearance."

The risk was trivial, and he might need that big dome in a hurry. Somehow, he had to provide air and shelter for twenty-two men and women out there on the Sea of Thirst. They couldn't all wear space suits from the time they left *Selene* until they were ferried back to Port Roris.

There was a "beep beep" from the communicator behind his left ear. He flicked the switch at his belt and acknowledged the call.

"C.E.E. speaking."

"Message from *Selene*, sir," said a clear, tiny voice. "Very urgent—they're in trouble."

# Chapter 19

Until now, Pat had scarcely noticed the man who was sitting with folded arms in window seat 3D, and had to think twice to remember his name. It was something like Builder—that was it, *Baldur*, Hans Baldur. He had looked like the typical quiet tourist who never gave any trouble.

He was still quiet, but no longer typical—for he was remaining stubbornly conscious. At first sight he appeared to be ignoring everything around him, but the twitching of a cheek muscle betrayed his tenseness.

"What are you waiting for, Mister Baldur?" asked Pat, in the most neutral tone that he could manage. He felt very glad of the moral and physical support ranged behind him; Baldur did not look exceptionally strong, but he was certainly more than Pat's Moon-born muscles could have coped with—if it came to that.

Baldur shook his head, and remained staring out of the window for all the world as if he could see something there besides his own reflection.

"You can't make me take that stuff, and I'm not going to," he said, in heavily accented English.

"I don't want to force you to do anything," answered Pat. "But can't you see it's for your own good—and for the good of everyone else? What possible objection do you have?"

Baldur hesitated and seemed to be struggling for words.

"It's—it's against my principles," he said. "Yes, that's it. My religion won't allow me to take injections."

Pat knew vaguely that there were people with such scruples. Yet he did not for a moment believe that Baldur was one of them. The man was lying. But why?

"Can I make a point?" said a voice behind Pat's back.

"Of course, Mister Harding," he answered, welcoming anything that might break this impasse.

"You say you won't permit any injections, Mister Baldur," continued Harding, in tones that reminded Pat of his cross-examination of Mrs. Schuster. (How long ago *that* seemed!) "But I can tell that you weren't born on the Moon. No one can miss going through Quarantine—so, how you get here without taking the usual shots?"

The question obviously left Baldur extremely agitated.

"That's no business of yours," he snapped.

"Quite true," said Harding pleasantly. "I'm only trying to be helpful." He stepped forward and reached out his left hand. "I don't suppose you'd let me see your Interplanetary Vaccination Certificate?"

That was a damn silly thing to ask, thought Pat. No human eye could read the magnetically inscribed information on an IVC. He wondered if this would occur to Baldur, and if so, what he would do about it.

He had no time to do anything. He was still staring, obviously taken by surprise, at Harding's open palm when Baldur's interrogator moved his other hand so swiftly that Pat never saw exactly what happened. It was like Sue's conjuring trick with Mrs. Williams—but far more spectacular, and also much deadlier. As far as Pat could judge, it involved the side of the hand and the base of the neck—and it was not, he was quite sure, the kind of skill he ever wished to acquire.

"That will hold him for fifteen minutes," said Harding in a matter-of-fact voice, as Baldur crumpled up in his seat. "Can you give me one of those tubes? Thanks." He pressed the cylinder against the unconscious man's arm; there was no sign that it had any additional effect.

The situation, thought Pat, had got somewhat out of his control. He was grateful that Harding had exercised his singular skills, but was not entirely happy about them.

"Now what was all that?" he asked, a little plaintively.

Harding rolled up Baldur's left sleeve, and turned the arm over to reveal the fleshy underside. The skin was covered with literally hundreds of almost invisible pinpricks.

"Know what that is?" he said quietly.

Pat nodded. Some had taken longer to make the trip than others, but by now all the vices of weary old Earth had reached the Moon.

"You can't blame the poor devil for not giving his reasons. He's been conditioned against using the needle. Judging from the state of those scars, he started his cure only a few weeks ago. Now it's psychologically impossible for him to accept an injection. I hope I've not given him a relapse, but that's the least of his worries."

"How did he ever get through Quarantine?"

"Oh, there's a special section for people like this. The doctors don't talk about it, but the customers get temporary deconditioning under hypnosis. There are more of them than you might think; a trip to the Moon's highly recommended as part of the cure. It gets you away from your original environment."

There were quite a few other questions that Pat would have liked to ask Harding, but they had already wasted several minutes. Thank heavens all the remaining passengers had gone under. That last demonstration of judo, or whatever it was, must have encouraged any stragglers.

"You won't need me any more," said Sue, with a small, brave smile. "Good-by, Pat—wake me when it's over."

"I will," he promised, lowering her gently into the space between the seat rows. "Or not at all," he added, when he saw that her eyes were closed.

He remained bending over her for several seconds before he regained enough control to face the others. There were so many things he wanted to tell her, but now the opportunity was gone, perhaps forever.

Swallowing to overcome the dryness in his throat, he turned to the five survivors. There was still one more problem to deal with, and David Barrett summed it up for him.

"Well, Captain," he said. "Don't leave us in suspense. Which of us do you want to keep you company?"

One by one, Pat handed over five of the sleep tubes.

"Thank you for your help," he said. "I know this is a little melodramatic, but it's the neatest way. Only four of those will work."

"I hope mine will," said Barrett, wasting no time. It did. A few seconds later, Harding, Bryan, and Johanson followed the Englishman into oblivion.

"Well," said Dr. McKenzie, "I seem to be odd man out. I'm flattered by your choice—or did you leave it to luck?"

"Before I answer that question," replied Pat, "I'd better let Port Roris know what's happened."

He walked to the radio and gave a brief survey of the situation. There was a shocked silence from the other end. A few minutes later, Chief Engineer Lawrence was on the line.

"You did the best thing, of course," he said, when Pat had repeated his story in more detail. "Even if we hit no snags, we can't possibly reach you in under five hours. Will you be able to hold out until then?"

"The two of us, yes," answered Pat. "We can take turns using the space-suit breathing circuit. It's the passengers I'm worried about."

"The only thing you can do is to check their respiration, and give them a blast of oxygen if they seemed distressed. We'll do our damnedest from this end. Anything more you want to say?"

Pat thought for a few seconds.

"No," he said, a little wearily. "I'll call you again on each quarter-hour. *Selene* out."

He got to his feet—slowly, for the strain and the carbon-dioxide poisoning were now beginning to tell heavily upon him—and said to McKenzie: "Right, Doc—give me a hand with that space suit."

"I'm ashamed of myself. I'd forgotten all about that."

"And I was worried because some of the other passengers might have remembered. They must all have seen it, when they came in through the air lock. It just goes to prove how you can overlook the obvious."

It took them only five minutes to detach the absorbent canisters and the twenty-four-hour oxygen supply from the suit; the whole breathing circuit had been designed for quick release, in case it was ever needed for artificial respiration. Not for the first time, Pat blessed the skill, ingenuity, and foresight that had been lavished on *Selene*. There were some things that had been overlooked, or that might have been done a little better—but not many.

Their lungs aching, the only two men still conscious aboard the cruiser stood staring at each other across the gray metal cylinder that held another day of life. Then, simultaneously, each said: "You go first."

They laughed without much humor at the hackneyed situation, then Pat answered, "I won't argue" and placed the mask over his face.

Like a cool sea breeze after a dusty summer day, like a wind from the mountain pine forests stirring the stagnant air in some deep lowlands valley—so the flow of oxygen seemed to Pat. He took four slow, deep breaths, and exhaled to the fullest extent, to sweep the carbon dioxide out of his lungs, Then, like a pipe of peace, he handed the breathing kit over to McKenzie.

Those four breaths had been enough to invigorate him, and to sweep away the cobwebs that had been gathering in his brain. Perhaps it was partly psychological—could a few cubic centimeters of oxygen have had so profound an effect?—but whatever the explanation, he felt like a new man. Now he could face the five—or more—hours of waiting that lay ahead.

Ten minutes later, he felt another surge of confidence. All the passengers seemed to be breathing as normally as could be expected—very slowly, but steadily. He gave each one a few seconds of oxygen, then called Base again.

"*Selene* here," he said. "Captain Harris reporting. Doctor McKenzie and I both feel quite fit now, and none of the passengers seem distressed. I'll remain listening out, and will call you again on the half-hour."

"Message received. But hold on a minute, several of the news agencies want to speak to you."

"Sorry," Pat answered. "I've given all the information there is, and I've twenty unconscious men and women to look after. *Selene* out."

That was only an excuse, of course, and a feeble one at that; he was not even sure why he had made it. He felt, in a sudden and uncharacteristic burst of rancor: Why, a man can't even die in peace nowadays! Had he known about that waiting camera, only five kilometers away, his reaction might have been even stronger.

"You still haven't answered my question, Captain," said Dr. McKenzie patiently.

"What question? Oh—*that*. No, it wasn't luck. The Commodore and I both thought you'd be the most useful man to have awake. You're a scientist, you spotted the overheating danger before anyone else did, and you kept quiet about it when we asked you to."

"Well, I'll try to live up to your expectations. I certainly feel more alert than I've done for hours. It must be the oxygen we're sniffing. The big question is: How long will it last?"

"Between the two of us, twelve hours. Plenty of time for the skis to get here. But we may have to give most of it to the others, if they show signs of distress. I'm afraid it's going to be a very close thing."

They were both sitting cross-legged on the floor, just beside the pilot's position, with the oxygen bottle between them. Every few minutes they would take turns with the inhaler—but only two breaths at a time. I never imagined, Pat told himself, that I should ever get involved in the number-one cliché of the TV space operas. But it had occurred in real life too often to be funny any more—especially when it was happening to you.

Both Pat and McKenzie—or almost certainly one of them—could survive if they abandoned the other passengers to their fate. Trying to keep these twenty men and women alive, they might also doom themselves.

The situation was one in which logic warred against conscience. But it was nothing new; certainly it was not peculiar to the age of space. It was as old as Mankind, for countless times in the past, lost or isolated groups had faced death through lack of water, food, or warmth. Now it was oxygen that was in short supply, but the principle was just the same.

Some of those groups had left no survivors; others, a handful who would spend the rest of their lives in self-justification. What must George Pollard, late captain of the whaler *Essex*, have thought as he walked the streets of Nantucket, with the taint of cannibalism upon his soul? That was a two-hundred-year-old story of which Pat had never heard; he lived on a world too busy making its own legends to import those of Earth. As far as he was concerned, he had already made his choice, and he knew, without asking, that McKenzie would agree with him. Neither was the sort of man who would fight over the last bubble of oxygen in the tank. But if it *did* come to a fight—

"What are you smiling at?" asked McKenzie.

Pat relaxed. There was something about this burly Australian scientist that he found very reassuring. Hansteen gave him the same impression, but McKenzie was a much younger man. There were some people you knew that you could trust, whom you were certain would never let you down. He had that feeling about McKenzie.

"If you want to know," he said, putting down the oxygen mask, "I was thinking that I wouldn't have much of a chance if you decided to keep the bottle for yourself."

McKenzie looked a little surprised; then he too grinned.

"I thought all you Moon-born were sensitive about that," he said.

"I've never felt that way," Pat answered. "After all, brains are more important than muscles. I can't help it that I was bred in a gravity field a sixth of yours. Anyway, how could you tell I was Moon-born?"

"Well, it's partly your build. You all have that same tall, slender physique. And there's your skin color—the U.V. lamps never seem to give you the same tan as natural sunlight."

"It's certainly tanned *you*," retorted Pat with a grin. "At night, you must be a menace to navigation. Incidentally, how did you get a name like McKenzie?"

Having had little contact with the racial tensions that were not yet wholly extinct on Earth, Pat could make such remarks without embarrassment—indeed, without even realizing that they might cause embarrassment.

"My grandfather had it bestowed on him by a missionary when he was baptized. I'm very doubtful if it has any—ah—genetic significance. To the best of my knowledge, I'm a full-blooded abo."

"Abo?"

"Aboriginal. We were the people occupying Australia before the whites came along. The subsequent events were somewhat depressing."

Pat's knowledge of terrestrial history was vague; like most residents of the Moon, he tended to assume that nothing of great importance had ever happened before 8 November 1967, when the fiftieth anniversary of the Russian Revolution had been so spectacularly celebrated.

"I suppose there was war?"

"You could hardly call it that. We had spears and boommerangs; they had guns. Not to mention T.B. and V.D., which were much more effective. It took us about a hundred and fifty years to get over the impact. It's only in the last century—since about nineteen forty—that our numbers started going up again. Now there are about a hundred thousand of us—*almost* as many as when your ancestors came."

McKenzie delivered this information with an ironic detachment that took any personal sting out of it, but Pat thought that he had better disclaim responsibility for the misdeeds of his terrestrial predecessors.

"Don't blame me for what happened on Earth," he said. "I've never been there, and I never will—I couldn't face that gravity. But I've looked at Australia plenty of times through the telescope. I have some sentimental feeling for the place—my parents took off from Woomera."

"And my ancestors named it; a woomera's a booster stage for spears."

"Are any of your people," asked Pat, choosing his words with care, "still living in primitive conditions? I've heard that's still true, in some parts of Asia."

"The old tribal life's gone. It went very quickly, when the African nations in the U.N. started bullying Australia. Often quite unfairly, I might add—for I'm an Australian first, and an aboriginal second. But I must admit that my white countrymen were often pretty stupid; they must have been, to think that *we* were stupid! Why, 'way into the last century some of them still thought we were Stone Age savages. Our technology was Stone Age, all right—but we weren't."

There seemed nothing incongruous to Pat about this discussion, beneath the surface of the Moon, of a way of life so distant both in space and time. He and McKenzie would have to entertain each other, keep an eye on their twenty unconscious companions, and fight off sleep, for at least five more hours. This was as good a way as any of doing it.

"If your people weren't in the Stone Age, Doc—and just for the sake of argument. I'll grant that *you* aren't—how did the whites get that idea?"

"Sheer stupidity, with the help of a preconceived bias. It's an easy assumption that if a man can't count, write, or speak good English, he must be unintelligent. I can give you a perfect example from my own family. My grandfather—the first McKenzie—lived to see the year two thousand, but he never learned to count beyond ten. And his description of a total eclipse of the Moon was 'Kerosene lamp bilong Jesus Christ he bugger-up finish altogether.'

"Now, I can write down the differential equations of the Moon's orbital motion, but I don't claim to be brighter than Grandfather. If we'd been switched in time, he might have been the better physicist. Our opportunities were different—that's all. Grandfather never had occasion to learn to count; and I never had to raise a family in the desert—which was a highly skilled, full-time job."

"Perhaps," said Pat thoughtfully, "we could do with some of your grandfather's skills here. For that's what we're trying to do now—survive in a desert."

"I suppose you could put it that way, though I don't think that boomerang and fire stick would be much use to us. Maybe we could use some magic—but I'm afraid I don't know any, and I doubt if the tribal gods could make it from Arnhem Land."

"Do you ever feel sorry," asked Pat, "about the breakup of your people's way of life?"

"How could I? I scarcely knew it. I was born in Brisbane, and had learned to run an electronic computer before I ever saw a corroboree—"

"A what?"

"Tribal religious dance—and half the participants in *that* were taking degrees in cultural anthropology. I've no romantic illusions about the simple life and the noble savage. My ancestors were fine people, and I'm not ashamed of them, but geography had trapped them in a dead end. After the struggle for sheer existence, they had no energy left for a civilization. In the long run, it was a good thing that the white settlers arrived, despite their charming habit of selling us poisoned flour when they wanted our land."

"They did *that*?"

"They certainly did. But why are you surprised? That was a good hundred years before Belsen."

Pat thought this over for a few minutes. Then he looked at his watch and said, with a distinct expression of relief: "Time I reported to Base again. Let's have a quick look at the passengers first."

# Chapter 20

There was no time now, Lawrence realized, to worry about inflatable igloos and the other refinements of gracious living in the Sea of Thirst. All that mattered was getting those air pipes down into the cruiser. The engineers and technicians would just have to sweat it out in the suits until the job was finished. Their ordeal would not last for long. If they could not manage inside five or six hours, they could turn round and go home again, and leave *Selene* to the world after which she was named.

In the workshops of Port Roris, unsung and unrecorded miracles of improvisation were now being achieved. A complete air-conditioning plant, with its liquid-oxygen tanks, humidity and carbon-dioxide absorbers, temperature and pressure regulators, had to be dismantled and loaded on to a sledge. So did a small drilling rig, hurled by shuttle rocket from the Geophysics Division at Clavius. So did the specially designed plumbing, which now had to work at the first attempt, for there would be no opportunity for modifications.

Lawrence did not attempt to drive his men; he knew it was unnecessary. He kept in the background, checking the flow of equipment from stores and workshop out to the skis, and trying to think of every snag that could possibly arise. What tools would be needed? Were there enough spares? Was the raft being loaded on to the skis last, so that it could be off-loaded first? Would it be safe to pump oxygen into *Selene* before connecting up the exhaust line? These, and a hundred other details—some trivial, some vital—passed through his mind. Several times he called Pat to ask for technical information, such as the internal pressure and temperature, whether the cabin relief valve had blown off yet (it hadn't; probably it was jammed with dust), and advice on the best spots to drill through the roof. And each time Pat answered with increasing slowness and difficulty.

Despite all attempts to make contact with him, Lawrence resolutely refused to speak to the newsmen now swarming round Port Roris and jamming half the sound and vision circuits between Earth and Moon. He had issued one brief statement explaining the position and what he intended doing about it; the rest was up to the administrative people. It was their job to protect him so that he could get on with his work undisturbed; he had made that quite clear to the Tourist Commissioner, and had hung up before Davis could argue with him.

He had no time, of course, even to glance at the TV coverage himself, though he had heard that Doctor Lawson was rapidly establishing a reputation as a somewhat prickly personality. That, he presumed, was the work of the Interplanet News man into whose hands he had dumped the astronomer; the fellow should be feeling quite happy about it.

The fellow was feeling nothing of the sort. High on the ramparts of the Mountains of Inaccessibility, whose title he had so convincingly refuted, Maurice Spenser was heading swiftly toward that ulcer he had avoided all his working life. He had spent a hundred thousand stollars to get *Auriga* here—and now it looked as if there would be no story after all.

It would all be over before the skis could arrive; the suspense-packed, breath-taking rescue operation that would keep billions glued to their screens was never going to materialize. Few people could have resisted watching twenty-two men and women snatched from death; but no one would want to see an exhumation.

That was Spenser's cold-blooded analysis of the situation from the newscaster's viewpoint, but as a human being he was equally unhappy. It was a terrible thing to sit here on the mountain, only five kilometers away from impending tragedy, yet able to do absolutely nothing to avert it. He felt almost ashamed of every breath he took, knowing that those people down there were suffocating. Time and again he had wondered if there was anything that *Auriga* could do to help (the news value of this did not, of course, escape him), but now he was sure that she could only be a spectator. That implacable Sea ruled out all possibility of aid.

He had covered disasters before, but this time he felt uncommonly like a ghoul.

It was very peaceful now, aboard *Selene*—so peaceful that one had to fight against sleep. How pleasant it would be, thought Pat, if he could join the others, dreaming happily all around him. He envied them, and sometimes felt jealous of them. Then he would take a few draughts from the dwindling store of oxygen, and reality would close in upon him as he recognized his peril.

A single man could never have remained awake, or kept an eye on twenty unconscious men and women, feeding them oxygen whenever they showed signs of respiratory distress. He and McKenzie had acted as mutual watchdogs; several times each had dragged the other back from the verge of sleep. There would have been no difficulty had there been plenty of oxygen, but that one bottle was becoming rapidly exhausted. It was maddening to know that there were still many kilograms of liquid oxygen in the cruiser's main tanks, but there was no way in which they could use it. The automatic system was metering it through the evaporators and into the cabin, where it was at once contaminated by the now almost unbreathable atmosphere.

Pat had never known time to move so slowly. It seemed quite incredible that only four hours had passed since he and McKenzie had been left to guard their sleeping companions. He could have sworn that they had been here for days, talking quietly together, calling Port Roris every fifteen minutes, checking pulses and respiration, and doling out oxygen with a miserly hand.

But nothing lasts forever. Over the radio, from the world which neither man really believed he would ever see again, came the news they had been waiting for.

"We're on the way," said the weary but determined voice of Chief Engineer Lawrence. "You only have to hang on for another hour—we'll be on top of you by then. How are you feeling?"

"Very tired," said Pat slowly. "But we can make it."

"And the passengers?"

"Just the same."

"Right—I'll call you every ten minutes. Leave your receiver on, volume high. This is Med Division's idea—they don't want to risk your falling asleep."

The blare of brass thundered across the face of the Moon, then echoed on past the Earth and out into the far reaches of the solar system. Hector Berlioz could never have dreamed that, two centuries after he had composed it, the soul-stirring rhythm of his "Rakoczy March" would bring hope and strength to men fighting for their lives on another world.

As the music reverberated round the cabin, Pat looked at Dr. McKenzie with a wan smile.

"It may be old-fashioned," he said, "but it's working."

The blood was pounding in his veins, his foot was tapping with the beat of the music. Out of the lunar sky, flashing down from space, had come the tramp of marching armies, the thunder of cavalry across a thousand battlefields, the call of bugles that had once summoned nations to meet their destiny. All gone, long ago, and that was well for the world. But they had left behind them much that was fine and noble—examples of heroism and self-sacrifice, proofs that men could still hold on when their bodies should have passed the limits of physical endurance.

As his lungs labored in the stagnant air, Pat Harris knew that he had need of such inspiration from the past, if he was to survive the endless hour that lay ahead.

Aboard the tiny, cluttered deck of Duster One, Chief Engineer Lawrence heard the same music, and reacted in the same fashion. His little fleet was indeed going into battle, against the enemy that Man would face to the end of time. As he spread across the Universe from planet to planet and sun to sun, the forces of Nature would be arrayed against him in ever new and unexpected ways. Even Earth, after all these aeons, still had many traps for the unwary, and on a world that men had known for only a lifetime, death lurked in a thousand innocent disguises. Whether or not the Sea of Thirst was robbed of its prey, Lawrence was sure of one thing—tomorrow there would be a fresh challenge.

Each ski was towing a single sledge, piled high with equipment which looked heavier and more impressive than it really was; most of the load was merely the empty drums upon which the raft would float. Everything not absolutely essential had been left behind. As soon as Duster One had dumped its cargo, Lawrence would send it straight back to Port Roris for the next load. Then he would be able to maintain a shuttle service between the site and Base, so that if he wanted anything quickly he would never have to wait more than an hour for it. This, of course, was taking the optimistic view; by the time he got to *Selene*, there might be no hurry at all.

As the Port buildings dropped swiftly below the sky line, Lawrence ran through the procedure with his men. He had intended to do a full-dress rehearsal before sailing, but that was another plan that had had to be abandoned through lack of time. The first count-down would be the only one that mattered.

"Jones, Sikorsky, Coleman, Matsui, when we arrive at the marker, you're to unload the drums and lay them out in the right pattern. As soon as that's done, Bruce and Hodges will fix the cross-members. Be very careful not to drop any of the nuts and bolts, and keep all your tools tied to you. If you accidentally fall off, don't panic; you can only sink a few centimeters. I know.

"Sikorsky, Jones, you give a hand with the flooring as soon as the raft framework's fixed. Coleman, Matsui, immediately there's enough working space, start laying out the air pipes and the plumbing. Greenwood, Renaldi, you're in charge of the drilling operation—"

So it went on, point by point. The greatest danger, Lawrence knew was that his men would get in each other's way as they worked in this confined space. A single trifling accident, and the whole effort would be wasted. One of Lawrence's private fears, which had been worrying him ever since they left Port Roris, was that some vital tool had been left behind. And there was an even worse nightmare—that the twenty-two men and women in *Selene* might die within minutes of rescue because the only wrench that could make the final connection had been dropped overboard.

On the Mountains of Inaccessibility, Maurice Spenser was staring through his binoculars and listening to the radio voices calling across the Sea of Thirst. Every ten minutes Lawrence would speak to *Selene*, and each time the pause before the reply would be a little longer. But Harris and McKenzie were still clinging to consciousness, thanks to sheer will power and, presumably, the musical encouragement they were getting from Clavius City.

"What's that psychologist disc jockey pumping into them now?" asked Spenser. On the other side of the control cabin, the ship's Radio Officer turned up the volume, and the Valkyries rode above the Mountains of Inaccessibility.

"I don't believe," grumbled Captain Anson, "that they've played anything later than the nineteenth century."

"Oh yes they have," corrected Jules Braques, as he made some infinitesimal adjustment to his camera. "They did Khachaturan's 'Sabre Dance' just now. That's only a hundred years old."

"Time for Duster One to call again," said the Radio Officer. The cabin became instantly silent.

Right on the second, the dust-ski signal came in. The expedition was now so close that *Auriga* could receive it directly, without benefit of the relay from Lagrange.

"Lawrence calling *Selene*. We'll be over you in ten minutes. Are you O.K.?"

Again that agonizing pause; this time it lasted almost five seconds. Then:

"*Selene* answering. No change here."

That was all. Pat Harris was not wasting his remaining breath.

"Ten minutes," said Spenser. "They should be in sight now. Anything on the screen?"

"Not yet," answered Jules, zooming out to the horizon and panning slowly along its empty arc. There was nothing above it but the black night of space.

The Moon, thought Jules, certainly presented some headaches to the cameraman. Everything was soot or white-wash; there were no nice, soft half tones. And, of course, there was that eternal dilemma of the stars, though that was an aesthetic problem, rather than a technical one.

The public expected to see stars in the lunar sky even during the daytime, because they were there. But the fact was that the human eye could not normally see them; during the day, the eye was so desensitized by the glare that the sky appeared an empty, absolute black. If you wanted to see the stars, you had to look for them through blinkers that cut off all other light; then your pupils would slowly expand, and one by one the stars would come out until they filled the field of view. But as soon as you looked at anything else—*phut*, out they went. The human eye could look at the daylight stars, *or* the daylight landscape; it could never see both at once.

But the TV camera could, if desired, and some directors preferred it to do so. Others argued that this falsified reality. It was one of those problems that had no correct answer. Jules sided with the realists, and kept the star gate circuit switched off unless the studio asked for it.

At any moment, he would have some action for Earth. Already the news networks had taken flashes—general views of the mountains, slow pans across the Sea, close-ups of that lonely marker sticking through the dust. But before long, and perhaps for hours on end, his camera might well be the eyes of several billion people. This feature was either going to be a bust, or the biggest story of the year.

He fingered the talisman in his pocket. Jules Braques, Member of the Society of Motion Picture and Television Engineers, would have been displeased had anyone accused him of carrying a lucky charm. On the other hand, he would have been very hard put to explain why he never brought out his little toy until the story he was covering was safely on the air.

"Here they are!" yelled Spenser, his voice revealing the strain under which he had been laboring. He lowered his binoculars and glanced at the camera. "You're too far off to the right!"

Jules was already panning. On the monitor screen, the geometrical smoothness of the far horizon had been broken at last; two tiny, twinkling stars had appeared on that perfect arc dividing Sea and space. The dust-skis were coming up over the face of the Moon.

Even with the longest focus of the zoom lens, they looked small and distant. That was the way Jules wanted it; he was anxious to give the impression of loneliness, emptiness. He shot a quick glance at the ship's main screen, now tuned to the Interplanet channel. Yes, they were carrying him.

He reached into his pocket, pulled out a small diary, and laid it on top of the camera. He lifted the cover, which locked into position just short of the vertical—and immediately became alive with color and movement. At the same time a faint gnat-sized voice started to tell him that this was a special program of the Interplanet News Service, Channel One Oh Seven—and We Will Now Be Taking You Over to the Moon.

On the tiny screen was the picture he was seeing directly on his monitor. No—not *quite* the same picture. This was the one he had captured two and a half seconds ago; he was looking that far into the past. In those two and a half million microseconds—to change to the time scale of the electronic engineer—this scene had undergone many adventures and transformations. From his camera it had been piped to *Auriga*'s transmitter, and beamed straight up to Lagrange, fifty thousand kilometers overhead. There it had been snatched out of space, boosted a few hundred times, and sped Earthward to be caught by one or another of the satellite relays. Then down through the ionosphere—that last hundred kilometers the hardest of all—to the Interplanet Building, where its adventures really began, as it joined the ceaseless flood of sounds and sights and electrical impulses which informed and amused a substantial fraction of the human race.

And here it was again, after passing through the hands of program directors and special-effects departments and engineering assist-ants—right back where it started, broadcast over the whole of Earthside from the high-power transmitter on Lagrange II, and over the whole of Farside from Lagrange I. To span the single hand's breadth from

Jules's TV camera to his pocket-diary receiver, that image had traveled three quarters of a million kilometers.

He wondered if it was worth the trouble. Men had been wondering that ever since television was invented.

# Chapter 21

Lawrence spotted *Auriga* while he was still fifteen kilometers away; he could scarcely have failed to do so, for she was a conspicuous object, as the sunlight glistened from her plastic and metal.

What the devil's that? he asked himself, and answered the question at once. It was obviously a ship, and he remembered hearing vague rumors that some news network had chartered a flight to the mountains. That was not his business, though at one time he himself had looked into the question of landing equipment there, to cut out this tedious haul across the Sea. Unfortunately, the plan wouldn't work. There was no safe landing point within five hundred meters of Sea leve the ledge that had been so convenient for Spenser was at too great an altitude to be of use.

The Chief Engineer was not sure that he liked the idea of having his every move watched by long-focus lenses up in the hills—not that there was anything he could do about it. He had already vetoed an attempt to put a camera on his ski—to the enormous relief, though Lawrence did not know it, of Interplanet News, and the extreme frustration of the other services. Then he realized that it might well be useful having a ship only a few kilometers away. It would provide an additional information channel, and perhaps they could utilize its services in some other way. It might even provide hospitality until the igloos could be ferried out.

Where was the marker? Surely it should be in sight by now! For an uncomfortable moment Lawrence thought that it had fallen down and disappeared into the dust. That would not stop them finding

*Selene*, of course, but it might delay them five or ten minutes at a time when every second was vital.

He breathed a sigh of relief; he had overlooked the thin shaft against the blazing background of the mountains. His pilot had already spotted their goal and had changed course slightly to head toward it.

The skis coasted to a halt on either side of the marker, and at once erupted into activity. Eight space-suited figures started unshipping roped bundles and large cylindrical drums at a great speed, according to the prearranged plan. Swiftly, the raft began to take shape as its slotted metal framework was bolted into position round the drums, and the light Fiberglas flooring was laid across it.

No construction job in the whole history of the Moon had ever been carried out in such a blaze of publicity, thanks to the watchful eye in the mountains. But once they had started work, the eight men on the skis were totally unconscious of the millions looking over their shoulders. All that mattered to them now was getting that raft in position, and fixing the jigs which would guide the hollow, life-bearing drills down to their target.

Every five minutes, or less, Lawrence spoke to *Selene*, keeping Pat and McKenzie informed of progress. The fact that he was also informing the anxiously waiting world scarcely crossed his mind.

At last, in an incredible twenty minutes, the drill was ready, its first five-meter section poised like a harpoon ready to plunge into the Sea. But this harpoon was designed to bring life, not death.

"We're coming down," said Lawrence. "The first section's much longer."

"You'd better hurry," whispered Pat. "I can't hold out much longer."

He seemed to be moving in a fog; he could not remember a time when it was not there. Apart from the dull ache in his lungs, he was not really uncomfortable—merely incredibly, unbelievably tired. He was now no more than a robot, going about a task whose meaning he had long ago forgotten, if indeed he had ever known it. There was a wrench in his hand; he had taken it out of the tool kit hours ago, knowing that it would be needed. Perhaps it would remind him of what he had to do when the time came.

From a great distance, it seemed, he heard a snatch of conversation that was obviously not intended for him. Someone had forgotten to switch channels.

"We should have fixed it so that the drill could be unscrewed from this end. Suppose he's too weak to do it?"

"We had to take the risk; the extra fittings would have delayed us at least an hour. Give me that—"

Then the circuit went dead; but Pat had heard enough to make him angry—or as angry as a man could be, in his half-stupefied condition. He'd show them—he and his good pal Doctor Mac—Mac what? He could no longer remember the name.

He turned slowly round in his swiveling seat and looked back along the Golgotha-like shambles of the cabin. For a moment he could not find the physicist among the other tumbled bodies; then he saw that he was kneeling beside Mrs. Williams, whose dates of birth and death now looked like being very close together. McKenzie was holding the oxygen mask over her face, quite unaware of the fact that the tell-tale hiss of gas from the cylinder had ceased, and the gauge had long ago reached zero.

"We're almost there," said the radio. "You should hear us hit at any minute."

So soon? thought Pat. But, of course, a heavy tube would slice down through the dust almost as quickly as it could be lowered. He thought he was very clever to deduce this.

Bang! Something had hit the roof. But where?

"I can hear you," he whispered. "You've reached us."

"We know," answered the voice. "We can feel the contract. But you have to do the rest. Can you tell where the drill's touching? Is it in a clear section of the roof, or is it over the wiring? We'll raise and lower it several times, to help you locate it."

Pat felt rather aggrieved at this. It seemed terribly unfair that he should have to decide such a complicated matter.

Knock, knock went the drill against the roof. He couldn't for the life of him (why did that phrase seem so appropriate?) locate the exact position of the sound. Well, they had nothing to lose.

"Go ahead," he murmured. "You're in the clear." He had to repeat it twice before they understood his words.

Instantly—they were quick off the pad up there—the drill started whirring against the outer hull. He could hear the sound very distinctly, more beautiful than any music.

The bit was through the first obstacle in less than a minute. He heard it race, then stop as the motor was cut. Then the operator lowered it the few centimeters to the inner hull, and started it spinning again.

The sound was much louder now, and could be pinpointed exactly. It came, Pat was mildly disconcerted to note, from very close to the main cable conduit, along the center of the roof. If it went through *that...*

Slowly and unsteadily he got to his feet and walked over to the source of the sound. He had just reached it when there was a shower of dust from the ceiling, a sudden spitting of electricity—and the main lights went out.

Luckily, the emergency lighting remained on. It took Pat's eyes several seconds to adapt to the dim red glow. Then he saw that a metal tube was protruding through the roof. It moved slowly downward until it had traveled half a meter into the cabin; and there it stopped.

The radio was talking in the background, saying something that he knew was very important. He tried to make sense of it as he fitted the wrench around the bit head, and tightened the screw adjustment.

"*Don't* undo the bit until we tell you," said that remote voice. "We had no time to fit a nonreturn valve—the pipe's open to vacuum at this end. We'll tell you as soon as we're ready. I repeat, *don't remove the bit until we say so.*"

Pat wished the man would stop bothering him; he knew exactly what to do. If he leaned with all his might on the handle of the wrench—so—the drill head would come off, and he'd be able to breathe again.

Why wasn't it moving? He tried once more.

"My God," said the radio. "Stop that! We're not ready! You'll lose all your air!"

Just a minute, thought Pat, ignoring the distraction. There's something wrong here. A screw can turn *this* way—or *that* way. Suppose I'm tightening it up, when I should be doing the opposite?

This was horribly complicated. He looked at his right hand, then his left; neither seemed to help. (Nor did that silly man shouting on the radio.) Well, he could try the other way and see if that was better.

With great dignity, he performed a complete circuit of the tube, keeping one arm wrapped around it. As he fell on the wrench from the other side, he grabbed it with both hands to keep himself from collapsing. For a moment he rested against it, head bowed.

"Up periscope," he mumbled. Now what on Earth did that mean? He had no idea, but he had heard it somewhere and it seemed appropriate.

He was still puzzling over the matter when the drill head started to unscrew beneath his weight, very easily and smoothly.

Fifteen meters above, Chief Engineer Lawrence and his assistants stood for a moment almost paralyzed with horror. This was something that no one could ever have imagined; they had thought of a hundred other accidents, but not *this*.

"Coleman—Matsui!" snapped Lawrence. "Connect up that oxygen line, for God's sake!"

Even as he shouted at them, he knew that it would be too late. There were two connections still to be made before the oxygen circuit was closed. And, of course, they were screw threads, not quick-release couplings. Just one of those little points that normally wouldn't matter in a thousand years, but now made all the difference between life and death.

Like Samson at the mill, Pat trudged round and round the pipe, pushing the handle of the wrench before him. It offered no opposition, even in his present feeble state. By now the bit had unscrewed more than two centimeters; surely it would fall off in a few more seconds.

Ah—almost there. He could hear a faint hissing, that grew steadily as the bit unwound. That would be oxygen rushing into the cabin, of course. In a few seconds, he would be able to breathe again, and all his troubles would be over.

The hiss had deepened to an ominous whistling, and for the first time Pat began to wonder if he was doing precisely the right thing. He stopped, looked thoughtfully at the wrench, and scratched his head. His slow mental processes could find no fault with his action; if the radio had given him orders then, he might have obeyed, but it had abandoned the attempt.

Well, back to work. (It was years since he'd had a hangover like this.) He started to push on the wrench once more—and fell flat on his face as the drill came loose.

In the same instant, the cabin reverberated with a screaming roar, and a gale started all the loose papers fluttering like autumn leaves. A mist of condensation formed as the air, chilled by its sudden expansion, dumped its moisture in a thick fog. When Pat turned over on his back, conscious at last of what had happened, he was almost blinded by the mist around him.

That scream meant only one thing to a trained spaceman, and his automatic reactions had taken over now. He must find some flat object that could be slid over the hole; anything would do, if it was fairly strong.

He looked wildly around him in the crimson fog, which was already thinning as it was sucked into space. The noise was deafening; it seemed incredible that so small a pipe could make such a scream.

Staggering over his unconscious companions, clawing his way from seat to seat, he had almost abandoned hope when he saw the answer to his prayer. There lay a thick volume, open face downward on the floor where it had been dropped. Not the right way to treat books, he thought, but he was glad that someone had been careless. He might never have seen it otherwise.

When he reached the shrieking orifice that was sucking the life out of the cruiser, the book was literally torn from his hands and flattened against the end of the pipe. The sound died instantly, as did the gale. For a moment Pat stood swaying like a drunken man; then he quickly folded at the knees and pitched to the floor.

# Chapter 22

The really unforgettable moments of TV are those which no one expects, and for which neither cameras nor commentators are prepared. For the last thirty minutes, the raft had been the site of feverish but controlled activity—then, without warning, it had erupted.

Impossible though that was, it seemed as if a geyser had spouted from the Sea of Thirst. Automatically, Jules tracked that ascending column of mist as it drove toward the stars (they were visible now; the director had asked for them). As it rose, it expanded like some strange, attenuated plant—or like a thinner, feebler version of the mushroom cloud that had terrorized two generations of mankind.

It lasted only for a few seconds, but in that time it held unknown millions frozen in front of their screens, wondering how a waterspout could possibly have reared itself from this arid sea. Then it collapsed and died, still in the same uncanny silence in which it had been born.

To the men on the raft that geyser of moisture-laden air was equally silent, but they felt its vibration as they struggled to get the last coupling into place. They would have managed, sooner or later, even if Pat had not cut off the flow, for the forces involved were quite trivial. But their "later" might have been too late. Perhaps, indeed, it already was....

"Calling *Selene*! Calling *Selene*!" shouted Lawrence. "Can you hear me?"

There was no reply. The cruiser's transmitter was not operating; he could not even hear the sounds her mike should be picking up inside the cabin.

"Connections ready, sir," said Coleman. "Shall I turn on the oxygen generator?"

It won't do any good, thought Lawrence, if Harris has managed to screw that damned bit back into place. I can only hope he's merely stuffed something into the end of the tube, and that we can blow it out.

"O.K." he said. "Let her go—all the pressure you can get."

With a sudden bang, the battered copy of *The Orange and the Apple* was blasted away from the pipe to which it had been vacuum-clamped. Out of the open oriflce gushed an inverted fountain of gas, so cold that its outline was visible in ghostly swirls of condensing water vapor.

For several minutes the oxygen geyser roared without producing any effect. Then Pat Harris slowly stirred, tried to get up, and was knocked back to the ground by the concentrated jet. It was not a particularly powerful jet, but it was stronger than he was in his present state.

He lay with the icy blast playing across his face, enjoying its refreshing coolness almost as much as its breathability. In a few seconds he was completely alert—though he had a splitting head-ache—and aware of all that had happened in the last half-hour.

He nearly fainted again when he remembered unscrewing the bit, and fighting that gusher of escaping air. But this was no time to worry about past mistakes; all that mattered now was that he was alive—and with any luck would stay so.

He picked up the still-unconscious McKenzie as though he were a limp doll, and laid him beneath the oxygen blast. Its force was much weaker now, as the pressure inside the cruiser rose back to normal; in a few more minutes it would be only a gentle zephyr.

The scientist revived almost at once, and looked vaguely round him.

"Where am I?" he said, not very originally. "Oh—they got through to us. Thank God I can breathe again. What's happened to the lights?"

"Don't worry about that—I'll soon fix them. We must get everyone under this jet as quickly as we can, and flush some oxygen into their lungs. Can you give artificial respiration?"

"I've never tried."

"It's very simple. Wait until I find the medicine chest."

When Pat had collected the resuscitator, he demonstrated on the nearest subject, who happened to be Irving Schuster.

"Push the tongue out of the way and slip the tube down the throat. Now squeeze this bulb—slowly. Keep up a natural breathing rhythm. Got the idea?"

"Yes, but how long shall I do it?"

"Five or six deep breaths should be enough, I'd guess. We're not trying to revive them, after all—we just want to get the stale air out of their lungs. You take the front half of the cabin; I'll do the rear."

"But there's only one resuscitator."

Pat grinned, without much humor.

"It's not necessary," he answered, bending over his next patient.

"Oh," said McKenzie. "I'd forgotten *that*."

It was hardly chance that Pat had headed straight to Sue, and was now blowing into her lips in the ancient—and highly effective—mouth-to-mouth method. But to do him justice, he wasted no time on her when he found that she was breathing normally.

He was just starting on his third subject when the radio gave another despairing call.

"Hello, *Selene*, is there anyone there?"

Pat took a few seconds off to grab the mike.

"Harris calling. We're O.K. We're applying artificial respiration to the passengers. No time to say more—we'll call you later. I'll remain on receive. Tell us what's happening."

"Thank God you're O.K.—we'd given you up. You gave us a hell of a fright when you unscrewed that drill."

Listening to the Chief Engineer's voice while he blew into the peacefully sleeping Mr. Radley, Pat had no wish to be reminded of that incident. He knew that, whatever happened, he would never live it down. Yet it had probably been for the best; most of the bad air had been siphoned out of *Selene* in that hectic minute or so of decompression. It might even have lasted longer than that, for it would have taken two or three minutes for a cabin of this size to lose much of its air, through a tube only four centimeters in diameter.

"Now listen," continued Lawrence, "because you've been overheating badly, we're letting you have your oxygen just as cold as we think it's safe. Call us back if it gets too chilly, or too dry. In five or ten minutes we'll be sinking the second pipe to you, so that we'll have a complete circuit and can take over your entire air-conditioning load. We'll aim this pipe for the rear of the cabin, just as soon as we've towed the raft a few meters. We're moving now. Call you back in a minute."

Pat and the Doctor did not relax until they had pumped the foul air from the lungs of all their unconscious companions. Then, very tired, yet feeling the calm joy of men who see some great ordeal approach its triumphant end, they slumped to the floor and waited for the second drill to come through the roof.

Ten minutes later, they heard it bang against the outer hull, just forward of the air lock. When Lawrence called to check its position, Pat confirmed that this time it was clear of obstructions. "And don't worry," he added. "I won't touch that drill until you tell me."

It was now so cold that he and McKenzie had put on their outer clothing once more, and had draped blankets over the sleeping passengers. But Pat did not call a halt; as long as they were not in actual distress, the colder the better. They were driving back the deadly heat that had almost cooked them—and, even more important, their own air purifiers would probably start working again, now that the temperature had dropped so drastically.

When that second pipe came through the roof, they would be doubly safeguarded. The men on the raft could keep them supplied with air indefinitely, and they would also have several hours—perhaps a day's—reserve of their own. They might still have a long wait here beneath the dust, but the suspense was over.

Unless, of course, the Moon arranged some fresh surprises.

"Well, Mr. Spenser," said Captain Anson, "looks as if you've got your story."

Spenser felt almost as exhausted, after the strain of the last hour, as any of the men out on the raft, two kilometers below him. He could see them there on the monitor, on medium close-up. They were obviously relaxing—as well as men could relax when they were wearing space suits.

Five of them, indeed, appeared to be trying to get some sleep, and were tackling the problem in a startling but sensible manner. They were lying beside the raft, half submerged in the dust, rather like floating rubber dolls. It had not occurred to Spenser that a space suit was much too buoyant to sink in this stuff. By getting off the raft, the five technicians were not only providing themselves with an incomparably luxurious couch; they were leaving a greatly enlarged working space for their companions.

The three remaining members of the team were moving slowly around, adjusting and checking equipment—especially the rectangular bulk of the air purifier and the big lox spheres coupled to it. At maximum optical and electronic zoom, the camera could get within ten meters of all this gear—almost close enough to read the gauges. Even at medium magnification, it was easy to spot the two pipes going over the side and leading down to the invisible *Selene*.

This relaxed and peaceful scene made a startling contrast with that of an hour ago. But there was nothing more to be done here until the next batch of equipment arrived. Both of the skis had gone back to Port Roris; that was where all the activity would now be taking place, as the engineering staff tested and assembled the gear which, they hoped, would enable them to reach *Selene*. It would be another day at least before that was ready. Meanwhile, barring accidents, the Sea of Thirst would continue to bask undisturbed in the morning sun, and the camera would have no new scenes to throw across space.

From one and a half light-seconds away, the voice of the program director back on Earth spoke inside *Auriga*'s control cabin.

"Nice work, Maurice, Jules. We'll keep taping the picture in case anything breaks at your end, but we don't expect to carry it live until the oh six hundred news spot."

"How's it holding up?"

"Supernova rating. And there's a new angle—every crackpot inventor who ever tried to patent a new paper clip is crawling out of the woodwork with ideas. We're rounding up a batch of them at six fifteen. It should be good fun."

"Who knows—perhaps one of them may have something."

"Maybe, but I doubt it. The sensible ones won't come near our program when they see the treatment the others are getting."

"Why—what are you doing to them?"

"Their ideas are being analyzed by your scientist friend Doctor Lawson. We've had a dummy run with him; he skins them alive."

"Not *my* friend," protested Spenser. "I've only met him twice. The first time I got ten words out of him; the second time, he fell asleep on me."

"Well, he's developed since then, believe it or not. You'll see him in—oh, forty-five minutes."

"I can wait. Anyway, I'm only interested in what Lawrence plans to do. Has he made a statement? You should be able to get at him, now the pressure's off."

"He's still furiously busy and won't talk. We don't think the Engineering Department has made up its mind yet, anyhow. They're testing all sorts of gadgets at Port Roris, and ferrying in equipment from all over the Moon. We'll keep you in touch if we learn anything new."

It was a paradoxical fact, which Spencer took completely for granted, that when you were covering a story like this you often had no idea of the big picture. Even when you were in the center of things, as he was now. He had started the ball rolling, but now he was no longer in control. It was true that he and Jules were providing the most important video coverage—or would be, when the action shifted back here—but the pattern was being shaped at the news centers on Earth and in Clavius City. He almost wished he could leave Jules and hurry back to headquarters.

That was impossible, of course, and even if he did so, he would soon regret it. For this was not only the biggest scoop of his career; it was, he suspected, the last time he would ever be able to cover a story out in the field. By his own success, he would have doomed himself irrevocably to an office chair—or, at best, a comfortable little viewing booth behind the banked monitor screens at Clavis Central.

# Chapter 23

It was still very quiet aboard *Selene*, but the quietness was now that of sleep, not of death. Before long, all these people would be waking, to greet a day few of them could really have expected to see.

Pat Harris was standing somewhat precariously on the back of a seat, mending the break in the overhead lighting circuit. It was fortunate that the drill had not been five millimeters to the left; then it would have taken out the radio as well, and the job would have been much worse.

"Throw in number-three circuit break, Doc," he called, winding up his insulating tape. "We should be in business now."

The main lights came on, blindingly brilliant after the crimson gloom. At the same time, there was a sudden, explosive sound, so unexpected and alarming that it shocked Pat off his unstable perch.

Before he reached the floor, he identified it. It was a sneeze.

The passengers were starting to waken, and he had, perhaps, slightly overdone the refrigeration, for the cabin was now extremely cold.

He wondered who would be the first to return to consciousness. Sue, he hoped, because then they would be able to talk together without interruption, at least for a little while. After what they had been through together, he did not regard Duncan McKenzie's presence as my interference—though perhaps Sue could hardly be expected to see it that way.

Beneath the covering of blankets, the first figure was stirring. Pat hurried forward to give assistance; then he paused, and said under his breath: "Oh, *no*!"

Well, you couldn't win all the time, and a captain had to do his duty, come what may. He bent over the scrawny figure that was struggling to rise, and said solicitously: "How do you feel, Miss Morley?"

To have become a TV property was at once the best and the worst thing that could have happened to Dr. Lawson. It had built up his self-confidence, by convincing him that the world which he had always affected to despise was really interested in his special knowledge and abilities. (He did not realize how quickly he might be dropped again, as soon as the *Selene* incident was finished.) It had given him an outlet for expressing his genuine devotion to astronomy, somewhat stultified by living too long in the exclusive society of astronomers. And it was also earning him satisfactory quantities of money.

But the program with which he was now involved might almost have been designed to confirm his old view that the men who weren't brutes were mostly fools. This, however, was hardly the fault of Interplanet News, which could not resist a feature that was a perfect fill-in for the long periods when nothing would be happening out at the raft.

The fact that Lawson was on the Moon and his victims were on Earth presented only a minor technical problem, which the TV technicians had solved long ago. The program could not go out live; it had to be taped beforehand, and those annoying two-and-a-half second pauses while the radio waves flashed from planet to satellite and back again had to be sliced out. They would upset the performers—nothing could be done about *that*—but by the time a skilled editor had anachronized the tape, the listener would be unable to tell that he was hearing a discussion that spanned almost four hundred thousand kilometers.

Chief Engineer Lawrence heard the program as he lay flat on his back in the Sea of Thirst, staring up into the empty sky. It was the first chance of resting he had had for more hours than he could remember, but his mind was too active to let him sleep. In any event, he had never acquired the knack of sleeping in a suit, and saw no need to learn it now, for the first of the igloos was already on the way from Port Roris. When that arrived, he would be able to live in well-earned, and much-needed, comfort.

Despite all the claims of the manufacturers, no one can function efficiently in a space suit for more than twenty-four hours, for several obvious reasons, and several that are not so obvious. There is, for example, that baffling complaint known as spaceman's itch, affecting the small of the back—or even less accessible spots—after a day's incarceration in a suit. The doctors claim that it is purely psychological, and several heroic space medicos have worn suits for a week or more to prove it. The demonstration has done nothing to affect the incidence of the disease.

The mythology of space suits is a vast, complex, and frequently ribald subject, with a nomenclature all of its own. No one is quite sure why one famous model of the 1970's was known as the Iron Maiden, but any astronaut will gladly explain why 2010's Mark XIV was called the Chamber of Horrors. There seems little truth, however, in the theory that it was designed by a sadistic female engineer, determined to inflict a diabolical revenge upon the opposite sex.

But Lawrence was reasonably at ease in his model, as he listened to these enthusiastic amateurs put forward their ideas. It was just possible—though very unlikely—that one of these uninhibited thinkers might come up with an idea that could be of practical use. He had seen it happen before, and was prepared to listen to suggestions rather more patiently than Dr. Lawson—who, it was obvious, would never learn to suffer fools gladly.

He had just demolished an amateur engineer from Sicily, who wanted to blow the dust away by means of strategically placed air jets. The scheme was typical of those put forward; even where there was no fundamental scientific flaw, most of these ideas fell to pieces when examined quantitatively. You *could* blow the dust away—if you had an unlimited supply of air. While the voluble flow of Italian-English was proceeding, Lawson had been doing some rapid calculations. "I estimate, Signor Gusalli," he said, "that you would need at least five tons of air a minute to keep open a hole large enough to be useful. It would be quite impossible to ship such quantities out to the site."

"Ah, but you could collect the air and use it over and over again!"

"Thank *you*, Signor Gusalli," cut in the firm voice of the master of ceremonies. "Now we have Mr. Robertson from London, Ontario. What's your plan, Mr. Robertson?"

"I suggest freezing."

"Just a minute," protested Lawson. "How can you freeze dust?"

"First I'd saturate it with water. Next I'd sink cooling pipes and turn the whole mass into ice. That would hold the dust in place, and then it would be easy to drill through it."

"It's an interesting idea," admitted Lawson, rather reluctantly. "At least it's not as crazy as some that we've had. But the amount of water needed would be impossibly large. Remember, the cruiser is fifteen meters down—"

"What's that in feet?" said the Canadian, in a tone of voice that made it clear that he was one of the hard-core antimetric school.

"Fifty feet—as I'm sure you know perfectly well. Now you'd have to deal with a column at least a meter across—yard, to you—so that would involve—ah—approximately fifteen times ten squared times ten to the fourth cubic centimeters, which gives—why, of course, fifteen tons of water. But this assumes no wastage at all; you'd really need several times as much as this. It might come to as much as a hundred tons. And how much do you think all the freezing gear would weigh?"

Lawrence was quite impressed. Unlike many scientists he had known, Lawson had a firm grasp of practical realities, and was also a rapid calculator. Usually when an astronomer or a physicist did a quick computation, his first attempt was out by a factor of anything from ten to a hundred. As far as Lawrence could judge, Lawson was always right the first time.

The Canadian refrigeration enthusiast was still putting up a fight when he was dragged off the program, to be replaced by an African gentleman who wanted to use the opposite technique—heat. He planned to use a huge concave mirror, focusing sunlight on the dust and fusing it into an immobile mass.

It was obvious that Lawson was keeping his temper only with the utmost difficulty; the solar-furnace advocate was one of those stubborn, self-taught "experts" who refused to admit that he could possibly have made an error in his calculations. The argument was getting really violent when a voice from much closer at hand cut across the program.

"The skis are coming, Mister Lawrence."

Lawrence rolled into a sitting position and climbed aboard the raft. If anything was already in sight, that meant it was practically on top of him. Yes, there was Duster One—and also Duster Three, which had made a difficult and expensive trip from the Lake of Drought, the Sea's smaller equivalent on Farside. That journey was a saga in itself, which would remain forever unknown except to the handful of men involved.

Each ski was towing two sledges, piled high with equipment. As they drew alongside the raft, the first item to be unloaded was the large packing case containing the igloo. It was always fascinating to watch one being inflated, and Lawrence had never anticipated the spectacle more eagerly. (Yes, he definitely had spaceman's itch.) The process was completely automatic; one broke a seal, turned two separate levers—as a safeguard against the disastrous possibility of accidental triggering—and then waited.

Lawrence did not have to wait for long. The sides of the box fell flat, revealing a tightly packed, convoluted mass of silvery fabric. It stirred and struggled like some living creature. Lawrence had once seen a moth emerging from the chrysalis, with its wings still crumpled, and the two processes bore an uncanny similarity. The insect, however, had taken an hour to reach its full size and splendor, but the igloo took only three minutes.

As the air generator pumped an atmosphere into the flaccid envelope, it expanded and stiffened in sudden jerks, followed by slow periods of consolidation. Now it was a meter high, and was spreading outward rather than upward. When it had reached the limits of its extension, it started to go upward again, and the air lock popped away from the main dome. The whole operation, one felt, should be accompanied by laborious wheezings and puffings; it seemed quite wrong that it was happening in utter silence.

Now the structure had nearly reached its final dimensions, and it was obvious that "igloo" was the only possible name for it. Though they had been designed to provide protection against a very different—though almost equally hostile—environment, the snow houses of the Eskimos had been of exactly the same shape. The technical problem had been similar; so was the solution.

It took considerably longer to install the fittings than to inflate the igloo, for all the equipment—bunks, chairs, tables, cupboards, electronic gear—had to be carried in through the air lock. Some of the larger items barely made it, having been designed with only centimeters to spare. But at last there was a radio call from inside the dome. "We're open for business!" is said. "Come on in!"

Lawrence wasted no time in accepting the invitation. He began to undo the fittings of his suit while he was still in the outer section of the two-stage air lock, and had the helmet off as soon as he could hear voices from inside the dome, reaching him through the thickening atmosphere.

It was wonderful to be a free man again, to be able to wriggle, scratch, move without encumbrance, talk to your fellows face to face. The coffin-sized shower removed the stink of the space suit and made him feel fit for human society once more. Then he put on a pair of shorts—all that one ever wore in an igloo—and sat down to a conference with his assistants.

Most of the material he had ordered had come in this consignment; the rest would be arriving on Duster Two in the course of the next few hours. As he checked the supply lists, he felt himself much more the master of the situation. Oxygen was assured—barring catastrophe. Water had been getting short down there; well, he could supply that easily enough. Food was a little more difficult, though it was merely a matter of packing. Central Catering had already supplied samples of chocolate, compressed meat, cheese, and even elongated French rolls—all packed into cylinders three centimeters wide. Presently he would shoot them down the air pipes, and give morale in *Selene* a big boost.

But this was less important than the recommendations of his brains trust, enbodied in a dozen blueprints and a terse six-page memorandum. Lawrence read it extremely carefully, nodding agreement from time to time. He had already come to the same general conclusions, and he could see no way of escaping from them.

Whatever happened to passengers, *Selene* had made her last voyage.

# Chapter 24

The gale that had swept through *Selene* seemed to have carried away with it more than the stagnant air. When he looked back on their first days beneath the dust, Commodore Hansteen realized that there had often been a hectic, even hysterical mood aboard, after the initial shock had worn off. Trying to keep up their spirits, they had sometimes gone too far in the direction of false gaiety and childish humor.

Now that was all past, and it was easy to see why. The fact that a rescue team was at work only a few meters away was part of the explanation, but only part of it. The spirit of tranquillity that they now shared came from their encounter with death; after that, nothing could be quite the same again. The petty dross of selfishness and cowardice had been burned out of them.

No one knew this better than Hansteen. He had watched it happen many times before, whenever a ship's company faced peril in the far reaches of the solar system. Though he was not philosophically inclined, he had had plenty of time to think in space. He had some-times wondered if the real reason why men sought danger was that only thus could they find the companionship and solidarity which they unconsciously craved.

He would be sorry to say good-by to all those people—yes, even to Miss Morley, who was now as agreeable and considerate as her tem-perament would allow. The fact that he could think that far ahead was the measure of his confidence; one could never be certain, of course, but the situation now seemed completely under control. No one knew exactly how Chief Engineer Lawrence intended to get them out, but that problem was now merely a choice between alternative methods. From now on, their imprisonment was an inconvenience, not a danger.

It was not even a hardship, since those food cylinders had started popping down the air tubes. Though there had never been any risk of starvation, the diet had grown extremely monotonous, and water had been rationed for some time. Now, several hundred liters had been pumped down, to refill the almost empty tanks.

It was strange that Commodore Hansteen, who usually thought of everything, never asked himself the simple question "Whatever happened to all the water we started with?" Though he had more immediate problems on his mind, the sight of that extra mass being taken aboard should have set him worrying. But it never did, until it was much too late.

Pat Harris and Chief Engineer Lawrence were equally to blame for the oversight. It was the one flaw in a beautifully executed plan. And one flaw, of course, was all that was needed.

The Engineering Division of Earthside was still working swiftly, but no longer in a desperate race against the clock. There was time now to construct mock-ups of the cruiser, to sink them in the Sea off Port Roris, and to try various ways of entering them. Advice, sensible and otherwise, was still pouring in, but no one took any notice of it. The approach had been decided, and would not be modified now, unless it ran into unexpected obstacles.

Twenty-four hours after the igloo had been set up, all the special gear had been manufactured and shipped out to the site. It was a record that Lawrence hoped he would never have to break, and he was very proud of the men who had made it possible. The Engineering Division seldom got the credit it deserved: like the air, everyone took it for granted, forgetting that the engineers supplied that air.

Now that he was ready to go into action, Lawrence was quite willing to start talking, and Maurice Spenser was more than willing to accommodate him. This was the moment Spenser had been waiting for.

As far as he could remember, it was also the first time that there had ever been a TV interview with camera and subject five kilometers apart. At this fantastic magnification the image was a little fuzzy, of course, and the slightest vibration in *Auriga*'s cabin set it dancing on the screen. For this reason, everyone aboard the ship was motionless, and all nonessential machinery had been switched off.

Chief Engineer Lawrence was standing on the edge of the raft, his space-suited figure braced against the small crane that had been swung over the side. Hanging from the jib was a large concrete cylinder, open at both ends—the first section of the tube that was now being lowered into the dust.

"After a lot of thought," said Lawrence for the benefit of that distant camera, but, above all, for the benefit of the men and women fifteen meters beneath him, "we've decided that this is the best way to tackle the problem. This cylinder is called a caisson"—he pronounced it "kasoon"—"and it will sink easily under its own weight. The sharp lower edge will cut through the dust like a knife through butter.

"We have enough sections to reach the cruiser. When we've made contact, and the tube is sealed at the bottom—its pressure against the roof will ensure that—we'll start scooping out the dust. As soon as that's done, we'll have an open shaft, like a small well, right down to *Selene*.

"That will be half the battle, but only half. Then we'll have to connect the shaft to one of our pressurized igloos, so that when we cut through the cruiser's roof there's no loss of air. But I think—I hope—that these are fairly straightforward problems."

He paused for a minute, wondering if he should touch on any of the other details that made this operation so much trickier than it looked. Then he decided not to; those who understood could see with their own eyes, and the others would not be interested, or would think he was boasting. This blaze of publicity (about half a billion people were watching, so the Tourist Commissioner had reported) did not worry him so long as things went well. But if they did not...

He raised his arm and signaled to the crane operator.

"Lower away!"

Slowly, the cylinder settled into the dust until its full fourmeter length had vanished, except for a narrow ring just protruding above the surface. It had gone down smoothly and easily. Lawrence hoped that the remaining sections would be equally obliging.

One of the engineers was carefully going along the rim of the caisson with a spirit level, to check that it was sinking vertically. Presently he gave the thumbs-up signal, which Lawrence acknowledged in the same manner. There had been a time when, like any regular spacehog, he could carry out an extended and fairly technical conversation by sign-language alone. This was an essential skill of the trade, for radio sometimes failed and there were occasions when one did not wish to clutter up the limited number of channels available.

"Ready for Number Two!" he said.

This would be tricky. The first section had to be held rigid while the second was bolted to it without altering the alignment. One really needed two cranes for this job, but a framework of I-beams, supported a few centimeters above the surface of the dust, could carry the load when the crane was otherwise engaged.

No mistakes now, for God's sake! he breathed silently. Number-two section swung off the sledge that had brought it from Port Roris, and three of the technicians manhandled it into the vertical. This was the sort of job where the distinction between weight and mass was vital. That swinging cylinder weighed relatively little, but its momentum was the same as it would be on Earth, and it could pulp a man if it managed to trap him on one of those sluggish oscillations. And that was something else peculiar to the Moon—the slow-motion movement of this suspended mass. In this gravity, a pendulum took two-and-a-half times as long to complete its cycle as it would on Earth. This was something that never looked quite right, except to a man who had been born here.

Now the second section was upended and mated to the first one. They were clamped together, and once again Lawrence gave the order to lower away.

The resistance of the dust was increasing, but the caisson continued to sink smoothly under its own weight.

"Eight meters gone," said Lawrence. "That means we're just past the halfway mark. Number-three section coming up."

After this, there would only be one more, though Lawrence had provided a spare section, just in case. He had a hearty respect for the Sea's ability to swallow equipment. So far, only a few nuts and bolts had been lost, but if that piece of caisson slipped from the hook, it would be gone in a flash. Though it might not sink far, especially if it hit the dust broadside on, it would be effectively out of reach even if it was only a couple of meters down. They had no time to waste salvaging their own salvage gear.

There went number three, its last section moving with almost imperceptible slowness. But it was still moving; in a few minutes, with any luck at all, they would be knocking on the cruiser's roof.

"Twelve meters down," said Lawrence. "We're only three meters above you now, *Selene*. You should be able to hear us at any minute."

Indeed they could, and the sound was wonderfully reassuring. More than ten minutes ago Hansteen had noticed the vibration of the oxygen inlet pipe as the caisson scraped against it. You could tell when it stopped, and when it started moving again.

There was that vibration once more, accompanied this time by a delicate shower of dust from the roof. The two air pipes had now been drawn up so that about twenty centimeters of their lengths projected through the ceiling, and the quick-drying cement which was part of the emergency kit of all space vehicles had been smoothed around their points of entry. It seemed to be working loose, but that impalpable rain of dust was far too slight to cause alarm. Nevertheless, Hansteen thought that he had better mention it to the skipper, who might not have noticed.

"Funny," said Pat, looking up at the projecting pipe. "That cement should hold, even if the pipe is vibrating."

He climbed up on a seat, and examined the air pipe more closely. For a moment he said nothing; then he stepped down, looking puzzled and annoyed—and more than a little worried.

"What's the trouble?" Hansteen asked quietly. He knew Pat well enough now to read his face like an open book.

"That pipe's pulling up through the roof," he said. "Someone up on the raft's being mighty careless. It's shortened by at least a centimeter, since I fixed that plaster." Then Pat stopped, suddenly aghast.

"My God," he whispere d, "suppose it's our own fault, *suppose we're still sinking.*"

"What if we are?" said the Commodore, quite calmly. "You'd expect the dust to continue settling beneath our weight. That doesn't mean we're in danger. Judging by that pipe, we've gone down one centimeter in twenty-four hours. They can always give us some more tubing if we need it."

Pat laughed a little shamefacedly.

"Of course—that's the answer. I should have thought of it before. We've probably been sinking slowly all the time, but this is the first chance we've had to prove it. Still, I'd better report to Mr. Lawrence—it may affect his calculations."

Pat started to walk toward the front of the cabin; but he never made it.

# Chapter 25

It had taken Nature a million years to set the trap that had snared *Selene* and dragged her down into the Sea of Thirst. The second time, she was caught in a trap that she had made herself.

Because her designers had no need to watch every gram of excess weight, or plan for journeys lasting more than a few hours, they had never equipped *Selene* with those ingenious but unadvertised arrangements whereby spaceships recycle all their water supply. She did not have to conserve her resources in the miserly manner of deep-space vehicles; the small amount of water normally used and produced aboard, she simply dumped.

Over the past five days, several hundred kilos of liquid and vapor had left *Selene*, to be instantly absorbed by the thirsty dust. Many hours ago, the dust in the immediate neighborhood of the waste vents had become saturated and had turned into mud. Dripping downward through scores of channels, it had honeycombed the surrounding Sea. Silently, patiently, the cruiser had been washing away her own foundations. The gentle nudge of the approaching caisson had done the rest.

Up on the raft, the first intimation of disaster was the flashing of the red warning light on the air purifier, synchonized with the howling of a radio klaxon across all the spacesuit wave bands. The howl ceased almost immediately, as the technician in charge punched the cutoff button, but the red light continued to flash.

A glance at the dials was enough to show Lawrence the trouble. The air pipes—*both* of them—were no longer connected to *Selene*. The purifier was pumping oxygen into the Sea through one pipe and, worse still, sucking in dust through the other. Lawrence wondered how long it would take to clean out the filters, but wasted no further time upon that thought. He was too busy calling *Selene.*

There was no answer. He tried all the cruiser's frequencies, without receiving even a whisper of a carrier wave. The Sea of Thirst was as silent to radio as it was to sound.

They're finished, he said to himself; it's all over. It was a near thing, but we just couldn't make it. And all we needed was another hour.

What could have happened? he thought dully. Perhaps the hull had collapsed under the weight of the dust. No—that was very unlikely; the internal air pressure would have prevented that. It must have been another subsidence. He was not sure, but he thought that there had been a slight tremor underfoot. From the beginning he had been aware of this danger, but could see no way of guarding against it. This was a gamble they had all taken, and *Selene* had lost.

Even as *Selene* started to fall, something told Pat that this was quite different from the first cave-in. It was much slower, and there were scrunching, squishing noises from outside the hull which, even in that desperate moment, struck Pat as being unlike any sounds that dust could possibly make.

Overhead, the oxygen pipes were tearing loose. They were not sliding out smoothly, for the cruiser was going down stern first, tilting toward the rear. With a crack of splintering Fiberglas, the pipe just ahead of the air-lock galley ripped through the roof and vanished from sight. Immediately, a thick jet of dust sprayed into the cabin, and fanned out in a choking cloud where it hit the floor.

Commodore Hansteen was nearest, and got there first, Tearing off his shirt, he swiftly wadded it into a ball and rammed it into the aperture. The dust spurted in all directions as he struggled to block the flow. He had almost succeeded when the forward pipe ripped loose—and the main lights went out as, for the second time, the cable conduit was wrenched away.

"I'll take it!" shouted Pat. A moment later, also shirtless, he was trying to stem the torrent pouring in through the hole.

He had sailed the Sea of Thirst a hundred times, yet never before had he touched its substance with his naked skin. The gray powder sprayed into his nose and eyes, half choking and wholly blinding him. Though it was as bone dry as the dust from a Pharaoh's tomb—dryer than this, indeed, for it was a million times older than the pyramids—it had a curiously soapy feeling. As he fought against it, Pat found himself thinking: If there is one death worse than being drowned, it's being buried alive.

When the jet weakened to a thin trickle, he knew that he had avoided that fate—for the moment. The pressure produced by fifteen meters of dust, under the low lunar gravity, was not difficult to overcome—though it would have been another story if the holes in the roof had been much larger.

Pat shook the dust from his head and shoulders, and cautiously opened his eyes. At least he could see again; thank heaven for the emergency lighting, dim though it was. The Commodore had already plugged his leak, and was now calmly sprinkling water from a paper cup to lay the dust. The technique was remarkably effective, and the few remaining clouds quickly collapsed into patches of mud.

Hansteen looked up and caught Pat's eye.

"Well, Captain," he said. "Any theories?"

There were times, thought Pat, when the Commodore's Olympian self-control was almost maddening. He would like to see him break, just once. No—that was not really true. His feeling was merely a flash of envy, even of jealousy—understandable, but quite unworthy of him. He should be ashamed of it, and he was.

"I don't know *what*'s happened," he said. "Perhaps the people on the top can tell us."

It was an uphill walk to the pilot's position, for the cruiser was now tilted at about thirty degrees from the horizontal. As Pat took his seat in front of the radio, he felt a kind of despairing numbness that surpassed anything he had known since their original entombment. It was a sense of resignation, an almost superstitious belief that the gods were fighting against them, and that further struggle was useless.

He felt sure of this when he switched on the radio and found that it was completely dead. The power was off; when that oxygen pipe had ripped out the roof cable conduit, it had done a thorough job.

Pat swiveled slowly around in his seat. Twenty-one men and women were looking at him, awaiting his news. But twenty of them he did not see, for Sue was watching him, and he was conscious only of the expression on her face. It held an anxiety and readiness—but, even now, no hint of fear. As Pat looked at her, his own feelings of despair seemed to dissolve. He felt a surge of strength, even of hope.

"I'm damned if I know what's happened," he said. "But I'm sure of this—we're not done for yet, by several light-years. We may have sunk a little farther, but our friends on the raft will soon catch up with us. This will mean a slight delay—that's all. There's certainly nothing to worry about."

"I don't want to be an alarmist, Captain," said Barrett, "but suppose the raft has sunk as well? What then?"

"We'll know as soon as I get the radio fixed," replied Pat, glancing anxiously at the wires dangling from the roof cable duct. "And until I get this spaghetti sorted out, you'll have to put up with the emergency lighting."

"I don't mind," said Mrs. Schuster. "I think it's rather cute."

Bless you, Mrs. S., said Pat to himself. He glanced quickly around the cabin; though it was hard to see all their expressions in this dim lighting, the passengers seemed calm enough.

They were not quite so calm a minute later; that was all the time it took to discover that nothing could be done to repair the lights or radio. The wiring had been ripped out far down inside the conduit, beyond reach of the simple tools available here.

"This is rather more serious," reported Pat. "We won't be able to communicate, unless they lower a microphone to make contact with us."

"That means," said Barrett, who seemed to like looking on the dark side of things, "that they've lost touch with us. They won't understand why we're not answering. Suppose they assume that we're all dead—and abandon the whole operation?"

The thought had flashed through Pat's mind, but he had dismissed it almost at once.

"You've heard Chief Engineer Lawrence on the radio," he answered. "He's not the sort of man who'd give up until he had absolute proof that we're no longer alive. You needn't worry on *that* score."

"What about our air?" asked Professor Jayawardene anxiouly. "We're back on our own resources again."

"That should last for several hours, now the absorbers have been regenerated. Those pipes will be in place before then," answered Pat, with slightly more confidence than he felt. "Meanwhile, we'll have to be patient and provide our own entertainment again. We did it for three days; we should be able to manage for a couple of hours."

He glanced again around the cabin, looking for any signs of disagreement, and saw that one of the passengers was rising slowly to his feet. It was the very last person he would have expected—quiet little Mr. Radley, who had uttered perhaps a dozen words during the entire trip.

Pat still knew no more about him than that he was an accountant, and come from New Zealand—the only country on Earth still slightly isolated from the rest of the world, by virtue of its position. It could be reached, of course, as quickly as any other spot on the planet, but it was the end of the line, not a way station to somewhere else. As a result, the New Zealanders still proudly preserved much of their individuality. They claimed, with a good deal of truth, to have salvaged all that was left of English culture, now that the British Isles had been absorbed into the Atlantic Community.

"You want to say something, Mister Radley?" asked Pat.

Radley looked around the dim-lit cabin, rather like a schoolmaster about to address a class.

"Yes, Captain," he began. "I have a confession to make. I am very much afraid that this is all my fault."

When Chief Engineer Lawrence broke off his commentary, Earth knew within two seconds that something had gone wrong—though it took several minutes for the news to reach Mars and Venus. But what had happened, no one could guess from the picture on the screen. For a few seconds there had been a flurry of frantic but meaningless activity, but now the immediate crisis seemed to be over. The space-suited figures were huddled together, obviously in conference—and with their telephone circuits plugged in, so that no one could overhear them. It was very frustrating in, so that no one could overhear them. It was very frustrating to watch that silent discussion, and to have no idea of what it was about.

During those long minutes of agonizing suspense, while the studio was trying to discover what was happening, Jules did his best to keep the picture alive. It was an extremely difficult job, handling such a static scene from a single camera position. Like all cameramen, Jules hated to be pinned down in one spot. This site was perfect, but it was fixed, and he was getting rather tired of it. He had even asked if the ship could be moved, but as Captain Anson put it, "I'm damned if I'll go hopping back and forth over the mountains. This is a spaceship, not a—chamois."

So Jules had to ring the changes on pans and zooms, though he used the latter with discretion, because nothing upset viewers more quickly than being hurled back and forth through space, or watching scenery explode in their faces. If he used the power-zoom flat out, Jules could sweep across the Moon at about fifty thousand kilometers an hour—and several million viewers would get motion sickness.

At last that urgent, soundless conference was breaking up; the men on the raft were unplugging their telephones. Now, perhaps, Lawrence would answer the radio calls that had been bombarding him for the last five minutes.

"My God," said Spenser, "I don't believe it! Do you see what they're doing?"

"Yes," said Captain Anson, "and I don't believe it either. But it looks as if they're abandoning the site."

Like lifeboats leaving a sinking ship, the two dust-skis, crowded with men, were pulling away from the raft.

# Chapter 26

Perhaps it was well that *Selene* was now out of radio contact; it would hardly have helped morale if her occupants had known that the skis, heavily overloaded with passengers, were heading away from the site. But at the moment, no one in the cruiser was thinking of the rescue effort; Radley was holding the center of the dimly lit stage.

"What do you mean—this is all *your* fault?" asked Pat in the baffled silence that followed the New Zealander's statement—only baffled as yet; not hostile, because no one could take such a remark seriously.

"It's a long story, Captain," said Radley, speaking in a voice that, though it was oddly unemotional, had undertones that Pat could not identify. It was almost like listening to a robot, and it gave Pat an unpleasant feeling somewhere in the middle of his spine. "I don't mean to say that I *deliberately* caused this to happen. But I'm afraid it is deliberate, and I'm sorry to have involved you all. You see—*they* are after me."

This is all we need, thought Pat. We really seem to have the odds stacked against us. In this small company we've got a neurotic spinster, a drug addict—and now a maniac. What other freaks are going to reveal themselves before we're finished?

Then he realized the unfairness of his judgment. The truth was that he had been very lucky. Against Radley, Miss Morley, and Hans Baldur (who had given on trouble after that single, never-mentioned incident), he had the Commodore, Dr. McKenzie, the Schusters, little Professor Jayawardene, David Barrett—and all the others who had done as they were asked, without making a fuss. He felt a sudden surge of affection—even of love—toward them all, for giving him their active or passive support.

And especially toward Sue, who was already one jump ahead of him, as she always seemed to be. There she was moving unobtrusively about her duties at the back of the cabin. Pat doubted if anyone noticed—certainly Radley did not—as she opened the medicine chest and palmed one of those cigarette-sized cylinders of oblivion. If this fellow gave trouble, she would be ready.

At the moment, trouble seemed the furthest thing from Radley's mind. He appeared to be completely self-possessed and perfectly rational; there was no mad gleam in his eye, or any other of the clichés of insanity. He looked exactly what he was—a middle-aged New Zealand accountant taking a holiday on the Moon.

"This is very interesting, Mister Radley," said Commodore Hansteen in a carefully neutral voice, "but please excuse our ignorance. Who are 'they,' and why should they be after you?"

"I am sure, Commodore, that you've heard of flying saucers?"

Flying *what*? Pat asked himself. Hansteen seemed better informed than he was.

"Yes, I have," he answered a little wearily. "I've come across them in old books on astronautics. They were quite a craze, weren't they, about eighty years ago?"

He realized that "craze" was an unfortunate word to use, and was relieved when Radley took no offense.

"Oh," he answered, "they go back much further than *that*, but it was only in the last century that people started to take notice of them. There's an old manuscript from an English abbey dated 1290 that describes one in detail—and that isn't the earliest report, by any means. More than ten thousand flying saucer sightings have been recorded prior to the twentieth century."

"Just a minute," interrupted Pat. "What the devil do you mean by 'flying saucer'? I've never heard of them."

"Then I'm afraid, Captain, that your education has been neglected," answered Radley in a sorrowful voice. "The term 'flying saucer' came into general use after 1947 to describe the strange, usually disc-shaped vehicles that have been investigating our planet for centuries. Some people prefer to use the phrase 'unidentified flying objects.'"

That aroused a few faint memories in Pat's mind. Yes, he had heard that term in connection with the hypothetical Outsiders. But there was no concrete evidence, of course, that alien space vessels had ever entered the solar system.

"Do you *really* believe," said one of the other passengers skeptically, "that there are visitors from space hanging round the Earth?"

"Much more than that," answered Radley. "They've often landed and made contact with human beings. Before we came here, they had a base on Farside, but they destroyed it when the first survey rockets started taking close-ups."

"How do you know all this?" asked someone else.

Radley seemed quite indifferent to the skepticism of his audience; he must have grown used to this response long ago. He radiated a kind of inner faith which, however ill-founded it might be, was oddly convincing. His insanity had exalted him into the realm beyond reason, and he was quite happy there.

"We have—contacts," he answered with an air of great importance. "A few men and women have been able to establish telepathic communication with the saucer people. So we know a good deal about them."

"How is it that no one else does?" asked another disbeliever. "If they're really out there, why haven't our astronomers and space pilots seen them?"

"Oh, but they have," Radley answered with a pitying smile, "and they're keeping quiet. There's a conspiracy of silence among the scientists; they don't like to admit that there are intelligences out in space so much superior to ours. So when a pilot does report a saucer, they make fun of him. Now, of course, every astronaut keeps quiet when he meets one."

"Have *you* ever met one, Commodore?" asked Mrs. Schuster, obviously half convinced. "Or are you in the—what did Mister Radley call it—conspiracy of silence?"

"I'm very sorry to disappoint you," said Hansteen. "You'll have to take my word for it that all the spaceships I've ever met have been on Lloyd's Register."

He caught Pat's eye, and gave a little nod that said, "Let's go and talk this over in the air lock." Now that he was quite convinced that Radley was harmless, he almost welcomed this interlude. It had, very effectively, taken the passengers' minds off the situation in which they now found themselves. If Radley's brand of insanity could keep them entertained, then good luck to it.

"Well, Pat," said Hansteen, when the air-lock door had sealed them off from the argument, "what do you think of him?"

"Does he *really* believe that nonsense?"

"Oh yes—every word of it. I've met his type before."

The Commodore knew a good deal about Radley's peculiar obsession; no one whose interest in astronautics dated back to the twentieth century could fail to. As a young man, he had even read some of the original writings on the subject—works of such brazen fraudulence or childish naïveté that they had shaken his belief that men were rational beings. That such a literature could ever have flourished was a disturbing thought, though it was true that most of those books had been published in that psychotic era, the Frantic Fifties.

"This is a very peculiar situation," complained Pat. "At a time like *this*—all the passengers are arguing about flying saucers."

"I think it's an excellent idea," answered the Commodore. "What else would you suggest they do? Let's face it, we've got to sit here and wait until Lawrence starts knocking on the roof again."

"If he's still here. Barrett may be right—perhaps the raft has sunk."

"I think that's very unlikely. The disturbance was only a slight one. How far would you imagine we went down?"

Pat thought this over. Looking back on the incident, it seemed to have lasted a long time. The fact that he had been in virtual darkness, and had been fighting that jet of dust, still further confused his memory. He could only hazard a guess.

"I'd say—ten meters."

"Nonsense! The whole affair only lasted a couple of seconds. I doubt if we dropped more than two or three meters."

Pat found this hard to believe, but he hoped that the Commodore was right. He knew that it was extremely difficult to judge weak accelerations, particularly when one was under stress. Hansteen was the only man aboard who could have had any experience of this; his verdict was probably correct—and was certainly encouraging.

"They may never have felt a thing on the surface," continued Hansteen, "and they're probably wondering why they can't make contact with us. Are you sure there's nothing we can do about the radio?"

"Quite sure. The whole terminal block's come loose at the end of the cable conduit. There's no way of reaching it from inside the cabin."

"Well, I suppose that's that. We might as well go back and let Radley try to convert us—if he can."

Jules had tracked the overcrowded skis for a hundred meters before he realized that they were not as overcrowded as they should have been. They carried seven men—and there had been eight on the site.

He panned swiftly back to the raft, and by the good luck or precognition that separates the brilliant cameraman from the merely adequate one, he arrived there just as Lawrence broke his radio silence.

"C.E.E. calling," Lawrence said, sounding as tired and frustrated as would any man who had just seen his carefully laid plans demolished. "Sorry for the delay, but as you'll have gathered, we have an emergency. There appears to have been another cave-in; how deep it is, we don't know—but we've lost physical contact with *Selene*, and she's not answering our radio.

"In case there's another subsidence. I've ordered my men to stand by a few hundred meters away. The danger's very slight—we hardly felt that last tremor—but there's no point in taking chances. I can do everything that's necessary for the moment without any help.

"I'll call again in a few minutes. C.E.E. out."

With the eyes of millions upon him, Lawrence crouched at the edge of the raft, reassembling the probe with which he had first located the cruiser. He had twenty meters to play with; if she had gone deeper than that, he would have to think of something else.

The rod sank into the dust, moving more and more slowly as it approached the depth where *Selene* had rested. There was the original mark—fifteen point one five meters—just disappearing through the surface. The probe continued to move, like a lance piercing into the body of the Moon. How much farther? whispered Lawrence to himself, in the murmurous silence of his space suit.

The anticlimax was almost laughable, except that this was no laughing matter. The probe penetrated an extra meter and a half—a distance he could comfortably span without straining his arms.

Far more serious was the fact that *Selene* had not sunk evenly, as Lawrence discovered after a few additional probings. She was much lower at the stern, being now tilted at an angle of about thirty degrees. That alone was enough to wreck his plan; he had relied upon the caisson making a flush contact with the horizontal roof.

He put that problem aside for the moment; there was a more immediate one. Now that the cruiser's radio was silent—and he had to pray that it was a simple power failure—how could he tell if the people inside were still alive? They would hear his probe, but there was no way in which they could communicate with him.

But of course there was. The easiest and most primitive means of all, which could be so readily overlooked after a century and a half of electronics.

Lawrence got to his feet and called the waiting skis.

"You can come back," he said. "There's no danger. She only sank a couple of meters."

He had already forgotten the watching millions. Though his new plan of campaign had still to be drawn up, he was going into action again.

# Chapter 27

When Pat and the Commodore returned to the cabin, the debate was still going full blast. Radley, who had said so little until now, was certainly making up for lost time. It was as if some secret spring had been touched, or he had been absolved from an oath of secrecy. That was probably the explanation; now that he was convinced that his mission was discovered, he was only too happy to talk about it.

Commodore Hansteen had met many such believers—indeed, it was in sheer self-defense that he had waded through the turgid literature of the subject. The approach was almost always the same. First would be the suggestion that "Surely, Commodore, you've seen some very strange things during your years in space?" Then, when his reply was unsatisfactory, there would be a guarded—and sometimes not so guarded—hint that he was either afraid or unwilling to speak. It was a waste of energy denying the charge; in the eyes of the faithful, that only proved that he was part of the conspiracy.

The other passengers had no such bitter experience to warn them, and Radley was evading their points with effortless ease. Even Schuster, for all his legal training, was unable to pin him into a corner; his efforts were as futile as trying to convince a paranoiac that he was not really being persecuted.

"Does it seem *reasonable*," Schuster argued, "that if thousands of scientists know this, not one of them will let the cat out of the bag? You can't keep a secret that big! It would be like trying to hide the Washington Monument!"

"Oh, there have been attempts to reveal the truth," Radley answered. "But the evidence has a way of being mysteriously destroyed—as well as the men who wanted to reveal it. They can be utterly ruthless when it's necessary."

"But you said that—*they*—have been in contact with human beings. Isn't that a contradiction?"

"Not at all. You see, the forces of good and evil are at war in the Universe, just as they are on Earth. Some of the saucer people want to help us, others to exploit us. The two groups have been struggling together for thousands of years. Sometimes the conflict involves Earth; that is how Atlantis was destroyed."

Hansteen was unable to resist a smile. Atlantis always got into the act sooner or later—or, if not Atlantis, then Lemuria or Mu. They all appealed to the same type of unbalanced, mystery-mongering mentality.

The whole subject had been thoroughly investigated by a group of psychologists during—if Hansteen remembered correctly—the 1970's. They had concluded that around the mid-twentieth century a substantial percentage of the population was convinced that the world was about to be destroyed, and that the only hope lay in intervention from space. Having lost faith in themselves, men had sought salvation in the sky.

The flying saucer religion flourished among the lunatic fringe of mankind for almost exactly ten years; then it had abruptly died out, like an epidemic that had run its course. Two factors, the psychologists had decided, were responsible for this: the first was sheer boredom; the second was the International Geophysical Year, which had heralded Man's own entry into space.

In the eighteen months of the IGY, the sky was watched and probed by more instruments, and more trained observers, than in the whole of previous history. If there had been celestial visitors poised above the atmosphere, this concentrated scientific effort would have revealed them. It did nothing of the sort; and when the first manned vehicles started leaving Earth, the flying saucers were still more conspicuous by their absence.

For most men, that settled the matter. The thousands of unidentified flying objects that had been seen over the centuries had some natural cause, and with better understanding of meteorology and astronomy there was no lack of reasonable explanations. As the Age of Space dawned, restoring Man's confidence in his own destiny, the world lost interest in flying saucers.

It is seldom, however, that a religion dies out completely, and a small body of the faithful kept the cult alive with fantastic "revelations," accounts of meetings with extraterrestrials, and claims of telepathic contacts. Even when, as frequently happened, the current prophets were proved to have faked the evidence, the devotees never wavered. They needed their gods in the sky, and would not be deprived of them.

"You still haven't explained to us," Mr. Schuster was now saying, "why the saucer people should be after *you*. What have you done to annoy them?"

"I was getting too close to some of their secrets, so they have used this opportunity to eliminate me."

"I should have thought they could have found less elaborate ways."

"It is foolish to imagine that our limited minds can understand their mode of thinking. But this would seem like an accident; no one would suspect that it was deliberate."

"A good point. Since it makes no difference now, could you tell us what secret you were after? I'm sure we'd all like to know."

Hansteen shot a quick glance at Irving Schuster. The lawyer had struck him as a rather solemn, humorless little man; irony seemed somewhat out of character.

"I'd be glad to tell you," answered Radley. "It really starts back in nineteen fifty-three, when an American astronomer named O'Neill observed something very remarkable here on the Moon. He discovered a small bridge on the eastern border of the Mare Crisium. Other astronomers, of course, laughed at him—but less prejudiced ones confirmed the existence of the bridge. Within a few years, however, it had vanished. Obviously, our interest had alarmed the saucer people, and they had dismantled it."

That "obvious," Hansteen told himself, was a perfect example of saucerite logic—the daring *non sequitur* that left the normal mind helplessly floundering several jumps behind. He had never heard of O'Neill's Bridge, but there had been scores of examples of mistaken observations in the astronomical records. The Martian canals were the classic case; honest observers had reported them for years, but they simply did not exist—at least not as the fine spider web that Lowell and others had drawn. Did Radley think that someone had filled in the canals between the time of Lowell and the securing of the first clear photographs of Mars? He was quite capable of it, Hansteen was sure.

Presumably O'Neill's Bridge had been a trick of the lighting, or of the Moon's perpetually shifting shadows—but such a simple explanation was not, of course, good enough for Radley. And, in any event, what was the man doing here, a couple of thousand kilometers from the Mare Crisium?

Someone else had thought of that, and had put the same question. As usual, Radley had a convincing answer at the tip of his tongue.

"I'd hoped," he said, "to divert their suspicions by behaving like an ordinary tourist. Because the evidence I was looking for lay on the western hemisphere, I went east. I planned to get to the Mare Crisium by going across Farside; there were several places there that I wanted to look at, too. But they were too clever for me. I should have guessed that I'd be spotted by one of their agents—they can take human form, you know. Probably they've been following me ever since I landed on the Moon."

"I'd like to know," said Mrs. Schuster, who seemed to be taking Radley with ever-increasing seriousness, "what they're going to do to us now."

"I wish I could tell you, ma'am," answered Radley. "We know that they have caves deep down inside the Moon, and almost certainly that's where we're being taken. As soon as they saw that the rescuers were getting close, they stepped in again. I'm afraid we're too deep for anyone to reach us now."

That's quite enough of this nonsense, said Pat to himself. We've had our comic relief, and now this madman is starting to depress people. But how can we shut him up?

Insanity was rare on the Moon, as in all frontier societies. Pat did not know how to deal with it, especially with this confident, curiously persuasive variety. There were moments when he almost wondered if there might be something in Radley's delusion. In other circumstances, his natural, healthy skepticism would have protected him, but now, after these days of strain and suspense, his critical faculties were dimmed. He wished there was some neat way of breaking the spell that this glib-tongued maniac was undoubtedly casting.

Half ashamed of the thought, he remembered the quick *coup de grâce* that had put Hans Baldur so neatly to sleep. Without intending to do so—at least, to his conscious knowledge—he caught Harding's eye. To his alarm, there was an immediate response; Harding nodded slightly and rose slowly to his feet. No! said Pat—but only to himself. I don't mean *that*; leave the poor lunatic alone; *what sort of man are you, anyway*?

Then he relaxed, very slightly. Harding was not attempting to move from his seat, four places from Radley. He was merely standing there, looking at the New Zealander with an unfathomable expression. It might even have been pity, but in this dim lighting Pat could not be sure.

"I think it's time to make my contribution." Harding said. "At least *one* of the things our friend was telling you is perfectly true. He has been followed—but not by saucerites. By me.

"For an amateur, Wilfred George Radley, I'd like to congratulate you. It's been a fine chase—from Christchurch to Astrograd to Clavius to Tycho to Ptolemy to Plato to Port Roris—and to here, which I guess is the end of the trail, in more ways than one."

Radley did not seem in the least perturbed. He merely inclined his head in an almost regal gesture of acknowledgment, as if he recognized Harding's existence, but did not wish to pursue his acquaintance.

"As you may have guessed," continued Harding, "I'm a detective. Most of the time I specialize in fraud. Quite interesting work, though

I seldom have a chance of talking about it. I'm quite grateful for this opportunity.

"I've no interest—well, no professional interest—in Mister Radley's peculiar beliefs. Whether they're true or not doesn't affect the fact that he's a very smart accountant, earning a good salary back in N.Z. Though not one good enough to pay for a month on the Moon.

"But that was no problem—because, you see, Mister Radley was senior accountant at the Christchurch branch of Universal Travel Cards, Incorporated. The system is supposed to be foolproof and double checked, but somehow he managed to issue himself a card—Q Category—good for unlimited travel anywhere in the solar system, for hotel and restaurant billings, for cashing checks up to five hundred stollars on demand. There aren't many Q cards around, and they're handled as if they're made of plutonium.

"Of course, people have tried to get away with this sort of thing before; clients are always losing their cards, and enterprising characters have a fine time with them for a few days before they're caught. But only a few days. The UTC central biling system is very efficient—it has to be. There are several safeguards against unauthorized use, and until now, the longest run anyone's had was a week."

"Nine days," Radley unexpectedly interjected.

"Sorry—*you* should know. Nine days, then. But Radley had been on the move for almost three weeks before we spotted him. He'd taken his annual leave, and told the office he'd be vacationing quietly on the North Island. Instead, he went to Astrograd and then on to the Moon, making history in the process. For he's the first man—and we hope the last one—to leave Earth entirely on credit.

"We still want to know exactly how he did it. How did he bypass the automatic checking circuits? Did he have an accomplice in the computer programing section? And similar questions of absorbing interest to UTC, Inc. I hope, Radley, you'll let down your hair with me, just to satisfy my curiosity. I think it's the least you can do in the circumstances.

"Still, we know *why* you did it—why you threw up a good job to go on a spree that was bound to land you in jail. We guessed the reason, of course, as soon as we found you were on the Moon. UTC knew all about your hobby, but it didn't affect your efficiency. They took a gamble, and it's been an expensive one."

"I'm very sorry," Radley replied, not without dignity. "The firm's always treated me well, and it did seem a shame. But it was in a good cause, and if I could have found my evidence—"

But at that point everyone, except Detective Inspector Harding, lost interest in Radley and his saucers. The sound that they had all been anxiously waiting for had come at last.

Lawrence's probe was scratching against the roof.

# Chapter 28

I seem to have been here for half a lifetime, thought Maurice Spenser, yet the sun is still low in the west, where it rises on this weird world, and it's still three days to noon. How much longer am I going to be stuck on this mountaintop, listening to Captain Anson's tall stories of the spaceways, and watching that distant raft, with its twin igloos?

It was a question that no one could answer. When the caisson had started to descend, it had looked as if another twenty-four hours would see the job finished. But now they were back where they had started—and, to make matters worse, all the visual excitement of the story was over. Everything that would happen from now on would be hidden deep in the Sea, or would take place behind the walls of an igloo. Lawrence still stubbornly refused to allow a camera out on the raft, and Spenser could hardly blame him. The Chief Engineer had been unlucky once, when his commentary had blown up in his face, and was not going to risk it happening again.

Yet there was no question of *Auriga* abandoning the site which she had reached at such expense. If all went well, there was one dramatic scene still to come. And if all went badly, there would be a tragic one. Sooner or later, those dust-skis would be heading back to Port Roris—with or without the men and women they had come to save. Spenser was not going to miss the departure of that caravan, whether it took place under the rising or the setting sun, or beneath the fainter light of the unmoving Earth.

As soon as he had relocated *Selene*, Lawrence had started drilling again. On the monitor screen, Spenser could see the thin shaft of the oxygen-supply tube making its second descent into the dust. Why was Lawrence bothering to do this, he wondered, if he was not even sure whether anyone was still alive aboard *Selene*? And how was he going to check this, now that the radio had failed?

That was a question that millions of people were asking themselves as they watched the pipe sink down into the dust, and perhaps many of them thought of the right answer. Yet, oddly enough, it never occurred to anyone aboard *Selene*—not even to the Commodore.

As soon as they heard that heavy thump against the roof, they knew at once that this was no sounding rod, delicately probing the Sea. When, a minute later, there came the unmistakable whirr of a drill chewing its way through Fiberglas, they felt like condemned men who had been granted a last-minute reprieve.

This time, the drill missed the cable conduit—not that it mattered now. The passengers watched, almost hypnotized, as the grinding sound grew louder and the first flakes planed down from the ceiling. When the head of the drill appeared and descended twenty centimeters into the cabin, there was a brief but heartfelt burst of cheering.

Now what? said Pat to himself. We can't talk to them; how will I know when to unscrew the drill? I'm not going to make *that* mistake a second time.

Startlingly loud in this tense, expectant silence, the metal tube resonated with the DIT DIT DIT DAH which, surely, not one of *Selene*'s company would forget, however long he lived. Pat replied at once, banging out an answering V with a pair of pliers. Now they know we're alive, he thought. He had never really believed that Lawrence would assume that they were dead and abandon them, yet at the same time there was always that haunting doubt.

The tube signaled again, this time much more slowly. It was a nuisance having to learn Morse; in this age, it seemed such an anachronism, and many were the bitter protests among pilots and space engineers at the waste of effort. In your whole lifetime, you might need it only once.

But that was the point. You would *really* need it then.

DIT DIT DAH, rapped the tube. DAH DIT...DIT DIT DIT...DAH DIT DAH DIT...DIT DAH DIT...DIT...DIT DAH DAH.

Then, so that there would be no mistake, it started to repeat the word, but both Pat and the Commodore, rusty though they were, had got the message.

"They're telling us to unscrew the drill," said Pat. "Well, here we go."

The brief rush of air gave everyone a moment of unnecessary panic as the pressure equalized. Then the pipe was open to the upper world, and twenty-two anxious men and women waited for the first breath of oxygen to come gushing down it.

Instead, the tube spoke. Out of the open orifice came a voice, hollow and sepulchral, but perfectly clear. It was so loud, and so utterly unexpected, that a gasp of surprise came from the company. Probably not more than half a dozen of these men and women had ever heard a speaking tube; they had grown up in the belief that only through electronics could the voice be sent across space. This antique revival was as much a novelty to them as a telephone would have been to an ancient Greek.

"This is Chief Engineer Lawrence speaking. Can you hear me?"

Pat cupped his hands over the opening, and answered slowly: "Hearing you loud and clear. How do you receive us?"

"Very clear. Are you all right?"

"Yes—what's happened?"

"You've dropped a couple of meters—no more than that. We hardly noticed anything up here, until the pipes came adrift. How's your air?"

"Still good—but the sooner you start supplying us, the better."

"Don't worry, we'll be pumping again as soon as we get the dust out of the filters, and can rush out another drill head from Port Roris. The one you've just unscrewed was the only spare; it was lucky we had that."

So it will be at least an hour, Pat told himself, before their air supply could be secured again. That, however, was not the problem that now worried him. He knew how Lawrence had hoped to reach them, and he realized that the plan would not work now that *Selene* was no longer on an even keel.

"How are you going to get at us?" he asked bluntly.

There was only the briefest of hesitations before Lawrence answered.

"I've not worked out the details, but we'll add another section to the caisson and continue it down until it reaches you. Then we'll start scooping out the dust until we get to the bottom. That will take us to within a few centimeters of you; we'll cross that gap somehow. But there's one thing I want you to do first."

"What's that?"

"I'm ninety per cent sure that you won't settle again—but if you're going to, I'd rather you did it now. I want you all to jump up and down together for a couple of minutes."

"Will that be safe?" asked Pat doubtfully. "Suppose this pipe tears out again?"

"Then you can plug it again. Another small hole won't matter—but another subsidence will, if it happens when we're trying to make a man-sized opening in the roof."

*Selene* had seen some strange sights, but this was undoubtedly the strangest. Twenty-two men and women were solemnly jumping up and down in unison, rising to the ceiling and then pushing themselves back as vigorously as possible to the floor. All the while Pat kept a careful watch on that pipe leading to the upper world; after a minute's strenuous exertion on the part of her passengers, *Selene* had moved downward by less than two centimeters.

He reported this to Lawrence, who received the news with thankfulness. Now that he was reasonably sure that *Selene* would not shift again, he was confident that he could get these people out. Exactly how, he was not yet certain, but the plan was beginning to form in his mind.

It took shape over the next twelve hours, in conferences with his brains trust and experiments on the Sea of Thirst. The Engineering Division had learned more about the dust in the last week than during the whole of its previous existence. It was no longer fighting in the dark against a largely unknown opponent. It understood which liberties could be taken, and which could not.

Despite the speed with which the changed plans were drawn up and the necessary hardware constructed, there was no undue haste and certainly no carelessness. For this was another operation that had to work the first time. If it failed, then at the very least the caisson would have to be abandoned and a new one sunk. And at the worst—those aboard *Selene* would be drowned in dust.

"It's a pretty problem," said Tom Lawson, who liked pretty problems—and not much else. "The lower end of the caisson's wide open to the dust, because it's resting against *Selene* at only one point, and the tilt of the roof prevents it from sealing. Before we can pump out the dust, we have to close that gap.

"Did I say 'pump'? That was a mistake. You can't pump the stuff; it has to be lifted. And if we tried that as things are now, it would flow in just as fast at the bottom of the tube as we took it out of the top."

Tom paused and grinned sardonically at his multimillion audience, as if challenging it to solve the problem he had outlined. He let his viewers stew in their own thoughts for a while, then picked up the model lying on the studio table. Though it was an extremely simple one, he was rather proud of it, for he had made it himself. No one could have guessed, from the other side of the camera, that it was only cardboard sprayed with aluminum paint.

"This tube," he said, "represents a short section of the caisson that's now leading down to *Selene*—and which, as I said, is full of dust. Now *this*—" with his other hand, he picked up a stubby cylinder, closed at one end—"fits snugly inside the caisson, like a piston. It's very heavy, and will try to sink under its own weight. But it can't do so, of course, while the dust is trapped underneath it."

Tom turned the piston until its flat end was toward the camera. He pressed his forefinger against the center of the circular face, and a small trap door opened.

"This acts as a valve. When it's open, dust can flow through and the piston can sink down the shaft. As soon as it reaches the bottom, the valve will be closed by a signal from above. That will seal off the caisson, and we can start scooping out the dust.

"It sounds very simple, doesn't it? Well, it's not. There are about fifty problems I haven't mentioned. For example, as the caisson is emptied, it will try to float up to the surface with a lift of a good many tons. Chief Engineer Lawrence has worked out an ingenious system of anchors to hold it down.

"You'll realize, of course, that even when this tube has been emptied of dust, there will still be that wedge-shaped gap between its lower end and *Selene*'s roof. How Mister Lawrence proposes to deal with that, I don't know. And please don't send *me* any more suggestions; we've already had enough half-baked ideas on this program to last a life-time.

"This—piston gadget—isn't just theory. The engineers here have built and tested it during the last twelve hours, and it's now in action. If I can make any sense of the signals the man's waving at me, I think we're now going over to the Sea of Thirst, to find out what's happening to the raft."

The temporary studio in the Hotel Roris faded from a million screens; in its place was the picture that, by this time, must have been familiar to most of the human race.

There were now three igloos of assorted sizes on or around the raft; as the sunlight glinted from their reflecting outer surfaces, they looked like giant drops of mercury. One of the dust-skis was parked beside the largest dome; the other two were in transit, still shuttling supplies from Port Roris.

Like the mouth of a well, the caisson projected from the Sea. Its rim was only twenty centimeters above the dust, and the opening seemed much too narrow for a man to enter. It would, indeed, have been a very tight fit for anyone wearing a space suit—but the crucial part of this operation would be done without suits.

At regular intervals, a cylindrical grab was disappearing into the well, to be hauled back to the surface a few seconds later by a small but powerful crane. On each withdrawal, the grab would be swung clear of the opening, and would disgorge its contents back into the Sea. For an instant a gray dunce's cap of dust would stand in momentary balance on the level plain; then it would collapse in slow motion, vanishing completely before the next load had emerged from the shaft. It was a conjuring trick being carried out in broad day-light, and it was fascinating to watch. More effectively than a thousand words of description, it told the viewers all that they needed to know about the Sea of Thirst.

The grab was taking longer on its journeys now, as it plunged deeper into the dust. And at last there came the moment when it emerged only half full, and the way to *Selene* was open—except for that roadblock at the end.

# Chapter 29

"We're still in very good spirits," said Pat, into the microphone that had now been lowered down the air shaft. "Of course, we had a bad shock after that second cave-in, when we lost contact with you—but now we're sure you'll soon have us out. We can hear the grab at work, as it scoops up the dust, and it's wonderful to know that help is so close. We'll never forget," he added, a little awkwardly, "the efforts that so many people have made to help us, and whatever happens we'd like to thank them. All of us are quite sure that everything possible has been done.

"And now I'll hand over the mike, since several of us have messages we want to send. With any luck at all, this will be the last broadcast from *Selene*."

As he gave the microphone to Mrs. Williams, he realized that he might have phrased that last remark a little better; it could be interpreted in two ways. But now that rescue was so close at hand, he refused to admit the possibility of further setbacks. They had been through so much that, surely, nothing more would happen to them now.

Yet he knew that the final stage of the operation would be the most difficult, and the most critical, of all. They had discussed it endlessly during the last few hours, ever since Chief Engineer Lawrence had explained his plans to them. There was little else to talk about now that, by common consent, the subject of flying saucers was vetoed.

They could have continued with the book readings, but somehow both *Shane* and *The Orange and the Apple* had lost their appeal. No one could concentrate on anything now except the prospects of rescue, and the renewal of life that lay before them when they had rejoined the human race.

From overhead, there was a sudden, heavy thump. That could mean only one thing; the grab had reached the bottom of the shaft, and the caisson was clear of dust. Now it could be coupled to one of the igloos and pumped full of air.

It took more than an hour to complete the connection and make all the necessary tests. The specially modified Mark XIX igloo, with a hole in its floor just large enough to accommodate the protruding end of the caisson, had to be positioned and inflated with the utmost care. The lives of *Selene*'s passengers, and also those of the men attempting to rescue them, might depend upon this air seal.

Not until Chief Engineer Lawrence was thoroughly satisfied did he strip off his space suit and approach that yawning hole. He held a floodlight above the opening and looked down into the shaft, which seemed to dwindle away to infinity. Yet it was just seventeen meters to the bottom; even in this low gravity, an object would take only five seconds to fall that distance.

Lawrence turned to his assistants; each was wearing a space suit, but with the face plate open. If anything went wrong, those plates could be snapped shut in a fraction of a second, and the men inside would probably be safe. But for Lawrence there would be no hope at all—nor for the twenty-two aboard *Selene.*

"You know exactly what to do," he said. "If I want to come up in a hurry, all of you pull on the rope ladder together. Any questions?"

There were none; everything had been thoroughly rehearsed. With a now to his men and a chorus of "Good lucks" in return, Lawrence lowered himself into the shaft.

He let himself fall most of the way, checking his speed from time to time by grabbing at the ladder. On the Moon it was quite safe to do this; well, *almost* safe. Lawrence had seen men killed because they had forgotten that even this gravity field could accelerate one to a lethal speed in less than ten seconds.

This was like Alice's fall into Wonderland (so much of Carroll might have been inspired by space travel), but there was nothing to see on the way down except the blank concrete wall, so close that Lawrence had to squint to focus upon it. And then, with the slightest of bumps, he had reached the bottom.

He squatted down on the little metal platform, the size and shape of a manhole cover, and examined it carefully. The trap-door valve that had been open during the piston's descent through the dust was leaking very slightly, and a trickle of gray powder was creeping round the seal. It was nothing to worry about, but Lawrence could not help wondering what would happen if the valve opened under the pressure from beneath. How fast would the dust rise up the shaft, like water in a well? Not as fast, he was quite certain, as he could go up that ladder.

Beneath his feet now, only centimeters away, was the roof of the cruiser, sloping down into the dust at that maddening thirty degrees. His problem was to mate the horizontal end of the shaft with the sloping roof of the cruiser—and to do it so well that the coupling would be dust-tight.

He could see no flaw in the plan; nor did he expect to, for it had been devised by the best engineering brains on Earth and Moon. It even allowed for the possibility that *Selene* might shift again, by a few centimeters, while he was working here. But theory was one thing—and, as he knew all too well, practice was another.

There were six large thumbscrews spaced around the circumference of the metal disc on which Lawrence was sitting, and he started to turn them one by one, like a drummer tuning his instrument. Connected to the lower side of the platform was a short piece of concertina-like tubing, almost as wide as the caisson, and now folded flat. It formed a flexible coupling large enough for a man to crawl through, and was now slowly opening as Lawrence turned the screws.

One side of the corrugated tube had to stretch through forty centimeters to reach the sloping roof; the other had to move scarcely at all. Lawrence's chief worry had been that the resistance of the dust would prevent the concertina from opening, but the screws were easily overcoming the pressure.

Now none of them could be tightened any further; the lower end of the coupling must be flush against *Selene's* roof, and sealed to it, he hoped, by the rubber gasket around its rim. How tight that seal was, he would very soon know.

Automatically checking his escape route, Lawrence glanced up the shaft. He could see nothing past the glare of the floodlight hanging two meters above his head, but the rope ladder stretching past it was extremely reassuring.

"I've let down the connector," he shouted to his invisible colleagues. "It seems to be flush against the roof. Now I'm going to open the valve."

Any mistake now, and the whole shaft would be flooded, perhaps beyond possibility of further use. Slowly and gently Lawrence released the trap door which had allowed the dust to pass through the piston while it was descending. There was no sudden upwelling; the corrugated tube beneath his feet was holding back the Sea.

Lawrence reached through the valve—and his fingers felt the roof of *Selene*, still invisible beneath the dust but now only a handsbreath away. Few achievements in all his life had ever given him such a sense of satisfaction. The job was still far from finished—*but he had reached the cruiser.* For a moment he crouched in his little pit, feeling as some old-time miner must have when the first nugget of gold gleamed in the lamplight.

He banged three times on the roof. Immediately, his signal was returned. There was no point in striking up a Morse conversation, for, if he wished, he could talk directly through the microphone circuit, but he knew the psychological effect that his tapping would have. It would prove to the men and women in *Selene* that rescue was now only centimeters away.

Yet there were still major obstacles to be demolished, and the next one was the manhole cover on which he was sitting—the face of the piston itself. It had served its purpose, holding back the dust while the caisson was being emptied, but now it had to be removed before anyone could escape from *Selene*. This had to be done, however, without disturbing the flexible coupling that it had helped to place in position.

To make this possible, the circular face of the piston had been built so that it could be lifted out, like a saucepan lid, when eight large bolts were unscrewed. It took Lawrence only a few minutes to deal with these and to attach a rope to the new loose metal disc; then he shouted, "Haul away!"

A fatter man would have had to climb the shaft while the circular lid came up after him, but Lawrence was able to squeeze against the wall while the metal plate, moving edge ways, was hoisted past him. There goes the last line of defense, he told himself, as the disc vanished overhead. Now it would be impossible to seal the shaft again if the coupling failed and the dust started to pour in.

"Bucket!" he shouted. It was already on its way down.

Forty years ago, thought Lawrence, I was playing on a California beach with bucket and spade, making castles in the sand. Now here I am on the Moon—Chief Engineer, Earthside, no less—shoveling in even deadlier earnest, with the whole human race looking over my shoulder.

When the first load was hoisted up, he had exposed a considerable area of *Selene's* roof. The volume of dust trapped inside the coupling-tube was quite small, and two more bucketfuls disposed of it.

Before him now was the aluminized fabric of the sun shield, which had long ago crumpled under the pressure. Lawrence cut it away without difficulty—it was so fragile that he could tear it with his bare hands—and exposed the slightly roughened Fiberglas of the outer hull. To cut through that with a small power saw would be easy; it would also be fatal.

For by this time *Selene's* double hull had lost its integrity; when the roof had been damaged, the dust would have flooded into the space between the two walls. It would be waiting there, under pressure, to come spurting out as soon as he made his first incision. Before he could enter *Selene*, that thin but deadly layer of dust would have to be immobilized.

Lawrence rapped briskly against the roof; as he had expected, the sound was muffled by the dust. What he did not expect was to receive an urgent, frantic tattoo in reply.

This, he could tell at once, was no reassuring "I'm O.K." signal from inside the cruiser. Even before the men overhead could relay the news to him, Lawrence had guessed that the Sea of Thirst was making one final bid to keep its prey.

Because Karl Johanson was a nucleonics engineer, had a sensitive nose, and happened to be sitting at the rear of the bus, he was the one who spotted the approach of disaster. He remained quite still for a few seconds, nostrils twitching, then said "Excuse me" to his companion in the aisle seat, and strolled quietly to the washroom. He did not wish to cause alarm if there was no need, especially when rescue seemed so near. But in his professional lifetime he had learned, through more examples than he cared to remember, never to ignore the smell of burning insulation.

He was in the washroom for less than fifteen seconds. When he emerged he was walking quickly, but not quickly enough to cause panic. He went straight to Pat Harris, who was deep in conversation with Commodore Hansteen, and interrupted them without ceremony.

"Captain," he said in a low, urgent voice, "we're on fire. Go and check in the toilet. I've not told anyone else."

In a second, Pat was gone, and Hansteen with him. In space, as on the sea, no one stopped to argue when he heard the word "Fire." And Johnson was not the sort of man to raise a false alarm; like Pat, he was a Lunar Administration tech, and had been one of those whom the Commodore had selected for his riot squad.

The toilet was typical of that on any small vehicle of land, sea, air, or space; one could touch every wall without changing position. But the rear wall, immediately above the wash-bowl, could no longer be touched at all. The Fiberglas was blistered with heat, and was buckling and bulging even while the horrified spectators looked at it.

"My God!" said the Commodore. "That will be through in a minute. What's causing it?"

But Pat had already gone. He was back a few seconds later, carrying the cabin's two small fire extinguishers under his arms.

"Commodore," he said, "go and report to the raft. Tell them we may only have a few minutes. I'll stay here in case it breaks through."

Hansteen did as he was told. A moment later Pat heard his voice calling the message into the microphone, and the sudden turmoil among the passengers that followed. Almost immediately the door opened again, and he was joined by McKenzie.

"Can I help?" asked the scientist.

"I don't think so," Pat answered, holding the extinguisher at the ready. He felt a curious numbness, as if this was not really happening to him, but was all a dream from which he would soon awaken. Perhaps by now he had passed beyond fear; having surmounted one crisis after another, all emotion had been wrung out of him. He could still endure, but he could no longer react.

"What's causing it?" asked McKenzie, echoing the Commodore's unanswered question and immediately following it with another. "What's behind this bulkhead?"

"Our main power supply. Twenty heavy-duty cells."

"How much energy in them?"

"Well, we started with five thousand kilowatt-hours. We probably still have half of it."

"There's your answer. Something's shorting out our power supply. It's probably been burning up ever since the overhead wiring got ripped out."

The explanation made sense, if only because there was no other source of energy aboard the cruiser. She was completely fireproof, so could not support an ordinary combustion. But there was enough electrical energy in her power cells to drive her at full speed for hours on end, and if this dissipated itself in raw heat the results would be catastrophic.

Yet this was impossible; such an overload would have tripped the circuit breakers at once—unless, for some reason, they had jammed.

They had not, as McKenzie reported after a quick check in the air lock.

"All the breakers have jumped," he said. "The circuits are as dead as mutton. I don't understand it."

Even in this moment of peril, Pat could hardly refrain from smiling. McKenzie was the eternal scientist; he might be about to die, but he would insist on knowing how. If he was being burned at the stake—and a similar fate might well be in store—he would ask his executioners, "What kind of wood are you using?"

The folding door creased inward as Hansteen came back to report.

"Lawrence says he'll be through in ten minutes," he said. "Will that wall hold until then?"

"God knows," answered Pat. "It may last for another hour—it may go in the next five seconds. Depends how the fire's spreading."

"Aren't there automatic fire-fighting appliances in that compartment?"

"There's no point in having them—this is our pressure bulkhead, and there's normally vacuum on the other side. That's the best fire fighter you can get."

"That's it!" exclaimed McKenzie. "Don't you see? The whole compartment's flooded. When the roof tore, the dust started to work its way in. It's shorting all the electrical equipment."

Pat knew, without further discussion, that McKenzie was right. By now all the sections normally open to space must be packed with dust. It would have poured in through the broken roof, flowed along the gap between the double hull, slowly accumulated around the open bus bars in the power compartment. And then the pyrotechnics would have started: there was enough meteoric iron in the dust to make it a good conductor. It would be arcing and shorting in there like a thousand electric fires.

"If we sprinkled water on that wall," said the Commodore, "would it help matters—or would it crack the Fiberglas?"

"I think we should try it," answered McKenzie, "but very carefully—not too much at a time." He filled a plastic cup—the water was already hot—and looked enquiringly at the others. Since there were no objections, he began to splash a few drops on the slowly blistering surface.

The cracklings and poppings that resulted were so terrifying that he stopped at once. It was too big a risk; with a metal wall, it would have been a good idea, but this nonconducting plastic would shatter under the thermal stresses.

"There's nothing we can do in here," said the Commodore. "Even those extinguishers won't help much. We'd better get out and block off this whole compartment. The door will act as a fire wall, and give us some extra time."

Pat hesitated. The heat was already almost unbearable, but it seemed cowardice to leave. Yet Hansteen's suggestion made excellent sense; if he stayed here until the fire broke through, he would probably be gassed at once by the fumes.

"Right—let's get out," he agreed. "We'll see what kind of barricade we can build behind this door."

He did not think they would have much time to do it; already he could hear, quite distinctly, a frying, blistering sound from the wall that was holding the inferno at bay.

# Chapter 30

The news that *Selene* was on fire made no difference at all to Lawrence's actions. He could not move any faster than he was doing now; if he attempted it, he might make a mistake, just when the trickiest part of the entire job was coming up. All he could do was to forge ahead, and hope that he would beat the flames.

The apparatus now being lowered down the shaft looked like an overgrown grease gun, or a giant version of those syringes used to put icing on wedding cakes. This one held neither grease nor icing, but an organic silicon compound under great pressure. At the moment it was liquid; it would not remain so for long.

Lawrence's first problem was to get the liquid between the double hull, without letting the dust escape. Using a small rivet gun, he fired seven hollow bolts into *Selene*'s outer skin—one in the center of the exposed circle, the other six evenly spaced around its circumference.

He connected the syringe to the center bolt, and pressed the trigger. There was a slight hiss as the fluid rushed through the hollow bolt, its pressure opening a tiny valve in the bullet-shaped nose. Working very swiftly, Lawrence moved from bolt to bolt, shooting equal charges of fluid through each. Now the stuff would have spread out almost evenly between the two hulls, in a ragged pancake more than a meter across No—not a pancake—a *soufflé*, for it would have started to foam as soon as it escaped from the nozzle.

And a few seconds later, it would have started to set, under the influence of the catalyst injected with it. Lawrence looked at his watch; in five minutes that foam would be rock-hard, though as porous as pumice—which, indeed, it would very closely resemble. There would be no chance of more dust entering this section of the hull; what was already there was frozen in place.

There was nothing he could do to shorten that five minutes; the whole plan depended upon the foam setting to a known consistency. If his timing and positioning had been faulty, or the chemists back at Base had made an error, the people aboard *Selene* were already as good as dead.

He used the waiting period to tidy up the shaft, sending all the equipment back to the surface. Soon only Lawrence himself was left at the bottom, with no tools at all but his bare hands. If Maurice Spenser could have smuggled his camera into this narrow space—and he would have signed any reasonable contract with the Devil to have done so—his viewers would have been quite unable to guess Lawrence's next move.

They would have been still more baffled when what looked like a child's hoop was slowly lowered down the shaft. But this was no nursery toy; it was the key that would open *Selene*.

Sue had already marshaled the passengers to the front—and now much higher—end of the cabin. They were all standing there in a tightly packed group, looking anxiously at the ceiling and straining their ears for every encouraging sound.

Encouragement, thought Pat, was what they needed now. And he needed it more than any of them, for he alone knew—unless Hansteen or McKenzie had guessed it—the real magnitude of the danger they were facing.

The fire was bad enough, and could kill them if it broke through into the cabin. But it was slow-moving, and they could fight it, even if only for a while. Against explosion, however, they could do nothing.

For *Selene* was a bomb, and the fuse was already lit. The stored-up energy in the power cells that drove her motors and all her electrical devices could escape as raw heat, but it could not detonate. That was not true, unfortunately, of the liquid-oxygen tanks.

They must still hold many liters of the fearfully cold, violently reactive element. When the mounting heat ruptured those tanks, there would be both a physical and a chemical explosion. A small one, it was true—perhaps equivalent to a hundred kilograms of T.N.T. But that would be quite enough to smash *Selene* to pieces.

Pat saw no point in mentioning this to Hansteen, who was already planning his barricade. Seats were being unscrewed from the rows near the front of the cabin, and jammed between the rear row and the toilet door. It looked as if the Commodore was preparing for an invasion rather than a fire—as indeed he was. The fire itself, because of its nature, might not spread beyond the power-cell compartment, but as soon as that cracked and blistered wall finally gave way, the dust would come flooding through.

"Commodore," said Pat, "while you're doing this, I'll start organizing the passengers. We can't have twenty people trying to get out at once."

That was a nightmare prospect that had to be avoided at all costs. Yet it would be hard to avoid panic—even in this well-disciplined community—if a single narrow tunnel was the only means of escape from a rapidly approaching death.

Pat walked to the front of the cabin; on Earth that would have been a steep uphill climb, but here a thirty-degree slope was barely noticeable. He looked at the anxious faces ranged in front of him and said: "We're going to be out of here very soon. When the ceiling opens, a rope ladder will be dropped down. The ladies will go first, then the men—all in alphabetical order. Don't bother to use your feet. Remember how little you weigh here, and go up hand over hand, as quickly as you can. But don't crowd the person in front; you should have plenty of time, and it will take you only a few seconds to reach the top.

"Sue, please sort everyone out in the right order. Harding, Bryan, Johanson, Barrett—I'd like you to stand by as you did before. We may need your help—"

He did not finish the sentence. There was a kind of soft, muffled explosion from the rear of the cabin—nothing spectacular; the popping of a paper bag would have made more noise. But it meant that the wall was down—while the ceiling, unfortunately, was still intact.

On the other side of the roof, Lawrence laid his hoop flat against the Fiberglas and started to fix it in position with quick-drying cement. The ring was almost as wide as the little well in which he was crouching; it came to within a few centimeters of the corrugated walls. Though it was perfectly safe to handle, he treated it with exaggerated care. He had never acquired that easy familiarity with explosives that characterizes those who have to live with them.

The ring charge he was tamping in place was a perfectly conventional specimen of the art, involving no technical problems. It would make a neat clean cut of exactly the desired width and thickness, doing in a thousandth of a second a job that would have taken a quarter of an hour with a power saw. That was what Lawrence had first intended to use; now he was very glad that he had changed his mind. It seemed most unlikely that he would have a quarter of an hour.

How true that was, he learned while he was still waiting for the foam to set. "The fire's through into the cabin!" yelled a voice from overhead.

Lawrence looked at his watch. For a moment it seemed as if the second hand was motionless, but that was an illusion he had experienced all his life. The watch had not stopped; it was merely that Time, as usual, was not going at the speed he wished. Until this moment it had been passing too swiftly; now, of course, it was crawling on leaden feet.

The foam should be rock-hard in another thirty seconds. Far better to leave it a little longer than to risk shooting too soon, while it was still plastic.

He started to climb the rope ladder, without haste, trailing the thin detonating wires behind him. His timing was perfect. When he had emerged from the shaft, uncrimped the short circuit he had put for the sake of safety at the end of the wires, and connected them to the exploder, there were just ten seconds to go.

"Tell them we're starting to count down from ten," he said.

As Pat raced downhill to help the Commodore—though just what he could do now, he had very little idea—he heard Sue calling in an unhurried voice: "Miss Morley, Mrs. Schuster, Mrs. Williams..." How ironic it was that Miss Morley would once again be the first, this time by virtue of alphabetical accident. She could hardly grumble about the treatment she was getting now.

And then a second and much grimmer thought flashed through Pat's mind. *Suppose Mrs. Schuster got stuck in the tunnel and blocked the exit.* Well, they could hardly leave her until last. No, she'd go up all right; she had been a deciding factor in the tube's design, and since then she had lost several kilos.

At first glance, the outer door of the toilet still seemed to be holding. Indeed, the only sign that anything had happened was a slight wisp of smoke curling past the hinges. For a moment Pat felt a surge of relief; why, it might take the fire half an hour to burn through the double thickness of Fiberglas, and long before that—

Something was tickling his bare feet. He had moved automatically aside before his conscious mind said, "*What's that?*"

He looked down. Though his eyes were now accustomed to the dim emergency lighting, it was some time before he realized that a ghostly gray tide was pouring beneath that barricaded door—and that the panels were already bulging inward under the pressure of tons of dust. It could be only a matter of minutes before they collapsed; even if they held, it might make little difference. That silent, sinister tide had risen above his ankles even while he was standing here.

Pat did not attempt to move, or to speak to the Commodore, who was standing equally motionless a few centimeters away. For the first time in his life—and now, it might well be, for the last—he felt an emotion of sheer, overwhelming hate. In that moment, as its million dry and delicate feelers brushed against his bare legs, it seemed to Pat that the Sea of Thirst was a conscious, malignant entity that had been playing with them like a cat with a mouse. Every time, he told himself, we thought we were getting the situation under control, it was preparing a new surprise. We were always one move behind, and now it is tired of its little game; we no longer amuse it. Perhaps Radley was right, after all.

The loud-speaker dangling from the air pipe roused him from his fatalistic reverie.

"We're ready!" it shouted. "Crowd at the end of the bus and cover your faces. I'll count down from ten.

"TEN."

We're already at the end of the bus, thought Pat. We don't need all that time. We may not even have it.

"NINE."

I'll bet it doesn't work, anyway. The Sea won't let it, if It thinks we have a chance of getting out.

"EIGHT."

A pity, though, after all this effort. A lot of people have half killed themselves trying to help us. They deserved better luck.

"SEVEN."

That's supposed to be a lucky number, isn't it? Perhaps we may make it, after all. Some of us.

"SIX."

Let's pretend. It won't do much harm now. Suppose it takes—oh, fifteen seconds to get through—

"FIVE."

And, of course, to let down the ladder again; they probably rolled that up for safety—

"FOUR."

And assuming that someone goes out every three seconds—no, let's make it five to be on the safe side—

"THREE."

That will be twenty-two times five, which is one thousand and—no, that's ridiculous; I've forgotten how to do simple arithmetic—

"TWO."

Say one hundred and something seconds, which must be the best part of two minutes, and that's still plenty of time for those lox tanks to blow us all to kingdom come—

"ONE."

ONE! And I haven't even covered my face; maybe I should lie down even if I have to swallow this filthy stinking dust—

There was a sudden, sharp *crack* and a brief puff of air; that was all. It was disappointingly anticlimactic, but the explosives experts had known their job, as is highly desirable that explosives experts should. The energy of the charge had been precisely calculated and focused; there was barely enough left over to ripple the dust that now covered almost half the floor space of the cabin.

Time seemed to be frozen; for an age, nothing happened. Then there was a slow and beautiful miracle, breath-taking because it was so unexpected, yet so obvious if one had stopped to think about it.

A ring of brilliant white light appeared among the crimson shadows of the ceiling. It grew steadily thicker and brighter—then, quite suddenly, expanded into a complete and perfect circle as the section of the roof fell away. The light pouring down was only that of a single glow tube twenty meters above, but to eyes that had seen nothing but dim redness for hours, it was more glorious than any sunrise.

The ladder came through almost as soon as the circle of roofing hit the floor. Miss Morley, poised like a sprinter, was gone in a flash. When Mrs. Schuster followed—a little more slowly, but still at a speed of which no one could complain—it was like an eclipse. Only a few stray beams of light now filtered down that radiant road to safety. It was dark again, as if, after that brief glimpse of dawn, the night had returned with redoubled gloom.

Now the men were starting to go—Baldur first, probably blessing his position in the alphabet. There were only a dozen left in the cabin when the barricaded door finally ripped from its hinges, and the pent-up avalanche burst forth.

The first wave of dust caught Pat while he was halfway up the slope of the cabin. Light and impalpable though it was, it slowed his movements until it seemed that he was struggling to wade through glue. It was fortunate that the moist and heavy air had robbed it of some of its power, for otherwise it would have filled the cabin with choking clouds. Pat sneezed and coughed and was partly blinded, but he could still breathe.

In the foggy gloom he could hear Sue counting—"Fifteen, sixteen, seventeen, eighteen, nineteen—" as she marshaled the passengers to safety. He had intended her to go with the other women, but she was still down here, shepherding her charges. Even as he struggled against the cloying quicksand that had now risen almost to his waist, he felt for Sue a love so great that it seemed to burst his heart. Now he had no possible doubt. Real love was a perfect balance of desire and tenderness. The first had been there for a long time, and now the second had come in full measure.

"Twenty—that's *you*, Commodore—quickly!"

"Like hell it is, Sue," said the Commodore. "Up you go."

Pat could not see what happened—he was still partly blinded by the dust and the darkness—but he guessed that Hansteen must have literally thrown Sue through the roof. Neither his age nor his years in space had yet robbed him of his Earth-born strength.

"Are you there, Pat?" he called. "I'm on the ladder."

"Don't wait for me—I'm coming."

That was easier said than done. It felt as if a million soft yet determined fingers were clutching at him, pulling him back into the rising flood. He gripped one of the seatbacks—now almost hidden beneath the dust—and pulled himself toward the beckoning light.

Something whipped against his face; instinctively, he reached out to push it aside, then realized that it was the end of the rope ladder. He hauled upon it with all his might, and slowly, reluctantly, the Sea of Thirst relaxed its grip upon him.

Before he entered the shaft, he had one last glimpse of the cabin. The whole of the rear was now submerged by that crawling tide of gray; it seemed unnatural, and doubly sinister, that it rose in such a geometrically perfect plane, without a single ripple to furrow its surface. A meter away—this was something Pat knew he would remember all his life, though he could not imagine why—a solitary paper cup was floating sedately on the rising tide, like a toy boat upon a peaceful lake. In a few minutes it would reach the ceiling and be overwhelmed, but for the moment it was still bravely defying the dust.

And so were the emergency lights; they would continue to burn for days, even when each one was encapsulated in utter darkness.

Now the dim-lit shaft was around him. He was climbing as quickly as his muscles would permit, but he could not overtake the Commodore. There was a sudden flood of light from above as Hansteen cleared the mouth of the shaft, and involuntarily Pat looked downward to protect his eyes from the glare. The dust was already rising swiftly behind him, still unrippled, still smooth and placid—and inexorable.

Then he was straddling the low mouth of the caisson, in the center of a fantastically overcrowded igloo. All around him, in various stages of exhaustion and dishevelment, were his fellow passengers; helping them were four space-suited figures and one man without a suit, whom he assumed was Chief Engineer Lawrence. How strange it was to see a new face, after all these days.

"Is everyone out?" Lawrence asked anxiously.

"Yes," said Pat. "I'm the last man." Then he added, "I hope," for he realized that in the darkness and confusion someone might have been left behind. Suppose Radley had decided not to face the music back in New Zealand...

No—he was here with the rest of them. Pat was just starting to do a count of heads when the plastic floor gave a sudden jump—and out of the open well shot a perfect smoke ring of dust. It hit the ceiling, rebounded, and disintegrated before anyone could move."

"What the devil was *that*?" said Lawrence.

"Our lox tank," answered Pat. "Good old bus—she lasted just long enough."

And then, to his helpless horror, the skipper of *Selene* burst into tears.

# Chapter 31

"I still don't think those flags are a good idea," said Pat as the cruiser pulled away from Port Roris. "They look so phony, when you know they're in vacuum."

Yet he had to admit that the illusion was excellent, for the lines of pennants draped around the Embarkation Building were stirring and fluttering in a nonexistent breeze. It was all done by springs and electric motors, and would be very confusing to the viewers back on Earth.

This was a big day for Port Roris, and indeed for the whole Moon. He wished that Sue could be here, but she was hardly in proper shape for the trip. Very literally; as she had remarked when he kissed her good-by that morning: "I don't see how women could ever have had babies on Earth. Fancy carrying all this weight around, in six times our gravity."

Pat turned his mind away from his impending family, and pushed *Selene II* up to full speed. From the cabin behind him came the "Oh's" and "Ah's" of the thirty-two passengers, as the gray parabolas of dust soared against the sun like monochrome rainbows. This maiden voyage was in daylight; the travelers would miss the Sea's magical phosphorescence, the night ride up the canyon to Crater Lake, the green glories of the motionless Earth. But the novelty and excitement of the journey were the main attractions. Thanks to her ill-fated predecessor, *Selene II* was one of the best-known vehicles in the solar system.

It was proof of the old saying that there is no such thing as bad publicity. Now that the advance bookings were coming in, the Tourist

Commissioner was very glad that he had taken his courage in both hands and insisted on more passenger space. At first he had had to fight to get a new *Selene* at all. "Once bitten, twice shy," the Chief Administrator had said, and had capitulated only when Father Ferraro and the Geophysics Division had proved, beyond reasonable doubt, that the Sea would not stir again for another million years.

"Hold her on that course," said Pat to his copilot. "I'll go back and talk to the customers."

He was still young enough, and vain enough, to savor the admiring glances as he walked back into the passenger cabin. Everyone aboard would have read of him or seen him on TV; in fact, the very presence of these people here was an implicit vote of confidence. Pat knew well enough that others shared the credit, but he had no false modesty about the role he had played during the last hours of *Selene I*. His most valued possession was the little golden model of the cruiser that had been a wedding present to Mr. and Mrs. Harris "From all on the last voyage, in sincere appreciation." That was the only testimonial that counted, and he desired no other.

He had walked halfway down the cabin, exchanging a few words with a passenger here and there, when he suddenly stopped dead in his tracks.

"Hello, Captain," said an unforgotten voice. "You seem surprised to see me."

Pat made a quick recovery and flashed his most dazzling official smile.

"It's certainly an unexpected pleasure, Miss Morley. I had no idea you were on the Moon."

"It's rather a surprise to me. I owe it to the story I wrote about *Selene I*. I'm covering this trip for *Life Interplanetary*."

"I only hope," said Pat, "that it will be a little less exciting than last time. By the way, are you in touch with any of the others? Doctor McKenzie and the Schusters wrote a few weeks ago, but I've often wondered what happened to poor little Radley after Harding marched him off."

"Nothing—except that he lost his job. Universal Travel Cards decided that if they prosecuted, everyone would sympathize with Radley, and it would also give other people the same idea. He makes a living, I believe, lecturing to his fellow cultists about 'What I Found on the Moon.' And I'll make you a prediction, Captain Harris."

"What's that?"

"Some day, he'll get back to the Moon."

"I rather hope he does. I never did discover just what he expected to find in the Mare Crisium."

They both laughed. Then Miss Morley said: "I hear you're giving up this job."

Pat looked slightly embarrassed.

"That's true," he admitted. "I'm transferring to the Space Service. *If* I can pass the tests."

He was by no means sure that he could, yet he knew that he had to make the effort. Driving a moon bus had been an interesting and enjoyable job, but it was also a dead end—as both Sue and the Commodore had now convinced him. And there was another reason.

He had often wondered how many other lives had been changed or diverted when the Sea of Thirst had yawned beneath the stars. No one who had been aboard *Selene I* could fail to be marked by the experience, in most cases for the better. The fact that he was now having this friendly talk with Miss Morley was sufficient proof of that.

It must also have had a profound effect on the men who had been involved in the rescue effort—especially Doctor Lawson and Chief Engineer Lawrence. Pat had seen Lawson many times, giving his irascible TV talks on scientific subjects; he was grateful to the astronomer, but found it impossible to like him. It seemed, however, that some millions of people did.

As for Lawrence, he was hard at work on his memoirs, provisionally entitled "A Man about the Moon"—and wishing to God he'd never signed the contract. Pat had already helped him on the *Selene* chapters, and Sue was reading the typescript while waiting for the baby.

"If you'll excuse me," said Pat, remembering his duties as skipper, "I must attend to the other passengers. But please look us up next time you're in Clavius City."

"I will," promised Miss Morley, slightly taken aback but obviously somewhat pleased.

Pat continued his progress to the rear of the cabin, exchanging a greeting here, answering a question there. Then he reached the air-lock galley and closed the door behind him—and was instantly alone.

There was more room here than in *Selene I*'s little air lock, but the basic design was the same. No wonder that memories came flooding back. That might have been the space suit whose oxygen he and McKenzie had shared while all the rest were sleeping; that could have been the wall against which he had pressed his ear, and heard in the night the whisper of the ascending dust. And this whole chamber, indeed, could have been where he had first known Sue, in the literal and Biblical sense.

There was one innovation in this new model—the small window in the outer door. He pressed his face against it, and stared across the speeding surface of the Sea.

He was on the shadowed side of the cruiser, looking away from the sun, into the dark night of space. And presently, as his vision adjusted itself to that darkness, he could see the stars. Only the brighter ones, for there was enough stray light to desensitize his eyes, but there they were—and there also was Jupiter, most brilliant of all the planets next to Venus.

Soon he would be out there, far from his native world. The thought exhilarated and terrified him, but he knew he had to go.

He loved the Moon, but it had tried to kill him; never again could he be wholly at ease out upon its open surface. Though deep space was still more hostile and unforgiving, as yet it had not declared war upon him. With his own world, from now on, there could never be more than an armed neutrality.

The door of the cabin opened, and the stewardess entered with a tray of empty cups. Pat turned away from the window, and from the stars. The next time he saw them, they would be a million times brighter.

He smiled at the neatly uniformed girl, and waved his hand around the little galley.

"This is all yours, Miss Johnson," he said. "Look after it well."

Then he walked back to the controls to take *Selene II* on his last voyage, and her maiden one, across the Sea of Thirst.

# Jupiter V

"Jupiter V," written in June 1951, belongs to that typical and often despised category of science fiction, the "gimmick" story, in which some little-known fact or natural law forms an essential part of the plot. The genre may well have originated (like much else) with Edgar Allan Poe; his "A Descent into the Maelstrom" is a classic example.

As I wrote on its first appearance in volume form (Reach for Tomorrow, 1956): "I am by no means sure that I could write 'Jupiter V' today; it involved twenty or thirty pages of orbital calculations and should by rights be dedicated to Professor G.C. McVittie, my erstwhile tutor in applied mathematics." Twenty-seven years later I'm completely sure on this point.

But during those years something has happened that, when I wrote the story, I would have dismissed as completely incredible. The photographer covering the satellites of Jupiter for a 2044 issue of Life Magazine (presumably a holographic, satellite-delivered edition) was sixty-five years too late. The Voyager spacecraft had already done the job, back in 1979...

Or at least the first part of it, for we will never finish unravelling the complexities of the mini-solar-system formed by Jupiter and his moons. And dated though this story has been by the astonishing speed of space exploration (it was written, please remember, when Sputnik I was still six years in the future!), it may yet contain some elements of truth.

Those fuzzy, long-range shots of little Jupiter V (now officially christened Amalthea) look very, very odd indeed...

Professor Forster is such a small man that a special space-suit had to be made for him. But what he lacked in physical size he more than made up—as in so often the case—in sheer drive and determination. When I met him, he'd spent twenty years pursuing a dream. What is more to the point, he had persuaded a whole succession of hard-headed business men, World Council Delegates and administrators of scientific trusts to underwrite his expenses and to fit out a ship for him. Despite everything that happened later, I still think that was his most remarkable achievement....

The "Arnold Toynbee" had a crew of six aboard when we left Earth. Besides the Professor and Charles Ashton, his chief assistant, there was the usual pilot-navigator-engineer triumvirate and two graduate students—Bill Hawkins and myself. Neither of us had ever gone into space before, and we were still so excited over the whole thing that we didn't care in the least whether we got back to Earth before the next term started. We had a strong suspicion that our tutor had very similar views. The reference he had produced for us was a masterpiece of ambiguity, but as the number of people who could even begin to read Martian script could be counted, if I may coin a phrase, on the fingers of one hand, we'd got the job.

As we were going to Jupiter, and not to Mars, the purpose of this particular qualification seemed a little obscure, though knowing something about the Professor's theories we had some pretty shrewd suspicions. They were partly confirmed when we were ten days out from Earth.

The Professor looked at us very thoughtfully when we answered his summons. Even under zero g he always managed to preserve his dignity, while the best we could do was to cling to the nearest hand-hold and float around like drifting seaweed. I got the impression—though I may of course be wrong—that he was thinking: What have *I* done to deserve this? as he looked from Bill to me and back again. Then he gave a sort of "It's too late to do anything about it now" sigh and began to speak in that slow, patient way he always does when he has something to explain. At least, he always uses it when he's speaking to *us*, but it's just occurred to me—oh, never mind.

"Since we left Earth," he said, "I've not had much chance of telling you the purpose of this expedition. Perhaps you've guessed it already."

"I think I have," said Bill.

"Well, go on," replied the Professor, a peculiar gleam in his eye. I did my best to stop Bill, but have you ever tried to kick anyone when you're in free fall?

"You want to find some proof—I mean, some *more* proof—of your diffusion theory of extraterrestrial culture."

"And have you any idea why I'm going to Jupiter to look for it?"

"Well, not exactly. I suppose you hope to find something on one of the moons."

"Brilliant, Bill, brilliant. There are fifteen known satellites, and their total area is about half that of Earth. Where would you start looking if you had a couple of weeks to spare? I'd rather like to know."

Bill glanced doubtfully at the Professor, as if he almost suspected him of sarcasm.

"I don't know much about astronomy," he said. "But there are four big moons, aren't there? I'd start on those."

"For your information, Io, Europa, Ganymede and Callisto are each about as big as Africa. Would you work through them in alphabetical order?"

"No," Bill replied promptly. "I'd start on the one nearest Jupiter and go outward."

"I don't think we'll waste any more time pursuing your logical processes," sighed the Professor. He was obviously impatient to begin his set speech. "Anyway, you're quite wrong. We're not going to the big moons at all. They've been photographically surveyed from space and large areas have been explored on the surface. They've got nothing of archaeological interest. *We're* going to a place that's never been visited before."

"Not to Jupiter!" I gasped.

"Heavens no, nothing as drastic as that! But we're going nearer to him than anyone else has ever been."

He paused thoughtfully.

"It's a curious thing, you know—or you probably don't—that it's nearly as difficult to travel between Jupiter's satellites as it is to go between the planets, although the distances are so much smaller. This is because Jupiter's got such a terrific gravitational field and his moons are traveling so quickly. The innermost moon's moving almost as fast as Earth, and the journey to it from Ganymede costs almost as much fuel as the trip from Earth to Venus, even though it takes only a day and a half.

"And it's *that* journey which we're going to make. No one's ever done it before because nobody could think of any good reason for the expense. Jupiter Five is only thirty kilometers in diameter, so it couldn't possibly be of much interest. Even some of the outer satellites, which are far easier to reach, haven't been visited because it hardly seemed worth while to waste the rocket fuel."

"Then why are *we* going to waste it?" I asked impatiently. The whole thing sounded like a complete wild-goose chase, though as long as it proved interesting, and involved no actual danger, I didn't greatly mind.

Perhaps I ought to confess—though I'm tempted to say nothing, as a good many others have done—that at this time I didn't believe a word of Professor Forster's theories. Of course I realized that he was a very brilliant man in his field, but I did draw the line at some of his more fantastic ideas. After all, the evidence was so slight and the conclusions so revolutionary that one could hardly help being skeptical.

Perhaps you can still remember the astonishment when the first Martian expedition found the remains not of one ancient civilization, but of two. Both had been highly advanced, but both had perished more than five million years ago. The reason was unknown (and still is). It did not seem to be warfare, as the two cultures appear to have lived amicably together. One of the races had been insect-like, the other vaguely reptilian. The insects seem to have been the genuine, original Martians. The reptile-people—usually referred to as "Culture X"—had arrived on the scene later.

So, at least, Professor Forster maintained. They had certainly possessed the secret of space travel, because the ruins of their peculiar cruciform cities had been found on—of all places—Mercury. Forster believed that they had tried to colonize all the smaller planets—Earth and Venus having been ruled out because of their excessive gravity. It was a source of some disappointment to the Professor that no traces of Culture X had ever been found on the Moon, though he was certain that such a discovery was only a matter of time.

The "conventional" theory of Culture X was that it had originally come from one of the smaller planets or satellites, had made peaceful contact with the Martians—the only other intelligent race in the known history of the System—and had died out at the same time as the Martian civilization. But Professor Forster had more ambitious ideas: he was convinced that Culture X had entered the Solar System from interstellar space. The fact that no one else believed this annoyed him, though not very much, for he is one of those people who are happy only when in a minority.

From where I was sitting, I could see Jupiter through the cabin porthole as Professor Forster unfolded his plan. It was a beautiful sight: I could just make out the equatorial cloud belts, and three of the satellites were visible as little stars close to the planet. I wondered which was Ganymede, our first port of call.

"If Jack will condescend to pay attention," the Professor continued, "I'll tell you why we're going such a long way from home. You know that last year I spent a good deal of time poking among the ruins in the twilight belt of Mercury. Perhaps you read the paper I gave on the subject at the London School of Economics. You may even have been there—I do remember a disturbance at the back of the hall.

"What I didn't tell anyone then was that while I was on Mercury I discovered an important clue to the origin of Culture X. I've kept quiet about it, although I've been sorely tempted when fools like Dr. Haughton have tried to be funny at my expense. But I wasn't going to risk letting someone else get here before I could organize this expedition.

"One of the things I found on Mercury was a rather well preserved bas-relief of the Solar System. It's not the first that's been discovered—as you know, astronomical motifs are common in true Martian and Culture X art. But there were certain peculiar symbols against various planets, including Mars and Mercury. I think the pattern had some historic significance, and the most curious thing about it is that little Jupiter Five—one of the least important of all the satellites—seemed to have the most attention drawn to it. I'm convinced that there's something on Five which is the key to the whole problem of Culture X, and I'm going there to discover what it is."

As far as I can remember now, neither Bill nor I was particularly impressed by the Professor's story. Maybe the people of Culture X had left some artifacts on Five for obscure reasons of their own. It would be interesting to unearth them, but hardly likely that they would be as important as the Professor thought. I guess he was rather disappointed at our lack of enthusiasm. If so it was his fault since, as we discovered later, he was still holding out on us.

We landed on Ganymede, the largest moon, about a week later. Ganymede is the only one of the satellites with a permanent base on it; there's an observatory and a geophysical station with a staff of about fifty scientists. They were rather glad to see visitors, but we didn't stay long as the Professor was anxious to refuel and set off again. The fact that we were heading for Five naturally aroused a good deal of interest, but the Professor wouldn't talk and we couldn't; he kept too close an eye on us.

Ganymede, by the way, is quite an interesting place and we managed to see rather more of it on the return journey. But as I've promised to write an article for another magazine about that, I'd better not say anything else here. (You might like to keep your eyes on the *National Astrographic* Magazine next Spring.)

The hop from Ganymede to Five took just over a day and a half, and it gave us an uncomfortable feeling to see Jupiter expanding hour by hour until it seemed as if he was going to fill the sky. I don't know much about astronomy, but I couldn't help thinking of the tremendous gravity field into which we were falling. All sorts of things could go wrong so easily. If we ran out of fuel we'd never be able to get back to Ganymede, and we might even drop into Jupiter himself.

I wish I could describe what it was like seeing that colossal globe, with its raging storm belts spinning in the sky ahead of us. As a matter of fact I *did* make the attempt, but some literary friends who have read this MS advised me to cut out the result. (They also gave me a lot of other advice which I don't think they could have meant seriously, because if I'd followed it there would have been no story at all.)

Luckily there have been so many color close-ups of Jupiter published by now that you're bound to have seen some of them. You may even have seen the one which, as I'll explain later, was the cause of all our trouble.

At last Jupiter stopped growing: we'd swung into the orbit of Five and would soon catch up with the tiny moon as it raced around the planet. We were all squeezed in the control room waiting for our first glimpse of our target. At least, all of us who could get in were doing so. Bill and I were crowded out into the corridor and could only crane over other people's shoulders. Kingsley Searle, our pilot, was in the control seat looking as unruffled as ever: Eric Fulton, the engineer, was thoughtfully chewing his mustache and watching the fuel gauges, and Tony Groves was doing complicated things with his navigation tables.

And the Professor appeared to be rigidly attached to the eyepiece of the teleperiscope. Suddenly he gave a start and we heard a whistle of indrawn breath. After a minute, without a word, he beckoned to Searle, who took his place at the eyepiece. Exactly the same thing happened, and then Searle handed over to Fulton. It got a bit monotonous by the time Groves had reacted identically, so we wormed our way in and took over after a bit of opposition.

I don't know quite what I'd expected to see, so that's probably why I was disappointed. Hanging there in space was a tiny gibbous moon, its "night" sector lit up faintly by the reflected glory of Jupiter. And that seemed to be all.

Then I began to make out additional markings, in the way that you do if you look through a telescope for long enough. There were faint crisscrossing lines on the surface of the satellite, and suddenly my eye grasped their full pattern. For it *was* a pattern: those lines covered Five with the same geometrical accuracy as the lines of latitude and longitude divide up a globe of the Earth. I suppose I gave my whistle of amazement, for then Bill pushed me out of the way and had his turn to look.

The next thing I remember is Professor Forster looking very smug while we bombarded him with questions.

"Of course," he explained, "this isn't as much a surprise to me as it is to you. Besides the evidence I'd found on Mercury, there were other clues. I've a friend at the Ganymede Observatory whom I've sworn to secrecy and who's been under quite a strain this last few weeks. It's rather surprising to anyone who's not an astronomer that the Observatory has never bothered much about the satellites. The big instruments are all used on extragalactic nebulae, and the little ones spend all their time looking at Jupiter.

"The only thing the Observatory had ever done to Five was to measure its diameter and take a few photographs. They weren't quite good enough to show the markings we've just observed, otherwise there would have been an investigation before. But my friend Lawton detected them through the hundred-centimeter reflector when I asked him to look, and he also noticed something else that should have been spotted before. Five is only thirty kilometers in diameter, but it's much brighter than it should be for its size. When you compare its reflecting power—its aldeb—its—"

"Its albedo."

"Thanks, Tony—it's albedo with that of the other Moons, you find that it's a much better reflector than it should be. In fact, it behaves more like polished metal than rock."

"So that explains it!" I said. "The people of Culture X must have covered Five with an outer shell—like the domes they built on Mercury, but on a bigger scale."

The Professor looked at me rather pityingly.

"So you still haven't guessed!" he said.

I don't think this was quite fair. Frankly, would you have done any better in the same circumstances?

We landed three hours later on an enormous metal plain. As I looked through the portholes. I felt completely dwarfed by my surroundings. An ant crawling on the top of an oil-storage tank might have had much the same feelings—and the looming bulk of Jupiter up there in the sky didn't help. Even the Professor's usual cockiness now seemed to be overlaid by a kind of reverent awe.

The plain wasn't quite devoid of features. Running across it in various directions were broad bands where the stupendous metal plates had been joined together. These bands, or the crisscross pattern they formed, were what we had seen from space.

About a quarter of a kilometer away was a low hill—at least, what would have been a hill on a natural world. We had spotted it on our way in after making a careful survey of the little satellite from space. It was one of six such projections, four arranged equidistantly around the equator and the other two at the Poles. The assumption was pretty obvious that they would be entrances to the world below the metal shell.

I know that some people think it must be very entertaining to walk around on an airless, low-gravity planet in space-suits. Well, it isn't. There are so many points to think about, so many checks to make and precautions to observe, that the mental strain outweighs the glamor—at least as far as I'm concerned. But I must admit that this time, as we climbed out of the airlock, I was so excited that for once these things didn't worry me.

The gravity of Five was so microscopic that walking was completely out of the question. We were all roped together like mountaineers and blew ourselves across the metal plain with gentle bursts from our recoil pistols. The experienced astronauts. Fulton and Groves, were at the two ends of the chain so that any unwise eagerness on the part of the people in the middle was restrained.

It took us only a few minutes to reach our objective, which we discovered to be a broad, low dome at least a kilometer in circumference. I wondered if it was a gigantic airlock, large enough to permit the entrance of whole spaceships. Unless we were very lucky, we might be unable to find a way in, since the controlling mechanisms would no longer be functioning, and even if they were, we would not know how to operate them. It would be difficult to imagine anything more tantalizing than being locked out, unable to get at the greatest archaeological find in all history.

We had made a quarter circuit of the dome when we found an opening in the metal shell. It was quite small—only about two meters across—and it was so nearly circular that for a moment we did not realize what it was. Then Tony's voice came over the radio:

"That's not artificial. We've got a meteor to thank for it."

"Impossible!" protested Professor Forster. "It's much too regular."

Tony was stubborn.

"Big meteors always produce circular holes, unless they strike very glancing blows. And look at the edges; you can see there's been an explosion of some kind. Probably the meteor and the shell were vaporized; we won't find any fragments."

"You'd expect this sort of thing to happen," put in Kingsley. "How long has this been here? Five million years? I'm surprised we haven't found any other craters."

"Maybe you're right," said the Professor, too pleased to argue. "Anyway, I'm going in first."

"Right," said Kingsley, who as captain has the last say in all such matters. "I'll give you twenty meters of rope and will sit in the hole so that we can keep radio contact. Otherwise this shell will blanket your signals."

So Professor Forster was the first man to enter Five, as he deserved to be. We crowded close to Kingsley so that he could relay news of the Professor's progress.

He didn't get very far. There was another shell just inside the outer one, as we might have expected. The Professor had room to stand upright between them, and as far as his torch could throw its beam he could see avenues of supporting struts and girders, but that was about all.

It took us about twenty-four exasperating hours before we got any further. Near the end of that time I remember asking the Professor why he hadn't thought of bringing any explosives. He gave me a very hurt look.

"There's enough aboard the ship to blow us all to glory," he said. "But I'm not going to risk doing any damage if I can find another way."

That's what I call patience, but I could see his point of view. After all, what was another few days in a search that had already taken him twenty years?

It was Bill Hawkins, of all people, who found the way in when we had abandoned our first line of approach. Near the North Pole of the little world he discovered a really giant meteor hole—about a hundred meters across and cutting through both the outer shells surrounding Five. It had revealed still another shell below those, and by one of those chances that must happen if one waits enough eons, a second, smaller, meteor had come down inside the crater and penetrated the innermost skin. The hole was just big enough to allow entrance for a man in a space-suit. We went through head first, one at a time.

I don't suppose I'll ever have a weirder experience than hanging from that tremendous vault, like a spider suspended beneath the dome of St. Peter's. We only knew that the space in which we floated was vast. Just *how* big it was we could not tell, for our torches gave us no sense of distance. In this airless, dustless cavern the beams were, of course, totally invisible and when we shone them on the roof above, we could see the ovals of light dancing away into the distance until they were too diffuse to be visible. If we pointed them "downward" we could see a pale smudge of illumination so far below that it revealed nothing.

Very slowly, under the minute gravity of this tiny world, we fell downward until checked by our safety ropes. Overhead I could see the tiny glimmering patch through which we had entered; it was remote but reassuring.

And then, while I was swinging with an infinitely sluggish pendulum motion at the end of my cable, with the lights of my companions glimmering like fitful stars in the darkness around me, the truth suddenly crashed into my brain. Forgetting that we were all on open circuit, I cried out involuntarily:

"Professor—I don't believe this is a planet at all! *It's a spaceship!*"

Then I stopped, feeling that I had made a fool of myself. There was a brief, tense silence, then a babble of noise as everyone else started arguing at once. Professor Forster's voice cut across the confusion and I could tell that he was both pleased and surprised.

"You're quite right, Jack. This is the ship that brought Culture X to the Solar System."

I heard someone—it sounded like Eric Fulton—give a gasp of incredulity.

"It's fantastic! A ship thirty kilometers across!"

"*You* ought to know better than that," replied the Professor with surprising mildness. "Suppose a civilization wanted to cross interstellar space—how else would it attack the problem? It would build a mobile planetoid out in space, taking perhaps centuries over the task. Since the ship would have to be a self-contained world, which could support its inhabitants for generations, it would need to be as large as this. I wonder how many suns they visited before they found ours and knew that their search was ended? They must have had smaller ships that could take them down to the planets, and of course they had to leave the parent vessel somewhere in space. So they parked it here, in a close orbit near the largest planet, where it would remain safely forever—or until they needed it again. It was the logical place: if they had set it circling the Sun, in time the pulls of the planets would have disturbed its orbit so much that it might have been lost. That could never happen to it here."

"Tell me, Professor," someone asked, "did you guess all this before we started?"

"I *hoped* it. All the evidence pointed to this answer. There's always been something anomalous about Satellite Five, though no one seems to have noticed it. Why this single tiny moon so close to Jupiter, when all the other small satellites are seventy times further away? Astronomically speaking, it didn't make sense. But enough of this chattering. We've got work to do."

That, I think, must count as the understatement of the century. There were seven of us faced with the greatest archaeological discovery of all time. Almost a whole world—a small world, an artificial one, but still a world—was waiting for us to explore. All we could perform was a swift and superficial reconnaissance: there might be material here for generations of research workers.

The first step was to lower a powerful floodlight on a power line running from the ship. This would act as a beacon and prevent us getting lost, as well as giving local illumination on the inner surface of the satellite. (Even now, I still find it hard to call Five a ship.) Then we dropped down the line to the surface below. It was a fall of about a kilometer, and in this low gravity it was quite safe to make the drop unretarded. The gentle shock of the impact could be absorbed easily enough by the spring-loaded staffs we carried for that purpose.

I don't want to take up any space here with yet another description of all the wonders of Satellite Five; there have already been enough pictures, maps and books on the subject. (My own, by the way, is being published by Sidgwick and Jackson next summer.) What I would like to give you instead is some impression of what it was actually *like* to be the first men ever to enter that strange metal world. Yet I'm sorry to say—I know this sounds hard to believe—I simply can't remember what I was feeling when we came across the first of the great mushroom-capped entrance shafts. I suppose I was so excited and so overwhelmed by the wonder of it all that I've forgotten everything else. But I can recall the impression of sheer size, something which mere photographs can never give. The builders of this world, coming as they did from a planet of low gravity, were giants—about four times as tall as men. We were pigmies crawling among their works.

We never got below the outer levels on our first visit, so we met few of the scientific marvels which later expeditions discovered. That was just as well; the residential areas provided enough to keep us busy for several lifetimes. The globe we were exploring must once have been lit by artificial sunlight pouring down from the triple shell that surrounded it and kept its atmosphere from leaking into space. Here on the surface the Jovians (I suppose I cannot avoid adopting the popular name for the people of Culture X) had reproduced, as accurately as they could, conditions on the world they had left unknown ages ago. Perhaps they still had day and night, changing seasons, rain and mist. They had even taken a tiny sea with them into exile. The water was still there, forming a frozen lake three kilometers across. I hear that there is a plan afoot to electrolize it and provide Five with a breathable atmosphere again, as soon as the meteor holes in the outer shell have been plugged.

The more we saw of their work, the more we grew to like the race whose possessions we were disturbing for the first time in five million years. Even if they were giants from another sun, they had much in common with man, and it is a great tragedy that our races missed each other by what is, on the cosmic scale, such a narrow margin.

We were, I suppose, more fortunate than any archaeologists in history. The vacuum of space had preserved everything from decay and—this was something which could not have been expected—the Jovians had not emptied their mighty ship of all its treasures when they had set out to colonize the Solar System. Here on the inner surface of Five everything still seemed intact, as it had been at the end of the ship's long journey. Perhaps the travelers had preserved it as a shrine in memory of their lost home, or perhaps they had thought that one day they might have to use these things again.

Whatever the reason, everything was here as its makers had left it. Sometimes it frightened me. I might be photographing, with Bill's help, some great wall carving when the sheer *timelessness* of the place would strike into my heart. I would look round nervously, half expecting to see giant shapes come stalking in through the pointed doorways, to continue the tasks that had been momentarily interrupted.

We discovered the art gallery on the fourth day. That was the only name for it; there was no mistaking its purpose. When Groves and Searle, who had been doing rapid sweeps over the southern hemisphere, reported the discovery we decided to concentrate all our forces there. For, as somebody or other has said, the art of a people reveals its soul, and here we might find the key to Culture X.

The building was huge, even by the standards of this giant race. Like all the other structures on Five, it was made of metal, yet there was nothing cold or mechanical about it. The topmost peak climbed half way to the remote roof of the world, and from a distance—before the details were visible—the building looked not unlike a Gothic cathedral. Misled by this chance resemblance, some later writers have called it a temple; but we have never found any trace of what might be called a religion among the Jovians. Yet there seems something appropriate about the name "The Temple of Art," and it's stuck so thoroughly that no one can change it now.

It has been estimated that there are between ten and twenty million individual exhibits in this single building—the harvest garnered during the whole history of a race that may have been much older than Man. And it was here that I found a small, circular room which at first sight seemed to be no more than the meeting place of six radiating corridors. I was by myself (and thus, I'm afraid, disobeying the Professor's orders) and taking what I thought would be a short-cut back to my companions. The dark walls were drifting silently past me as I glided along, the light of my torch dancing over the ceiling ahead. It was covered with deeply cut lettering, and I was so busy looking for familiar character groupings that for some time I paid no attention to the chamber's floor. Then I saw the statue and focused my beam upon it.

The moment when one first meets a great work of art has an impact that can never again be recaptured. In this case the subject matter made the effect all the more overwhelming. I was the first man ever to know what the Jovians had looked like, for here, carved with superb skill and authority, was one obviously modeled from life.

The slender, reptilian head was looking straight toward me, the sightless eyes staring into mine. Two of the hands were clasped upon the breast as if in resignation; the other two were holding an instrument whose purpose is still unknown. The long, powerful tail—which, like a kangaroo's, probably balanced the rest of the body—was stretched out along the ground, adding to the impression of rest or repose.

There was nothing human about the face or the body. There were, for example, no nostrils—only gill-like openings in the neck. Yet the figure moved me profoundly; the artist had spanned the barriers of time and culture in a way I should never have believed possible. "Not human—but humane" was the verdict Professor Forster gave. There were many things we could not have shared with the builders of this world, but all that was really important we would have felt in common.

Just as one can read emotions in the alien but familiar face of a dog or a horse, so it seemed that I knew the feelings of the being confronting me. Here was wisdom and authority—the calm, confident power that is shown, for example, in Bellini's famous portrait of the Doge Loredano. Yet there was sadness also—the sadness of a race which had made some stupendous effort, and made it in vain.

We still do not know why this single statue is the only representation the Jovians have ever made of themselves in their art. One would hardly expect to find taboos of this nature among such an advanced race; perhaps we will know the answer when we have deciphered the writing carved on the chamber walls.

Yet I am already certain of the statue's purpose. It was set here to bridge time and to greet whatever beings might one day stand in the footsteps of his makers. That, perhaps, is why they shaped it so much smaller than life. Even then they must have guessed that the future belonged to Earth or Venus, and hence to beings whom they would have dwarfed. They knew that size could be a barrier as well as time.

A few minutes later I was on my way back to the ship with my companions, eager to tell the Professor about the discovery. He had been reluctantly snatching some rest, though I don't believe he averaged more than four hours sleep a day all the time we were on Five. The golden light of Jupiter was flooding the great metal plain as we emerged through the shell and stood beneath the stars once more.

"Hello!" I heard Bill say over the radio, "the Prof's moved the ship."

"Nonsense," I retorted. "It's exactly where we left it."

Then I turned my head and saw the reason for Bill's mistake. We had visitors.

The second ship had come down a couple of kilometers away, and as far as my non-expert eyes could tell it might have been a duplicate of ours. When we hurried through the airlock, we found that the Professor, a little bleary-eyed, was already entertaining. To our surprise, though not exactly to our displeasure, one of the three visitors was an extremely attractive brunette.

"This," said Professor Forster, a little wearily, "is Mr. Randolph Mays, the science writer. I imagine you've heard of him. And this is—" He turned to Mays. "I'm afraid I didn't quite catch the names."

"My pilot, Donald Hopkins—my secretary, Marianne Mitchell."

There was just the slightest pause before the word "secretary," but it was long enough to set a little signal light flashing in my brain. I kept my eyebrows from going up, but I caught a glance from Bill that said, without any need for words: If you're thinking what I'm thinking, I'm ashamed of you.

Mays was a tall, rather cadaverous man with thinning hair and an attitude of bonhomie which one felt was only skin-deep—the protective coloration of a man who has to be friendly with too many people.

"I expect this is as big a surprise to you as it is to me," he said with unnecessary heartiness. "I certainly never expected to find anyone here before me; and I certainly didn't expect to find all *this*."

"What brought you here?" said Ashton, trying to sound not too suspiciously inquisitive.

"I was just explaining that to the Professor. Can I have that folder please, Marianne? Thanks."

He drew out a series of very fine astronomical paintings and passed them round. They showed the planets from their satellites—a common-enough subject, of course.

"You've all seen this sort of thing before," Mays continued. "But there's a difference here. These pictures are nearly a hundred years old. They were painted by an artist named Chesley Bonestell and appeared in *Life* back in 1994—long before space-travel began, of course. Now what's happened is that *Life* has commissioned me to go round the Solar System and see how well I can match these imaginative paintings against the reality. In the centenary issue, they'll be published side by side with photographs of the real thing. Good idea, eh?"

I had to admit that it was. But it was going to make matters rather complicated, and I wondered what the Professor thought about it. Then I glanced again at Miss Mitchell, standing demurely in the corner, and decided that there would be compensations.

In any other circumstances, we would have been glad to meet another party of explorers, but here there was the question of priority to be considered. Mays would certainly be hurrying back to Earth as quickly as he could, his original mission abandoned and all his film used up here and now. It was difficult to see how we could stop him, and not even certain that we desired to do so. We wanted all the publicity and support we could get, but we would prefer to do things in our own time, after our own fashion. I wondered how strong the Professor was on tact, and feared the worst.

Yet at first diplomatic relations were smooth enough. The Professor had hit upon the bright idea of pairing each of us with one of Mays's team, so that we acted simultaneously as guides and supervisors. Doubling the number of investigating groups also greatly increased the rate at which we could work. It was unsafe for anyone to operate by himself under these conditions, and this had handicapped us a great deal.

The Professor outlined his policy to us the day after the arrival of Mays's party.

"I hope we can get along together," he said a little anxiously. "As far as I'm concerned they can go where they like and photograph what they like, as long as *they don't take anything*, and as long as they don't get back to Earth with their records before we do."

"I don't see how we can stop them," protested Ashton.

"Well, I hadn't intended to do this, but I've now registered a claim to Five. I radioed it to Ganymede last night, and it will be at The Hague by now."

"But no one can claim an astronomical body for himself. That was settled in the case of the Moon, back in the last century."

The Professor gave a rather crooked smile.

"I'm not annexing an *astronomical body*, remember. I've put in a claim for salvage, and I've done it in the name of the World Science Organization. If Mays takes anything out of Five, he'll be stealing it from them. Tomorrow I'm going to explain the situation gently to him, just in case he gets any bright ideas."

It certainly seemed peculiar to think of Satellite Five as salvage, and I could imagine some pretty legal quarrels developing when we got home. But for the present the Professor's move should have given us some safeguards and might discourage Mays from collecting souvenirs—so we were optimistic enough to hope.

It took rather a lot of organizing, but I managed to get paired off with Marianne for several trips round the interior of Five. Mays didn't seem to mind: there was no particular reason why he should. A space-suit is the most perfect chaperon ever devised, confound it.

Naturally enough I took her to the art gallery at the first opportunity, and showed her my find. She stood looking at the statue for a long time while I held my torch beam upon it.

"It's very wonderful," she breathed at last. "Just think of it waiting here in the darkness all those millions of years! But you'll have to give it a name."

"I have. I've christened it 'The Ambassador.'"

"Why?"

"Well, because I think it's a kind of envoy, if you like, carrying a greeting to us. The people who made it knew that one day someone else was bound to come here and find this place."

"I think you're right. 'The Ambassador'—yes, that was clever of you. There's something noble about it, and something very sad, too. Don't you feel it?"

I could tell that Marianne was a very intelligent woman. It was quite remarkable the way she saw my point of view, and the interest she took in everything I showed her. But "The Ambassador" fascinated her most of all, and she kept on coming back to it.

"You know, Jack," she said (I think this was sometime the next day, when Mays had been to see it as well) "you must take that statue back to Earth. Think of the sensation it would cause."

I sighed.

"The Professor would like to, but it must weigh a ton. We can't afford the fuel. It will have to wait for a later trip."

She looked puzzled.

"But things hardly weigh anything here," she protested.

"That's different," I explained. "There's weight, and there's iner-tia—two quite different things. Now inertia—oh, never mind. We can't take it back, anyway. Captain Searle's told us that, definitely."

"What a pity," said Marianne.

I forgot all about this conversation until the night before we left. We had had a busy and exhausting day packing our equipment (a good deal, of course, we left behind for future use). All our photographic material had been used up. As Charlie Ashton remarked, if we met a *live* Jovian now we'd be unable to record the fact. I think we were all wanting a breathing space, an opportunity to relax and sort out our impressions and to recover from our head-on collision with an alien culture.

Mays's ship, the "Henry Luce," was also nearly ready for take-off. We would leave at the same time, an arrangement which suited the Professor admirably as he did not trust Mays alone on Five.

Everything had been settled when, while checking through our records. I suddenly found that six rolls of exposed film were missing. They were photographs of a complete set of transcriptions in the Temple of Art. After a certain amount of thought I recalled that they had been entrusted to my charge, and I had put them very carefully on a ledge in the Temple, intending to collect them later.

It was a long time before take-off, the Professor and Ashton were canceling some arrears of sleep, and there seemed no reason why I should not slip back to collect the missing material. I knew there would be a row if it was left behind, and as I remembered exactly where it was I need be gone only thirty minutes. So I went, explaining my mission to Bill just in case of accidents.

The floodlight was no longer working, of course, and the darkness inside the shell of Five was somewhat oppressive. But I left a portable beacon at the entrance, and dropped freely until my hand torch told me it was time to break the fall. Ten minutes later, with a sigh of relief, I gathered up the missing films.

It was a natural-enough thing to pay my last respects to The Ambassador: it might be years before I saw him again, and that calmly enigmatic figure had begun to exercise an extraordinary fascination over me.

Unfortunately, that fascination had not been confined to me alone. For the chamber was empty and the statue gone.

I suppose I could have crept back and said nothing, thus avoiding awkward explanations. But I was too furious to think of discretion, and as soon as I returned we woke the Professor and told him what had happened.

He sat on his bunk rubbing the sleep out of his eyes, then uttered a few harsh words about Mr. Mays and his companions which it would do no good at all to repeat here.

"What I don't understand," said Searle "is how they got the thing out—if they have, in fact. We should have spotted it."

"There are plenty of hiding places, and they could have waited until there was no one around before they took it up through the hull. It must have been quite a job, even under this gravity," remarked Eric Fulton, in tones of admiration.

"There's no time for post-mortems," said the Professor savagely. "We've got five hours to think of something. They can't take off before then, because we're only just past opposition with Ganymede. That's correct, isn't it, Kingsley?"

Searle nodded agreement.

"Yes. We must move round to the other side of Jupiter before we can enter a transfer orbit—at least, a reasonably economical one."

"Good. That gives us a breathing space. Well, has anyone any ideas?"

Looking back on the whole thing now, it often seems to me that our subsequent behavior was, shall I say, a little peculiar and slightly uncivilized. It was not the sort of thing we could have imagined ourselves doing a few months before. But we were annoyed and over-wrought, and our remoteness from all other human beings somehow made everything seem different. Since there were no other laws here, we had to make our own...

"Can't we do something to stop them from taking off? Could we sabotage their rockets, for instance?" asked Bill.

Searle didn't like this idea at all.

"We mustn't do anything drastic," he said. "Besides, Don Hopkins is a good friend of mine. He'd never forgive me if I damaged his ship. There'd be the danger, too, that we might do something that couldn't be repaired."

"Then pinch their fuel," said Groves laconically.

"Of course! They're probably all asleep, there's no light in the cabin. All we've got to do is to connect up and pump."

"A very nice idea," I pointed out, "but we're two kilometers apart. How much pipeline have we got? Is it as much as a hundred meters?"

The others ignored this interruption as though it was beneath contempt and went on making their plans. Five minutes later the technicians had settled everything: we only had to climb into our spacesuits and do the work.

I never thought, when I joined the Professor's expedition, that I should end up like an African porter in one of those old adventure stories, carrying a load on my head. Especially when that load was a sixth of a space-ship (being so short, Professor Forster wasn't able to provide very effective help). Now that its fuel tanks were half empty, the weight of the ship in this gravity was about two hundred kilograms. We squeezed beneath, heaved, and up she went—very slowly, of course, because her inertia was still unchanged. Then we started marching.

It took us quite a while to make the journey, and it wasn't quite as easy as we'd thought it would be. But presently the two ships were lying side by side, and nobody had noticed us. Everyone in the "Henry Luce" was fast asleep, as they had every reason to expect us to be.

Though I was still rather short of breath, I found a certain schoolboy amusement in the whole adventure as Searle and Fulton drew the refueling pipeline out of our airlock and quietly coupled up to the other ship.

"The beauty of this plan," explained Groves to me as we stood watching, "is that they can't do anything to stop us, unless they come outside and uncouple our line. We can drain them dry in five minutes, and it will take them half that time to wake up and get into their space-suits."

A sudden horrid fear smote me.

"Suppose they turned on their rockets and tried to get away?"

"Then we'd both be smashed up. No, they'll just have to come outside and see what's going on. Ah, there go the pumps."

The pipeline had stiffened like a fire-hose under pressure, and I knew that the fuel was pouring into our tanks. Any moment now the lights would go on in the "Henry Luce" and her startled occupants would come scuttling out.

It was something of an anticlimax when they didn't. They must have been sleeping very soundly not to have felt the vibration from the pumps, but when it was all over nothing had happened and we just stood round looking rather foolish. Searle and Fulton carefully uncoupled the pipeline and put it back into the airlock.

"Well?" we asked the Professor.

He thought things over for a minute.

"Let's get back into the ship," he said.

When we had climbed out of our suits and were gathered together in the control room, or as far in as we could get, the Professor sat down at the radio and punched out the "Emergency" signal. Our sleeping neighbors would be awake in a couple of seconds as their automatic receiver sounded the alarm.

The TV screen glimmered into life. There, looking rather frightened, was Randolph Mays.

"Hello, Forster," he snapped. "What's the trouble?"

"Nothing wrong here," replied the Professor in his best deadpan manner, "but you've lost something important. Look at your fuel gauges."

The screen emptied, and for a moment there was a confused mumbling and shouting from the speaker. Then Mays was back, annoyance and alarm competing for possession of his features.

"What's going on?" he demanded angrily. "Do you know anything about this?"

The Prof let him sizzle for a moment before he replied.

"I think you'd better come across and talk things over," he said. "You won't have far to walk."

Mays glared back at him uncertainly, then retorted, "You bet I will!" The screen went blank.

"He'll have to climb down now!" said Bill gleefully. "There's nothing else he can do!"

"It's not so simple as you think," warned Fulton. "If he really wanted to be awkward, he could just sit tight and radio Ganymede for a tanker."

"What good would that do him? It would waste days and cost a fortune."

"Yes, but he'd still have the statue, if he wanted it that badly. And he'd get his money back when he sued us."

The airlock light flashed on and Mays stumped into the room. He was in a surprisingly conciliatory mood; on the way over, he must have had second thoughts.

"Well, well," he said affably. "What's all this nonsense in aid of?"

"You know perfectly well," the Professor retorted coldly. "I made it quite clear that nothing was to be taken off Five. You've been stealing property that doesn't belong to you."

"Now, let's be reasonable. Who *does* it belong to? You can't claim everything on this planet as your personal property."

"This is *not* a planet—it's a ship and the laws of salvage operate."

"Frankly, that's a very debatable point. Don't you think you should wait until you get a ruling from the lawyers?"

The Professor was being icily polite, but I could see that the strain was terrific and an explosion might occur at any moment.

"Listen, Mr. Mays," he said with ominous calm. "What you've taken is the most important single find we've made here. I will make allowances for the fact that you don't appreciate what you've done, and don't understand the viewpoint of an archaeologist like myself. Return that statue, and we'll pump your fuel back and say no more."

Mays rubbed his chin thoughtfully.

"I really don't see why you should make such a fuss about one statue, when you consider all the stuff that's still here."

It was then that the Professor made one of his rare mistakes.

"You talk like a man who's stolen the Mona Lisa from the Louvre and argues that nobody will miss it because of all the other paintings. This statue's unique in a way that no terrestrial work of art can ever be. That's why I'm determined to get it back."

You should never, when you're bargaining, make it obvious that you want something really badly. I saw the greedy glint in Mays's eye and said to myself, "Uh-huh! He's going to be tough." And I remembered Fulton's remark about calling Ganymede for a tanker.

"Give me half an hour to think it over," said Mays, turning to the airlock.

"Very well," replied the Professor stiffly. "Half an hour—no more."

I must give Mays credit for brains. Within five minutes we saw his communications aerial start slewing round until it locked on Ganymede. Naturally we tried to listen in, but he had a scrambler. These newspaper men must trust each other.

The reply came back a few minutes later; that was scrambled, too. While we were waiting for the next development, we had another council of war. The Professor was now entering the stubborn, stop-at-nothing stage. He realized he'd miscalculated and that had made him fighting mad.

I think Mays must have been a little apprehensive, because he had reinforcements when he returned. Donald Hopkins, his pilot, came with him, looking rather uncomfortable.

"I've been able to fix things up, Professor," he said smugly. "It will take me a little longer, but I can get back without your help if I have to. Still, I must admit that it will save a good deal of time and money if we can come to an agreement. I'll tell you what. Give me back my fuel and I'll return the other—er—souvenirs I've collected. But I insist on keeping Mona Lisa, even if it means I won't get back to Ganymede until the middle of next week."

The Professor then uttered a number of what are usually called deep-space oaths, though I can assure you they're much the same as any other oaths. That seemed to relieve his feelings a lot and he became fiendishly friendly.

"My dear Mr. Mays," he said, "You're an unmitigated crook, and accordingly I've no compunction left in dealing with you. I'm prepared to use force, knowing that the law will justify me."

Mays looked slightly alarmed, though not unduly so. We had moved to strategic positions round the door.

"Please don't be so melodramatic," he said haughtily. "This is the twenty-first century, not the Wild West back in 1800."

"1880," said Bill, who is a stickler for accuracy.

"I must ask you," the Professor continued, "to consider yourself under detention while we decide what is to be done. Mr. Searle, take him to Cabin B."

Mays sidled along the wall with a nervous laugh.

"Really, Professor, this is *too* childish! You can't detain me against my will." He glanced for support at the Captain of the "Henry Luce."

Donald Hopkins dusted an imaginary speck of fluff from his uniform.

"I refuse," he remarked for the benefit of all concerned, "to get involved in vulgar brawls."

Mays gave him a venomous look and capitulated with bad grace. We saw that he had a good supply of reading matter, and locked him in.

When he was out of the way, the Professor turned to Hopkins, who was looking enviously at our fuel gauges.

"Can I take it, Captain," he said politely, "that you don't wish to get mixed up in any of your employer's dirty business?"

"I'm neutral. My job is to fly the ship here and take her home. You can fight this out among yourselves."

"Thank you. I think we understand each other perfectly. Perhaps it would be best if you returned to your ship and explained the situation. We'll be calling you in a few minutes."

Captain Hopkins made his way languidly to the door. As he was about to leave he turned to Searle.

"By the way, Kingsley," he drawled. "Have you thought of torture? Do call me if you get round to it—I've some jolly interesting ideas." Then he was gone, leaving us with our hostage.

I think the Professor had hoped he could do a direct exchange. If so, he had not bargained on Marianne's stubbornness.

"It serves Randolph right," she said. "But I don't really see that it makes any difference. He'll be just as comfortable in your ship as in ours, and you can't do anything to him. Let me know when you're fed up with having him around."

It seemed a complete impasse. We had been too clever by half, and it had got us exactly nowhere. We'd captured Mays, but he wasn't any use to us.

The Professor was standing with his back to us, staring morosely out of the window. Seemingly balanced on the horizon, the immense bulk of Jupiter nearly filled the sky.

"We've got to convince her that we really *do* mean business," he said. Then he turned abruptly to me.

"Do you think she's actually fond of this blackguard?"

"Er—I shouldn't be surprised. Yes, I really believe so."

The Professor looked very thoughtful. Then he said to Searle, "Come into my room. I want to talk something over."

They were gone quite a while. When they returned they both had an indefinable air of gleeful anticipation and the Professor was carrying a piece of paper covered with figures. He went to the radio, and called the "Henry Luce."

"Hello," said Marianne, replying so promptly that she'd obviously been waiting for us. "Have you decided to call it off? I'm getting so bored."

The Professor looked at her gravely.

"Miss Mitchell," he replied. "It's apparent that you have not been taking us seriously. I'm therefore arranging a somewhat—er—drastic little demonstration for your benefit. I'm going to place your employer in a position from which he'll be only too anxious for you to retrieve him as quickly as possible."

"Indeed?" replied Marianne noncommittally—though I thought I could detect a trace of apprehension in her voice.

"I don't suppose," continued the Professor smoothly, "that you know anything about celestial mechanics. No? Too bad, but your pilot will confirm everything I tell you. Won't you, Hopkins?"

"Go ahead," came a painstakingly neutral voice from the background.

"Then listen carefully, Miss Mitchell. I want to remind you of our curious—indeed our precarious—position on this satellite. You've only got to look out of the window to see how close to Jupiter we are; and I need hardly remind you that Jupiter has by far the most intense gravitational field of all the planets. You follow me?"

"Yes," replied Marianne, no longer quite so self-possessed. "Go on."

"Very well. This little world of ours goes round Jupiter in almost exactly twelve hours. Now there's a well-known theorem stating that if a body *falls* from an orbit to the center of attraction, it will take point one seven seven of a period to make the drop. In other words, anything falling from here to Jupiter would reach the center of the planet in about two hours seven minutes. I'm sure Captain Hopkins can confirm this."

There was a long pause. Then we heard Hopkins say, "Well, of course I can't confirm the exact figures, but they're probably correct. It would be something like that, anyway."

"Good," continued the Professor. "Now I'm sure you realize," he went on with a hearty chuckle, "that a fall to the *center* of the planet is a very theoretical case. If anything really was dropped from here, it would reach the upper atmosphere of Jupiter in a considerably shorter time. I hope I'm not boring you?"

"No," said Marianne, rather faintly.

"I'm so glad to hear it. Anyway, Captain Searle has worked out the actual time for me, and it's one hour thirty-five minutes—with a few minutes either way. We can't guarantee complete accuracy, ha, ha!

"Now, it has doubtless not escaped your notice that this satellite of ours has an extremely weak gravitational field. It's escape velocity is only about ten meters a second, and anything thrown away from it at that speed would never come back. Correct, Mr. Hopkins?"

"Perfectly correct."

"Then, if I may come to the point, we propose to take Mr. Mays for a walk until he's immediately under Jupiter, remove the reaction pistols from his suit, and—ah—launch him forth. We will be prepared to retrieve him with our ship as soon as you've handed over the property you've stolen. After what I've told you, I'm sure you'll appreciate that time will be rather vital. An hour and thirty-five minutes is remarkably short, isn't it?"

"Professor!" I gasped, "You can't possibly do this!"

"Shut up!" he barked. "Well, Miss Mitchell, what about it?"

Marianne was staring at him with mingled horror and disbelief.

"You're simply bluffing!" she cried. "I don't believe you'd do anything of the kind! Your crew won't let you!"

The Professor sighed.

"Too bad," he said. "Captain Searle—Mr. Groves—will you take the prisoner and proceed as instructed."

"Aye-aye, sir," replied Searle with great solemnity.

Mays looked frightened but stubborn.

"What are you going to do now?" he said, as his suit was handed back to him.

Searle unholstered his reaction pistols. "Just climb in," he said. "We're going for a walk."

I realized then what the Professor hoped to do. The whole thing was a colossal bluff: of course he wouldn't *really* have Mays thrown into Jupiter; and in any case Searle and Groves wouldn't do it. Yet surely Marianne would see through the bluff, and then we'd be left looking mighty foolish.

Mays couldn't run away; without his reaction pistols he was quite helpless. Grasping his arms and towing him along like a captive balloon, his escorts set off toward the horizon—and towards Jupiter.

I could see, looking across the space to the other ship, that Marianne was staring out through the observation windows at the departing trio. Professor Forster noticed it too.

"I hope you're convinced, Miss Mitchell, that my men aren't carrying along an empty space-suit. Might I suggest that you follow the proceedings with a telescope? They'll be over the horizon in a minute, but you'll be able to see Mr. Mays when he starts to—er—ascend."

There was a stubborn silence from the loudspeaker. The period of suspense seemed to last for a very long time. Was Marianne waiting to see how far the Professor really would go?

By this time I had got hold of a pair of binoculars and was sweeping the sky beyond the ridiculously close horizon. Suddenly I saw it—a tiny flare of light against the vast yellow back-cloth of Jupiter. I focused quickly, and could just make out the three figures rising into space. As I watched, they separated: two of them decelerated with their pistols and started to fall back toward Five. The other went on ascending helplessly toward the ominous bulk of Jupiter.

I turned on the Professor in horror and disbelief.

"They've really done it!" I cried. "I thought you were only bluffing!"

"So did Miss Mitchell, I've no doubt," said the Professor calmly, for the benefit of the listening microphone. "I hope I don't need to impress upon you the urgency of the situation. As I've remarked once or twice before, the time of fall from our orbit to Jupiter's surface is ninety-five minutes. But, of course, if one waited even half that time, it would be much too late..."

He let that sink in. There was no reply from the other ship.

"And now," he continued, "I'm going to switch off our receiver so we can't have any more arguments. We'll wait until you've unloaded that statue—*and* the other items Mr. Mays was careless enough to mention—before we'll talk to you again. Goodbye."

It was a very uncomfortable ten minutes. I'd lost track of Mays, and was seriously wondering if we'd better overpower the Professor and go after him before we had a murder on our hands. But the people who could fly the ship were the ones who had actually carried out the crime. I didn't know *what* to think.

Then the airlock of the "Henry Luce" slowly opened. A couple of space-suited figures emerged, floating the cause of all the trouble between them.

"Unconditional surrender," murmured the Professor with a sigh of satisfaction. "Get it into our ship," he called over the radio. "I'll open up the airlock for you."

He seemed in no hurry at all. I kept looking anxiously at the clock; fifteen minutes had already gone by. Presently there was a clanking and banging in the airlock, the inner door opened, and Captain Hopkins entered. He was followed by Marianne, who only needed a bloodstained axe to make her look like Clytaemnestra. I did my best to avoid her eye, but the Professor seemed to be quite without shame. He walked into the airlock, checked that his property was back, and emerged rubbing his hands.

"Well, that's that," he said cheerfully. "Now let's sit down and have a drink to forget all this unpleasantness, shall we?"

I pointed indignantly at the clock.

"Have you gone crazy!" I yelled. "He's already halfway to Jupiter!"

Professor Forster looked at me disapprovingly.

"Impatience," he said, "is a common failing in the young. I see no cause at all for hasty action."

Marianne spoke for the first time; she now looked really scared.

"But you promised," she whispered.

The Professor suddenly capitulated. He had had his little joke, and didn't want to prolong the agony.

"I can tell you at once, Miss Mitchell—and you too, Jack—that Mays is in no more danger than we are. We can go and collect him whenever we like."

"Do you mean that you lied to me?"

"Certainly not. Everything I told you was perfectly true. You simply jumped to the wrong conclusions. When I said that a body would take ninety-five minutes to fall from here to Jupiter, I omitted—not, I must confess, accidentally—a rather important phrase. I should have added "*a body at rest with respect to Jupiter.*" Your friend Mr. Mays was sharing the orbital speed of this satellite, and he's still got it. A little matter of twenty-six kilometers a second, Miss Mitchell.

"Oh yes, we threw him completely off Five and toward Jupiter. But the velocity we gave him then was trivial. He's still moving in practically the same orbit as before. The most he can do—I've got Captain Searle to work out the figures—is to drift about a hundred kilometers inward. And in one revolution—twelve hours—*he'll be right back where he started*, without us bothering to do anything at all."

There was a long, long silence. Marianne's face was a study in frustration, relief, and annoyance at having been fooled. Then she turned on Captain Hopkins.

"You must have known all the time! Why didn't you tell me?"

Hopkins gave her a wounded expression.

"You didn't ask me," he said.

We hauled Mays down about an hour later. He was only twenty kilometers up, and we located him quickly enough by the flashing light on his suit. His radio had been disconnected, for a reason that hadn't occurred to me. He was intelligent enough to realize that he was in no danger, and if his set had been working he could have called his ship and exposed our bluff. That is, if he wanted to. Personally, I think I'd have been glad enough to call the whole thing off even if I had known that I was perfectly safe. It must have been awfully lonely up there.

To my great surprise, Mays wasn't as mad as I'd expected. Perhaps he was too relieved to be back in our snug little cabin when we drifted up to him on the merest fizzle of rockets and yanked him in. Or perhaps he felt that he'd been worsted in fair fight and didn't bear any grudge. I really think it was the latter.

There isn't much more to tell, except that we did play one other trick on him before we left Five. He had a good deal more fuel in his tanks than he really needed, now that his payload was substantially reduced. By keeping the excess ourselves, we were able to carry The Ambassador back to Ganymede after all. Oh, yes, the Professor gave him a check for the fuel we'd borrowed. Everything was perfectly legal.

There's one amusing sequel I must tell you, though. The day after the new gallery was opened at the British Museum I went along to see The Ambassador, partly to discover if his impact was still as great in these changed surroundings. (For the record, it wasn't—though it's still considerable and Bloomsbury will never be quite the same to me again.) A huge crowd was milling around the gallery, and there in the middle of it were Mays and Marianne.

It ended up with us having a very pleasant lunch together in Holborn. I'll say this about Mays—he doesn't bear any grudges. But I'm still rather sore about Marianne.

And, frankly, I can't imagine *what* she sees in him.